THE STRANGE LAND

HAMMOND INNES's highly individual and successful novels are the result of travel in outback parts of the world. Many of them follow the central character to strange countries where the forces of nature, as much as people, provide the conflict. He has also written two books of travel and one of history. His international reputation as a storyteller keeps his books in print; they have been translated into over thirty foreign languages.

The origins of this story of the French in Morocco go back to an 'Arabian Nights' journey Hammond Innes made in 1952, when all the south was known as the Zone of Insecurity. He and his wife lived in Beau Geste forts, were entertained by the Glaoui— the Great Caid—in his kasbah strongholds, rendezvoused with the elusive Taouregs in the Sahara, and watched Berber dancing in a Biblical setting high up under a snow peak of the Haut Atlas.

The story is as strange as the setting. It starts in Tangier with a yacht driving ashore in a gale and only one survivor. Was it the yacht's English owner Latham had pulled out of the water, or was it the Czech doctor whose reasons for coming to Morocco were as mysterious as his past?

HAMMOND INNES

The Strange Land

FONTANA/Collins

First published in 1954 by William Collins Sons & Co Ltd
First issued in Fontana Books 1964
Seventeenth Impression May 1979

Made and printed in Great Britain by
William Collins Sons & Co Ltd, Glasgow

L & M

For
DOROTHY
This book in particular, because she acted
as interpreter in addition to her usual
role of reader and critic

AUTHOR'S NOTE TO THE NEW
FONTANA EDITION

The Strange Land was first published in 1954. The setting is
Tangier and Morocco and was the result of journeys my wife
and I had made in North Africa two years previously.
Morocco is now an independent kingdom, but at that time
it was still a French Protectorate. The Protectorate dated from
1912, but in point of fact the final pacification of the remote
south was not completed until the middle 30's. It was in this
southern area—between the mountains of the High Atlas and
the deserts of the Sahara—that we spent most of our time.
In 1952 it was still known as the Zone of Insecurity and still a
military area administered by *Les Officiers des Affairs
Indigènes* through the Sheriffian Government of the Sultan.
These officers supervised the building of roads, schools,
hospitals, the collection of the Sultan's taxes, the tribunals
of justice and arbitrated in the constant land disputes that had
previously been settled by inter-tribal war. They were an élite
corps, speaking both Berber and Arab and relying solely on
the force of their personalities. They were the equivalent of
our D.C.s except that they acted always *in loco parentis* to the
Sheriffian Government and had no direct powers of enforce-
ment.

The story of *The Strange Land* is, of course, fiction. But in
the third section particularly I hope I have managed to convey
not only the atmosphere of this primitive and exciting country
on the edge of a vast desert, but also something of the work and
achievements of a dedicated group of French officers who
sacrificed their health and sometimes their lives for a people
not their own.

Hammond Innes
Kersey, 1963

CONTENTS

PART ONE

International Zone

I

The rain came in gusts out of a leaden sky. The flat-topped houses of the old Arab town climbed the hill like a cemetery of close-packed gravestones, windowless, lifeless, their whiteness accentuated by the dusk. There was still light enough for me to see the solitary palm tree above the old Sultan's Palace thrashing its fronds. It was straight like a flagstaff and black against the fading light of the western sky. Down in the harbour a siren blared, the sound of it cut off abruptly as the wind clutched at it. The wide, open space of the Zocco Grande —the big market—was deserted and runnelled by muddy streams of water. Naked lights already glimmered in the squalid huts, revealing the cracked mud of the walls and the still, wrapped bodies of the men who sat there drinking mint tea and smoking their tiny-bowled pipes of kif. An Arab passed me, carrying his slippers in his hand. His djellaba flapped in the wind and his bare feet were wide and splayed as they scuffed through the mud.

The Air France flight from Paris went over, a dull roar of engines in the murk of low-hung cloud. The plane was over two hours late, delayed by bad weather. Even so, it had left Paris only that morning. A day's flying and I could be in England. The rain would be soft and gentle there with the smell of things growing and the promise of spring. I hunched my shoulders into my raincoat and tried not to think of England. My home was Enfida now, close under the mountains of the High Atlas looking out across the flat, brown plain of Marrakech.

But Tangier is a restless, transient place. I had already been waiting three days; and all the time I had carefully avoided my old haunts, trying to tell myself that it was a sordid, unreal city, a sort of international Sodom and Gomorrah, and that the past was all done with. After all, it was here that I had made the big decision. It was here in Tangier that I had thought it all out and taken the plunge. It was crazy perhaps, but at least I was doing something real. And I had made some progress in the last five years; the French no longer regarded me with suspicion and the Berbers of the High Atlas accepted me without hostility. When Kavan arrived. . . .

I half shrugged my shoulders. The sooner I got out of Tangier the better. It was an unsettling place and already the old fever, the desire for excitement, for taking a chance, had got hold of me. But Kavan would be in tonight, and tomorrow we should leave for Enfida where the white mountain peaks are seen through the grey mist of the olive trees and there are no planes roaring over to remind one of England.

The arch of the medina loomed ahead, the entrance to the Arab town and Es Siaghines, the street of the money changers. There were lights in some of the shops, but the street itself was deserted, the steep slope of the asphalt shining blackly. The money changers—operators of one of the world's few free bourses—were gone, and the narrow street was strangely silent. A bundle of rags, propped against a shuttered jeweller's shop, stirred and extended a brass bowl held in two filthy arm stumps.

The forgotten beggar and the deserted bourse seemed somehow symbolic of the bubble nature of Tangier, and I found myself suddenly loathing the place for what it was— crooked and greedy and shallow, a harlot city in a world at grips with the reality of a cold war.

The Zocco Chico was empty, the tables glistening forlornly in the light from the deserted cafés that surrounded it. The little market place was like an Italian piazza in the rain. I took the alley that leads past the grand mosque and went down the steps. The fronds of the palm trees lining the Avenue d'Espagne were waving wildly and the sea roared white along the sands; the noise of it mingled with the wind, so that the whole front was one continuous murmur of sound. Out in the harbour the lights of the anchored freighters shone on heaving, white-capped water. A plume of smoke rose from above the roof of the railway station and was whipped out across the mole in a long, white streamer. I pitied the poor devil I was waiting for and turned into José's Bar.

After all these years the place smelt the same—a combination of coffee, garlic, sour wine and bad sanitation. José was standing behind the bar counter. He looked fatter, greasier, more shifty, and his black hair was grizzled now. " Muy buenas, señor." And then he stared. " Señor Latham!" His face lit up with a smile, his brown teeth showing a grin that cracked the grey stubble. He wiped his hand on his apron and extended it to me across the counter. " It is good to see you, señor. It is a long time—five, six years ; I do not remember. Time goes so quick."

" You've got a good memory, José," I said.

" Si, si. A good memory is necessary in my business." He turned and reached for a bottle. " It is a Fundador, si?"

" No, José. A coffee, that's all."

" Ah, no, no, no." He shook his head. " I do not forget what you drink, and this is with me." He poured two glasses. " Salud!"

" Salud!" I raised my glass. It was like old times. It seemed a long, long time ago.

" A terrible night, señor."

" Terrible." I glanced at my watch. It was nearly six. Youssef was late. But that meant nothing. Time meant nothing in an Arab world. " How's business, José?" I asked. The place was almost empty.

He shrugged his shoulders. " The season, she is finish now." He meant the smuggling season. Not for nothing was José's called the " Smuggler's Bar." It used to be the haunt of half the riff-raff of the port, probably was still. But the Mediterranean in December is no place for small boats. The business would be confined now to the bigger boats and the short runs across to Gib and Algeciras.

I turned and glanced round the café. It was a dreary little place. Yet there were times I could remember when it had seemed gay and bright and cheerful—but then that had been just after the war, late at night when the boys were in after a successful run and José sweating like a bull to keep the glasses filled. Now the piano in the corner was closed and the only music came from the radio, the tinkle of a guitar from some

Spanish station. José's wife, Maria, hummed the tune tonelessly as she sat mending a shirt and watching the pots on the battered range. A child sat at her feet, cross-legged like an Arab and sucking a cork. The place had a tired, run-down air. Two sailors sat at a table engrossed in a game of cards and in the far corner, beyond the door, a girl sat alone, toying with a half-empty glass, whilst two tables away one of the currency boys, with long sideboards and a wide-brimmed hat, sat eyeing her speculatively. There was nobody else in the bar.

" Who's the girl?" I asked José. It was unusual for a girl to sit drinking alone in a place like José's.

He shrugged his shoulders. " I never see her before, señor. I think she is new in Tangier."

" She certainly must be," I said. Didn't she know the sort of place José's was? " You ought to have a notice up outside, José," I said. " ' Abandon hope all girls who enter here.' "

He frowned. " I do not understand, señor."

" Oh, yes you do."

He glared at me angrily, and then he showed his decayed teeth like a bull terrier shifting a snarl to a smirk. " Si, si— always you are the joker, señor."

I turned and glanced at the girl. She had a small, pinched, rather serious face with a finely shaped nose and an attractive mouth. Her skin was pale, accentuating her dark hair, and she had a high, rather bony forehead. She sat with her head a little on one side, staring out of the window, her mouth tightly puckered. There was something of the gamine about her that was appealing, and she wore no make-up, which again was something unusual.

She was apparently aware of my interest, for she glanced at me quickly out of the corners of her eyes. Then she was looking down at her fingers, which were twined round the stem of her glass as though to shatter it. Something about that quick, surreptitious glance had given her face an odd, almost furtive look. Perhaps it was the slant of her eyes. She was frowning now and her lips were no longer puckered, but compressed into a thin, hard line.

" She is not a Tangeroise," José whispered across the bar.

" Of course not."

" She is Inglés perhaps?"

But I shook my head. She didn't look English. I turned back to José. He still had that ugly smirk on his face. " You are married per'aps now, señor?" he suggested.

" No."

" You are still in the business then?"

" Smuggling?" I laughed. " No," I said. " I'm a missionary now."

" A missionary? You?" He let out a great guffaw that came to me hot with the smell of bad breath and garlic. " You a missionary! Si, si. I understand. An Inglés joke, eh?"

I didn't say anything. He'd never understand. How should he when I didn't understand myself? It was just that a man changed as he got older, that excitement palled—that kind of excitement anyway. It had happened to Paul. It had happened to any number of men.

" You are serious, señor?" His tone had changed.

" Yes, José—quite serious."

He mumbled an apology and crossed himself, his fat face sagging. " It is this place, señor. God is not here in Tangier." And he crossed himself again.

And then the door swung open and Youssef came in.

" You're late, Youssef."

He hung his head. " Is wet, m'soor," was all he said. His brown eyes stared up at me. The brown eyes and the big, hooked nose were all that was visible of him. The hood of his djellaba muffled his pock-marked features. He pushed the hood back with long, stained fingers till it showed the red of his tarbush. Little pools of water formed on the floor at his feet. " Very wet, m'soor," he said and shook his djellaba. " Very bad night. Boat not come here. Stop other side, in Spain, I think."

" Well, I don't," I said. " The weather's no worse than they'll have had in the Bay of Biscay. You have a drink, Youssef, and then get back to the douane."

" Okay," he said. " But is no good, m'soor. Boat not in Spain, then is finish."

There was a sudden tinkle of glass. It came from the corner where the girl was sitting. The stem of her glass had snapped. She sat, staring down at the dribble of wine that spilled across the oilcloth covering the table. Her long fingers still gripped

the broken stem. Her face was very white. Again her eyes
darted in my direction, apprehensive, furtive. Then she was
picking up the pieces, her hand trembling slightly, and José
was at her side, explaining volubly that glasses were difficult
to get, that they were expensive. She fumbled in her bag and
brought out a hundred-peseta note, which she handed to him,
at the same time ordering another drink in English that was
too grammatical, as though it were a language learned long ago
and now unfamiliar. She had a soft, slightly husky voice, a
whisper that was as pale and thin as her face.

" I take a café with you, m'soor," Youssef said. " After, I
return to the douane. But is no good."

" They'll come," I said.

" *Insh'Allah*." He shrugged his shoulders. He was a
Christian, one of the few Arab Christians in Tangier, but he
still used that inevitable, fatalistic phrase—*If Allah wills it*.

I was still watching the girl, wondering about her, and when
José returned to the bar, I ordered two coffees and asked him
what nationality he thought she was. He shrugged his shoulders. " You are right," he said. " She speaks your language,
señor, but she is not Inglès. She is not Spanish or French
and she is not an indigène. Perhaps she is Mexican."
He grinned. He had once had a Mexican girl to serve drinks,
but his wife had thrown her out.

Youssef drank his coffee noisily, standing at the bar. He
drank like a horse, sucking it up through his thick lips. Then
he left. I went with him to the door and watched his flapping
figure scurry down to the wharf like a rag blown on the wind.
He was a clerk in the Customs office. He would know sooner
than I could when the boat was sighted.

I stood there for a moment with the rain beating down on
me, listening to the roar of the sea along the beach and
thinking of the two men somewhere out there in the night,
beating into the shelter of Tangier in a 15-ton ketch, fighting
their way through the breaking seas towards the safety of the
harbour. They had been sighted off Cape St. Vincent the day
I had arrived in Tangier and yesterday a freighter had reported
them forty miles south-west of Cadiz. I prayed God that they
would reach Tangier safely. It wasn't only a prayer for two
men in peril on the sea. I needed Dr. Kavan. I knew nothing

about him, had never seen him, and I didn't understand why he had to come out to Tangier in an undermanned yacht, but I needed a doctor, a man who would give his life to the people I lived and worked among, who would give it for a pittance because it was what he wanted to do.

I went slowly back into the bar, conscious of the girl's eyes following me as I crossed the room. The place brought back old memories and I felt a momentary impatience, wishing Kavan would come so that I could get out of the town. José picked the bottle up. "Don't you ever feel you want to go back to Spain?" I asked him.

"Spain?" He stared at me, the bottle poised in his hand. "I fight in the Republican Army. What the hell for I go back to Spain, uhn?" The bottle tinkled against the rim of the glass as he poured. He pushed the drink across to me, not saying anything, his black eyes morose and withdrawn.

"I'm sorry," I said. "I didn't know." I sipped the drink, looking across at him, seeing more now than the fat paunch held in by a leather belt and the matted, hairy chest and the grey, unshaven face, seeing for the first time the man behind the crumbling exterior, the man who had fought for an ideal.

I was still thinking about this, thinking how blind people are, seeing only the ugliness—until suddenly you catch a glimpse of the likeness of God in a man—and then the door was thrust open and the bar was suddenly full of noise. It was Big Harry and his crew. With them were the Galliani brothers and Kostos, the Greek. I had known them all in the old days. "Muy buenas, José," Harry roared. "Set 'em up. Drinks for everybody. The kid, too." He bent down, swept José's little boy up and set him on the bar top. The child gurgled, putting his fat arms round the giant's neck, while the mother smiled coyly. "Come on, José. Make it snappy. We're wet and tired and dam' thirsty. We just got in. An' we got somep'n to celebrate, ain't we, boys?" He grinned round at his crew and there was a murmur of assent.

He was a huge rock of a man dressed in a reefer jacket with a peaked cap that looked several sizes too small for him crammed on to his cannon-ball of a head. He was an ex-Navy petty officer, one of the last of the big-time smugglers who had given Tangier the reputation it had had immediately after the war. Now it was all banking and export-import crookery and he was left to rule a roost that had become no more than a dung heap for Mediterranean small fry to root in. It was sad in a way.

He saw me and grinned and came staggering through the whole bunch of them like a tramp ploughing through a litter of bum boats. " Well, Phip. Good God! Long time no see, eh? What you do for a living these days?" The big hand gripped my shoulder and the round, unshaven face was thrust close to mine. He still had a boyish look, even when liquored up— except for the eyes. " Watcher drinking, cocker?"

" Same as you," I said. " Fundador."

" Ca va. Make it eight, José. An' one fer yourself. We're celebrating."

" Good run?" I asked him.

" Sure we had a good run. We always have good runs. Wet, that's all. Molto bloody wet." He seized hold of the bottle on the counter and took a swig at it. " Only we ain't the only ones to get wet tonight," he said, grinning and wiping his mouth. " There's a poor bastard out there . . . Christ! You never saw such a sight. We picked him up against the beam of Malabata. All plain sail an' going like a train. Couldn't see the boat fer spray. Jesus! There are some crazy bastards! Single-handed and full sail!"

I caught his elbow as he turned back to join his crew. " What sort of boat was she?" I asked him.

" Ketch or yawl—couldn't be certain in the spotlight."

" About fifteen tons?"

" Yeah, about that. Why? You know the boat?"

" If it's the boat I'm expecting, there should be two men on board her."

" Well, this bloke was single-handed."

" How do you know?"

" How do I know? Because there was only one bloke in the Goddamned boat, that's how."

" In the cockpit?"

" Well, he wasn't standing in the bows, I can tell you. She was taking it green, right back as far as the coach-roofing."

" The other fellow was probably below," I said. " In a storm that'd be the sensible——"

"What do you know about it?" He thrust his face close to mine. "In a storm you shorten sail. This crazy bastard had full main and mizzen set, Number One jib and stays'l. If you don't believe me, ask one of the boys. They all saw it. He was a single-hander all right."

Kostos thrust his long nose between us. He had a thin, acquisitive face and dark, restless eyes. "How far is he, this boat?"

"About five miles."

The Greek nodded. "Good. That will be him. And you are right. He is alone—one man."

"Well, that's fine." Big Harry grinned. "Kostos agrees with me. He's never seen the boat, but he agrees with me. That means I'm right, eh?"

Kostos smiled and tapped the side of his nose. "Not a sparrow falls," he said.

Big Harry roared with laugher and clapped him on the back. Then he turned and rolled back along the bar to join his crew. The Greek stared at me. He had grown sleeker and fatter with the years. When I had first come to Tangier he had been a pale, under-nourished little runt of a man, inquisitive, restless, his grubby fingers prodding energetically into every pie. Now his hands were manicured, his clothes well cut and he had an air of flashy opulence. "What do you want with Wade?" he asked me curiously.

"Wade?"

"Yes, Wade: the man who sails this boat into Tangier. What do you want with him?"

"Nothing."

"Then why are you asking about the boat?"

"That's my business."

He stared at me hard. The pupils of his eyes were the colour of sloes when the bloom has been rubbed off. An unpleasant silence stretched between us. I watched him trying to sum me up, trying to understand what I was doing back here in Tangier. "You have been away from here a long time, Captain Lat'am," he said, smiling. "Things have changed. I have an organisation here now, several companies." He paused significantly and then said, "You like a drink?"

"No thank you," I said.

He nodded and smiled. " All right, Lat'am. But don't do nothing foolish." He went back to his drink then and I wondered what his interest was in *Gay Juliet* and her skipper. I was wishing Dr. Kavan had chosen a more conventional method of travelling out. I was wishing, too, that I hadn't decided to wait for the boat at this bar.

I seated myself at one of the tables. A newspaper lay there, the black print of the headlines ringed by the base of a wine glass. Idly, I picked it up. There had been trouble at Casablanca. There was always trouble at Casa, for it grew too fast and the people of the *bled* were herded in packing-case slums of indescribable squalor. And then I noticed the weather report. There was a gale warning, and heavy falls of snow were reported in the High Atlas. The pass of Tizi N Tichka, which linked Marrakech with Ouarzazate, was closed. I had never known the pass blocked so early in the year and I wondered if there had been snow at Enfida. I started thinking of the Mission then, wondering if it was all right and how Julie Corrigan was making out with the kids. George would be painting, of course. He never stopped painting. But Julie . . .

And then I was thinking of the girl again, alone there in the far corner of the bar. The rings of spilled wine had reminded me of how she had snapped the stem of her glass. I lowered the paper. She was still there, and she was staring out of the window, just as she had been when I had first noticed her. But there was nothing to see there; only the rain drops glistening on the glass and the lights of the ships out there in the blackness of the harbour. Her face and neck were reflected in the dark surface of the glass, disembodied and blurred, like the face and neck of a girl in an old painting.

And then I realised that it wasn't the world outside nor the reflection of her own image that she saw there, but the bar and the men ranged along it under the naked lights, the whole room. I couldn't see her eyes, but somehow I knew that she was watching us all surreptitiously. And suddenly I knew, too, that she wasn't here by chance—she was here because she was waiting for somebody, or something. She had the tension and watchfulness and the resignation of a woman waiting. She was massaging nervously at the fingers of her left hand. I couldn't see whether she wore a wedding ring or not, but that was the finger she was massaging.

She turned her head then and our eyes met again. I heard Big Harry shouting to his crew, telling them to drink up and get the hell out of here and go on up to Maxie's with him, and all the time she seemed to be measuring me, trying to make up her mind about something.

Finally she got slowly to her feet. I watched her all the time she was coming across the café towards me. Her clothes were poor and did not fit very well, yet she moved easily and she had a good figure. She didn't smile as she reached my table. She just kept her eyes on mine and said, " Do you mind please if I ask you something?"

" Go ahead," I said, wondering what was coming.

She was nervous and her eyes looked scared. It gave her face a sort of beauty, that and the way her mouth puckered at the corners. " You talk about a boat with the big sailor over there." She nodded towards Big Harry. " When will it come, please?"

" The boat?"

" Yes, the boat."

A chair overturned with a crash as one of the crowd stumbled drunkenly. Harry was leading them out of the bar now.

" Are you waiting for *Gay Juliet,* too?"

She nodded her head solemnly. " Yes, that is the name. When will it come please?"

The street door was wide open now and the wind was blowing sand and dust along the floor. Surprisingly a glint of moonlight streaked the roadway outside. " Soon," I said. " Big Harry saw her five miles out. That was probably an hour ago, maybe more." The street door shut with a bang. " Would you like to join me whilst you're waiting?" I suggested. And when she didn't answer I said, " Why are you interested in the boat? Do you know one of them?"

She shook her head uncertainly, as though bewildered by the question.

" Who is it you're waiting for?" I asked. " Is it Wade or Dr. Kavan?"

Her eyes widened fractionally and her mouth opened as

though she had caught her breath, but she still said nothing and I asked her whether she would like a drink.

" It is kind of you. No." She turned quickly and her heels click-clacked across the wooden floor to her table by the window.

I called to José for another coffee. It came in a cracked cup. A violent gust of wind shook the building. It went tearing and screaming round the walls, tugging at the tin roof. The door burst open and sand blew in along the floor in little, sifting runnels, bringing with it the wild sound of the sea along the beach. The girl shivered. I caught a glimpse of a big, bright moon sailing swiftly amongst torn fragments of cloud, and then José had shut the door again.

" A bad night, señor." José crossed himself and I remembered that he'd been a fisherman in his youth.

Kostos hadn't left with Big Harry and his crowd. He was still standing at the bar, his long, thin nose dipping every now and then to the little glass of liqueur he held in his hand.

There was a conscious stillness about the half-empty bar. It was a silent watchful stillness, as though the whole place were waiting for something to happen. The girl glanced nervously at her watch and then stared resolutely out of the window. Moonlight filtered through on to her face, making it pale like a mask instead of living flesh and blood.

She was waiting for the boat. Kostos was waiting for it, too. All three of us were waiting for the boat, and I wondered what it was like out there in the wind and the waves. Tomorrow it would be hot again with that blazing North African sun heat that bleaches the houses of the kasbah whiter than bone. But right now it was gusting fifty or sixty knots and Big Harry had said the boat was being sailed single-handed. Suppose he were right? Suppose Kavan . . . I felt the need for prayer, but I couldn't, for I was thinking of my plans, not of the man. I didn't know the man. What I did know was that I'd never get another doctor for my Mission on my own terms the way I'd got Kavan. There was something odd about the man, of course. There had to be for him to come a thousand miles to a remote hill village for next to no money. But he had written—*I have the need to lose myself in work that is quite*

*remote from everything that I have been striving for over
many years. That part of my life is finished. Now I wish to
make use of the art of healing I learned as a young man. It
is better so and all I ask is that the work shall absorb me
utterly . . .*

That section of his letter I knew by heart, for when you live
a lonely life, cut off from the world among an alien people, and
you plan to share that life with another man, a man you do
not know, then you search urgently for any scrap that may
give you some clue to the sort of person he is.

I was still wondering about him when the door opened and
Youssef burst in. " Come quick, m'soor," he called, flapping
urgently across to me, his hooked nose moist and blue with the
wind. " Quick. Is finish, the boat. Is to be a tragedy." He
caught hold of my arm. " Quick. I show you." The words
spilled out of him in breathless puffs. The whole café was
silent, listening.

I pulled him down into the chair beside me. " Just tell me
quietly what happened."

He caught his breath. " Is the wind—a terrible blow of
wind. It take the roof from one of the warehouses and there
is a little house down near the——"

" The boat," I said, shaking him. " Tell me about the boat."

" Oui, m'soor. I tell you. Is finish—no good—*kaput*."

" You mean it's sunk?"

" Non, non. Not sink. Is finish."

" For Heaven's sake, Youssef—what's happened?"

" Is the wind, m'soor. Is coming into Tangier, the boat, and
I am watching it and there is terrible blow of wind and—
pouff." He blew out his lips and shrugged his shoulders. " The
big sail is finish and the boat is blown away."

" Where? Where is it now?"

" Below the kasbah, m'soor. Per'aps he obtain the Baie des
Juifs. I do not know."

" What are they doing about it—the port authorities?"

" Nothing. They can do nothing. They have telephone to
the police." He shrugged his shoulders again. " Is to be a
tragedy." He seemed to like the word. " You come quick
now. You see. I do not lie."

I followed him out of the café then. The girl was standing, wide-eyed and shaken, by the door as I opened it. "You'd better come, too," I suggested.

Outside, the wind and the sea still roared along the beach, but the sky was clear now, a blue-black sky, studded with stars and dominated by the white orb of the moon which flung a glittering pathway across wind-white waters. Youssef clutched my arm and pointed. Beyond the roof of the Customs House, against the black blur of the sea, a patch of white showed, a rag hung momentarily above the waves and then lost in spray. It emerged again and, shielding my eyes from the wind, I saw vaguely the shape of a boat with heads'ls set and drawing. And then it was gone again, like a phantom boat, as the spray smothered it.

"Oh, God!" the girl whispered, and when I looked at her I saw her eyes were closed and her lips were moving silently.

I told Youssef to phone for a taxi and then I took her arm. "Would you like a drink?" I had half turned her back towards the bar and, as Youssef opened the door, I saw Kostos momentarily outlined against the rectangle of light. He was staring along the line of the cliffs, watching the death struggles of the boat, and his hands were clasped together, the fingers pressed against the knuckles as though by mere physical effort of thrusting at his hands he could pull the boat through.

"Come on," I said to the girl. "A drink will do you good."

But she remained quite still, resisting the pressure of my hand. "No," she whispered. "I do not want a drink."

She was trembling. I could feel her body shaking. "Who do you know on the boat?" I asked her. She wasn't English. It had to be Kavan. "Is it Dr. Kavan?"

She nodded dumbly.

"You're a Czech then?" I said.

"My mother was Irish," she answered as though that made some sort of difference.

I stared out across the docks to the moonlit fury of the sea. It was a wild, terrifying sight. The cliffs were black in shadow and the sea was white with driven spray and the backlash of the tide running around Cape Spartel. I was thinking about Kavan and how little I knew about him—just that he was a Czech and was thirty-eight years old and that he had been trained in his youth as a doctor. The Mission authorities in London had not been involved. This was a purely personal arrangement and the only information I had on him was what he had given me in those two letters—the first applying for the post in answer to my advertisement and the second informing me that he was sailing with a man called Wade in the fifteen-ton ketch *Gay Juliet*. I hadn't dared ask questions, for his had been the only application I had received. "How did you know he was on the boat?" I asked the girl.

I thought for a moment that she hadn't heard my question and I glanced at her face. It was very pale in the moonlight and there were lines of strain at the corners of eyes and mouth. "He told me," she whispered. "We still have means of communicating." And her mouth was shut in a tight, hard line and I felt her body shake again, though she wasn't crying.

Youssef came back to us out of the bar. "The taxi is coming, m'soor."

The girl didn't move, didn't look at him. She was staring at the point where we'd last seen the boat. I wanted to ask her about Kavan, but it would have to wait. This wasn't the moment. She was racked with fear and there was a sort of desperate bitterness about her face. I looked round for Kostos, but he'd gone. And then a police jeep drove past and went through the dock gates and stopped at the Customs House.

The girl stopped trembling. She was suddenly incredibly still. And when I looked at her, she wasn't staring at the sea any more, but at the little group that had gathered about the jeep, gesticulating and pointing towards the cliffs where the boat had disappeared. Customs officers and police piled into the jeep and it turned and came racing past us again and disappeared down the Avenue d'Espagne, the red tail-light dwindling to a pinpoint. The girl found her voice then. "What are the police going to do? Why have they been called?" Her voice was scared, a little breathless.

"The boat's in distress," I reminded her.

"That is purely a job for the coastguards, not for the police."

I shrugged my shoulders, not understanding her concern. "There's a lot of smuggling goes on in Tangier," I told her.

" Smuggling?" She repeated the word slowly as though she'd never heard it before. " But if they——" She stopped suddenly as though biting back her words. And then she said, " I suppose it does not matter. So long as they get him safe ashore. Nothing else matters." But there was an odd reservation on her voice as though there were things worse than drowning.

The taxi arrived then and we got in and I ordered the driver to take us to the Pension de la Montagne. From the terrace there we should have a clear view right across Jews' Bay where the oued that the Europeans call Jews' River runs out into the sea. To go up to the kasbah meant walking and would take too long, and if we drove to the Marchan on this side of the bay, we should lose ourselves in a tangle of undergrowth and villas.

The girl sat very still as we drove up through the Place de France and out along the route de la Montagne. She didn't talk. She had her hands clasped tightly on her lap and her face, in the flash of the street lamps, was set and tense. We crossed the Pont des Juifs, and then the headlights were cutting up through a narrow road hemmed in by steep, walled banks, where the bougainvillea showed as splashes of bright purple on the walls of villas. At the bend halfway up la Montagne, we turned off on to a track, and in a moment we were in bright moonlight with a clear view of the sea below.

We left the taxi then and walked through the arched gateway of the pension and out on to the terrace. The wind caught us there, driving the breath back into our throats. The view was magnificent. On the dark slopes of the Marchan opposite, the lights of the villas shone like glow-worms, and beyond, the kasbah sprawled over its hill like a bone-white cemetery. Below us, the sea was deeply ridged and flecked with white. I shaded my eyes from the moon's glare and stared down along the line of the cliffs beyond to Marchan.

" Do you see it?" the girl asked.

" No."

It was dark below the Marchan and all I could see was the white of the waves breaking. Then Youssef was pointing and I thought I saw the triangle of a sail. But it vanished as though it were a trick of the light. The girl saw it, too, and said,

"We must do something. Please can you do something."
There was a desperate urgency in her plea.

"There's nothing we can do," I said. "We can only wait
until . . ." And then, suddenly, I saw the boat quite clearly.
It had emerged from the shadow of the Marchan and was out
in the moonlight. It was edging along the coast, close in and
half-smothered by the break of the waves. The wind was
driving it straight into the bay. "They'll beach her in the bay,"
I said. The yacht hadn't a hope of wearing the headland below
us. "Come on." I caught her arm and we ran back to the
taxi.

"Is there any hope for him?" she asked as the taxi turned
and started back down the hill.

"I don't know," I said. "The sea looks pretty bad down
there. But if the boat comes in close . . ." She was looking at
me and there was a desperate pleading in her eyes, so that I
felt her fear as though it were my own. "Why does he mean
so much to you?" I asked gently.

"He is my husband." She said it so quietly, so softly, that I
scarcely caught the words, only the meaning. And then in a
sudden rush she added, "We were engaged before the war.
Christmas, 1938. And then in March the Germans came and,
because he was a scientist, they forced him to go to Germany.
We didn't see each other until after the war. Then he came
back and we were married. We were married two years. Then
the Russians came and he escaped to England. We only had
those two years." There was no bitterness in the way she said
it, only a sort of hopeless resignation.

It seemed odd her talking about him whilst the man himself
was fighting for his life down there in the bay and we were
careering down the hill to be there when the boat struck.
"Why didn't you go to him in England?" I asked. "If you
could get to Tangier . . ." I felt the sentence unfinished, for
she was staring at me, sudden fear and suspicion in her eyes.

"Who are you? Why are you here, waiting for him?" It
was the same breathless rush of words, but difficult now, harder
and more withdrawn.

"I'm Philip Latham," I said. And then I began to explain
about the Mission and my need of a hospital and how we had
so little money that I had despaired of ever getting a doctor

out from England. And before I had finished, the taxi had
swung off the road on to a track that ran down through a
squalid, mud-walled village and finished on the banks of the
oued.

The police jeep was parked there. And beside it was a big
American car, its chromium glinting in the moonlight. She
gave a little gasp and clutched my arm. She was staring at
the jeep. "Why can't they leave him alone?" she whispered.
I stared at her, not understanding the cause of her outburst.

It was the car that puzzled me. The village was half a mile
away and there was no villa near. "Do you know whose car
this is?" I asked Youssef.

But he shook his head. "There are many American cars in
Tangier, m'soor. Very expensive, very nice. Per'aps I have
American car one day." He grinned at me from beneath the
hood of its djellaba. An American car was the dream of every
Arab in Tangier.

We pushed past the jeep and hurried along the path that ran
beside the oued. The pounding of the sea was hurled at us on
the wind and soon a fine spray was drifting across our faces.
Then we were out on a little bluff that was all coarse grass and
sand, and there, straight ahead of us, was the yacht, its jib
bellied out as it ran for the shore with the wind and sea behind
it. A lone figure stood on the edge of the bluff, curiously
insubstantial and ghostly in the driven spume and the moonlight. He turned as we came up. It was Kostos.

"What are you doing here?" I shouted to him.

His long face smiled at me. But he didn't say anything, only
turned and stared out across the surging, foaming surf to
where the boat was piling in, its bows lifting to a wave and
then creaming forward on the break of it.

"Who is that man?" the girl asked me. "He was there in
the café. What does he want?"

"His name is Kostos," I said. "I think he's waiting for
Wade."

"Wade?"

"The owner of the boat."

"Oh, I see." She was staring down at the beach where a
little group of officials stood at the water's edge, watching the
boat. It was in the broken water now and I wondered how the

poor devils who sailed her expected to get ashore through those thundering acres of surf.

A hand gripped my elbow and I turned to find Kostos at my side. "Why do you come here, Lat'am?" he shouted at me. "What is your interest in the boat?"

"What's yours?" I demanded.

He stared at me hard and then asked about the girl.

"She's come here to meet Kavan," I told him.

"Who?"

"Dr Kavan," I shouted.

"Kavan? But there is only Wade on the boat."

"No. A Dr. Kavan is with him."

"I don't believe it." He stared at me. "Why should he bring Kavan? He would not be such a fool." And then he caught hold of my arm. "What do you know about this, Lat'am?"

But my attention switched to the boat then as she lifted high on the curling crest of a breaker. I thought for a moment that she was going to broach-to; she swung almost broadside and then twisted back on to her pell-mell course of destruction, steadying in the surf and driving forward through the broken water, her bows half buried by the press of canvas for'ard. She was surging straight in towards us and I realised that the man at the helm had seen the channel cut by the oued and was driving her towards it. But the oued was only a trickle. The channel did not extend into the sands.

The tall mainmast quivered as she struck. She held there for a moment, her waterline showing like a red wound in the backwash, and then the next wave had piled in on top of her, jerking her forward, covering her with a seething cataract of foam like a half-submerged rock. And as the wave receded, a lone man fought his way for'ard to the bows. He wore a life jacket and for a moment he stood there, his head turned, watching the next wave climb and curl above the stern of the boat. I heard the girl give a cry that was as wild and forlorn as a sea bird's, and then the wave was breaking and the figure of the man plunged into the surf of it and was lost.

I ran down to the sands then. The little group by the water's edge had a rope, but they were arguing and gesticulating. They weren't going to risk their necks in that sea. I stripped off my

clothes and seized the end of the rope and tied it round my
waist. I could see the swimmer's head now. He was halfway
between the yacht and the beach and he was being swept out
again in the backwash of a wave. " Hold that," I shouted to
one of the gendarmes, thrusting the end of the rope into his
hand. And then I was wading out through the warmth of the
water, letting the backwash carry me towards the dark head of
the swimmer where he was being sucked into the break of the
next wave.

I called to him as my legs were swept from under me, and
then I was swimming. I met the on-coming breaker with my
body flat, spearing through it, coming up with my ears
singing with the rush of it, and then swimming hard with the
rope tugging at my belly.

The yacht wasn't far now. It shifted in the break of a wave.
The waves seemed huge in the moonlight. They piled in, one
after the other, growing, white-capped mountains that rose
up as though from some subterranean commotion, rose up to
impossible heights and then toppled and fell with the crushing
weight of tons of water. Their surf piled over me, flinging
me shorewards, filling mouth, ears, eyes and nose full of the
burning, sand-laden salt of the water.

I prayed to God that they would keep a firm hold on the
rope, knowing no swimmer could get ashore through this
unaided, and then I came up gasping for breath, searching
desperately for the man I'd come in after. The tug of a
backwash got me, tossed me into the maw of a breaker, which
toyed with me and spewed me up out of its creaming back,
and there he was, lying like a log not twenty yards to my left.

I put my head down and began to swim. Another wave
piled over me and then I was seaward of him, treading water,
waiting to hold him in the backwash. I caught him just as the
next wave engulfed us. I got my fingers into his life jacket and
kicked with all my strength. And as we broke surface, I felt
the rope tighten round my body, biting into my flesh as they
held the two of us against the back-surge. And then they were
dragging us in, my lungs fighting for breath against the
constriction of the rope and the tug of the man's waterlogged
body.

After what seemed an age there came a wave that rolled us forward like logs before a wall of broken water, engulfed us and then subsided to leave my feet scrabbling desperately in a moving tide of sand.

After that there wasn't any danger any more, only the leaden weakness of my legs as I forced them to drag myself and my burden clear of the pull of the surf. Where the sea ended and the sands showed hard and white in the moonlight I staggered and fell forward on to my hands. I was completely drained of energy, utterly exhausted. They dragged us higher up the sands to safety and then fingers unknotted the rope from around my waist and began to rub my body to restore the circulation.

Slowly the blood pumped energy back into my limbs and I pulled myself into a sitting position. I saw the bay and the white surf in the moonlight and the lank hair lying across the man's bloodless face. He was short and thick-set and he had a round head set close into broad, powerful shoulders. One arm was bent across his chest. He looked like a little bearded Napoleon.

And then everything was blurred and I retched, emptying myself of the sea water that was in my lungs and stomach. I was sweating suddenly and very cold.

One of the Spanish Customs officers helped me to my feet. And then Youssef was there. He had slipped out of his djellaba and he thrust it down over my head, whether to cover my nakedness or to keep me warm I don't know. The cloth was soft and it kept out the wind. I pulled it close round me, trying to control the shivering of my body. The girl was still standing up there on the bluff, her hands clasped together, her body leant forward as though she were on the point of rushing down on to the beach; but yet she did not move. She stayed up there as though her feet were somehow rooted to the spot.

The officials were all bending over the man I had pulled out of the sea. One of them had turned him over on his face and had begun to work on him, kneeling astride him and pressing rhythmically with the palms of his hands against the man's shoulders, thrusting down with all his weight. Kostos hovered uncertainly in the background. One of the police, a sergeant, caught hold of my hand and pumped it up and down and slapped me on the back as though by shaking my hand and congratulating me and telling me I was a brave man he could absolve himself from his failure to enter the water.

And all the time I stood there, feeling dazed, staring down at the face of the stranger that was pressed against the sand. It was a round, white face under the dark stubble of the beard, the lips slightly parted, blowing frothy bubbles. Then the eyes opened and they were bloodshot and wild in the moonlight. He began to retch with a ghastly concentration, and a pool of water appeared where his mouth touched the sand and trickled away under his body. He groaned, shook himself, and crawled slowly to his feet, swaying slightly and blinking his eyes. He stared at us for a moment, rubbed at the salt in his eyes with his knuckles, and then looked back at the yacht where it lay, canted over, the waves thundering across its decks.

"What about the other man?" I asked him.

He didn't seem to hear, so I caught him by the arm and repeated my question.

He looked at me then. There was blood trickling down from a cut on his head, a bright scarlet runnel of blood in the sand that covered his temple. His eyes were half closed and his mouth was a thin line as though compressed by pain. Then he looked past me at the police and the Customs officers and his eyes were wide open and I saw that he was fully conscious, his brain alive again.

The sergeant saw it, too. He stepped forward. "Your name please, Señor?" he asked in Spanish. The man didn't reply and the sergeant said, "Are you Señor Kavan? Señor Jan Kavan, a resident of Great Britain?"

The man made some sort of sound, inarticulate as a grunt, as though somebody had punched him in the solar plexus. He was staring at the police, swaying slightly, his eyes immensely blue and wide open, dazed with shock. And then Kostos pushed his way through the little circle of officials. "You are Mr. Wade, yes?" He gripped the man's arm, shaking him. "You do not bring anybody else with you, eh?"

The man shook his head dumbly.

"Good. I thought not. You are very fortunate man, Mr.

Wade. One time I do not think you make it. But now, everything is all right, eh? I am Kostos."

The man stared at him with the same concentration with which he had stared at the police. He was puzzled and uneasy. The sergeant cleared his throat and addressed Kostos. "You know this man, Señor Kostos?"

" Si, si." The Greek nodded emphatically. " He is Mr. Roland Wade—an Englishman. The yacht out there is called *Gay Juliet*. He has sailed it direct from England."

" Is this correct, señor?" the sergeant asked.

The man I had pulled out of the sea stared wildly round the group, half-nodded and pushed his hand wearily through his hair. " Please I am cold. I must get some clothes. I'm very tired."

The sergeant was sympathetic, but he was also correct. " Have you anything by which to identify yourself, Señor Wade? Your passport? The certificate of registration of your boat? Entry into the International Zone of Tangier, you must understand, can only be permitted on production of the necessary passport." It was really rather ridiculous, the pompous little sergeant demanding a passport from the poor devil there on the sands in the roar of the wind and the sea.

The man moved his hand in a vague, automatic gesture towards his breast pocket and let it fall limp at his side. His eyes closed and he swayed. I thought he was going to pass out. So did Kostos. We both caught hold of him at the same time. " Can't you settle this in the morning, sergeant?" I said. " The man is in no state to go through the immigration formalities now."

The sergeant hesitated, frowning. He stared at the stranger, whose body sagged heavily between the two of us. His eyes ceased to be impersonal, official, became sympathetic. "Si, si." He nodded energetically. " The formalities will be dealt with in the morning. For the moment, señor, I permit you to land." He made an expansive, accommodating gesture, and looked round for confirmation from the Customs officers, who nodded agreement. They crowded round him then, bowing and offering him their congratulations at his miraculous escape from death.

" Help me get him out of here, Lat'm," Kostos hissed.

" Mr Wade." He shook the man's arm. " I have a car waiting for you. Can you walk to my car?"

The officials had broken away from us and were going down the beach to recover their rope. The man seemed to pull himself together. " I'm all right," he mumbled. He had his eyes open again and was standing more firmly.

" What about the other man?" I asked him again.

" What other man?" His voice was slurred, almost inaudible against the sound of the surf.

" There were two of you on the boat."

He shook his head slowly. " No. Only myself. I am single-handed—all the way from England." He spoke quickly, violently.

" You see," Kostos said to me. " It is as I tell you in the café. There is only Wade on the boat." He tightened his hold on the man's arm. " I have been expecting you."

" Expecting me?" The man stared at him, his expression one of bewilderment. " I don't understand."

" I tell you. I am Kostos."

" Leave it at that," I said. " He's about all in."

" You keep out of this, Lat'am. Mr Wade."

But the man had turned and was staring up the beach. And then he saw the girl and stopped. She was standing about ten yards away. She had her back to the moonlight and I couldn't see the expression on her face, but her hands were held slightly forward, her body too, as though she were entreating him to say he was her husband.

And for a moment I thought he knew her. His eyes had come suddenly alive and his mouth opened, but all he uttered was a sort of groan and then his eyes closed and his knees buckled slowly under him. The police sergeant ran forward, clicking his tongue. He bent over the man's body lying there in the sand and then he looked up at the girl. " You know Señor Wade?" he asked.

She backed away slowly and shook her head. " No. I do not know him." Her body seemed suddenly slack as though all the strength had gone out of her with the realisation that the man was a stranger. She turned, slowly, reluctantly, her head bowed, and walked back alone across the bluff, back towards the taxi.

So Kostos was right. Kavan wasn't on the boat. I went and got my clothes and pulled them on. By the time I was dressed, the little party of officials, carrying the unconscious body of the man I had rescued, was climbing the bluff. Only Kostos still remained there on the wet, gleaming stretch of the sands. He was staring after the little cavalcade. I stared at them, too, wondering about Kavan. Had he changed his mind? Had he decided at the last minute not to sail in *Gay Juliet*? I felt tired and dispirited. And as I walked up the beach, I wasn't thinking about the girl. I was thinking of myself, of the people of Enfida and the mountain villages who needed a doctor, of the fact that the way to their confidence, to the success of my work, lay through medical aid.

Youssef was waiting for me at the foot of the bluff. I gave him his djellaba and we climbed through the wet sand. At the top of the bluff, I turned to look at the yacht again. A glint of metal caught my eye. Kostos was still there on the beach and he was ripping open the discarded life jacket with a knife. As I watched him, he flung the jacket down and started up the beach towards us.

I glanced at the yacht. The starboard shrouds had already parted and the mast was swaying wildly. It was only a matter of time before the whole thing broke up. It was cold there in the wind and spray and I turned and hurried after Youssef along the path beside the oued. We caught up with the others just as they reached the cars. They had halted beside the jeep, the half-conscious man held up between them. He was shivering violently and I suggested that he'd better come with me in the taxi. It would be warmer. The sergeant nodded. "You will take him to the hospital, señor?"

Apparently the poor devil understood Spanish, for he caught hold of my arm in a quick, urgent movement. "Not a hospital," he said. "There's nothing wrong with me. I just want some sleep, that's all." He was scared of something. It was there in his eyes. They were imploring like the eyes of a stray dog. And I heard myself tell the sergeant that I would take him to my hotel. He asked me the name of it and I told him the Hotel Malabata. He glanced at the man and then nodded and climbed into his jeep.

I saw the look of relief in the man's eyes and then he had

closed them and his body sagged as though he had suddenly relaxed his hold on consciousness. Youssef and I had to carry him to the taxi.

I had expected the girl to be sitting there, waiting for us. But she wasn't in the taxi and when I asked the driver whether he had seen her, he said " No." I turned and stared back along the path but there was no sign of her. I wondered whether to go and look for her, but I was cold and the man was just about all in. I decided the girl would have to look after herself and I got into the taxi. As we drove off I caught a glimpse of Kostos running towards us. He shouted something. I think it was the man's name. And then we were bumping our way back to the village and the road to Tangier, the police jeep following behind us.

II

It seemed a long drive back to Tangier. I felt tired and sick and dispirited, and the taste of the salt water I had swallowed was like a thick, furry film on my tongue. The man I had pulled out of the water lay slumped in his corner and I sat and stared at him, almost hating him. Why couldn't it be Kavan? If only one man was going to arrive in that boat, why couldn't it be . . . We were on a bend and his eyes suddenly flicked open and he grabbed at me. " Look out! Hold on!" His voice was thick and blurred. He was back on the boat. Then he slumped back in the seat again and his head was lolling and he was mumbling to himself.

I should have realised the significance of his words immediately. But my brain was dulled with the cold and it only came to me slowly. That warning had been shouted to somebody. If in his mind he were back on the boat then he couldn't have been alone; there would have been no reason in shouting a warning if he were single-handed. In a sudden surge of anger I caught hold of him and shook him and shouted, " What happened to Kavan? What have you done with him?" I was convinced now that Kavan had been on that boat.

But the man was dazed and only half conscious. He mumbled something I couldn't understand and then his head was lolling again to the movement of the car. The blood was caked on his temple and his face was grey with exhaustion. My mood changed from anger to pity and I leaned back and closed my eyes. I could find out about Kavan later. I was thinking what it must have been like at the helm of that yacht coming down through the Bay of Biscay and along the coasts of Spain and Portugal in winter. And then I began to think about Enfida again and how I had told the chiefs of all the villages about my plans and had persuaded them to send men down to help me build an extension to the house to act as a surgery and dispensary. They would shrug their shoulders and murmur *insh'Allah.* But it was a serious blow to my work. And it was no use pretending I should get another doctor. Kavan alone had replied to my advertisements. The salary I was able to offer was too small. I would be able to have stayed on here in Tangier and run a few more cargoes. If I had done that . . .

It was stupid to think like that, but my mind was confused and angry. In my loneliness and isolation I had built too much upon Kavan, upon this idea of getting a doctor out to the mountain villages. I closed my eyes wearily, sinking back into a lassitude of exhaustion, too tired to face the thought of planning for the future again.

And then the taxi stopped and we were at the Hotel Malabata. It was a small, cheap hotel occupying a part of one of those grey blocks of cracking concrete that cling to the escarpment above the Avenue d'Espagne. I pushed open the taxi door and stumbled out. The police jeep had parked behind us and they came and lifted the unconscious man out and carried him into the hotel. As I paid off the driver, an American car rolled quietly down the cobbled street, paused beside the taxi and then drove on. It was Kostos, and in the gleam of the street lighting I saw the hard, inquisitive stare of his eyes.

The hotel was full, but the patrone agreed to let the man share my room and they carried him up the stairs and laid him on the stiff, horse-hair couch at the foot of the bed. The police and Customs officers left then with little bows, each of them shaking me by the hand and commending me for having saved the man's life. "We will return in the morning, señor," the sergeant said. "For the formalities, you understand." The Customs officers nodded. "Buenas noches, señor."

"Buenas noches."

They were gone and the door shut behind them and I stood there, shivering and staring down at the man on the couch. His eyes were closed and his body trembled uncontrollably with the cold. His skin had a wax-like transparency and the blue veins of his forehead showed through like the marks of an indelible pencil. I felt deathly tired. All I wanted to do was to get into my bed and sleep, and I wished I had ignored his plea and taken him straight to the French hospital. But he was here now and I was responsible for him. I sent Youssef for hot-water bottles and began to strip off his sodden clothing.

Below his oilskin jacket I found a waterproof bag hung by a line round his neck. It had the hard compactness of documents; the ship's papers presumably and the log. I tossed it on to the bed, making a mental note to have a look at it later. His sodden clothes I piled on the floor where they formed a little pool of water that trickled away across the bare tiles under the bed.

I was struggling to pull off his blue seaman's jersey when his eyes flicked open. They were incredibly blue. His hair was lank and his beard all grey with salt. Combined with the marble pallor of his face, it made him look like a corpse given back by the sea. He stared up at me. It was a fixed, glazed stare, without expression. His mouth opened, but no sound emerged from the cracked lips. He wiped his hand across his face, slowly, wearily, and then reached out automatically for something he imagined to be hanging above his head. "Is it my watch already? I'm just coming." His voice was dead and quite toneless.

Then, suddenly, there was consciousness in his eyes as they stared up at me and his forehead creased in a puzzled frown. He pushed himself up on his elbow with a quick-violent movement and stared wildly around the room. "Who are you? What am I doing here?" His eyes had come back to my face and his voice was hard and urgent.

I started to explain and he nodded as though it were all coming back to him. "Have the police gone?"

"Yes."

"You were down on the beach, waiting for me, weren't you?"

"I was waiting for Kavan," I said.

He nodded. "Then you must be Philip Latham."

"You know my name?" I stared at him. And then I caught hold of him, gripping his arm. "How do you know my name's Philip Latham? Did Kavan tell you I'd be waiting here for him?" I shook him violently. "What happened to him? He was on the boat, wasn't he? What happened to him?"

He stared at me. His eyes had a dazed look and he was frowning as though trying to concentrate his thoughts.

"What happened to Jan Kavan?" I repeated.

"Nothing." His voice sounded dazed, and then in the same flat tone he added, "I am Jan Kavan."

"What?" I didn't understand for the moment. "What was that you said?"

His eyes were suddenly wide open and he fought to raise himself. "It's true, isn't it? You are Latham?"

"Yes."

"What did you mean just now?" I shouted at him. "You said you were Kavan. What did you mean?"

"Yes. I am Kavan." He said it wearily.

"But——" I stared at him stupidly. "You're not Wade at all then," I heard myself say.

"No. I told you. I'm Jan Kavan. I've come here to act as a doctor . . ."

"But you said you were Wade. Down there on the beach——"

"I never said I was Wade," he said quickly.

"But you let Kostos think——" I stopped there. It was so unbelievable.

"I'm sorry," he murmured. "I wanted to tell you, but——" He frowned. "Who is that man Kostos? What did he want—do you know?"

"Nothing," I said. "He was meeting Wade, that's all." It didn't matter about Kostos. It didn't matter about anything. Kavan was alive. He was here in my room. "Did you check up on trachoma?" I asked. It was a stupid thing to ask of a man who was so utterly exhausted, but I couldn't help it. I couldn't think of anything but the fact that he was alive, that my dream of a doctor at the Mission was coming true. Eye diseases were the bane of the Berber people in their fly-ridden villages.

"Yes," he said wearily. "I checked up on everything—all the things I have forgotten." He sighed and then said, "When do we leave for your Mission?"

"As soon as you're fit enough to travel," I said.

"Good." He nodded and closed his eyes. I thought for a moment that he had lost consciousness again, but then his eye-lids flicked back and he was looking up at me again. "Is Kasbah Foum anywhere near your Mission?" he asked.

"Kasbah Foum?" It was an Arab name, meaning fort at the entrance. Probably it was somewhere down in the south, in the kasbah country beyond the High Atlas. "No," I replied. "Why?"

"I have to go there. It's important. I have to go to Kasbah Foum." He spoke in a whisper, his voice urgent. "Wade told me that the Caid's son . . ." He stopped there and his eyes closed again.

That mention of Wade brought me back to the problems of the moment. "What happened to him?" I demanded. "What happened to Wade?"

But he didn't answer. His eyes remained closed. It was then I began to get uneasy. The police would have to be informed that he was Kavan. And then there would be an investigation. It might take some days. . . . "Where's Wade?" I asked him again. And when he still didn't answer, I took hold of him and shook him. "What happened to Wade?" I was certain he wasn't unconscious, and yet . . . "You'll have to explain to the police," I told him.

"The police?" His eyes flicked open again and he stared up at me. There was something near to panic in his face.

"They're coming here tomorrow."

"Tomorrow." He said it as though it were some distant thing like a mountain peak that had to be faced and overcome.

"It was Wade's boat," I said. "You couldn't have left England without him. He was the skipper. What happened? You must tell me what happened."

"Wade's dead." He said it in a flat, toneless voice. There was a sort of hopelessness in the way he said it.

So Wade was dead. Somehow I wasn't surprised or even shocked. Maybe I was too tired and my senses were dulled. All I knew was that if this was Kavan, then Wade had to be dead. And then I remembered how he'd said he was alone on the boat, that he'd come single-handed from England and an awful thought came into my mind. "What happened?" I asked. "For God's sake tell me what happened."

He stared at me, his eyes clouded as though he were looking back through time to a scene that was indelibly imprinted on his mind. "I don't know. I don't know how it happened. He just seemed to jump over the guardrail into the sea."

There was a pause and then he lifted his head and stared up at me and it all came out of him in a rush. "It was off Cape St. Vincent. It had been blowing. The seas were terrible; great big seas, but not breaking then. It was night and I remember the St. Vincent light was winking at us on the port quarter. There had been a bad storm, but the wind had dropped and it was a clear night. The sea was big and confused and there was a lot of movement And we were tired. I was just coming on watch to relieve him. We were both of us in the cockpit. Then the jib sheet broke. The sail was flapping about and I had hold of the helm. It was difficult to hold the boat. She was yawing wildly and Wade jumped out of the cockpit to get the sail down. He was tired, that was the trouble. We were both of us tired. He jumped out of the cockpit straight into the sea. That was the way it seemed. He just jumped straight over the guardrail."

He pushed his hand through his hair and glanced up at me. "You believe me, don't you?" His voice was agitated. "There was nothing I could do The boat sunk away into a trough and then he was in the water. I saw him reach up to catch hold of the side and a wave came and he disappeared. I threw the lifebelt to him I think he got hold of it. I don't know. It was dark. The moon had set. It took me a long time to go about single-handed and I didn't see him again, though I sailed round and round that area till dawn and for a long time after."

He lay back, exhausted. "That's all," he said. "That's how

it happened. There was nothing I could do. . . ." His voice trailed away. His eyes closed and he drifted into unconsciousness again, or maybe it was sleep. His face was relaxed, his breathing easier and more regular.

Youssef came back then with four wine bottles filled with hot water. I got some underclothes from my suitcase, wrapped them round the bottles and slipped them into the bed. Then we got Kavan stripped and I washed his body with hot water, rubbing hard with a towel to restore the circulation. His back and buttocks were covered with salt water sores, little nodules of suppuration that bled when I rubbed them. Patches of white, scabrous skin flaked away and his feet and hands were soft and wrinkled with long immersion.

" Is going to die?" Youssef asked.

" Of course not." I spoke sharply, conscious of the Arab's fascination at the white European body lying naked and hurt and helpless. We got him on to the bed and I piled the blankets on top of him and then I sent Youssef for a doctor I had known, a Frenchman who had lived just across the Boulevard Pasteur.

Then at last I was free to slip out of my own damp clothes. I put on a dressing-gown and lit a cigarette. I would have liked a bath, but the hotel was inexpensive and Spanish and its occupants were expected to use the public baths or go without. I sat on the bed, thinking of the girl and their meeting on the beach. Of course, they had recognised each other. That was why he had collapsed. It was the shock of recognising her. He had said he was Wade and then she had turned away and disappeared. There was no longer any doubt in my mind. This man lying on my bed really was Jan Kavan. But why had he said he was Wade? That was the thing I couldn't understand. And he'd been scared of the police. Why?

I dragged myself to my feet and went over to the chair where my clothes lay. Both his letters were in my wallet—his original application and his note saying that he would be sailing with Wade on *Gay Juliet*.

Youssef returned as I was getting out my wallet. The French doctor had moved. Nobody seemed to know where he now lived. I looked at Kavan lying there on the farther side of the big double bed. His eyes were closed and he was breathing peacefully. It was sleep he needed more than a doctor. I let it go at that and paid Youssef off with two hundred peseta notes. Then I switched over to the bedside lamp and checked through the letters.

It was the one in which he had applied for the post of doctor to the Mission that chiefly interested me. I knew it all, of course, but I was hoping that perhaps there was something I had missed, some little point that would now prove significant. I ran through it quickly. . . .

I will be quite frank. I am 38 years old and I have not looked at a medical book since I obtained my degree. Nor have I at any time practised as a doctor. I studied at Prague, Berlin and Paris. My father was a specialist in diseases of the heart, and it was for him I passed my examinations. Already I was primarily interested in physics. All my life since then has been devoted to scientific research.

Normally I would not think of applying for a position as doctor, but I gather from your advertisement that you are in desperate need of one, that you can pay very little and that your Mission is in a remote area amongst backward people. I am a man of some brilliance. I do not think I should let you down or prove inadequate for the task. I am a Czech refugee and for personal reasons I wish to get out of England. I have the need to lose myself in work quite remote . . .

I folded the letter up and put it back in my wallet. He was a Czech refugee. He had been a scientist. He had personal reasons for wanting to leave England.

There was nothing there I had missed.

He had cabled acceptance of my offer. The final letter had merely announced that the French had given him a visa to work as a doctor in Morocco and that he would be sailing with Wade in the fifteen-ton ketch, *Gay Juliet*, leaving Falmouth on November 24, and arriving Tangier by December 14, all being well. He hadn't mentioned his wife, or even the fact that he was married. He hadn't explained his reasons for wanting such remote and out-of-the-way employment and he hadn't haggled over the ridiculously small salary which was all I had been able to offer him.

Then I remembered the oilskin bag. The answer to some, at any rate, of the things that were puzzling me might lie in the documents he'd salvaged. It's not a very nice thing to go prying into another man's papers, but in this case, I felt it was justified. I got up and began searching through the bedclothes. But I couldn't find it and I was afraid of waking him.

I didn't persist in the search. It was very cold in the room. North African hotels, with their bare, plaster walls and tiled floors are designed for the summer heat. Also I was tired. It could wait till morning. There was no point in trying to work it out for myself. When he was rested, he'd be able to explain the whole thing. I lay back again and switched off the light, pulling the blankets up round me. The moonlight cast the pattern of the window in a long, sloping rectangle on the opposite wall. I yawned and closed my eyes and was instantly asleep.

But it was only my body that was tired and probably this accounts for the fact that I awoke with such startling suddenness at the sound of movement in the room. The moonlight showed me a figure stooped over the couch at the foot of the bed. "Who's that?" I called out.

The figure started up. It was one of the Arab hotel boys. I switched on the light. "What are you doing in here?" I asked him in Spanish. "I didn't send for you."

"No, señor." He looked scared and his rather too thick lips trembled slightly. He looked as though he had negro blood in him; so many of them did who came from the south. "The patrone sent me to collect the clothes that are wet." He held up some of Kavan's sodden garments. "They are to be made dry."

"Why didn't you knock and switch on the light?"

"I do not wish to disturb you, señor." He said it quickly as though it were something he had expected to have to say, and then added, "May I take them please?"

"All right," I said. "And you can take my jacket. That needs drying, too." I got out of bed and emptied the pockets. Then I ran through Kavan's things. I thought he might have his wallet in one of the pockets of his windbreaker, but there was nothing but a jack-knife, an old briar, matches—the usual odds and ends of a man sailing a boat. "Thank the patrone

for me, will you." The boy nodded and scurried out of the
room. The door closed with a slam.

"Who was that? What is it?"

I turned quickly towards the bed and saw that Kavan was
sitting bolt upright, a startled look on his face. "It's all right,"
I said. "It was one of the hotel boys. He came for your
wet things."

Relief showed on his face and his head sank back against
the pillows. "I thought I was back on the boat," he murmured. Though he was utterly exhausted, his mind still
controlled his body, forcing it to react to unusual sounds, as
though he were still at the yacht's helm. I thought of how it
must have been at night out there in the Atlantic after Wade
had gone overboard, and I crossed over to the window to
draw the curtains and shut out the moonlight.

As I pulled the curtains, I glanced down into the street
below. A movement caught my eyes. There was somebody
standing down there in the shadow of a doorway on the
opposite side of the street, standing quite still, staring up at the
window. I could see the pale circle of a face, nothing more.
And then the figure moved, walking quickly away, keeping to
the shadows of the buildings. It was a European girl and where
an alley entered the street, she crossed a patch of moonlight.

It was Kavan's wife.

She was in the shadows again now, walking quickly. I
watched her until she turned at the end of the street, up
towards the Boulevard Pasteur. I could have been mistaken,
of course. But I knew I wasn't—the suède jacket and the
crumpled skirt, the way she walked, the shape of the face with
its high, bony forehead as she had stared up at me from the
shadows. What had she wanted? She hadn't come into the
hotel. She hadn't asked to see him. The natural thing . . .

"What is it? What are you staring at?"

I swung away from the window and saw that his eyes were
watching me, and there was the same fearfulness in them that
I had seen in his wife's eyes when she asked me who I was.
"I've just seen your wife," I said. "She was out there, looking
up at the hotel."

"My wife?"

"The girl who was on the beach."

He stared at me. "How do you know she is my wife?" For the first time I noticed the trace of a foreign accent.

"She told me," I said.

He started to get out of bed then, but I stopped him. "She's gone now." And then I said, "Why didn't you tell me you were Kavan down there on the beach? Surely you must have guessed who I was?"

"How should I? Besides——" He hesitated and shrugged his shoulders. "It is not the moment to say who I am."

"Because of the police?" I asked. "And then, when you saw your wife . . ." I hesitated, wondering how best to put it. "She loves you," I said. "Surely you must know that? Somehow she got out of Czechoslovakia and came here to meet you, and when you saw her you turned your back on her. Surely you could have——"

His eyes suddenly blazed at me. "For Christ's sake, stop it!" he cried out. "Stop it! Do you hear? How do I know they don't arrange for her to come here to Tangier? They may be watching her, trying to follow me. They are there in the background always." The words tumbled wildly out of his mouth, and then he steadied himself and pushed his hands up over his face and through his hair. "I have not seen Karen for more than four years." His voice was gentle, but with a note of bitterness in it. "And then suddenly we meet . . ." He stared at me. "Do you think I like to have to turn my back on her?" He shrugged his shoulders angrily. "I have had too much of this—during the German occupation and after, when the Russians walk in. You don't understand. You were born British. You don't understand what it is to be a middle-European—always to be escaping from something, always to go in fear—the knock on the door, the unopened envelope, the glance of a stranger in the street—to have people checking on you, spying on you, coming between you and your work, never to be trusted or to trust anybody. God! If only I'd been born British." There were tears of anger and frustration in his eyes and he lay back, exhausted.

"Why did you leave England then?" I asked. "Why didn't you become naturalised?"

"Naturalised!" He laughed. It wasn't a pleasant sound, for there was a note of hysteria in it. "How can I become naturalised when they . . ." He closed his mouth abruptly, his eyes suddenly watchful. "Don't ask me any more questions," he said. "You want a doctor for your Mission. All right, you have one. I am here. But don't ask me any questions. I don't want any questions." His voice shook with the violence of his feeling.

I stood for a moment staring at him. I didn't like it. I knew too little about the man. I'd been prepared for a failure. What else could I expect of a qualified doctor who was willing to come out to North Africa and bury himself in a village in the Atlas? But I hadn't been prepared for this.

"All right," I said. "I won't ask any more questions." And then to ease the tension between us I asked him if he'd like some food.

"No. No, thank you. A little cognac. That's all."

I got some dry clothes from my suitcase, put them on and went down to the Cypriot café at the corner. When I returned I found he had been sick. His face was ghastly white and he was sweating and shivering. I poured him a little cognac, added some water and handed it to him. His hands were trembling uncontrollably as he took the tumbler from me. "Shall I get a doctor?" I asked.

He shook his head, quickly and emphatically. "No. I'll be all right in a minute." He sipped at the cognac. "I'm just exhausted physically."

But it was more than that. It was nervous exhaustion.

"Can I have a cigarette please?"

I gave him one and when I had lit it for him, he drew on it, quickly, eagerly, like a man whose nerves are crying out for a sedative. I stayed with him whilst he smoked. He didn't talk and a heavy silence lay over the room. I watched him covertly, wondering how this odd, excitable man would settle in to the quiet, lonely life that I had become accustomed to. It wasn't lonely, of course. There was too much to do, too many demands on one's time and energy. But for a man who wasn't accustomed to it, who wasn't accepting the life voluntarily . . . I had been so engrossed in the idea of getting a doctor out there that I hadn't really given much thought to the fact that he would also be a man, with a personality of his own, a past and all the inevitable human complications and peculiarities. I had thought about it only as it would affect me, not as I and the conditions of life down at Enfida would affect him.

"Have you ever been to Morocco before?" I asked him. He shook his head. "No. Never."

I gave him a little more cognac and then I began to talk about Enfida. I told him how the olives were just being gathered and piled in heaps in the open space outside the auberge and how we would soon be thrashing our own trees to harvest the crop that was part of the tiny income of the Mission. I described the mountain villages to him; how they were flat-roofed, like Tibetan villages, and clung precariously to the sides of great ravines that cut back to the base of the peaks that rose twelve and thirteen thousand feet to form the backbone of the Atlas Mountains. And I tried to give him an idea of what it was like, travelling every day from village to village, sometimes on foot, sometimes by mule, living in the Berber huts and sitting around at night, drinking mint tea and listening to their stories and the gossip of the village.

And then, suddenly, his hand fell limp at the edge of the bed and he was asleep. I got up and took the cigarette from between his fingers and picked up the empty tumbler which lay on his chest. His face had more colour in it now, and it was relaxed. The nerve at the corner of his mouth no longer twitched and his features were smoothed out as though his mind were at rest.

I put his arms inside the bedclothes and then I switched out the light and went out to the café for some food. When I returned he was still lying exactly as I had left him. His mouth was slightly open and he was snoring gently. I went to bed by the moon's light that filtered in through the half-drawn curtains and lay there, wondering about him and about his wife and whether I had bitten off more than I could chew financially, for I would have to get her to join us at the Mission.

In thinking about the Mission, I forgot to some extent the strangeness of his arrival and drifted quietly off to sleep.

I awoke to a tap on the door and a shaft of sunlight cutting across my face. "Entrez!" I sat up and rubbed my eyes. It was one of the hotel boys to say that the police and the douane had arrived. "All right. Show them up." I got out of bed and slipped my dressing gown on. Kavan was still fast asleep. He didn't seem to have moved all night. He still lay on his back, quite motionless, his mouth slightly open and his breathing regular and easy. I looked at my watch. It was almost ten o'clock. He had had more than a dozen hours' sleep. He should be fit enough now to cope with the immigration formalities.

The door opened and they came in. It was the same sergeant and he had with him one of the Customs officers. I glanced back at the bed, wishing that I'd told them to wait. I'd have to wake him now and he'd be suddenly confronted with them. I hoped he'd be clear in his mind what he was going to tell them. He ought to have mentioned Wade's death to them the night before.

" Muy buenas, señor."

" Muy buenas." I gave the sergeant a chair. The Customs officer sat on the couch. They both stared at Kavan. I felt uneasy and only half awake.

" So, he is still sleeping, eh?" The sergeant clicked his tongue sympathetically. " I am sorry to disturb him, but it is the formalities, you understand." He shrugged his shoulders to make it clear that he was not responsible for drawing up the regulations.

" You want me to wake him?"

" Si, si—if you please. He is all right, eh?"

" Yes, he's all right," I said. " He was just exhausted. He had a bad trip."

The sergeant nodded. " Of course. And to wreck the ship— terrible. We will be very quick. Then he can sleep again."

I went over to the bed and shook Kavan gently. His eyelids flicked back almost immediately. " What is it?" And then he saw the police and there was instant panic in his eyes. " What do they want? Why are they here?"

" It's all right," I said. " It's about the immigration details. They said they'd come this morning. Remember?"

He nodded, but all the blood seemed to have drained out of his face so that it looked as white as it had done the previous night.

" Señor Wade." The sergeant had got to his feet.

I started to explain that he wasn't Wade, but Kavan checked

me, gripping hold of my arm. I could feel him trembling. His eyes switched from the police sergeant to the door and then back again to the sergeant. "What do you want?" he asked in fair Spanish and his voice shook slightly and I could feel him trying desperately to get control of himself.

The sergeant was standing at the foot of the bed now. "You are captain of the boat that is wrecked last night in the Baie des Juifs?"

Kavan hesitated, glancing up at me, and his tongue licked along the sore edges of his lips. "Yes." His voice was little more than a whisper. But then he added in a firmer tone. "Yes, I'm the captain of the boat."

"What is the name of the boat please?"

"*Gay Juliet.*"

The sergeant had his notebook out now. He was leaning over the end of the bed, his round, rather chubby face with its blue jowls puckered in a frown of concentration as he licked his pencil and wrote down the name of the boat. "And you are from where?"

"Falmouth."

"You come direct, señor?"

"Yes."

"And your name is Señor Roland Wade?"

Again Kavan hesitated and then he nodded. "Yes."

"Just a moment," I said, speaking to him in English. "This is absurd, you know. You can't go on trying to pretend you're Wade."

"Why not? Are you going to stop me? Listen." He grabbed hold of my arm again. "You want a doctor for your Mission, don't you? It's important to you. It must be or you wouldn't be taking somebody you know nothing about."

"Yes, it's important to me."

"Well then, you tell these men the truth and you won't get your doctor. Not me anyway. So you'd better choose. If you want your doctor, don't interfere. If you do, I'll get sent back to England and you'll never see me again." Though he was blackmailing me, his face had a desperate, pleading look. "It's only until we get out of Tangier." He stared up into my face for a moment and then turned back to the sergeant. "I'm sorry," he said, reverting to Spanish.

"You sail here alone?" the sergeant asked.

"Yes."

"There is nobody with you?"

"No."

He looked up from his notebook then and stared at Kavan. "Do you know a man called Dr. Jan Kavan?"

I heard the slight hissing intake of Kavan's breath and felt the muscles of his hand tense. "Yes."

"We were told that he was sailing with you."

"Who told you?" The sergeant didn't answer, but his small, brown eyes stared at Kavan watchfully. "No, he didn't sail with me," Kavan added quickly. "He—changed his mind."

I felt sure that slight hesitation must have been as noticeable to the sergeant as it was to me. But all he said was, "Can you tell me, señor, why he changed his mind?"

"He wouldn't tell me," Kavan said. "He came on board the night before I was due to sail. I was leaving with the tide at 4 a.m. and when I woke him, he said he had changed his mind and wanted to be put ashore."

The sergeant nodded and wrote it all down. "So you sailed alone, señor?"

Kavan nodded. His eyes were fixed on the sergeant and little beads of sweat had broken out on his forehead.

"That was very dangerous, surely, señor—to sail alone? It is a big ship for one man."

"I have sailed a great deal—often single-handed."

The sergeant turned to me. "Twice last night you asked the señor here about another man. You thought there were two of them on the yacht."

"Yes," I said. "That's correct."

"Who was the second man?' Was it Dr. Kavan?"

"Yes."

"Why were you so sure that Dr. Kavan was on board the boat?"

"He wrote to me to tell me he was sailing with Mr. Wade."

"I see. Do you know of any reason why he should have changed his mind?"

I shrugged my shoulders. "No, but there are easier methods of reaching Tangier than by sailing in a yacht."

"Of course." He nodded towards the bed. "Can you confirm the identity of the señor here?"

"No. I had never seen him before last night."

"Si, si, it is understood. So you think Dr. Kavan changed his mind?"

I glanced down at Kavan. His eyes were watching me, very blue and with the same expression in them that they'd had when he'd implored me not to take him to a hospital. "Yes," I said. "I think he must have changed his mind."

I felt the grip of Kavan's fingers on my arm relax. "Bueno!" The sergeant closed his notebook. "You have the papers for this boat?" he asked.

Kavan nodded.

"I would like to have the papers. What is the port of registration?"

"Southampton." Kavan's voice had dropped to a whisper.

"Also we would like to have your passport, señor. And if you have the record of the voyage . . ." He stopped then, for Kavan had suddenly closed his eyes. He leaned over, clutching at me and retching violently. His hand reached out automatically for the pot, gripped it and the retching sound went on and on—dry, rasping and foodless, a horrible sound in the sullen stillness of the room. And then he dropped the pot and keeled over, his body suddenly limp.

I got hold of him and pushed him back into the bed. He was sweating and his face was ashen. I wiped his lips with my handkerchief. His eyes opened and he stared past me at the sergeant. "I'll bring the papers later," he whispered, and then he closed his eyes again and seemed to pass into unconsciousness.

I glanced at the sergeant. He was shaking his head and making little clicking sounds with his tongue. "He is bad, very bad. I am sorry, señor."

"I'll get a doctor," I said.

"Si, si. That is what he need—a doctor." He turned to the Customs officer and they began talking quickly, shrugging their shoulders and gesticulating. Several times they glanced at the man's body lying there on the bed, and their expressions were sympathetic. At length the sergeant turned to me. "Señor. Do you know if he has his passport?"

"No," I said. "I don't know. I think he had some papers with him, but I don't know what they are. If you like I can bring them down to you?"

The sergeant nodded. "Bueno. If you will take them to the office of the douane down by the harbour, señor, they will be stamped. There is no necessity for him to come himself. Also, there is this paper to be completed." He handed me the usual immigration form. "As soon as he is sufficiently recovered, perhaps you will have him fill it in and bring it with you to the douane."

"Very well." As I opened the door for them, I asked the sergeant why the police were interested in Dr. Kavan.

"Oh, it is not we who are interested," he replied. "It is the British Consulate. It is they who ask us to watch for him."

"But why?" I asked. "Were you going to arrest him or something?"

"No. They just wish us to check his papers and report to them. I will inform them that he did not sail after all. Muy buenas, señor."

"Muy buenas"

I closed the door and turned to Kavan. His eyes were open now and he was listening to the tramp of their feet as they descended the stairs. He was still pale, but his eyes were alert. "Were you shamming?" I said.

"Ssh!" He gestured for me to be quiet. "Go to the window and check that both of them leave the hotel."

I walked to the window and pulled the curtains. A jeep was parked down in the street. As I peered out, the sergeant and the Customs officer came out of the hotel and got into it. There was the sound of a starter and then it drove off, turning down towards the plage. "They've gone," I said.

He breathed a sigh of relief and pulled himself up in the bed. "Now we'll fix Wade's passport. After that everything is straightforward. Will you telephone for a doctor, please?"

He was suddenly calm. He seemed to have no conception of the position he had put me in. I was angry and a little scared. Why couldn't foreigners behave rationally? And now there was the problem of papers, passports, and official documents. I had committed myself without thinking about that. "You know the British Consulate are making inquiries about you?" I said. And then, when he didn't answer, I asked him why he'd had to pretend to be Wade. "What have you done that you have to hide your own identity?"

He looked at me then and said quietly, "I haven't done anything."

"I don't believe you," I said sharply. "When you saw the police, you panicked. You must have done something. If you want my help, you'd better tell me——"

"I have done nothing," he repeated. "Absolutely nothing. Please, you must believe me. I have done nothing that you or any other British person can object to. I give you my word."

"Then why pretend to be Wade?"

He pushed his hands through his hair, which was still dull and sticky with salt water. "No," he said. "Not yet. Maybe when I know you better—when we are out of Tangier." He lifted his head and stared at the window. "I came here to start a new life. I have to sail here because it's the only way I can get out of England. I am a stateless person, you see. And then the owner is lost overboard, the yacht is wrecked and, when I'm brought ashore, I find the police waiting for me there on the beach and asking me if I am Dr. Jan Kavan. And then the man Kostos mistakes me for Wade." He looked up at me quickly. "What would you do? What would you do if you were in my shoes? It's a gift from the Gods. I accept it." His shoulders sagged and his voice fell away to a whisper: "And then I find my wife waiting there to greet me also—and she turns away because I have said I am Wade."

He stared down at his feet, his pale hands gripped convulsively round his knees. "Last night—I thought and thought, trying to find a way out. And then, this morning, I wake up and find the police here, and I'm scared. When you're scared, the mind works very fast. I suddenly knew this was the only way out. I must be Wade. I must continue to be Wade until I am safe inside French Morocco. If I admit I am Jan Kavan, then there will be an enquiry into Wade's disappearance and——"

"Why should that worry you?" I demanded. "You said last night——"

"I told you the truth," he cut in quickly, and then glanced at me nervously as though trying to discover whether I believed him or not. "But I can't tell them the truth," he added. "Once they know I'm Jan Kavan——" He hesitated. "They will send me back to England. I know they will. I feel it. And I must get to Morocco. I must get to Morocco." He looked at me. "Please. You want a doctor, don't you? You want a doctor for your Mission?"

"Yes, but——"

"Then you must let me enter French Morocco on Wade's passport."

"But why should they send you back to England? What makes you think——"

"Oh, for God's sake!" he shouted at me. His voice had that upward trend that it had had the night before when he'd been half hysterical with exhaustion. "Just leave it at that. Leave it at that."

"All right," I said, for he was in a desperately nervous state. "But if you enter Morocco on Wade's passport, your own papers will have no entry stamp. You can't work at the Mission unless your papers are in order."

"I understand." He nodded, his forehead wrinkled in thought. "But that is something we can sort out later. Maybe I lose my papers, maybe I forge the necessary stamp. I don't know. But first I must get to Morocco. That is the important thing. And I can't do that except on Wade's passport."

"But, good Heavens, man!" I said. "You're not Wade's double, surely. There's the photograph—the description and his signature, too—you'd never get away with it."

"Nonsense," he said, his tone suddenly more confident. "Do you think I learned nothing during the war? I was six years working in the laboratories at Essen and passing information to the British. Besides, don't forget I have been shipwrecked." He dragged himself to his feet, standing a little unsteadily. And then his voice was suddenly agitated again. "Where's the oilskin bag? I had a little oilskin bag tied round my neck. I had all the papers in it—everything. Did you see it? It wasn't left on the beach, was it?"

"No, it's here somewhere," I said. I crossed over to the bed, wishing now that I'd had a look at it last night. "It's among the bedclothes. I threw it here last night."

But it wasn't on the bed. It had slipped off on to the couch and was lying under the counterpane. He almost snatched it out of my hand as I held it out to him. "You'd better have some food," I suggested.

But he shook his head. "Not until I've seen a doctor." He suddenly smiled. It was almost as though the feel of that oilskin bag in his hands had given him back his confidence. "If he's a good doctor, he'll tell me I'm suffering from lack of food and if the police bother to enquire, they will not be surprised if I recover quickly."

Curiously, I found myself liking him. Behind the nervous tension and the almost neurotic fear of the authorities was a man of considerable personality, a man of drive and energy. Whatever he had done, whatever he was afraid of, he had guts. "What are you going to do about the passport?" I asked.

"Oh, that's not too difficult," he said, shaking the contents of the oilskin bag out on to the bed. "Wade was about my build and colouring. He even had blue eyes. He was thinner and more wiry, that's all." He tossed the blue-covered British passport across to me. "I'll have to fix the photograph, of course."

The passport was slightly damp, othewise there was nothing to show that it had come through the surf of Jew's Bay. On the first page there was the man's name—Mr. Roland Tregareth Wade—and on the next his description: Profession —Company director; Place of birth and date—St. Austell, 10th April, 1915; Residence—France; Height—5 ft. 11 ins.; Colour of eyes—blue; Colour of hair—black. I turned the page and looked at the photograph. It showed him to be a rather good-looking man with a square forehead and black hair. But the cheeks were a little heavy, the broad, full-lipped mouth rather too easy-going, and there were little pouches under the eyes. It wasn't a dissipated face and it wasn't a dishonest face, but somehow it wasn't quite frank— it was the face of a man about whom one would have reservations.

I looked across at Kavan. "What about the photograph?" I asked him.

But it didn't seem to worry him. "They're not to know that the passport was wrapped in oilskin," he said. "By the time they get it the pages will be damp and very dirty. The beard helps, too." He rasped his hand over his chin.

"You seem to have it all worked out," I said.

He shrugged his shoulders. "A kindly Providence worked it all out for me."

"Well, I hope Providence realises its responsibility." My mind was running over the possible snags, conscious that I was thoroughly implicated in the whole business. I glanced down at the passport again, turning the pages. The visa section showed that Wade had travelled extensively—Germany, Austria, Czechoslovakia, Roumania—most of the satellite countries—and Egypt, as well as Britain and France. He had visas for French Morocco, Algeria and Spanish Morocco, but these were not counter-stamped with dates of entry. The final pages for currency were a mass of entries. I tossed the passport back on to the bed beside him. "I'll go and get the patrone to ring for a doctor," I said.

He nodded. He had already picked up the passport and was padding across the room to the wash-basin.

By the time the doctor arrived Kavan was back in bed and the passport, now crumpled and dirty, was drying in the sun by the open window. I checked it through. The ink on Wade's signature on the first page had run badly, so had the figures giving his height which was a good two inches taller than Kavan, and the upper half of the face in the photograph was almost obliterated by a dirty stain. The yacht's certificate of registration had been treated in the same way, and Kavan had completed the form which the police sergeant had left, the signature shaky, but not unlike what could be deciphered of Wade's signature

The doctor was a young, thoroughly efficient Frenchman. He examined Kavan carefully and, after questioning him about what had happened, wrote a prescription for a tonic and advised a diet of meat broth and steak for the next two or three days. He left with a little bow and a handshake, and I went across to the Cypriot restaurant and got Kavan a tray of food. It was the first hot food he had had for over sixty hours.

The passport was almost dry and I took it, together with the other papers, down to the Customs House. There was no difficulty. The sergeant was there and he only gave a cursory glance at the passport before stamping it. Officially Kavan was now Wade and I walked out into the hot sunshine with a light heart and a feeling of relief. The way was now clear for me to return to Enfida.

It was odd, but I felt no qualms, no sense of apprehension. Just as soon as Kavan was fit to travel, I could shake the dust of Tangier off my feet. That was all I was thinking about as I walked back to the hotel. Wade was dead. An investigation into how it happened would serve no useful purpose. There remained only the yacht. The waves were still pounding heavily at the sands and one of the Customs officers had told me that the wreck was breaking up fast. Lloyds' representative would have to be contacted about the insurance to avert suspicion. After that, the Wade who had arrived in Tangier could simply disappear.

I imagined Kavan would be sleeping after his food, but instead there was the sound of somebody talking beyond the closed door of my room. I hesitated, and then I heard a voice that I recognised say, "What you are running is no business of mine. I am interested only in the deeds of Kasbah Foum." It was Kostos.

Kavan made some reply that was inaudible, and then the Greek's voice cut in: "You are lying. I know that you visited Marcel Duprez's lawyers in Rouen. I know that—" He stopped abruptly as I pushed open the door.

Kavan was sitting up in the bed, the blankets pulled tightly round his naked body. Kostos was standing by the couch. They were both looking towards the door as I entered. They were quite still like a tableau, and the tension in the room was something that you could feel. "What are you doing here, Kostos?" I demanded angrily.

"Nothing. Nothing that is to do with you. You keep out of this, Lat'am." His eyes switched to Kavan. "Think it over, my friend." He began buttoning up his raincoat. "Ali is a fool. I tell him that when I know that in Cairo he arranges for you to act as the contact man. Your reputation is no dam' good. But you double-cross me and you find yourself out on the Marchan with a knife in your back." He fished in the pocket of his waistcoat and flipped a piece of pasteboard on to the blankets of Kavan's feet. "Come to my office as soon as you are recovered. An' no more nonsense, you see. This is not Europe. This is North Africa, and all out there——" he waved his hand towards the uncurtained windows—" it is an Arab world with only a thin layer of white peoples who tread a careful step." He put his hat on, pulling it down with a quick tug at the brim, and then turned to go.

As he passed me, he paused, tapping the side of his nose. "Not a sparrow falls. Remember, Lat'am. An' don't do nothing silly, eh?" He pushed past me and went out, slamming the door behind him.

I turned to face Kavan, who was still sitting up in the bed. "What's all this about?" I demanded. "What did Kostos want?"

"Some papers—a cargo. How the hell do I know? Kostos is a part of Wade's world." He shrugged his shoulders. He wasn't scared; not the way he had been when the police had been in the room. But there was a tautness in his voice that showed his uneasiness. "Wade was a crook," he added.

"Then why in God's name did you sail with him?"

"I told you before—because I am a Czech and a refugee and it's the only way I can get out of England."

"But if you knew he was a crook——?"

"I didn't discover that till later." He lay back and put his hands behind his head. "He came and saw me in London and it was agreed that I should sail with him to Tangier. I knew nothing about him, except that he wanted——" He stopped there. "Can I have a cigarette please?"

I handed him the packet and lit one myself. "Well, when did you discover he was running something?" I asked.

"We ran into a gale off Ushant," he said. "We could easily have slipped into the lee of the islands through the Chenal du Four and put into Brest. Instead, he stood out into the Atlantic, beating into the teeth of it to clear the coast of France. He said he wasn't taking any chances. That's how I knew."

"But what about the Customs when you left Falmouth?"

"We didn't clear Customs. He said there was no need."

"What was he running?"

He shrugged his shoulders. "Currency, securities—how do I know? When I asked him, he told me to mind my own damn business. He didn't talk about his own affairs."

"Did you know Kostos would be waiting for you when you arrived?"

"Of course not."

"But when he came up to you on the beach—why didn't you tell him you weren't Wade?"

He pushed himself up on to his elbow. "Because the police are there. Because I have to escape from myself, from all the past. Now leave it at that, will you?" He lay back, breathing heavily. "I'm sorry, Latham," he murmured. "It's just that I'm tired. As soon as we're clear of Tangier——"

"But we're not clear of Tangier yet," I reminded him. "What exactly did Kostos say? Had he been here long?"

"No." He hesitated, looking at me uncertainly out of the corners of his eyes. "He wanted some documents. He said that I'd been employed by an Arab to get them. He meant, of course, that Wade had." He paused and then asked me if I knew anything about an Arab called Ali d'Es-Skhira.

"Yes," I said. "He's a nationalist; a fanatic. The French deported him from Morocco after he'd caused serious rioting in Marrakech. He lives in Tangier now. Why?"

"Nothing. It doesn't matter."

"What happened next?"

"I told Kostos I hadn't been able to get the documents, and he got angry and called me a liar. Then you came in."

"Did Wade mention these documents to you?"

"I told you, Wade didn't talk about his affairs."

He was trying to hide something. I could sense it. "Kostos described them as the deeds of Kasbah Foum." He stared at me sullenly, not saying anything. I went over and sat on the bed. "Now look here," I said. "You're getting yourself mixed up in something dangerous. I know this town. I've been part of it—that was what turned me into a missionary. Kostos is not a man to play around with. And if you're mixed up with Ali d'Es-Skhira as well . . ."

"But I'm not," he protested. "I don't know anything about it."

"Oh yes, you do. You know all about this place Kasbah

Foum. When you regained consciousness in this room last night, one of the first things you asked me——"

"All right. I do know about Kasbah Foum. But it's nothing to do with you, Latham." He was sitting up again and his voice was angry. We stared at each other for a moment and the atmosphere between us had grown suddenly tense. Then he gradually relaxed. "I'm sorry," he murmured. "Maybe later, when we're out of this place, I'll explain. . . ." He lay back and closed his eyes. There was an obstinate set to his mouth.

I hesitated. Maybe I could shock the truth out of him. "Tell me one thing," I said. "Did you get possession of those deeds after Wade went overboard—or before?"

His eyes flicked open and there was a surprised look on his face. "You mean——" His mouth stayed open slightly, and then he rolled over in the bed so that he faced me. "Now listen, Latham. I didn't kill Wade, if that's what you're getting at. It happened just as I told you."

"It was the deeds I asked about."

"The deeds?" He stared at me.

"When did you get them out of him?"

"I didn't get them out of him." His voice was angry. "How could I? He never had them."

"How do you know?"

"Oh, for God's sake!" he shouted at me. "Leave it at that, will you. Wade didn't have them."

"All right," I said, getting to my feet. "But it's a pity you didn't bother to convince Kostos of that." I stubbed out my cigarette. It was no good worrying about it. The thing to do was to get out of Tangier as quickly as possible. "How do you feel?" I asked him. "I see you ate the steak I brought you."

"Yes." He smiled and added quickly, "It was the most wonderful steak I have ever eaten."

"And you weren't sick?"

"No."

"How do you feel then?"

"Not too bad. A little tired, and my body's still sore. Otherwise, I'm all right. I think I'll try and get some sleep."

"Do you think you'll be fit enough to travel tonight?

There's a train at nine thirty-five. We could be in Casablanca tomorrow morning in time to catch the day train to Marrakech."

" Is there a sleeper on the train tonight?"

" Yes. I'll try and book berths."

There was a knock at the door. It was one of the hotel boys. The patrone had sent him up for Kavan's passport. " What's he want the passport for?" Kavan asked. I explained that it was the custom in Tangier for the hotelier to hold visitors' passports and he let the boy have it. " And bring the señor's clothes up, will you?" I told him.

" Si, si, señor."

When he had gone, Kavan began rummaging in the oilskin bag and produced a rather battered book that looked something like a ledger. " Do you think you could dispose of that for me?" He held it out to me.

" What is it?" I asked.

" It's the log of the *Gay Juliet*. I brought it ashore with me as evidence of what happened to Wade. It should be burned now. Do you think you can manage that?"

" Are you sure you want it destroyed?" I asked him. " I could leave it with a friend of mine—just in case."

" No. I'm sure your friend is reliable, but——" He shrugged his shoulders. " And I daren't take it with me, just in case the douane decide to search me. Burn it, will you."

" I'll see what I can do," I said. " What else did you bring ashore with you?"

" My own papers and visas. There's some money, too."

" How much?"

He glanced at me quickly. " Quite a lot."

I explained to him then that the regulations only permitted him to take so much in cash into French Morocco. I suggested that I bank the excess for transfer to the Banque d'Etat at Marrakech and he agreed. Altogether there was over four hundred pounds, mainly in English notes. " Is this Wade's or yours?" I asked.

He looked at me hard. " Does it matter? Wade wasn't the sort to have dependants."

There was a knock at the door and the boy came in with his clothes and my jacket. I slipped the notes into my hip pocket.

The boy paused as he was arranging the clothes on a chair. He was staring at the oilskin bag which Kavan still held in his hands. The dark, Arab eyes met mine and then he turned abruptly and hurried out. " You said you'd lived in Tangier," Kavan said as the door closed. " You know it well?"

" Well enough to want to get out of it," I answered.

" Can you find Karen for me then?" His voice was suddenly urgent. " I must get in touch with her before we leave. I must tell her where I'm going. Can you do that for me?"

" I don't know." Tangier wasn't a big place, not the European section of it. But there wasn't much time. " The best chance would be through the immigration authorities."

" No, no. Don't do that. Not the authorities. But you must know people here—somebody would know about her in a place like this. Please. Find out where she's living and give her the address of the Mission. Tell her to write to me there as soon as she's convinced that she's not being watched. No, not to me. Tell her to write to you. That would be safer. Will you do that?"

" I'll try." I got my hat. " Better lock the door behind me," I said, and left him and went down the stairs and out into the bright sunlight of the streets.

I went first to Cook's in the rue de Statut and was lucky enough to get two wagon-lit berths on the night train. Then I crossed the Zocco Grande to the British bank in the Siaghines where I arranged for Kavan's money to be changed into Moroccan francs and transferred to the Mission's account in Marrakech. It was then past midday and I cut up a side street to a small Italian café, and there I sat over my lunch and read *Gay Juliet's* log.

Until then I think Wade had appeared to me as an almost mythical character. But he was real enough by the time I had finished his record of that winter voyage out from Falmouth. As a kid I had done a lot of sailing—that was back in the days when my father was alive, before he'd gone bankrupt. I knew enough about the sea to be able to interpret, in terms of physical conditions, such laconic statements as: " *Wind Force 7, gusting 8. Direction S.W. Waves 20 feet, breaking heavily. Lay to under bare sticks, everything battened down.*

Jan very sick. Pumping every half hour." This was off Ushant
and continued for fifteen hours. Sometimes he was less
factual, more descriptive, as in the entry for November 30:
*" Light S.E. breeze off the land. Heavy swell with sea oily
and black. Moon just lipping horizon. Ghosting along under
Genoa—no sound except the grunt of porpoises. They have
been with us all night, their movements visible on account of
the phosphorescence, which is unusual at this time of the year.
Jan fit now and has the makings of a good seaman. Pray God
it doesn't start to blow again. Both of us very tired."*

The log was something more than a bare record of speed,
course and conditions. It was Wade's personal record,
entered up daily from the chart table data and going back over
several voyages: Cannes to Naples and back—Cannes to
Palermo and on to the Piraeus, across to Alexandria and back
to Nice by way of Valetta—Nice to Gibraltar. The yachts
were all different, so were the crews. Sometimes he sailed
single-handed. But always the same flowing, easy handwriting,
the same graphic descriptive details running through the
Mediterranean voyages and on to the final trip out from
England. And then, suddenly, two pages from the last entry,
the writing changed, becamee finer, neather, more exact.
*" Dec. 12—0245: Course 195°. Wind S.S.E. Force 3-4. Speed
5 knots. A terrible thing has happened. Roland lost overboard
shortly after I relieved him. Time 0205 approx. Heavy swell
running. Threw lifebelt to him and gybed to bring ship
round . . ."*

Wade was dead and Kavan was writing up his log. There
was a rather touching finality about that abrupt change in the
writing. After all those hundreds of sea miles, logged and
recorded between the brown board covers of the book, this
bald statement that the sea had claimed him.

Whatever else the man had been, he was a fine yachtsman.

I rifled through the remaining twenty or so pages of the
book. They were blank, except for the last two which
contained odd jottings, reminders of things he had probably
planned on the long night watches. They were under port
headings, such as Naples—*see Borgioli—Ring Ercoli—Vomero
23-245—Cheaper to slip here and get topsides blown off and*

repainted (*Luigi Cantorelli's yard*), *etc*. I glanced quickly to the last entry and there, sure enough, was the heading *TANGIER* and underneath—*Michel Kostos, 22 rue de la Grande Mosquèe.* Tel. 237846. There were several other names and telephone numbers and then a note—*Try to contact Ed White. Wazerza*t 12 (*Lavin, Roche et Lavin*).

I sat drinking my coffee and wondering about this last entry. Lavin, Roche et Lavin was obviously the name of a French firm and Wazerzat looked like the phonetic spelling of an Arab town—Ouarzazate, for instance.

I closed the book slowly and finished my coffee. Reading that log had brought the man to life in my mind. Reluctantly, I called the patrone and had him take me through into the kitchen, and there I thrust the book down into the red hot coals of the range. I found myself muttering a prayer for him as it burst into flames. The book should have been consigned to the sea.

Coming back into the café, I noticed an Arab sitting in the far corner, by the window. I hadn't seen him come in. I suppose I had been too engrossed in the story of Wade's voyages. There was something familiar about his face. I paid my bill and, as I walked out, our eyes met and I remembered that he had been in the bank when I had arranged for the transfer of Kavan's money. He had quick, intelligent eyes and a hard, aquiline face. His djellaba was of the smooth, grey gaberdine favoured by the richer guides and pimps and he wore brown European shoes.

I turned up into the Arab town, climbing quickly towards the kasbah. I wanted to take a look at Jews' Bay—and I wanted to quash the suspicion that had suddenly crossed my mind.

From the Naam Battery I looked down to the sea and across the width of Jews' Bay. The sea was blue and sparkled in the sunshine. The water of the bay was faintly corrugated and there was a fringe of white where the swell broke on the golden sand. It was a quiet, peaceful scene, utterly at variance with my memories of what it had been like down there less than twenty-four hours ago. There was no sign of the wreck, but a small motor launch was hovering around the spot where the yacht had struck. I turned and walked back to the Place du Tabor, and there was the Arab I had left sitting in the café.

It was just possible, of course, that it was a coincidence. There were always guides hanging around the Place du Tabor. I cut down the rue Raid-Sultan, past the old palace—the Dar el Makhzen—and the treasury and into the labyrinth of alleys that run steeply down to the Zocco Chico. It was cool and quiet, but the roar of the markets drifted up to me on the still air like the murmur of a hive. I reached an intersection where the main alley descended in shallow steps through a tunnel formed by the houses. A narrower passage, leading I knew to a cul-de-sac, ran off at right angles and close by a baby sunned itself in an open doorway. I slipped into the doorway and waited.

Almost immediately I heard the patter of slippers hurrying down to the intersection. It was the same Arab. He hesitated an instant, glancing along the empty passage of the cul-de-sac. Then he dived into the tunnel of the main alley and went flapping down the steps like an ungainly bird.

There was no doubt about it now. I was being followed. The thought that a man like Kostos was now in a position to do this to me made me unreasonably angry. I went on down the alley and came out into the Zocco Chico. The Arab was waiting for me there. His face showed relief as he saw me, and then he looked away. I went straight up to him. "Who told you to follow me?" I asked him angrily in Spanish. He started to walk away, but I caught hold of him by the arm and swung him round. "Was it Señor Kostos?" Recognition of the name showed in his eyes. "All right," I said. "We're going back to the Hotel Malabata now." I let him go and turned up by the Spanish Church, walking fast.

He was close behind me as I entered the hotel. I went straight over to the reception desk where the patrone was sitting and demanded my bill and both our passports.

"You are leaving Tangier, señor?" He was a sallow-faced, oily little man with discoloured teeth and a large, hooked nose. I think he was of mixed Arab-Spanish blood. His eyes stared at me inquisitively over the rim of deep, fleshy pouches. His interest made me suspicious. " My bill," I said. " I'm in a hurry."

He glanced up at the clock above his head. It was just after three. " Already you have missed the train, señor. The next one does not depart until twenty-one hundred thirty-five."

" I'm still in a hurry," I said.

He shrugged his shoulders and started making out the bill. His eyes kept shifting to my face as he wrote. They were full of curiosity. Through the open doorway I could see the Arab waiting patiently across the street. " There will be a small addition for the other señor."

" That's all right."

He put down his pen. " He can have your room if he wishes." He stared at me. " Or do you both leave Tangier together?"

" Give me the bill," I said. He met my gaze for an instant and then his eyes dropped shiftily.

I settled the bill and he gave me my passport with the change. " It is necessary for you to complete this paper, señor. It is for the police." He was smiling at me craftily as he handed me the printed form which I should have filled in on arrival. He knew that the information I had to give included the address of my destination. When I had completed it, all but this one item, I hesitated. Then I wrote in the Pension de la Montagne. It was the pension from which we had seen the yacht being blown into Jews' Bay. In the old days there had been no telephone there. I handed the form back to him and he glanced at it quickly, almost eagerly. " I'd like my friend's passport, too," I said.

But he shook his head. " I am sorry, señor. He must collect it himself and complete the paper for the police."

I nodded. " All right," I said, and went up to the room. Kavan unlocked the door for me. He had had a wash and was dressed in his underclothes. " I'm glad you're up," I said. " Get dressed quickly. We're leaving at once."

He reacted instantly to the urgency in my voice. " Why? What's happened?"

" It's your friend Kostos." And I explained how I had been followed. " The man's waiting for us outside now. We've got to lose him before we get on that train. And I don't trust the patrone here either."

"Did you find Karen?" he asked.

"No. We can do that later when we've got rid of this Arab. Come on. Hurry." Thank heavens he looked a lot better.

He didn't argue and when he'd got into his clothes, I sent him down to get his passport while I finished packing my case. "There's a form to fill in." I told him as he was going out. "For destination put the Pension de la Montagne. It's out of town and it'll take them some time to check that we're not there."

He nodded, stuffing the oilskin bag into his pocket. "I'll wait for you downstairs."

When I went down to join him, I heard his voice raised in altercation with the patrone. It was something to do with the passport and they were shouting at each other in French. "Then why did Monsieur Latham tell me to come down here to get it?" Kavan demanded agitatedly. He caught sight of me then and said, "This idiot says he gave you my passport."

The patrone nodded his head emphatically. "Si, si, señor. Did you not ask for both the passports—yours and that of señor here?"

"Yes." I said. "But you refused to give me his. You said he must collect it personally and fill in the form at the same time."

"No, no. It is true about the paper. But I give you the passport." He turned to the hotel boy standing by the desk. "Did I not give the señor both the passports?"

"Si, si, si." The Arab nodded.

It was the same boy who had come up to my room the previous night to collect Kavan's wet clothes. And suddenly I knew why the patrone had wanted these clothes. He had been told to check through the pockets. "Do you know a Greek called Kostos?" I asked him.

The man's eyes narrowed slightly. He didn't say anything, but I knew I was right. Kostos was at the back of this passport nonsense, too. I sent the Arab boy for a taxi. "If you haven't produced that passport by the time the taxi arrives." I told the patrone, "I'm going straight to the British Consul."

He shrugged his shoulders, but there was a frightened look in his shifty eyes.

"Now come on," I said. "Hand it over."

But he shook his head obstinately and reiterated his statement that he'd already given it to me.

"All right," I said. "We'll see what the Consul and the police think of that story."

Kavan plucked at my arm. "It doesn't matter," he whispered urgently. "I've still got my own papers." His face was white and the twitch at the corner of his mouth had started again.

"That's no good," I said. "They're not stamped as having entered Tangier. You'd never get across the frontier."

"But——" His mouth stayed open. He was trembling. I thought he was scared because he was a refugee and in a bureaucratic world; refugees have no existence unless their papers are in order. But it wasn't that. "I'm not going to the Consulate," he hissed. "Whatever happens, I'm not going to the Consulate. We've got to get that passport."

I glanced at the patrone. His greasy face was sullen and obstinate and frightened. "It's no good," I said. "Kostos must have some kind of hold over him. We're not going to get it."

"But we must. We must."

"If you hadn't called yourself Wade and got mixed up with Kostos," I said angrily, "this would never have happened." The taxi arrived then and I turned to the patrone, giving him one more chance to produce it. But he only shrugged his shoulders and called on the saints to witness the truth of what he was saying.

"All right," I said, and I got Kavan out to the taxi and bundled him in. The Arab moved towards us from the opposite corner of the street. "Le Consulat Britannique," I ordered the driver. "Vite, vite!"

Kavan caught hold of my arm as the taxi drove off. "It's no good," he cried. "I won't go to the Consulate. I won't go, I tell you." He was wrought up to a point of hysteria. "Tell him to stop." He leaned quickly forward to tap on the glass partition.

But I pulled him back, struggling with him. "Don't be a fool!" I shouted at him. "You wanted to call yourself Wade. Well, now you've got to be Wade until we're out of Tangier. And you won't get out till we've recovered that passport."

"There must be some other way. I could slip across the frontier. . . ." He reached forward to the partition again, but I flung him back into his seat. "What are you scared of?" I demanded, shaking him. I was suddenly furiously angry, fed up with the whole wretched business. "Why are you frightened of the Consul? What is it you've done?"

"Nothing. I told you before. I've done nothing. Absolutely nothing." His voice was trembling. He seemed on the verge of tears he was so wrought up. "I promise you. Please. Tell the driver to stop."

"No," I said, holding him down. "I've had enough of this." My voice sounded hard. "We're going to see the Consul. Either that or you tell me why you're scared to go there. Did you kill Wade?"

"No." He stared at me, his body shocked rigid. "It happened just as I said."

"Then what the devil is it you're scared of? Why did you insist on taking his name? Come on now," I added, gripping hold of his arm. "If you want any more help from me, you'd better give me the whole story."

He stared at me, his white, frightened face outlined against the dark leather of the cab. "All right," he whispered, and his body relaxed under my hand as though a weight had been lifted from him. "All right, I'll tell you." He leaned back in his seat as though exhausted. "I have told you I am a scientist." I nodded. "Have you lived here so long in North Africa that you don't know what that means?" He leaned quickly forward, his face becoming excited again. "It means you have something here——" He tapped his forehead. "And because of that your life is not your own any more. It belongs to the State. I am a Czech. If you take me to the Consulate, then I shall be sent back to England, and sooner or later they will get me. Or else life will become so insupportable . . ."

"Who will get you?" I asked.

"Who? The Communists, of course. The Czech Communists."

"But for Heaven's sake!" I exclaimed. "You're a refugee. You've been given political asylum. You were perfectly safe in England."

"Safe?" He laughed. "You say that because you are English, because you have never been a refugee! Listen. When I fled to England in 1949, everything was all right. But then, after the Fuchs business, there was a new screening and it was discovered I had been a Communist."

"But if you were a Communist——"

"I was not a Communist," he declared violently. "I have never been a Communist—not in the sense of the word as it is used now. But I joined the Party in 1938, after Munich. A great many of us joined then. It seemed our only hope. And afterwards, when the war was over, I forgot all about it. I didn't think it mattered after I had fled from Czechoslovakia. I had left my wife to escape the Communists. I thought that was sufficient."

"I still don't see what you're frightened of," I said. "Are you trying to tell me that our people were going to send you back to Czechoslovakia?"

"No, no, of course not. Oh, God! I knew you wouldn't understand. The British refused to let me leave the country. That's why I had to come with Wade in a boat. It isn't the British I am afraid of. But if I go back there . . . Listen, please. When I ignored the offers from Prague, they began sending me Party literature as though I were a member, they stopped me in the street, phoned me at the office, sent anonymous letters to the authorities denouncing me as a paid Communist agent. They even sent me letters in code from Prague. Finally they began to threaten. They were going to arrest Karen and my father. They would have been sent to the uranium mines or, worse still, into Russia, to Siberia."

"But your wife's here now," I said.

"I know, I know. But how do I know she is here of her own free will?" He caught hold of my arm, shaking it excitedly. "Please, please, try to understand. If I am sent back to England, it will start all over again. I couldn't stand it. No man's nerves could stand it. But here . . . Wade will disappear and there is nothing, absolutely nothing, to connect an obscure doctor at a Mission in the Atlas Mountains with the scientist who is missing in England." He was sweating and his face was all puckered up with the urgency of what he was trying to convey. " Please. You must help me. There must be some way out of Tangier. There must be some way."

The taxi was just turning into the rue d'Angleterre. I could see the arched entrance to the Consulate. " Maybe there is,' I said and leaned forward and slid back the glass partition. "Drive down to the Zocco Grande," I told the driver. I couldn't very well do anything else. Half of his fears were probably imaginary, but they were real enough to him. The taxi turned the corner by the entrance to the Consulate and drove on down the hill, and he was suddenly crying. Tears of relief were welling out of his eyes. " Thank you," he breathed. " Thank you."

Poor devil! I leaned back in my seat, thinking back over the events of the past twenty-four hours. If I hadn't pulled him out of the sea . . . But I had and now he was my responsibility. Somehow I'd got to get him out of the International Zone and into Morocco. It was a problem—the sort of problem that required inside knowledge of the working of Tangier. There had been a time . . .

I glanced at my watch. It was ten past three. Unless they had altered the flight schedules, we could still be at the Airport in time to meet the Paris-Casablanca plane. I hesitated, wondering whether Vareau was still a clerk at the Airport. Once, a long time back, I had got a man out that way, and his papers had lacked the necessary entry stamp. It was worth trying. "We'll get another taxi in the Zocco Grande," I said, more to myself than to him. " And we'll have to hurry. We've got to buy you a new suit and be out at the Airport before four."

He gripped my hand. " I shall never be able to thank you," he said.

" You haven't thanked me yet for saving your life," I said harshly. " Better leave thanksgiving until we're both of us safely out of Tangier."

III

We left Tangier by the rue de Fez, along a dirt-edged road where strings of asses trotted through the dust kicked up by battered French trucks driven fast. Out on the outskirts of the Mountain it was all rickety, new-grown development—an ugly pattern of telegraph poles and tin shacks and brand-new concrete factories. And the old ran side-by-side with the new ; the over-burdened asses, the bare-legged, turbaned men driving wooden ploughs through hard, dry ground, and the women, shrouded and veiled so that they looked like perambulating bundles of old clothes.

Beyond the development area, a ridge of grey-brown hills covered with stones and scrub ran out to Cap Spartel and the Atlantic. We passed a gang of convicts picking desultorily at the road and there were herds of black goats and drifts of white that were flocks of the stork-like birds that the French call pique-bœuf. It was all just as I remembered it, even to the nervous void in my stomach and Kavan sitting tense and rigid beside me as that other man had done.

It was not quite four when we reached the Airport. The field was empty. The Paris flight had not yet landed. I told Kavan to wait in the taxi and slipped over the white-painted fence and round to the back of the Airport buildings where the buffet was. I was in luck. Vareau was there. " Monsieur Latham!" He came waddling over to me, a fat, slightly shabby man with a face like a bloodhound. " Comment ça va, eh, eh? You wish me to arrange a seat for you on the plane, yes?"

" Not for me," I said. " For a friend." And I drew him aside and explained the situation to him. But he shook his head. " You know, mon ami, I would do anything to help you. But it is too dangerous. The regulations are most strict now. I must put his name on the Paris list and then what happens when the office in Casablanca see that, eh? Non, non, it is impossible."

" Nonsense," I said. " It's not impossible. The Casablanca

office wouldn't even notice. And if they did, then you made a mistake, that's all. You've got to help me, Vareau." There was no other way of getting Kavan out, not with his papers correct. And they had to be correct if he were to work with me at Enfida. I pleaded, threatened, cajoled, and in the end he agreed to do it for twice the sum I originally offered him. Even then he wouldn't have done it but for one thing—for personal reasons the air hostesses were being changed at Tangier. It was this factor that made the thing possible.

We went through the details carefully and then I returned to Kavan. He was sitting exactly as I had left him, his body rigid, his face tense. He looked dazed and desperately tired, oddly unfamiliar in his new suit. "Is it all right?" he asked urgently as I climbed in beside him. "Did you fix it?"

"Yes," I said. "I fixed it." But all the same I was wondering whether he could carry it through. His nerves were on edge and beneath the stubble of his beard I saw that the corner of his mouth was twitching.

"What do I have to do?" he asked. "Tell me what I'm to do."

I hesitated. I was wondering just how much I needed a doctor, for this business involved me deeper than I cared to go. But it was no good getting cold feet now. The man would just have to pull himself together. "All right," I said. "Now listen. This is the drill. As soon as the Paris plane is sighted, Vareau, the French clerk, will come for you. He'll take you to the lavatory and there you'll shave off that beard, so that your appearance coincides with the photograph on your papers. By the way, I suppose your visa for entry into French Morocco is okay?"

"Yes, yes." He nodded. "That was all arranged at the French Consulate in London."

"And you have a labour permit?"

"Yes."

"Good. You'll stay in the lavatory until Vareau collects you. By then the passengers who are going through to Casablanca will be congregated in the buffet. You will join them. Have a drink or something to occupy yourself. Talk to nobody. If anybody speaks to you, reply in Czech. Vareau will bring you your ticket and anything else you need to get on to the plane. When the Paris passengers are instructed to return to the plane, you will go with them. There will be a different air hostess and your name will be on the list of passengers travelling direct from Paris to Casablanca. If the air hostess or the immigration official asks you anything, you don't understand—you speak nothing but Czech. Is all that clear?"

He nodded and I had him repeat the instructions word for word.

"When Vareau takes you to the lavatory, he will give you an immigration form to fill in. You will complete it in the lavatory and return it to him when he comes to collect you. Only one question on that form is not straightforward. Against *Where have you come from*? you will put Heath Row, London, via Paris. For destination and purpose of visit you state the exact truth—that you are going to work as a doctor in Morocco and that your address will be the English Mission at Enfida. Any questions about that?"

"No. No, I don't think so." He was frowning. "But I don't understand how it helps. The authorities at Casablanca will want to know why my papers are not stamped as having come from Paris. When they find they are not stamped, they will know——"

"There's no difficulty there," I said, and I pulled out my own passport. "Look!" I had come out to Morocco by air from England in July, 1949, yet the only indication was the entry stamp of the immigration authorities at Casablanca. Though I had stopped off two days in Paris no entry had been made in my passport. "You see. All you have to say is that you've come from England. You left London by the night flight yesterday. All right?" He nodded uneasily. "You've nothing to worry about once you're on that plane," I assured him.

"But you're not coming with me?"

"No. I shall go by train. We'll meet in Casablanca."

He gripped my arm. "Come with me on the plane. You could get a ticket here. There's nothing to stop you. Why must you go by train?" He was like a child afraid of being left.

" Because I reserved two berths in the wagon-lit. It would look odd if neither of us turned up."

He nodded unhappily and stared out across the airfield, his fingers drumming nervously on his knee. " Isn't there some way we could both go together?"

" No. This is the only way that gets you into Morocco with your papers in order. I should warn you there's a French Civil Control office at Enfida."

" I don't like it," he said, shaking his head. " It's dangerous. And if I'm caught——"

" Oh, for heaven's sake!" I said, and took hold of him and swung him round so that he faced me. " Now just listen. I'm in this as deep as you are. If you're caught, then I'll be in trouble, too. If you don't like this arrangement, then I'm through with you. Understand?"

" Yes. Yes, of course. I'm sorry." He half shrugged his shoulders. " Well, if it's the only way . . ." He nodded slowly. " Very well. I'll do what you say."

"Fine. You've nothing to worry about. Just convince yourself that you really have come direct from England."

" I'll try." He nodded and then asked me where he should meet me in Casablanca.

" At the railway station," I said. " The train for Marrakech leaves at 8.45 a.m. to-morrow."

" And your train arrives when?"

" At seven twenty."

" I shall be at the station in time to met your train then."

" All right. But if we do happen to miss each other, we'll rendezvous in the foyer of the Hotel Metropole."

" If I'm not there to meet your train," he said, " you'd better look for me in the prison." He said it unsmilingly.

The taxi driver, who had been standing talking to one of the baggage checkers, called out to us and pointed. The silver glint of wings showed above the hills behind us. I pulled open my case and handed Kavan my shaving things. As we got out of the taxi, Vareau appeared round the corner of the Airport building and signalled to us. I gripped Kavan's hand. " Good luck!" I said. " You're clear on what you have to do?"

" Quite clear." He nodded and then said urgently, " You'll

contact Karen, won't you? You'll let her know where I am?"

" I'll get in touch with her somehow," I assured him.

" Promise you won't leave Tangier without——"

" Of course," I said. "Now hurry. Vareau's waiting."

I watched him climb the fence and disappear round the front of the building with the clerk and then I got back into the taxi and sat there, watching the airfield, whilst the Constellation landed and taxied over. It was about ten minutes before the passengers emerged from the plane and came across the brown, burnt-up grass to the Airport building.

I was nervous and the minutes dragged by. Cars came and went and my eyes remained on the corner of the building, my mind trying to visualise the scene inside. It was a modern brick building and on the side facing the airfield was a buffet with tall windows looking out to the runway. The baggage counter was between the buffet and the entrance hall, enclosed by doors. The officials would be fully occupied with the papers and baggage of the passengers stopping at Tangier. Kavan should have finished shaving by now. He should be sitting in the buffet with the rest of the passengers bound for Casablanca. The air hostess had gone into the building with the air crew several minutes ago. Vareau should have added Kavan's name to the list by now. He should have got Kavan's immigration form, too.

I got out of the taxi and began pacing up and down. If I could only have been in the buffet to keep an eye on things, to keep Kavan's mind occupied . . . I was afraid his nervousness would give him away, sitting there alone. I tried not to think what would happen if they started questioning him.

I kept glancing at my watch, but it seemed ages before the hands pointed to four forty-five. The air crew strolled out to the plane, their flat hats and dark blue uniforms looking oddly naval. A mechanic was clambering along one wing. Then he jumped down and the air crew disappeared inside the fuselage. It was ten to five. Were they interrogating Kavan now? I went to the rail, craning my head forward to see farther round the corner of the building.

And then the air hostess came out, the board with her list of passengers swinging in her hand. The passengers followed in a long, straggling line. I didn't recognise Kavan at first. He was near the end of the line, walking close to a French family. He looked quite different without his beard. He was walking jerkily, a little nervously, his head thrust forward, his eyes on the ground. Once he half-turned and glanced in my direction. His face looked stronger, more positive without the beard. He had a strong jaw and somehow the sight of him looking like that made me feel it would be all right.

The passengers were bunching up now, queueing at the foot of the steps into the fuselage. Gradually the little crowd thinned. I could see the immigration official. He was talking to the hostess, only half his attention on the passengers. And then he was looking at Kavan and my muscles tensed and my mouth felt dry. The air hostess glanced down at her list and I breathed a sigh of relief. Kavan was climbing the steps. I watched him disappear into the fuselage and then I turned and walked rather shakily back to the taxi.

Five minutes later the plane taxied out to the end of the runway. It stood there for a moment, revving its engines, and then it took off, the under-carriage retracting and the starboard wing dipping as it swung south and disappeared in the direction of Morocco.

I told the driver to take me back to Tangier and I lay back in my seat and closed my eyes. In little more than an hour Kavan would be through the airfield immigration check and on his way into Casablanca in the Air France bus—so long as nothing went wrong. But I couldn't do anything about it now. I would mail Vareau his money from Marrakech and that, I hoped, would be the end of the whole business.

For the first time since I had pulled Kavan out of the sea I felt relaxed. Lying back, watching the dusty road stream by, my mind turned to Enfida. Now at last I was able to think and plan again for the future.

The next thing I knew we were back in Tangier and a horn was blaring at us. We had stopped at some traffic lights and somebody was gesticulating and shouting to me from a car drawn up alongside. It was Kostos, and he leaned across the Arab he had with him and wound down the window. "Lat'am!" he called across to me. "I like to talk to you. Tell your driver to stop opposite the British Post Office, eh?"

"And I'd like a word with you," I shouted at him. The sight of him had suddenly made me angry. If it hadn't been for that nonsense about the passport, I shouldn't have had to run the risk of getting Kavan out of the Zone illegally. He could have travelled with me on the train. I leaned forward and told the driver to stop opposite the B.P.O. The lights changed and we moved forward. Through the rear window I saw Kostos nose his car in behind us. I sat back again, thinking how dangerous it could be to take another man's name when you knew nothing about him—especially when the destination was Tangier. I was consumed with sudden curiosity to discover what it was all about. What were these documents that Kostos was so anxious to get hold of? And this place Kasbah Foum—it had an oddly sinister sound.

The taxi stopped and I paid the driver off. Kostos and the Arab were waiting for me on the curb. "Where have you been?" Kostos demanded. "You don't go to the British Consulate. I check that. An' you don't go to the Pension de la Montagne. I just come from there. Where do you go?"

"That's none of your business," I said. "There are one or two questions I want to ask you. First, I want that passport. What have you done with it?"

"The passport?" He smiled at me. "You heard what Lopez say. He give it to you." He leaned closer to me, still smiling. "You tell me where Wade is, Lat'am, an' I make it worth your while, eh?"

"He's left Tangier," I told him.

"Left the Zone? Oh no." He shook his head, looking down at the suitcase I was carrying. "He don't leave the Zone with you—not now. So you better cancel that other berth in the wagon-lit. He don't leave till I get what I want."

"And that is the deeds of Kasbah Foum?"

He nodded, watching me closely. "Strictly between you an' me, Lat'am. I trade the papers for his passport. You tell him."

"And if he hasn't got them?"

"Oh, he has them."

"How do you know?"

"I know because . . ." He stopped there and took hold of my arm. "Come. We cannot talk 'ere. You come to the Café Normandie and have a drink with me, eh?"

" All right," I said.

He nodded towards the Arab, who was about thirty, tall and well-built, but carrying a little too much flesh under his djellaba. " This is Si Ali bel-Caid El Hassan d'Es-Skhira." His use of the man's full title rather than the way he said it conveyed his contempt of everything indigène. " Maybe he persuade you, eh?" He smiled slyly, convinced that only money or power would persuade anybody.

I glanced at his companion with renewed interest. So this was the man who had employed Wade to get the deeds. At the mention of his name he had turned towards me and now that I could see his face I realised that he was Berber, not Arab. His features were long and pale, like a European's, with prominent cheek bones and a high-bridged, aquiline nose. It would have been a fine face but for the cruelty of the mouth and a slight craftiness of the eyes. " Are you from the Atlas?" I asked him in French.

" From the Anti-Atlas. My father is Caid of Kasbah Foum-Skhira."

" Poor fellow, he is an exile, you see." Kostos tightened his grip on my arm with unpleasant familiarity. " Come, Lat'am. We go where we can talk." And he led me to one of the pavement tables of the Café Normandie, where he ordered two cognacs and a coffee for Ali, and then sat watching me uncertainly. The Berber stared out across the Place de France, his face impassive, his eyes remote. I was thinking they were typical of the cosmopolitan world of Tangier—the crook lured there by easy money and the Berber nationalist deported from his own country because he had been too actively anti-French. The roar of the traffic lapped round us, mingling with the shrill cries of the Arab news-vendors and the sound of Spanish music from the café radio.

The drinks came and Kostos raised his glass. " Salud!" He was looking at me with a sly grin. Then he set his glass down and leaned towards me across the table. " Lat'am. You do something for me, will you—for the sake of old times. You tell me where Wade is."

" I don't know," I replied, amused that it was the exact truth.

" Now don't be silly, please." The smile had gone from his

mouth. The lips were compressed into a hard line. His small, dark eyes had hardened, too. " I am going to have those papers. He is somewhere here in the Zone. If I do not get them, he never get out. Why do you smile? Do you think I don't tell you the truth? Maybe you think to help him slip across the frontier with some Berber caravan. Well, you try. That's all. You try an' get him out like that. You see——" He jabbed a tobacco-stained forefinger at me—"it is not only me he have to reckon with. It is Ali, also. The word has gone out to the souks." He tapped the side of his nose and smiled. " He don't get out of Tangier till Ali has those papers."

I was almost tempted to tell him how the man he thought was Wade had got out of the Zone. I would like to have seen his face. But it was too dangerous. Instead, I said, " He hasn't got the papers you want."

" Then what is your interest in him?" He said it with something near to a sneer. " Now come, Lat'am. Let us not waste time. I know he has the papers."

" How do you know?" I asked again.

" How? Because he come alone." He leaned forward across the table. " Down on the beach las' night you are asking about this man Kavan. Well, Kavan is not on the boat. He do not come. Wade is alone an' he has the papers. He must have."

" Why? What's Kavan got to do with it?"

He stared at me and then shrugged his shoulders. " Come, my friend. We are getting nowhere." His voice hardened. " We talk business now, eh? 'Ow much? 'Ow much you want?"

I suppose I should have told him then and there what Kavan had told me—that Wade never had the papers. I should have tried to convince him. But I couldn't tell him that Wade was dead, lost overboard during the voyage, and I hesitated. The trouble was that I was consumed with curiosity about this place Kasbah Foum. Curiosity is something you suck up out of the atmosphere of Tangier. " It might help," I said, " if I knew something about Kasbah Foum."

" Ah, I understand. You wish to know what these papers are worth to us, eh?" Kostos chuckled. " All right, Lat'am. I tell you. To me they are worth nothing. Nothing at all. It is to Ali only that they are important." He turned to the

Berber and spoke quickly in French, explaining what had been said.

Ali nodded. "Kasbah Foum is part of the land that will come to me when my father, Allah preserve him, is dead," he said, speaking directly to me. "It is our own land, you understand, not collective land belonging to the tribe. But when the French come into the south of Morocco; what they call the Pacification"—there was the suggestion of a sneer in the way he said it—" my father is forced to surrender Kasbah Foum to them. A Capitaine Marcel Duprez demand it of him as a personal gift. Now Duprez is dead and my people need that land because the trees are dying of some pest in the palmerie of Foum-Skhira. The date crop has failed and there is little food. But at Kasbah Foum there is water. New trees could be planted and the land tilled."

"The place is of no real value," Kostos cut in quickly.

"C'est ça." Ali nodded. "It is about a thousand hectares of land, mostly mountain, and there is a kasbah, an old mud fort, at the entrance to a gorge. It is of no value, except to my father's people."

I looked across at Kostos. I didn't believe him. Why should he trouble himself about this if there was nothing more to it than a matter of planting a few date palms? "Suppose you tell me the truth," I said, reverting to English.

"You think we lie to you?" His eyes had narrowed.

I didn't say anything for a moment. I was thinking I ought to convince him I knew nothing about the papers and leave it at that. But I was back in the mood of Tangier and I was thinking of that entry at the end of Wade's log. "Does the name Ed White mean anything to you?" I asked him.

The Greek's eyes were suddenly hard and angry. "So you know all about it, eh? You sit there laughing at us——" His hand gripped my arm across the table. "All right, Lat'am. We talk business now. 'Ow much?"

I pulled my arm away. To gain time I turned to Ali and complimented him on his French. The Berber smiled so that his teeth showed through his rather thick lips. "I was educated in Paris." He said it with pride.

"And now you are a nationalist."

His eyes lighted up. "I have dedicated myself before Allah

to the task of driving the French out of my country." He started on a tirade against the Protecting Power, but Kostos cut him short. "This doesn't get us nowhere." He leaned towards me across the table. "Listen, Lat'am. You an' I, we understand each other, eh? You get Wade to hand over those papers an' there is a hundred thousand francs for you. Understand? A hundred pounds sterling, if you like. That's what I bring you 'ere to tell you."

"It's no good," I said. "He's out of the Zone now."

"That is a lie. He cannot be out of the Zone." He finished his drink and nodded to Ali. The two of them got to their feet and Kostos came round to my side of the table, leaning over me, his hand resting on my shoulders. "Tell him I expect him at my office by midday tomorrow. If he comes before midday, I see you get the money. Okay? And don't get some foolish ideas, Lat'am. He is in a fix, and there is nobody will lift a little finger to help him get out of 'ere— not Arab, Berber or Jew. You tell him that." He tapped the side of his nose and smiled. It wasn't a friendly smile.

They left then and I watched them drive past. Kostos was staring at me, hard-faced and angry. Then they were gone, swallowed up in the whirl of traffic in the Place de France, and I sat there, smoking a cigarette, whilst dust descended on Tangier and the lights came on in the shops. Finally I picked up my suitcase and went across to the British Post Office and phoned the one man I could trust to do something for me and not talk about it, a retired Indian Civil Servant who had been a friend of my father's. But he was out and his servant didn't expect him back till late. It didn't really matter. I could write to him about Karen Kavan from Enfida.

I went to a French restaurant and had some food and after that I walked down to the station and joined the queue waiting in the booking hall to go through the passport check. I wondered whether Kostos would have somebody follow me on the train and I looked about for the Arab who had kept watch outside the hotel. But I couldn't see him. I wasn't really surprised, for Kostos was essentially a Tangerois.

The minutes ticked slowly by on the station clock and the queue moved forward only a pace at a time. As always, it was a strangely mixed crowd—tourists and Spaniards and native tribesmen all jam-packed together. There were several Americans in gaily-coloured shirts and lumber-jackets—construction men from the big new Moroccan air bases. There were two Jews with grey beards and little black skull caps on their heads. And close beside me was a Berber chieftain with fierce, swarthy features and a black beard. The curved sheath of his knife was beautifully worked in silver.

The queue shuffled forward and one of the Americans said, " Jesus, these Goddamned Spaniards! The way they behave, you'd think we were on Ellis Island." He had a hard, braying laugh. Beyond his wide-brimmed hat, I could see the face of one of the passport officials framed in the oval of the hatch. And then a hand plucked at my arm and I turned, startled, thinking it was Kostos or perhaps the police to say that Kavan had been stopped at Casa.

Instead, I found Karen Kavan's grey eyes looking up at me. " I'm so glad I found you." Her voice was breathless with relief. " I was afraid I might miss you in all this crowd, or else that you would have arrived early and be on the train." She was nervous and her face was as pale and strained as it had been the previous night.

" How did you know where to find me?" I asked.

" I telephoned to your hotel. Then I try Cook's, just in case. I wanted to know——" She stopped there, uncertain how to go on.

" It's all right," I said. " I know who he is. And you needn't worry. Your husband left for Casablanca by plane this afternoon."

" Oh." She closed her eyes momentarily. " Oh, thank God. I was so afraid. You see, when I telephoned to the hotel, they said he had gone to the Pension de la Montagne. It's not far from where I work, so I walked there. But no guests had arrived there this afternoon and I was afraid the police . . ." The rush of words stopped abruptly and her eyes stared at me uncertainly. " Where has he gone please? Last night, you said something about him working for you, but I don't remember —I am too distrait."

I gave her my address and explained that her husband would be working as a doctor at the Mission. " You'll always be welcome there," I added. "When you're ready to come to him, you've only to write and let me know."

"Thank you. You're very kind." She breathed a little sigh. "I was so afraid I shouldn't find you, that I shouldn't know where he had gone. I felt so alone."

I glanced quickly at my watch. It was already nine thirty. "How long have you been in Tangier?" I asked her.

"Just two weeks now. I am working as governess for an American family—Mr. and Mrs. Schulborg."

Just two weeks! It was an odd coincidence. "Straight from Czechoslovakia?"

"No. From the American Zone of Austria." And then her eyes widened as she understood the drift of my questions. "Surely Jan doesn't think I am here because they——" She stopped there and then added quickly, "Please. You must explain to him that I received his message and that is why I am here." Her voice was desperately urgent. "His message arrived the 15th November. A week later, on the night of the 23rd, I escape across the border into Upper Austria on ski. That is in the American Zone. It was the Americans who find me this job here in Tangier. Please explain to him."

"Of course, I will," I said. And then I added, "You must love your husband very much."

"Yes. Yes, I do." The shadow of a smile suddenly touched her lips. "But I hardly know him any more, you know."

"Well, that's something that can be altered now. But it was a brave thing to do."

She shook her head. "No, not brave. It was dangerous, yes, but . . . You see, I was desperate. They had already arrested Pan Rudolph Kavan—that is his father. Fortunately I am away from Prague, staying with friends. When I returned, I was warned that our house was being watched and that I should be arrested also. That is what made me try to cross the border. I had no alternative. Explain to him, will you, please."

I nodded. I was thinking of what Jan Kavan had told me in the taxi going up to the British Consulate. So it was all true. "I'll tell him," I said. "Come to Enfida and join him as soon as you can." And I added, "You'd better write to me, not to him—just in case."

She nodded. "Yes, I will write to you."

"And your address?"

"The Villa da Vinci on La Montagne."

"Señor! Deprisa, deprisa, señor!" It was the passport officer telling me to hurry. I handed him my passport and went through the barrier to the next hatch where I got the necessary forms. I turned to speak to Karen again. A whistle shrilled. A voice called, "En voiture! En voiture!" There was the sound of running feet. "Give Jan my love," she called to me.

"I will. He will be expecting you. Come when you . . ." A blast of steam cut short my words and I saw the train begin to move. I waved to her and dashed on to the platform and scrambled on board.

My last memory of Tangier was Karen's small, pale face staring after me, her hand fluttering as she waved farewell to the only link she had with her husband. I found my sleeper and slumped into my seat, thinking about how she must feel, having come so far, still to be separated from him by two frontiers.

At El Ksar el Kebir there is a long wait. It's the frontier station between Spanish and French Morocco. I hung about in the cool night air until the frontier police returned my passport and then I went to bed. I was tired and I remember little except the usual vague noises of night travel by train— the rattle of the wheels on the rail points and the sudden, deathly silence of the stations where isolated noises become magnified.

When I woke it was daylight. The country was flat and there were glimpses of the sea through the ragged ribbon of factory buildings that lined the coast. We were approaching Casablanca. The buildings became taller, springing up all round the tracks—white concrete gleaming in the sunshine— and then the train was slowing down and we were running in to the station.

I rubbed the condensation from the window and peered at the people standing on the half-deserted platform, suddenly fearful that Kavan might not be there. But as the train jerked to a halt, I saw him a little farther down, standing alone beside some crates of oranges. He was smoking a cigarette and his face looked hard and set as he scanned the length of the train, watching the doors open and the passengers begin to alight.

He saw me as soon as I got off the train, and he rushed over to me and seized hold of my hand, pumping it up and down.

" You got through the immigration officials all right then?" I said.

" Of course, of course. There was no difficulty at all. They asked me whether I'd come straight from England and I nodded and talked to them in Czech and they stamped my papers and that was that. They're like little lambs." He grinned and put his hand on my shoulder, patting me as though I were a dog. " First you save my life. Then you get me out of Tangier. You are a wonderful man! Wonderful!" He was bubbling over with excitement. " And now, here I am in Morocco. My new country! My new life!" His hand gripped my shoulder. " I shall always be grateful. Always."

" Wait till you've walked twenty miles in the mountains," I said, " and attended dozens of children half blind with trachoma."

" You think I can't start my life again? I tell you I can. I'm tough. I have a stake in this country now. I shall learn Arabic and soon I shall be more Moroccan than the Moors." He laughed and then stopped abruptly and said, " Did you see Karen?"

" Yes." And I told him how she had met me at Tangier station. He had me repeat everything she had said, and when I had finished, he stood there with bowed head. " So my father has been arrested." He blinked his eyes. " He is an old man, so maybe they will . . ." But then he gave a little shrug. " He was a fine man." He used the past tense. " He did much good in Prague. I'm sorry." He straightened up and looked at me. " Thank God Karen got out in time. I was afraid that perhaps . . . But never mind that now. *Give Jan my love!*" He murmured the words to himself and then gave a little awkward laugh that was so near to a sob. " And she really said that? You heard her?" And when I nodded, he smiled a little sadly and said, " You know, it is hard to believe that you have actually heard her voice. You're the first person to give me actual words she has spoken in all these four years. There have been messages, of course—through the underground. But you are telling me her actual words." He cleared his throat briefly. " Come on. Let's get some breakfast. Now you are here, I find I'm hungry."

The difference in the man was extraordinary. He'd waited for my train in an all-night café near the station, but, though he was hollow-eved, he didn't seem tired. And without the beard he looked somehow younger. But it wasn't just his appearance. His whole attitude to life had changed. His mind looked forward now, not backwards, and he was no longer frightened. It was as though the ordeal of passing through the immigration check at Casablanca had destroyed all the nerves in his system. He had arrived in Morocco. His papers were in order. All the past seemed to have been swept out of his mind, except for one thing.

We had barely settled down to our breakfast in a nearby café when he began talking of Kasbah Foum. " I must go down there and see the place," he said, and he pulled a map from his pocket. It was Michelin Map No. 171, covering the area of Marrakech and south to the Sahara. " I got it last night," he said. " But it doesn't mark Kasbah Foum."

"I think you'd better forget all about Kasbah Foum."

He reacted at once to the sharpness of my tone. " Why? Did something happen after I left? Was it Kostos?"

"Yes," I said. " I had a meeting with him and Ali d'Es-Skhira."

" You mean you actually met Ali d'Es-Skhira?" He was suddenly excited. " What was he like? What happened? What did they say?" I started to tell him, but he interrupted me. " First, is Caid Hassan of Foum-Skhira still alive?"

It irritated me to have him thinking of nothing but this confounded Wade business. He had come out to be a doctor at Enfida. He should have been thinking about that. " How the devil do you know the Caid's name? I thought you said Wade didn't talk about his affairs?"

" Wade?" He sounded surprised. " Oh, I see. No. he didn't talk about his affairs, but . . ." He shrugged his shoulders. " It doesn't matter." He hesitated and then, as though he couldn't leave the subject alone, he said, " Well, is he alive? "

" As far as I know. Why? "

" Nothing, nothing. But go on. Tell me what they said. "

To satisfy him I gave a brief summary of that meeting in the Boulevard Pasteur. When I had finished he said, " So Kostos thinks I won't be able to get out of the Zone, eh? " He was smiling to himself. And then he looked at me, still smiling, and said, " What do you think he'll do when he finds I've disappeared? "

" I don't know, " I said shortly. " Nothing, probably. "

" Yes, he must do something. Ali, anyway. I think they'll go straight to Foum-Skhira. " He nodded his head thoughtfully, peering down at the map. " Yes, that's what I think they'll do. Look. Here is Foum-Skhira. " He twisted the map round for me to see, pointing to a spot about 150 miles south-west of Marrakech. " Kasbah Foum will be quite near it, I imagine. "

" Now just listen to me, " I said, pushing the map aside angrily. " I don't know what Wade told you. Something obviously. But whatever it was that's got you so interested in the place, forget about it. You're not Wade any longer. You're Jan Kavan again. You ceased to have any connection with Wade the moment you stepped on that plane. From what you've told me, you've got quite enough worries without getting involved in another man's affairs. "

" But if Kostos follows me—— "

" Why should he? He's not interested in you. He's only interested in Wade. Now just try and understand who you are. You're coming with me to Enfida to act as Mission doctor. That should be enough to occupy your mind. And your wife's going to join you there later. Now just shut up about Kasbah Foum. Okay? "

He nodded slowly. " Yes, of course. I understand. " He folded the map up, but his eyes kept straying towards it as we ate our food in silence, and when we were on the train and steaming out of Casablanca he opened it up again and sat with it spread out on his knees, staring out of the window at the brown, rolling country where camels and mules, harnessed together, pulled primitive ploughs across the arid landscape.

" It's like the Old Testament come to life," he said, and then added, " And I suppose it gets even more Biblical as you go south towards the desert."

" You'll find all you want of the Old Testament in the souks of Marrakech," I told him.

We didn't talk much after that and I drowsed off. When I woke we were running out of the Djebilet hills, down into the flat plain of Marrakech, and there, ahead of us, were the Atlas Mountains. An hour later we were sitting at a table, drinking coffee and looking out at the teeming mass of humanity that packed the Djemaa el Fna. The mountains and the plain had gone. We were swallowed up in the dusty hubbub of the great, red-walled Berber city. We went to the bank and then found a cheap little French hotel in the rue Bab Aguenaou.

In the late afternoon I took Jan to the roof-top of the Café de France. The place was full of tourists, rich people from all over the world who had come to drink mint tea on that roof and watch the sky flare to Technicolor and to look down on the seething acres of tribesmen packed into the great square of the Djemaa el Fna. The tide of humanity ebbed and flowed out of the narrow, covered alleys of the souks and the noise of it came up to us in a steady roar of sound. It was evening now and the flat, white roof tops and the red walls and the graceful tower of the Katoubia were flushed with the pink of the sunset and all the sky was an incredible spectrum of pastel shades. Away to the south the Atlas Mountains glistened like sugar icing, a towering rampart of fairy beauty.

" And that's where we're going?" Jan asked. He was staring towards the mountains.

I nodded.

" It's unbelievable," he murmured. " Marcel described all this to me so often. And now I am really here——"

" Marcel?"

He glanced at me quickly. " A man I met during the war." He turned back towards the mountains and added, " It was when I was working with Krupps. I was on secret work and I was getting information out to the British. I used the French forced labour battalions and Marcel was my chief contact. He'd lived out here and he talked of nothing but this country and the people. He was a fine man. He believed in victory always, right from the beginning." He paused and then added, "He died of pneumonia in a cellar in Essen. I was sorry when he went." His tone was sad as though he were speaking of somebody who had died only yesterday. "And now I am here and it's all just as he described it to me. It doesn't seem possible." His voice was almost awed. He hunched his shoulders and leaned forward, staring down into the huge square.

I was used to it now, but I could remember how I had felt when I first saw it. There were thousands of people down there ; people from all over South Morocco—from the desert and the palmeries and from the most inaccessible villages of the Atlas. They crowded in circles round story-tellers and the snake charmers and the troops of dancers, or wandered hand-in-hand among the booths of doctors and barbers and letter-writers. Among them moved the water-boys, festooned with brass cups, their bells ringing an insistent water-note of sound. It was a shifting pattern of colour that sent up a continuous, inhuman roar. And over all the hubbub of the crowds there rose the ceaseless beat of the tam-tams— rhythmic and urgent ; the sound that beats like the pulsing of the blood through the high mountains and along all the valley arteries of the south.

"It's wonderful," Jan breathed. "Wonderful. Karen will love it."

I laughed. "The glamour of it doesn't last," I said. "Not when you discover the poverty and disease and inert stupidity that lies behind it all. This is the thousand and one nights, the city of delight, the sweets of a year's labour in a hard, naked land. And the place is rotten with venereal disease, with tuberculosis, dysentery and conjunctivitis, with every running sore that Job was plagued with."

"You want I show you souks?" A young Arab boy was standing at our table, his dark eager eyes watching us hope-fully. "You come. Jus' look. No buy. Jus' look."

I glanced at Jan. "Would you like to see the markets?"

His eyes went momentarily to the tinted crystal of the mountains and then he nodded and got to his feet. A gleam of triumph showed in the little Arab's eyes as he turned away towards the stairs. " Do we need him to guide us round?" Jan asked.

" Not necessarily," I said. " But these boys are good value. It's getting late, too, and you can easily get lost." We went down the concrete steps and out into the roar of the Djemaa el Fna, skirting the crowds.

" Philip!"

Jan had stopped, his head turned, staring towards the C.T.M. bus terminal building. " What is it?" I asked.

"Look!" He pointed. " Do you see? That man." His tone was urgent.

I followed the line of his outstretched hand, but all I could see was the shifting pattern of the human tide. " What man?"

" He's gone now." He lowered his arm slowly.

"Who was it?" I asked.

He shook his head. " I don't know. Maybe it was the light. I thought for a moment it was Kostos."

I laughed. " Nonsense," I said. " Kostos is a Tangerois. There's nothing for him in Marrakech."

The boy tugged at my sleeve. " Quick, m'soor. Is late. You come quick."

"Come on," I said to Jan. " It'll be dark soon. If you want to see the souks . . ."

He nodded and we plunged into the maelstrom that swirled around the dark mouth of the covered way that led down into the first of the souks. Here were dates and dried fruit and herbs and spices piled in little pyramids on open counters and Arab merchants squatting behind mountains of nuts in the gloom of their stalls. We went through the meat market and then we were in a long, narrow street thatched with palm fronds. The crowds were moving homewards from the souks now and we were fighting our way through a packed mass of people that flowed steadily towards the Djemaa el Fna. " What you want, eh?" our guide asked, grinning up at us, eyes sparkling and his teeth showing white against the shadowed darkness of his small face. " You like Berber silver? I show you bracelets. All good work. Very cheap."

" You speak Arab, don't you?" Jan said. " Tell him we just want to have a quick look round."

"No," I said. "You tell him in English. I'm just going to be a tourist for once. Besides it's not many boys of his age speak English."

"Ess, spik good English." The boy grinned at us. "I show you fine silver. Is not dear, m'soor. I fix."

"We don't want to buy," I said. "We just want to look around."

His mouth puckered sulkily and he shrugged his shoulders. "Okay. You look. I take you good leather shop. No cheat." We forged ahead slowly against the mass of people. There were only a few Europeans. Night was closing in and already the lights were on in the bigger shops, the shops that were marble-floored and had their walls covered with Moroccan rugs or finely stamped leather pouffes. "You like carpet? Real Persian. I fix good price for you."

"No," I said. "Take us to the street of the silversmiths."

"You want silver, eh? Okay." His eyes brightened.

The crowds were thinning now. A bicycle flashed past us, its bell ringing furiously as the Berber boy with a woolly cap on his head weaved dexterously in and out amongst the people. We turned into the little street where men sat cross-legged in workshops no bigger than cubby-holes stamping out the intricate designs of the bracelets, pouring the inlay from little iron pots of molten metal. There were still a few plump Arab women there, well dressed in grey or brown gabardine djellabas with silk veils over nose and mouth and naughty little gold-embroidered slippers peeping from beneath their voluminous skirts. Some of them already wore an armload of gold and silver bracelets, but they still stood and stared with longing.

As we left the street of the silversmiths, we met five blind beggars weaving their way home through the crowds, loosely linked like a sightless chain gang. They had the tortured, cadaverous features of the crucified and they were singing tonelessly, bobbing along with their shaven heads drawn back as though they'd all been hanged by ropes battened under the chin. They were led by a man with a wooden bowl who had the pitiless eyes of the professional beggar. His five freaks, strung out behind him, were all of them mutilated by disease besides having the blank, staring eyes of the blind. I stopped to put money in the bowl. As I did so there was a cry of warning, the crowd opened out and a small donkey piled high with Moroccan rugs went trotting past. The crowd closed up and surged forward. I was pushed to the wall and when at last I could make headway, I couldn't see Jan or our guide.

I hurried then, fighting my way through the crush and craning my neck to see ahead. But there wasn't a sign of him. I couldn't see a single European.

I began to get worried. He didn't know the language and I wasn't sure about the boy. It's easy to get lost in the souks. The place is an absolute rabbit warren. I fought my way through the silk market to the point where the souks divided. A narrow alley forked right. It was the street of the shoe-makers, a dark tunnel crammed with people. I turned back then. The boy must have led him off into one of the side markets. I cut through a wide souk where silks were displayed in the few shops that weren't already shuttered and came out into the parallel street, where the makers of brass had their stalls. But it was impossible to find anybody in the brush of people going home.

For a while I rushed madly up every side alley, searching for him in the intermittent patches of lighting. But in the end I gave it up and made my way slowly back towards the centre of the city, moving with the steadily-flowing tide of humanity, the murmur of the great square acting as a guide. He couldn't really get lost. He'd only to follow the crowd. It was annoying, that was all.

It was quite dark when I reached the Djemaa el Fna and the booths were lit by the smoking jets of a hundred acetylene flares. The whole place, with its milling thousands of tribes-men and its tented booths, had the appearance of an army encamped for the night. The hotel was opposite the Tazi cinema where harsh Arab music blared at the packed crowd waiting to see an American Western.

As I approached the alley-way leading to the hotel, the little Arab boy who had been our guide came out of it. He stopped at the sight of me and his eyes widened. He looked scared and I caught hold of his arm before he could run away. "Why didn't you wait for me?" I asked angrily, speaking to him in Arab.

He stared at me with hurt brown eyes, shocked into immobility by the realisation that I spoke his language. " *Allah ishet elik!* " I cried, shaking him. " Speak, boy. Why didn't you wait for me? "

" You no come, m'soor, " he said, sticking obstinately to his English. " We look all souks, but no see. Is late, very late for souks. " His voice sounded scared and his eyes searched the street as though looking for somebody to help him. " Is no good staying in souk. " He suddenly jerked away from me, wriggling out of my grasp, and with one frightened look at my face, disappeared into the crowd across the road, a small, scampering figure in a brown djellaba and heel-less slippers.

I went straight up to the room we were sharing and found Jan sitting on the bed staring down at the suitcase full of clothes that he'd bought that afternoon. He looked up quickly at my entrance. " Oh, here you are. Thank God! " His voice sounded nervous. " I was getting worried about you. Do you think that boy did it on purpose? "

" How do you mean? " I asked, too surprised at his question to express the annoyance I had felt at finding him back here in the hotel ahead of me when I'd been getting worried and searching all through the souks.

" When we got separated by those beggars, he wouldn't go back for you, " he said. " He insisted you'd cut down one of the side alleys. We went through it and came out into the brass market. But you weren't there and he got very excited, jabbering away at me in Arab, and led me into a maze of streets so that I didn't know where I was. All I knew was that he was leading me deeper and deeper into the souks. "

" Well, at least he brought you back, " I said, sinking into a chair.

" He certainly didn't. I had to find my own way back. "

I stared at him. " Do you mean to say the boy just left you? "

" Well, not quite. It was really the other way round. I left him. "

" Where? "

" It was in an alley full of those gold-embroidered slippers. He kept on trying to drag me along the whole length of it. But by then I knew the only sensible thing was to come back

to the hotel. I told him that and he tried to convince me the
best way back was straight down that alley. I knew it wasn't.
That way we should have been going against the crowd and I
was certain they were making for the Djemaa el Fna."

"And the boy left you to make your own way?"

"He came a little way with me. Then he gave it up."

"But I've just seen him outside the hotel."

Jan shrugged his shoulders. "Then he must have followed
me, that's all."

"You're certain he was trying to lead you the wrong way?"

"Yes, I'm pretty certain. I always have a shrewd idea
where I am in a strange city." He hesitated and then said,
"There's another thing, too. The room has been searched
whilst we've been out."

"Oh, for heaven's sake!" I said. I felt tired. "How do
you know?"

"The hasps of my case were undone. I didn't leave them
like that. And when I got here, the Arab porter couldn't find
the key. He was gone about five minutes before he produced
it." He was wrought up about it, his nerves on edge.

I pulled myself to my feet and examined my case. As far
as I could tell everything was just as I'd left it. "Let's go
down and have some food," I said.

He stared at me angrily for a moment and then he turned
away. "Perhaps you're right." But he said it without con-
viction.

However, he seemed to relax in the warmth of the
restaurant, and next day, after a long night's sleep, he was
quite a different person. In fact, he was almost exuberant
when we were finally seated in the Enfida bus, packed in like
sardines amongst a crowd of Berber men returning from a
night out in the great city. He talked excitedly, asking
questions, and when we drove out past the traceried gateway
of the Bab Aguenaou on to the road that runs out into the
flat plain, he sat quite still without talking, staring at the
mountains. Behind us Marrakech, with its nine kilometres of
red mud walls and its flat-roofed houses dotted with storks'
nests, lay sprawled out in the clear morning sunlight, a sleepy
pattern of red and brown and white.

I didn't talk to him on that two-hour journey out to Enfida.

I thought if I didn't talk, maybe he'd find it easier to adjust himself to his new surroundings. Also, I had my own problems. I hadn't given much thought to the Mission whilst I had been in Tangier. Now I needed to plan. There was the surgery to organise and people I wanted to see—people who had been sick or had suffered some misfortune like Yakoub at the olive factory who had lost his little son. And Jan would have to be introduced to Frehel, the Civil Controller, and to the Caid, and then I'd have to take him on a tour of the villages. I had hardly got all these matters sorted out in my mind before the bus was climbing up out of the plain to the fringe of the foothills and we had come to the first of the olive plantations.

Everything looked very wet. There were pools of water steaming in the sunshine and the roadway itself was creamed with mud. "There's been a lot of rain up here," Jan said.

I nodded, remembering the paper I had picked up in José's bar. It seemed ages ago. I wondered whether it could have snowed here.

"Have you had somebody looking after the mission whilst you've been away?" he asked.

"Yes," I said. "Two English people—a painter named George Corrigan and his sister, Julie. I think you'll like them. They run an old single-decker bus which they converted into a caravan. They've been touring Morocco in it."

"Do they know the south at all?"

"Still thinking about Kasbah Foum?" I said. And then, because my tone had sounded angry, I added, "If anybody knows it, they will. They've been all over the country. For all I know, George may have done a painting of it. One room of the Mission is stacked with his paintings. There are a lot of kasbahs amongst them."

We had turned up into Enfida now and a moment later we drew up at the bus stop behind a truck piled high with a load of black olives going down to the press. There was a little crowd standing in the mud waiting for the bus and the rushing sound of the river flooding under the bridge filled the town.

Yakoub, the man who had lost his little son, was standing talking to the driver of the olive truck, his woolly cap and ragged djellaba black and stiff with the rancid oil of the press.

" *Salaam ealykum!* " I called to him, but he didn't answer. And when I went up to him, he seemed ill-at-ease and refused to look me in the face. " What's the trouble?" I asked him.

He moved his shoulders awkwardly and mumbled something about the wrath of Allah being terrible.

" What is it?" I said. " What's happened?"

" It is the mountain, sidi," he murmured. " It has fallen into the valley. It has fallen upon the Dar el Mish'n."

" What's he saying?" Jan asked me.

" Something about the Mission." Yakoub had turned away now. The people by the bus were all standing watching me. " Come on," I said. " We'd better get up there right away." And we began walking up towards the open space by the Auberge de la Ravine, where the track into the mountains started. There was something about the atmosphere of the place and the way the people stood silently watching us that scared me. The air was heavy with the humid heat of mud steaming in the sunshine and the river roared in a brown flood under the bridge. And in the place of olives outside the auberge, the drivers of the asses and then men who bent over the scales stopped and stared, and when I spoke to them they were silent as though they had been struck dumb. A feeling of disaster hung over the place.

PART TWO

The Mission

We came out above the olive trees on to the hillside and
everything looked quiet and peaceful in the midday sun. The
mountains were a massive line of white shouldering up into
the blue sky and the air was still and calm and crystal-clear.
Down below us the river wound through the valley, a turgid,
brown flood of water, and the only sound was the persistent
braying of a donkey. The slope of the ground ahead screened
the Mission, but soon I could see the creamy white of the
Corrigans' caravan parked in an olive grove down to the left
and then I breasted a rise and all the hillside above the Mission
came suddenly into view, and I stopped.

Above the road there was a great, raw gash of newly-
exposed rock and rubble. It ran from the very top of the
sheer hill-slope, broadening out as it swept down, and
disappeared beyond the next rise of the road. I stood there,
my chest heaving, my whole body suddenly paralysed at what
I saw. It was a landslide, and I was rooted to the spot by fear
of what I should find when I topped the final rise.

Jan joined me. He didn't say anything, but just stood there
beside me, breathing heavily. There was nothing to be said.
I started forward again, slowly now, reluctantly. As we
climbed the rise, more and more of the hillside became
exposed, showing a broader, more chaotic tumble of
heaped-up debris. And then, suddenly, we were over the rise
and the full extent of the disaster was revealed. A quarter
of a mile ahead of us the road ceased, swept away and
overlaid by tons of wet, red earth and rock. The Mission
had vanished utterly, blotted out as though it had never been.
And where the olive trees had stood and the children's play-
ground and the stables I had built for sick donkeys, there was
nothing—nothing but raw, broken earth.

The landslide had swept over it all, obliterating five years'
work and all my hopes.

I didn't know what to do. I seemed suddenly without feeling. It just didn't seem real to me. This spot was my home, my whole life. It had been beautiful—a long, white-washed building looking out across the olive groves to the valley and across to the mountains. It was as much a part of me as my body.

I stared uncomprehendingly at the gang of labourers with their long-handled shovels already at work on the road. They were like pygmies trying to shift a mountain. I felt I must have come to the wrong place, that this couldn't really be Enfida, couldn't be Le Mission Anglais—the Dar el Mish'n.

I followed the great red sweep of the landslide down the slopes to the valley bottom and understood why the river had seemed so brown. It was pouring in a white cascade over the base of the landslide.

I felt dazed—bewildered by the violence, the utter ruthless-ness of it all. If it had left something—a wall, part of a building . . . But there was nothing; not a tree, not a stone, not a single vestige of the place. All my personal things were gone, my books, my notes, my clothes, George's pictures, the medical stores, the van . . . every single thing completely and utterly vanished below that ghastly, piled-up chaos of broken hillside.

Jan touched my arm. "It's no good looking at it," he said quietly. "Better come down to the auberge and have a drink."

No good looking at it! That was true. "I never want to see the damned place again," I said savagely. "All the time, all that effort! You'd think if God . . ." I stopped myself there and pushed my hand through my hair. Then I turned my back abruptly on the spot that had been my home and walked slowly down with Jan to the inn.

And that was where we met Julie, by the piled-up heaps of olives in the open space by the inn. She came towards us, walking slowly, her black hair hanging limp, her face white and strained. I was too dazed by the disaster of it all to notice then how desperately tired she was. I only knew I was glad she was there.

"You've seen?" she asked as she reached us.

I nodded, afraid to trust myself to speak.

"I was hoping to catch you before you went up there, to break it to you gently. But you didn't tell me you were coming back today." Her voice sounded flat and lifeless.

"When did it happen?"

"Two days ago; just after three o'clock in the afternoon."

"Thank God you weren't in the house," I said. "Where were you? Did you see it?"

She nodded, her lip trembling. She was suddenly on the verge of tears. "I was at the caravan, turning out a drawer. George . . . George was doing a painting of the house. He was sitting at his easel down near the donkey stable. He wanted the house and the hills in shadow behind it. It was to be a surprise for you, Philip. A welcome-home present. And then . . ." She closed her eyes and shook her head, the tears welling slowly, uncontrollably from between her tight-pressed eyelids.

"You mean—George?" I was too horrified to move.

She nodded slowly. "He was there—just below the house. I saw him." She opened her eyes, staring at me. "There was a sort of rumble . . . like thunder. I went to the door. I thought it might be another heavy downpour and I had some washing out. But it was clear and sunny. I heard George shout. He shouted to me and then he began to run and I looked up and saw the whole hillside pouring down. I couldn't run. I just stood there and saw the first wave of rocks pour over the roadway, down to the house and then . . . then George fell and the whole ghastly landslide rolled over him. And then it hit him and . . . and suddenly he wasn't there any more."

I said something. I don't know what it was, but she was suddenly clinging to me, sobbing hysterically. "It was horrible. Horrible. And I couldn't do anything." She was trembling and all I could do was stroke her head the way you do a sick animal.

Gradually she stopped trembling and her grip on my arm relaxed. "I'm sorry." Her voice was steadier, more controlled. "It happened two days ago. I should have got used to it by now." She straightened up and dried her eyes. "It was just that there was nobody . . ." She blew her nose hard. "Ever since it happened I've just felt screwed up tight inside. And then, when I saw you . . ." She shook her head as though trying to shake the picture out of her mind. " I'm all right now."

" Where are you staying—at the auberge?" I asked her.

She shook her head. " No. I'm still living in the caravan. I didn't want to see any strangers. I wanted my own things round me. Oh, Philip—why did it have to be George? Why did he have to choose that afternoon? . . . He'd been painting up in the hills for days."

I took her arm. She was still trembling. " I think perhaps some tea would help."

" Yes, of course." She nodded, clutching at the suggestion. " If you come back to the caravan I'll make you some." As she turned, she came face-to-face with Jan. I don't think she'd noticed him till then. The sight of a stranger seemed to brace her. " You must be Dr. Kavan." Her voice was steadier as she held out her hand to him. " I'm sorry. This isn't a very pleasant welcome. . . ." She let her hand drop to her side.

He didn't say anything and she turned quickly and led us down to the caravan.

The bus had been converted into two rooms with a shower bath and kitchenette between. She led us through into the front half, which was bedroom, living-room and studio combined and which merged into the driver's seat. It had been George's room. His things were everywhere, his clothes, his paints, the inevitable stack of canvasses. It was impossible not to imagine that he was away painting somewhere in the hills and would return today or tomorrow or the next day.

I sat down, feeling dazed, thinking how senseless it was. There were hundreds of square miles of mountains. Why did it have to be here, in this exact spot? I looked up and stared out through the windscreen. The bus was parked facing towards Enfida. I was looking out on to a pattern of silver grey against the sky with the holes of the olive trees dark streaks in the shade. But the tranquillity of the scene only sharpened the memory of that broken slash of rubble lying over the Mission.

Julie came in then with the tea. " It's no good brooding over it, Philip," she said in a small, taut voice. " We must think of the future, both of us. Think of the new Mission you'll build."

"The new Mission?" I stared at her. She didn't understand. "There won't be any new Mission," I said. "I've no money to start again."

"But weren't you insured?" Jan asked.

"Against fire and theft. Not against an Act of God."

"But your Mission Society?" His voice was suddenly tense. "Surely they will help——"

"Why should they? I put up most of the capital. The Society isn't really interested in a Mission here." And then I realised what was worrying him. "You'll be all right," I added. "You're a doctor. They need doctors out here in Morocco."

He gave a nervous little shrug. "It's not the same. Here I would have been lost to the world."

We sat in silence after that, drinking tea, wrapped in our own thoughts. For each of us that landslide meant something different. And for each of us the future was uncertain.

As soon as I finished my tea, I got up and went out into the hard, bright sunshine, walking through the shade of the olives until I came to where they ceased abruptly and there was nothing but great, piled-up heaps of mud and stone. It rose higher than the trees, the surface of it drying and caking in the sunshine.

Insh'Allah! I kicked out viciously at a clod of earth. That's what they'd be saying, here in Enfida and up the valleys at Kef and Tala and all the other mountain villages. Like disease and poverty and the loss of crops through water, it was the will of Allah and you shrugged your shoulders and did nothing about it.

I clenched my fists. Somehow I must fight back ; show them that disaster wasn't something to accept, but a thing to struggle against.

But how? How?

I bowed my head then, praying to God for some guidance for the future, for some hope ; praying that I'd have the strength to go on, that I wouldn't have to turn my back on it and admit that I'd wasted five years of my life.

But the answer to one's prayers comes from inside, not from outside, and I was too raw and hurt by the shock of what had happened to feel any revival of spirit.

A hand slipped under my arm and Julie was standing there beside me. She didn't say anything and we stood there, looking at what the giant force of Nature had done to the hillside. Twenty thousand bulldozers couldn't have done it in a year, and yet it had happened in a few moments—in less time than it had taken a man to try and run half the width of it.

The slide stretched like a giant scar from the valley bottom to the very summit of the sheer hillside.

"You mustn't be too bitter about it," Julie said. She had seen my face, knew what I was thinking.

"I don't know where to begin," I said.

"Something will turn up."

I stared at her, seeing her standing there, straight and firm-lipped, remembering what she had lost there under that landslide. I should have been comforting her. "I'm sorry," I said.

She smiled and shook her head. "We'd better go down to the auberge now and see Madame Gast." Her voice was suddenly practical, though it trembled slightly. "I expect she'll have rooms for you both."

The news that I'd returned had spread and the open space outside the auberge was crowded with people. There were women there, as well as men—Arab women, their eyes watching us curiously from the safety of their veils; Berber women in their gaily-coloured cottons. The men, standing in little huddles by the heaped-up piles of black olives, carefully avoided my gaze. They were superstitious—curious but frightened; Allah had struck down the Dar el Mish'n and to talk to the Englishman would be unlucky. Men I had helped, whose sons I had trained as mechanics and joiners in my workshops, averted their gaze, afraid to speak to me, afraid to give me even a word of sympathy. They still believed in the Evil Eye. They wore charms to protect themselves against it—the charm of the Hand of Fatima. "Damn them all to hell!" I muttered with sudden, pointless anger.

Julie's grip on my arm tightened. "It's not their fault," she said.

No, it wasn't their fault. But what was the point of going on? Why bother to struggle against centuries of ignorance?

And then we were in the cold, dark interior of the auberge and Madame Gast was sitting, waiting for us, with her cat. She was a Frenchwoman who had married a German in the Legion. But, sitting there in her ugly, Victorian chair, there was no indication of a colourful background. The girl who had followed the Legion had been obliterated by the widow who for twenty years had run an auberge in Enfida and now she was like a huge-bodied female spider huddled in the centre of her web. She fed on gossip and her little eyes sparkled as she saw us. Both she and her cat were immense and shapeless, like the old carpet slippers she wore. Little grey eyes stared at us curiously out of the big, sagging face.

" I have rooms ready for you, mes enfants," she said. She had known we must come to her.

" I'll leave you now," Julie said quickly. " Come and see me in the morning."

Madame Gast watched her go and then she shouted to the Berber kitchen boy to bring us some wine. The room was big and dreary. Down one side ran the bar and in the corner, where Madame Gust sat, was a big white-tiled Austrian stove. The walls were decorated with discoloured posters of French holiday resorts and there was a rack of faded postcards.

The wine came and we sat and drank it, listened to Madame's account of the disaster. Three farms had been destroyed as well as the Mission and the landslide had dammed up the river and flooded several olive groves. " And they blame me for the disaster?" I said.

She nodded. " Oui, monsieur."

" What else do they say?" This old woman knew everything that was said in Enfida.

She shrugged her shoulders. " Does it matter, monsieur?" She hesitated and her eyes softened. " Tell me, what are you going to do now?"

" What are the people expecting me to do?" I asked her.

" They think you will leave Enfida and go back to your country across the sea. They say that it is the will of Allah."

" And if I stay?"

She folded her thick, work-stained hands in her lap. " They

do not expect you to stay." There was silence between us for a moment and then she said, " Monsieur Frehel telephoned about an hour ago. He would like to see you."

" What's he want to see me about?" I asked.

She shrugged her shoulders. " I expect, like everybody else, he is curious to know what you are going to do."

So they were all waiting for me to admit defeat. Frehel was all right. We got on quite well together. But officially he didn't approve of an English missionary at Enfida. A bitter sense of loneliness had come over me.

I got up then. I felt I couldn't stay in that room any longer. It was so cold and dreary. And I wanted to think. " I'm going for a walk," I told Jan.

It was brighter outside. A cool wind blew down off the mountains, but the sun was warm. I walked up through the place of the olives, conscious of the stares and whispers of the crowd. I walked steadily up the road until I came to where the landslide had spilled across it and the gang of workmen were cutting into it with their shovels. I turned off to the right then and began to climb up through the olive groves, climbing towards the top of the slide. Maybe the attitude of the Berbers of the mountain villages would be different. There were too many Arabs in Enfida. Tomorrow I would go up to the villages at the head of the ravine.

It was dusk when I got back to the auberge. The single electric light bulb under its white porcelain shade barely illuminated the big, empty room. A table had been laid for the two of us in a corner. I stopped to warm myself at the stove. The cat was sitting in Madame's chair half-concealing a copy of *La Vigie*. A headline caught my eye: *TANGIER YACHT MYSTERY—What Happened to Second Man?—Police Search for Missing Captain Intensified.*

I pulled the paper out from beneath the recumbent cat and glanced quickly through the news story. It was date-lined Tangier. . . . *and it is now known that there was a second man on board the yacht. His identity is being kept secret, but the police state that the search for M. Roland Wade, captain and owner of the Gay Juliet, who disappeared from the Hotel Malabata in Tangier two days ago, has been intensified. They wish to question him about the fate of this second man. Wade stated, when he was rescued from the wreck, that he was the only person on board. It is thought that Wade, who is a short, dark-haired man, may have slipped across the International Frontier at some unguarded point into Spanish or French Morocco. A close watch is being kept on all forms of transport and a description has been ...* There followed a description of Jan as he was when he had shared my room at the Malabata and a brief account of how the yacht was wrecked in the gale. And then: *Wade was last seen when he left the Hotel Malabata in the company of M. Philip Latham, the Englishman who rescued him from the sea. M. Latham is believed to have returned to French Morocco where he is living. Enquiries are being made by the Moroccan police.*

I sat down in a chair and stared at that last line. So they would be coming here to question me! First the landslide, and now this! I dropped my head into my hands. It was too much. Everything seemed to have gone wrong. And then I was staring at that news story again, suddenly conscious of the significance of that word FATE. *They wish to question him about the fate of this second man.* I wondered how they knew for certain that there had been two men on the boat. But it didn't matter. The point was that they knew. I licked my lips, which had suddenly gone dry. The police had leapt to the same conclusion that I had.

I grabbed the paper again and ran up the stairs. It was inevitable. What else could they think? The man they thought was Wade had disappeared and his companion on the boat had never arrived. On the face of it, it could only add up to murder and now they'd go searching and questioning until they found him. I ran quickly from bedroom to bedroom. But they were all empty. Jan wasn't there. I went back down the stairs and shouted for Madame. The kitchen door opened. " Dinner is almost ready," she said.

" Where's Doctor Kavan?" I asked her breathlessly.

" He has gone out."

" Where? Did he say where?" I got a grip on myself and added more calmly. " When did he leave?"

"About half an hour ago." She paused and I was conscious of her beady eyes watching me curiously. "He has gone to see Monsieur Frehel."

"Frehel?" Had the police traced Jan already? Had they guessed at the truth? Oh God! What a mess! And then I pulled myself together and asked Madame to bring me a fine à l'eau. They'd discover that he was the man who'd come ashore from the wreck. I crossed the room and sat down at the table that had been laid for us. They'd think he'd taken Wade's identity for fear of being accused of killing the man. What else could they think? I rubbed my hand across my eyes. Poor devil! And there was his wife, waiting in Tangier. She would be brought into it, too. I tried desperately to think of a way out for him, but it was no good. The only hope was to tell them the truth. It would involve Vareau, but that couldn't be helped. They would have to be told the truth.

Madame brought me my drink and settled herself in her chair, holding the cat in her lap, stroking it gently and watching me with a gossip-greedy look in her small eyes. "Alors, monsieur—about this affair in Tangier. I see your name is mentioned in the paper."

But I was saved her cross-examination by the arrival of a car. It was a Frenchman wanting a room for the night. He was a man of medium height and he wore a grey felt hat and a raincoat over a light suit. I didn't really take much notice of him then. He was one of these men who fit quietly into their surroundings. He might have been a commercial traveller. Madame took him up to show him his room and I sat staring down at the paper, not reading it, just wishing I was done with the whole business.

And then Jan came in. "I had to go down and see the Civil Controller," he said.

"What happened?" I asked quickly. "What did he want? Does he know who you are?"

"Of course. I showed him my papers and we talked——"

"I don't mean that. Does he know you're the man who posed as Wade in Tangier?"

"No. Why should he?" He seemed surprised.

"Why? Because the police . . ." But of course, they

couldn't know all that yet. "Have you seen this?" I thrust the paper across to him.

He picked it up and I heard the quick intake of his breath, saw the knuckles of his hand whiten as his grip tightened on the pages. He dropped into the chair beside me. "How do they *know* I was on the boat? They can't know. It was dark when I joined *Gay Juliet* and we sailed in the early hours of the morning, before it was light. I'm certain I wasn't followed." He didn't say anything more for a moment as he read the whole story through. Then he put the paper down and looked at me. "This is how it started before," he said. "There was a lot of publicity about my being taken off secret work, that was how they knew I was worth bringing back to Czechoslovakia. Once the International Police reveal my name to the newspapers . . ." He gave a little sigh and shrugged his shoulders hopelessly. "They'll be coming here to question you, I suppose."

I nodded.

"What are you going to do? Frehel wants to see you in the morning. At ten o'clock. He asked me to let you know." He stared at me. "What are you going to tell him?"

"The truth," I said.

"No. You can't do that. Not yet." His voice was urgent, his grip on my arm like a vice. "I need time."

"Don't be a fool," I said. "The truth is your only help."

"How do you mean?" He had completely failed to understand the implication of the story.

But when he asked me to put my thoughts into words, I couldn't do it. He didn't see it the way I did—the way the police must see it. Perhaps it was better if he didn't. That way his denial would be more convincing. And then he said something that put the thing out of my mind for the moment. He said, "Philip. I want you to do something for me. I want you to confirm what I have just told Frehel—what you arranged back there in Tangier. I want you to tell the police when they come that I flew out from England direct to Casablanca."

"It's no good," I said. "They've only to check at Paris or London."

"I know. But I still want you to do it. All I need is four days. In four days I can get down to Foum-Skhira."

"Foum-Skhira?" I stared at him.

"I have to see Caïd Hassan d'Es-Skhira. It's about Kasbah Foum."

"What's Kasbah Foum got to do with you?" I demanded. And then I was suddenly angry. All the bitterness of the last few hours was concentrated on this one thing. "You never intended to work at the mission, did you?" I accused him. "It was just an excuse. You used my need of a doctor——" But I stopped there. How could he have known then about Wade and Kasbah Foum? I was tired and my mind was confused.

He leaned forward, his hand on my arm again. "Please, Philip. Listen. I have a proposition——" He stopped abruptly as footsteps sounded on the stairs behind him.

It was the Frenchman. He stood at the foot of the stairs for an instant, staring at us. Then he went over to the table in the far corner.

Jan picked up the paper again. I saw him glance several times at the newcomer. Then he leaned towards me. "We've got to talk this over. There's something I haven't told you."

But Madame came in then and I motioned him to be silent. She went through into the kitchen and for a while the only sound was the ticking of an alarm clock somewhere behind the bar. The darkness and the dreariness of the room, combined with Jan's tenseness, began to get on my nerves. The room had an unreal quality. It looked like a stage set, with its bar and its white-tiled stove and the faded posters on the flimsy wooden walls.

The soup arrived, and then Madame waddled in, carrying a special bottle of wine carefully in her two fat hands. She took it across to the Frenchman. Monsieur Bilvidic she called him, and her throaty voice smarmed over the hard syllables of his name as she bent obsequiously over his table. Evidently he wasn't just an ordinary traveller. He was someone of importance—an official. His face was pale, almost sallow, and there were little pouches under his eyes, like half spectacles on either side of his thin, sharp nose.

Once our eyes met. It was a quick, appraising glance, and

it left me with a faint feeling of hollowness in the pit of my stomach.

Madame had seated herself by the stove again. For a while she concentrated on her food, but once or twice she glanced in my direction. At length she said, "I was asking you, monsieur, about that affair in Tangier." And when I didn't say anything, she added, "You've read the paper, haven't you? What happened to this man after he left the Hotel Malabata with you?"

I glanced quickly across at the Frenchman. But he was concentrating on his food. He might not have heard her question. "Until I read the paper I hadn't realised the police were looking for Wade," I told her.

"But what happened to him?"

"That's something I shall have to tell Monsieur Frehel in the morning," I said. A cold sweat had broken out on my forehead. The man was concentrating too much on his food. He must be listening.

But Madame was persistent. She sat there, feeding the cat pieces of fish in her fingers and asking questions. And because I couldn't just sit there and refuse to say anything, I told her about how I had seen the wreck and brought Wade back to my room at the hotel, all the things, in fact, that the International Police already knew. And whilst I was talking I was conscious of Jan's growing nervousness.

The meal was over at last and I got to my feet, excusing myself by saying I was tired. Jan rose, too, and Madame saw us to the foot of the stairs. "Dormez bien, mes enfants." Her little beady eyes smiled at me maliciously.

We went upstairs to the narrow landing that ran the length of the inn. "Who was that man?" Jan asked.

"Your guess is as good as mine," I answered.

"You mean——"

"We'll know in the morning," I said and pushed open the door of my room.

"Philip. I want to talk to you about Kasbah Foum."

"Oh, damn Kasbah Foum!" I said. "I'm tired now." And I went into the bedroom and closed the door behind me.

What did he want to keep talking about Kasbah Foum for?

Hadn't he got enough problems without trying to involve
himself in something that concerned people like Kostos and
Ali d'Es-Skhira? I was thinking of the Frenchman back there
in the bar, talking to Madame, learning all the gossip of the
place.

I sat down on the bed and stared miserably round the room.
It was a sordid little box of a place with a big, brass-railed
double bed that sagged in the middle and the bare minimum
of furniture—a wash-stand, a tin slop pail, a chest of drawers,
a wooden chair and a small built-in cupboard. The flaking
paint patterned the walls with a stipple of little shadows cast
by the naked electric light bulb. I shivered in the cold that
struck up from the concrete floor.

I had a quick wash and went to bed. Somewhere out in
the darkness a tam-tam throbbed, accompanying the queer,
wailing cry of women singing. It went on and on, and then a
donkey began to bray, a harsh, sobbing note as though it were
slowly being strangled. I heard Bilvidic come to bed and then
the auberge settled down to sleep and the only sound was the
tam-tam beating out there in the night.

Gradually the moonlight filtered into the room. A little
wind had got up and I listened to it moaning round the
galvanised iron roof, searching for cracks in the old building.

And then I heard a movement in the passage outside. The
catch of the door scraped as the handle was turned and the
door opened and Jan's voice whispered, ". Are you asleep,
Philip?"

" No," I said. " What is it?"

He came in and shut the door gently behind him. " Mind if
I put the light on?" There was a click and I blinked my eyes.
" What the trouble?" I asked.

" Nothing. I wanted to show you something." He came and
sat on the bed. He was still dressed and he had the raincoat
he'd bought in Marrakech wrapped tightly round him. " I've
been thinking," he said. His manner was quiet as though he'd
made up his mind about something.

" Well?"

" I'm leaving for the south tomorrow. I would like you to
come with me. No," he added quickly. " Don't say anything.

Have a look at this first." He pulled an envelope out of his pocket and handed it to me. " Please. Examine it."

It was one of those stiff linen envelopes, but it had been softened and creased with age. It was damp, too, and the remains of the broken seal were indecipherable. Inside was a bulky document to which had been attached a note in French scrawled on a sheet of cheap notepaper that was torn and dirty along the creases where it had been folded. I sat up in bed and twisted round so that the light fell across my shoulder on to the document. It opened out into a stiff sheet of parchment covered with Arab writing. The ink was faded with age, but the words KASBAH FOUM, written in capitals, caught my eye. And then, farther down, I saw the name Marcel Duprez. The name occurred several times and the document was signed *Caïd El-Hassan l'Es-Skhira,* and some sort of seal had been affixed.

" But this is the document Kostos wanted," I exclaimed.

" Yes."

" You crazy fool! " I said, staring up at him. " Why didn't you let him have it? If you'd given it to him——"

" Kasbah Foum belongs to me."

But I didn't believe him. How could it belong to him? " You took those deeds from Wade," I said. " Wade was acting for Ali and you took them——"

" No," he said. " Wade never had the deeds. He offered me five hundred pounds if I'd give them to him and renounce my claim to the place. But I wouldn't sell. Kasbah Foum is mine." He said it fiercely, possessively.

I pushed my hand across my eyes. " I don't understand," I said. " How can this place belong to you? You've never been in Morocco before. Land like that isn't bought and sold——"

" Those deeds were given me by Marcel Duprez. He was the man I told you about in Marrakech, the man who died in that cellar in Essen." He stared at me, frowning angrily. " You don't believe me, do you? Why do you think Wade agreed to take me on his boat? How do you think we met in the first place? I didn't contact Wade. He contacted me." He pointed to the note pinned to the document. " If you still don't believe me, take a look at that note. It was written by Marcel Duprez to the lawyers just before he died."

I smoothed out the tattered note attached to the document.
It was written in French in a shaky hand and addressed to
Lavin, Roche et Lavin, of Rouen:

Dear Monsieur Roche,
    *The bearer of this note is Dr. Jan Kavan, who is here
with me in this abominable town of Essen. In the event
of my death, he will come to you after the war. You will
give him the document relating to Kasbah Foum in
French Morocco. This note you will regard as a codicil
to my will. Being unable at this time to write to you
direct, I hereby instruct you to ignore any illegality there
may be in this method of making my wishes known to
you and to carry out these instructions. Dr. Kavan knows
that Caid Hassan's confirmation of this bequest is necessary to substantiate his claim to the ownership of Kasbah
Foum and he holds the necessary letter to Caid Hassan,
which he will show to you on request.*

The note was signed *Marcel Duprez* and dated 22nd
September, 1944. So the Marcel Duprez who had fought at
Foum-Skhira with the legion and the man who had died
in a cellar at Essen were the same! And Kasbah Foum,
subject to Caid's confirmation, belonged to Jan. " But if you're
so interested in the place, why didn't you get your title to it
confirmed before?" I asked him.

" That's what I should have done. It's what I promised
Marcel. As soon as the Allies arrived in Essen and I was
released, I went to Rouen. I saw Monsieur Roche and he
gave me the deeds. But——" He shrugged his shoulders
awkwardly. " There was so much to do in Czechoslovakia.
I returned to Skoda and there was my research work, and
then Karen and I were married. To be the owner of a little
patch of desert somewhere in Morocco——". He gave a short
laugh. " It was absurd, you know. Even if there was silver
there . . . I had plenty of money and I was happy. I put
the deeds away and forgot all about them. Also I forgot
about my promise. The Berbers meant nothing to me." He
paused and then added, " But afterwards, when I was in
England, I found those deeds among some papers Karen

smuggled out to me. And then it wasn't absurd any more.
It was all I owned in the world."

He was staring at me and his voice trembled slightly with the
effort of trying to make me understand. "When you have no
country—nothing . . . to be the owner of a piece of land
becomes desperately important. It's a refuge, something to
dream about. I remembered my promise then and I wrote to
Caid Hassan."

"And he confirmed your title?"

"No. He didn't reply to my letter. And then, a few months
later, just after I'd decided to get out of England and had
answered your advertisement—Wade arrived. I knew then
that my letter had never reached the Caid, but had been sent
on to his son, Ali."

"Wade told you that?"

"No, no, of course not. But I knew, because of what
Marcel had told me. Marcel loved the Berber people. He
gave his whole life, and his health, to them." He shifted his
position, leaning towards me. "Listen, Philip. There's an
ancient, ruined city at Kasbah Foum. That was why Marcel
was interested in the place. And it was whilst he was doing
excavation work there that he came upon the entrance of some
old mine workings. It was blocked and he never had a chance
to open it up because, shortly after he discovered it, there was
a landslide and it was buried, just as your Mission is buried
here. But there is a local legend that silver was once mined
at Kasbah Foum. That was what worried him when he was
dying."

"Why should it?" I asked.

"The terms of those deeds are rather peculiar. Whoever
inherited from Marcel had to get his title confirmed by the
Caid and ownership registered with the Sultan's Government.
If no new ownership were confirmed, then when Caid Hassan
died, Kasbah Foum would belong to his son, Ali. Marcel
wanted to prevent that. In his view Ali was a fanatic—not
interested in the welfare of his people, only in fighting the
French. He was afraid that if Ali discovered the mine and
developed it, or sold it, he would use those funds to buy
arms. At all costs he wanted to prevent unnecessary blood-
shed."

"And he made you promise to get your title to the place confirmed by the old Caid before he died?"

"Yes." He stared down at the deeds lying on the blankets in front of him. "I thought it was just a whim—you know how people build things up in their minds when they're feverish. And back there at Skoda after the war it all seemed so remote and unreal." He looked up at me suddenly and said, "But it's real enough now—now that I know Ali is trying to get those deeds. When Wade came to me in England, he said he had seen the lawyers in Rouen and they'd told him a man named White had been making enquiries——" He stopped, his head on one side. "What was that?" His voice shook a little.

"It's only in the wind," I said.

But he got up quietly and went to the door and pulled it open. There was nothing there. He stood listening for a moment and then shut it. "That man," he said. "That Frenchman. He's a member of the security police. I know he is." He started pacing up and down. "Karen and Kasbah Foum—they're all I've got in the world. And they're both here in North Africa. I've got to stay in North Africa." He was talking to himself, gesturing urgently. He looked suddenly quite wild with his black hair standing on end.

He swung round abruptly and came back to the bed, leaning down and catching hold of my arm. "Don't tell them the truth tomorrow. Give me a week. A week is all I need. And you've got to come with me. You know the people. You speak the language. We'll see the old Caid. Maybe there is silver there. If so, you'll get your Mission. I promise you. You'll have all the money you need. It's what Marcel wanted; exactly what he wanted. I was to take what I needed and the rest was to go to the Berber people—hospitals and schools." He stopped abruptly, staring at me, panting slightly with the effort of his sudden outburst. Then he picked up the deeds and thrust them into their envelope. "Think it over." His voice had steadied. "A few days is all I ask. Afterwards——" He shrugged his shoulders. He stared at me a moment as though trying to will me to agree, and then, when I still didn't say anything, he crossed to the door. "Good night," he said and switched out the light."

"Good night."

The door closed and I was alone again. I lay in the darkness, thinking about it all, trying to make up my mind what to do. But my brain wouldn't concentrate and gradually I fell asleep through sheer exhaustion.

The Berber boy didn't wake me until after nine and when I went into the bar room, Bilvidic was already there, sitting at the same table, writing. He looked up as I entered, murmured " Bon jour" and went back to his notes. Jan came in a few minutes later and we breakfasted in silence. Only once did he say anything and then he leaned close to me and whispered, " What have you decided?"

" I don't know," I answered. I hadn't decided anything.

At ten minutes to ten Bilvidic put his notebook away and came over to me. " I believe you have an appointment with Monsieur le Controller at ten," he said. " Since I am also going to see him, perhaps you would care to come in my car."

I thanked him and got up, conscious of Jan watching me nervously. He went out to his Citroën and as he drove me down through Enfida he talked of nothing more alarming than mountain plants. He was a keen horticulturist.

The administration block of Civil Control was a low, brick building and the offices opened off a single long passage. The Tribunal was sitting that morning and the whole length of the passage was crowded with indigènes from the country round. As I walked down to the Controller's office I was conscious of a sudden hush. The men stopped talking and stared at me curiously. Many of them I knew, but they looked away as I approached.

And then suddenly an old man stood in front of me. It was the chef de village from Tala. He touched me and kissed my hand, bowing formally, and then in a clear voice he welcomed me back to Enfida and expressed his deep distress at what had happened. I caught his hand and gripped it, and his old eyes smiled at me behind the glasses. " We understand each other," he said quietly. " You will have help from the villages of the Ravine if you build your house again."

" There are few, like you, who understand," I said. And I thanked him and we parted. But somehow the morning had changed completely now. I felt suddenly warm inside and full of vigour.

I was shown into an empty office and though Frehel kept me waiting almost twenty minutes, I didn't mind. I was thinking that if I had the villages of the Ravine with me—the very ravine where the disaster had happened—then it was worth fighting to start again. And then I began thinking about Kasbah Foum. Julie had said something would turn up. Maybe this was it. . . .

The door opened and Frehel came in. He was a tall, rather stooped man with lined, leathery features. He looked more like a professor than an administrator and, as always, his Civil Control uniform looked oddly out of place on his long, loose-jointed figure. He shook my hand and apologised for keeping me waiting. And then he began talking about the disaster and about the Mission. " A terrible tragedy, Latham." He shook his head and clicked his tongue. " Will you tell Mademoiselle Corrigan how sad I am about the death of her brother. Terrible! And he was a fine painter." And then he wanted to know what my plans were and I began to think that that was the only reason he asked me down to his office. " And this Doctor Kavan?" he asked. " You went to Tangier to meet him, I believe?"

I nodded, conscious that there was suddenly more interest in his voice, a look of curiosity in his eyes. He hesitated, his hands in his pockets, rattling his keys. Then he said, " I am sorry to trouble you at a time like this, but I have a member of the Sûreté here who has come to ask you some questions. It is about something that happened in Tangier." He opened the door for me. " If you will come through to my office——"

Bilvidic was seated beside Frehel's desk, tapping his teeth with a silver pencil. " Monsieur l'Inspecteur tells me you have already met," Frehel murmured. Bilvidic got up and brought a chair for me. Frehel seated himself at the desk. He was obviously curious and his eyes glanced quickly at each of us in turn.

Bilvidic turned his chair so that he faced me. " I think you understand, monsieur, why I am here."

I nodded.

He produced a pack of American cigarettes and handed them round. " You were telling Madame last night how you rescued this Monsieur Wade from the wreck and took him back to your hotel." His manner was friendly, his tone almost conversational. " Would you kindly repeat the story so that I can check it against my notes. I would like every detail, if you please. You understand, of course, that this man has disappeared completely."

" I read the newspaper story," I said.

He nodded. " Alors, monsieur."

So I went through the whole sequence of events from the moment I had sighted the yacht trying to make for the harbour at Tangier. He had his notebook in his hand and a sheaf of typewritten pages, and he constantly referred to these, checking my story with neat little ticks in the margin. He didn't interrupt me until I came to the loss of the passport and the odd behaviour of the patrone at the Hotel Malabata. " Un moment, monsieur. The patrone says only that Wade had mislaid his passport."

" That's not true," I said, and I explained what had actually happened. I was sweating a little and the palms of my hands were moist. I was reaching the difficult part and I found I still hadn't really made up my mind.

" Can you explain why the patrone should attempt to retain Wade's passport illegally?"

" Yes," I said, seeing an opportunity to gain time. " I think he had been bribed by a man called Kostos."

" Kostos?"

" He's a Greek," I said. " He used to be involved in smuggling, but now——"

" Yes, yes. I know about Kostos." His tone was impatient. " But what is he to do with Wade?"

" He came to see him at the hotel."

" Ah, oui. I wished to ask you about that. We are curious about this Greek. He left Tangier suddenly two days ago. I think we trace him to Marrakech, but we are not——"

" To Marrakech?" I stared at him. Had Jan been right after all?

" Oui, to Marrakech." Bilvidic nodded. " We believe he was accompanied by a notorious agent povocateur."

" You mean Ali d'Es-Skhira?"

The name slipped out and he pounced on it. " How did you know that?"

" Kostos mentioned the name that time he came to see Wade in my room," I said quickly to cover myself.

" Ah, yes. Will you tell me exactly what Kostos said?"

I gave him the gist of it without mentioning Kasbah Foum. And whilst I was talking, I was thinking that it must be true, the whole incredible story that Jan had told me. Ali d'Es-Skhira would never return to Morocco and risk being arrested by the French unless the matter was urgent. There was no doubt in my mind that the pair of them were headed for Foum-Skhira. It was this that finally decided me.

" And now, monsieur," Bilvidic said when I had finished, " let us go back to your departure from the hotel. The patrone has withheld Wade's passport and you have ordered the driver of the taxi to take you to the British Consulate. You were going to make a protest, eh?"

I nodded.

" But you did not go there, monsieur. Why? Where do you go after you leave the hotel?"

" Wade changed his mind," I said. " He decided not to go to the Consulate after all. He asked me to drop him in the Zocco Grande."

" Why?"

" I don't know."

" What happened then?"

"Nothing. I was leaving Tangier by the evening train. I never saw him again."

He glanced down at the typewritten notes. " This would be about fifteen-thirty hours, eh? And your train did not leave until twenty-one thirty. Would you please tell me what you did during the rest of the day?"

I filled in as best I could. And then, suddenly, he said, " Why did you book two berths on the wagon-lit?"

In all my concern that he might know about my visit to the Airport, I had forgotten all about the problem of explaining that extra berth. I improvised quickly: I had booked the extra sleeper for the man I had gone to Tangier to meet and afterwards I had found a letter waiting for me at the British Post Office saying that he was flying direct to Casa and would I meet him there. I think my hesitation could only have been fractional, for he didn't seem to have noticed it. "And the man you went to meet was this Dr. Kavan?"

I nodded.

"And that is the man who is here now, the man you were dining with at the auberge last night? You met him at Casa?"

"Yes," I said.

"Bon." He seemed relieved. He looked across at Frehel. "At least there is no mystery about the disappearance of this Dr. Kavan from the boat. The British security officers have made an error. He was never on the boat." He chuckled, and then checked himself as though remembering he was on official business. "In fact, there is no mystery at all. There are not two men on the boat, only one. There remains only the disappearance of this man Wade." He glanced down at his notes, and then went back over my statement of what Kostos had said on the occasion he had come to the hotel. I knew it was all right then. Jan was clear for the moment.

We went over several points and then finally he sat back and lit another cigarette. "You say you have checked Dr. Kavan's papers?" he asked Frehel suddenly.

The Civil Controller nodded.

"And they are in order?"

"Oui, Monsieur l'Inspecteur."

"Bon." He looked across at me. "What do you know about this doctor, monsieur?"

"Not very much," I said, keeping a tight hold on my voice. "He's a Czech refugee."

"Is that all he has told you about himself?"

I didn't say anything and he shrugged his shoulders as though glad not to have to go further into the matter. "Alors, monsieur—the statement . . ."

It was almost midday before the statement was typed. When I had signed it, he drove me back to the auberge himself. "Au revoir, monsieur," he said as I got out. "I am going back to Casablanca now." His hard, grey eyes looked at me fixedly. "There is nothing you wish to alter?"

"No," I said.

"You realise that it will all be checked?"

I nodded.

" Bien, monsieur. We will hope there are no inaccuracies, eh?" He gave me a thin-lipped smile. And then he asked me if I should be leaving Enfida during the next few days.

" I don't know," I said.

He nodded. " I quite understand. In view of the catastrophe . . ." He gave a little shrug. " But if you do leave, monsieur, I should be grateful if you would inform Monsieur Frehel and give him your new address. You understand?"

" Yes," I said.

He nodded again and turned the Citroën in a tight circle, disappearing in a cloud of dust down the road towards the bridge. I turned and went into the auberge, but Jan wasn't there. I called Madame out of the kitchen and she told me that Julie had arrived shortly after I had left. She and Jan had gone off together.

I went up the mountain road then and cut down to the caravan. They must have been watching the track, for they both came out to meet me. But then Jan stopped and Julie came on alone. She looked very pretty with her black hair hanging down over her orange shirt. She was wearing slacks. She looked slender and graceful and cool. " Is it all right?" she asked. Her voice sounded nervous and I knew Jan must have explained the situation to her. I didn't say anything and she took my arm. " I'll get you a drink." And then she added, " Don't keep him waiting, Philip. It's important to him."

" All right," I said. And I called out to Jan and told him he needn't worry for the moment.

It was extraordinary. The man seemed suddenly to come to life. It was as though I had released a spring inside him. He caught hold of my hand and his grip was so tight it hurt. " I'll never forget this, Philip. I'll never forget it." He was like a man reprieved. " What decided you? All through breakfast this morning . . . I wanted to get a decision out of you, but that man Bilvidic was sitting there. What decided you?"

" Kostos was in Marrakech two days ago," I said.

" So, I was right. How do you know this?"

" Bilvidic told me. And Ali d'Es-Skhira is with him."

Sitting in the caravan over a large cognac I told them about the interview. And when I had finished Jan said, " Well, that settles it. We slip out of Enfida tonight. Julie says if we leave shortly after midnight we'd be across the pass by dawn. By to-morrow night, if we drive hard, we can be at Foum-Skhira."

"We'll need a car," I said.

It was Julie who answered. "We'll take the bus." She was smiling a little sadly. "I don't want to stay here—not alone. And there's no hotel south of Ouarzazate; not until you get to Zagora, and you aren't going there."

I sat and looked at her. I thought I ought to say "No"—that it was stupid for her to get mixed up in it. But seeing the way she looked—keyed up and excited—I thought maybe it was a good idea. It would take her mind off George's death.

There were a great many things to be done if we were to start that night—stores to get and the bus to be literally dug out. We agreed that Jan and I should feed at the auberge and retire to bed there in the ordinary way. We would slip out of Enfida at night, just in case.

It seemed a long evening, sitting there in that dreary bar room, talking with Madame, watching the Arabs who guarded the olive piles at night drift in and out for coffee. But at last it was ten o'clock and Madame was seeing us to the door to the stairs. "Dormez bien, mes enfants. Dormez bien." Her deep, throaty voice was like a benediction and I heaved a sigh of relief. From the window of my room I saw that a light rain was falling. The night was black and quiet.

Two hours later we slipped out by the terrace and the gate leading on to the road. Julie had the old bus waiting for us just below the road. It was exactly twelve as we drove down the winding road and across the bridge and up through the deserted street of Enfida on the Marrakech road. We left the olive trees behind, and the road and the red earth of the plain stretched ahead of us in the headlights. It was like that for hour after hour, except that the plain gave way to mountain-sides that loomed like dark shadows on either side of us as the road began to climb.

The first grey light of dawn found us grinding up the hair-pin bends to the top of the pass. Julie was at the wheel and the bus swayed heavily on the incessant bends, the wheels skidding in the loose slush of melted snow that covered the road. And then at last we were at the top and there were the gaunt pylons of the teleferrique marching like Wellsian monsters through the cleft in the mountains. We drew in beside a big stone notice—TIZI N TICHKA, alt. 2,250 m., and below were recorded the Army units who had slaved to build the road through the pass.

We were at the top of the High Atlas. We were astride the shining white barrier of the mountains that hide the strange, desert lands of the south. I had never crossed them, but I knew that beyond lay a different world, a world of kasbahs and dusty palmeries set in a land of black stone hills, rounded with age. And beyond those black hills of the Anti-Atlas was nothing—only the limitless wastes of the Sahara, a sea of sand.

We sat there and stared at the pale dawn sky ahead, conscious of a sense of the unknown, as though we were on a peak looking out across a strange sea. I was conscious, too, of a stillness within myself, and within my two companions. I glanced at Jan. His face was tense, his blue eyes fixed with a sort of desperate eagerness. He stood there upon what was for him the threshold of a Promised Land—the thing he dreamed of for himself and his wife, Karen—his last chance of a refuge from the nightmare in which he had lived.

The sun rose and touched the first of the mountain tops. Without a word Julie started the engine and we began the long run down to Ouarzazate. Nobody spoke. Our eyes were fixed on the sky ahead and the road winding down through the mountains. Somewhere, down there among the black stone hills, was Kasbah Foum.

PART THREE

Zone of Insecurity

I

The mountains changed abruptly the moment we were across
the divide as though to emphasise that we were entering upon
a wild, strange land. Where, on the northern side, there had
been scrub and small trees and slopes of snow glimmering
white in the dawn, there was nothing now but naked rock.
The sky was pale, a duck's egg, pastel blue, and above us
to the left rose piled-up cliffs of sand-blasted stone that
flanked the valley in a long ridge, their battlements picked out
in gold as the sun rose in the east.

It was a beautiful, pitiless country.

We stopped for breakfast where the road crossed the first
big torrent of melted snow. It was bitterly cold with a chill
wind whistling down the valley from the peaks behind us.
Yet, by the time the tea was made, the sun had risen above
the red rock fortresses of the ridge, the wind had gone, and it
was suddenly hot. The abruptness of the change was startling.

It was then that Julie remembered she had some letters for
me. There were two from England—a Bible Society tract and
an offer of old clothes from some association I had never
heard of. The third was post-marked Tangier and was from
Karen Kavan. As we had agreed, she had written to me, not
to Jan. It simply announced that her employers were taking
a trip south and would be staying at the Hotel Mamounia for
Christmas and then going on to Ouarzazate and Tinerhir. She
was travelling with them and she gave the telephone numbers
of the hotels they were staying at. The number of the Gîte
d'étapes at Ouarzazate was 12. It was the same number that
Wade had noted down in the back of his log against the name
of Ed White.

I was still thinking about this as I handed Jan the letter.

123

" It's from your wife," I said. He scanned it eagerly and then asked the date.

" To-day is the twenty-third," Julie said.

He folded the letter slowly and put it away in his breast pocket, staring out through the side window along the grey ribbon of the road leading south towards Ouarzazate.

" Is she all right?" Julie asked.

" Yes." He nodded quickly. " Yes, she's all right. She'll be in Ouarzazate on the twenty-sixth." There was a sort of wonder in his voice as though he couldn't believe it was true.

" Then you'll see her."

He looked across at Julie and smiled. " Yes. Yes, I hope so. It would be wonderful!"

He was thinking of his wife, stopping there at the Gîte d'étapes. And I was thinking of this man White. If Wade had planned to phone him there . . . " You remember you mentioned a man called White," I said to him. " When you were telling me about Kasbah Foum." He nodded. " Do you know anything about him?"

" No, nothing. Except that he'd tried to contact me through the lawyers."

" Wade told you that?"

" Yes."

" You don't know why?"

" No."

" Weren't you curious about it?"

" Yes. I asked Wade. But he wouldn't tell me. Why do you ask?"

I didn't say anything. I was thinking that perhaps it was White who had started this whole chain of interest in Kasbah Foum. He had been down the south here. He might even have been to Kasbah Foum. Was that the reason Ali had instructed Wade to purchase the deeds from Jan? " Was White ever at Kasbah Foum?" I asked.

" I don't know." He shook his head, staring at me with a puzzled frown.

" Wade told you nothing about him?"

" No, nothing. Only what I've told you."

I hesitated and then said, " What about Wade? Had he ever visited Kasbah Foum?"

" No." He said it slowly and then added, " But I think he intended to." He paused for a moment before saying, " As I told you, Wade was a crook. I have an idea he didn't intend to play straight with Ali."

" How do you mean?"

" I think, if he had got the deeds, he would have gone straight to Kasbah Foum. When he discovered I wouldn't sell, he tried to persuade me to go into some sort of partnership with him. He said there was money in it. I think he knew about the possibilities of silver. Right up to the end I think he believed that when we reached Tangier I would agree to his proposition. I didn't discourage him. I wanted that passage out and I didn't trust him. If I had definitely refused . . ." He shrugged his shoulders. " Anyway, it doesn't matter now." He glanced at his watch. " It's time we went on." He said it almost brusquely, as though he didn't want to think about what had happened on the boat.

The road ran gently down the valley of the Imini and emerged on to an arid, stony plain. The mountains dropped behind until I could see them in the mirror as a long, brown wall topped with snow. I was driving. The others were asleep —Julie in her own compartment at the back of the caravan, Jan sprawled out on the berth behind me. I was alone at the wheel with the road reeling out ahead of me and the blazing sun and the blue sky and the parched earth stretching brown to the horizon—just the two colours, blue and brown, and the grey ribbon of the road. I had an odd sense of space coming down out of the mountains. It was as though I could feel by the lie of the land that the way was open to the south. Ahead were the humped shapes of a range of low, dark hills. Beyond them was the Sahara.

It was strange and a little frightening. This was the most recently conquered part of Morocco. Barely twenty years ago Marshal Lyautey and his troops had still been fighting there. The whole area was run by the military—by les officiers des Affaires Indigènes. There were few Europeans and until quite recently it had been known as the Zone of Insecurity.

We passed the turning to the manganese mines of Imini and then we were running through Amerzgane and El Mdint. The white kasbah of Tifoultout stood like a fairy castle on a little rise on the far side of the river and after that the road was straight and tree-lined, ending abruptly in a hill with a fort on it. We were driving into Ouarzazate. The town was largely French, a single street pushed between two small hills. On the right was the Military Post. The road leading up to it was signposted TERRITOIRE. And then I saw a second signpost—GITE D'ETAPES. I turned up a sharp hill, climbing to a long, low building with a tower built like a kasbah.

"Why have you turned up here?" Jan asked, roused from his sleep by the change in the engine note.

"I want to phone Frehel," I said. "Also, your friend Ed White stayed here."

I told him about the telephone number noted down at the back of Wade's log as we went into the hotel. The place was centrally heated and very warm. Beyond the reception desk was a bar and on either side were two big glass cabinets, one displaying Berber jewellery—silver bangles and coin head-dresses, blanket pins and long necklaces of intricately-worked silver and beads—the other filled with specimens of minerals found locally. A French officer seated at a table reading a magazine glanced at us idly. Then Madame appeared and I asked her whether she knew a Mr. White.

"Mais oui, monsieur. An American. He has stayed here several times."

"On holiday?" I asked.

"En vacance? Non, non, monsieur. He is a prospector."

"A prospector!" Jan's voice was suddenly interested.

"Is this Monsieur's first visit to Ouarzazate?" Madame asked. And when Jan nodded, she said, "Ah, well then, you must understand that all this country south of here is very rich in minerals. We have many prospectors who stay——"

"Is he staying here now, madame?" Jan asked her.

"Monsieur White? Non, monsieur. He has not been here for several weeks now."

"Do you know where he is?"

"Un moment." She went behind the desk and picked up a notebook, running her finger down the passages. "Ah, oui. He left instructions for us to forward his letters to the office of Monsieur le Capitaine at the Military Post of Foum-Skhira."

So, Ed White was at Kasbah Foum!

"I suppose he didn't say what he was prospecting for?" Jan asked.

"Non, non." Madame laughed. "Prospectors do not talk about what they are searching for. But probably it is uranium." She shrugged her shoulders. "Always they dream of uranium now."

"Did a Monsieur Kostos stay here last night or the night before?" I asked her.

"Non, monsieur."

I phoned Frehel then and told him where he could find us. And whilst I was doing that, Jan wrote a note for his wife. He left it with Madame and we went back to the bus, driving out of Ouarzazate by a road that forded the river not far from the great Kasbah of Taourirt. Everything was very still in the sunlight and as the wheels splashed and bumped over the stones of the river bed, we could see the kasbah reflected in the water. It was a completely walled town, crowding up out of the palmerie in tower after tower, standing out against the blue of the sky like a part of the desert country in which it was built.

And then we were clear of the water and climbing the narrow, ploughed-up surface of the piste, climbing up through a long valley that led into the foothills of the Anti-Atlas. All about us were dark, sombre hills, shadowed by the stones that littered their slopes, closing up behind us and hemming us in so that we could no longer see the clean, white wall of the High Atlas. A little wind rose and drifted dust between the stones. Gaunt skeletons of heath and tamarisk marked out the drainage courses in dusty green.

"Marcel called this country Le Pays Noir," Jan murmured. "He said it was geologically much older than the High Atlas and full of undeveloped mineral resources." He was dreaming of Kasbah Foum again.

All afternoon we struggled through those dark, satanic hills. Dust seeped up through the floorboards in choking clouds from the fine-ground powder of the piste. It got in our clothes and in our nostrils. It powdered our hair grey. Once a jeep passed us, and for an hour after that we caught glimpses of it, a little cloud of dust far ahead. We climbed steadily upwards and then dropped down to a rocky basin in which a lonely kasbah stood subsisting on a few dusty palms and the herds of black goats that roamed the stunted vegetation. After that we climbed again, up a steep escarpment to a lonely watch tower and the pass of Tizi N Tinififft, more than five thousand feet up. Here we were in a land of sudden deep gorges, dark in shadow, that descended in shelves of rock. For an hour we wound round the tops of these gorges until, as the sun set, we came out on to a hill-top, and far below us saw the Draa Valley, a green ribbon of palm trees. And there, on a little hill, was the Military Post of Agdz.

We had a meal then and slept, and at two in the morning we drove through the sleeping Post of Agdz and down the valley of the Draa. The piste was white and ground as fine as talcum powder. It followed the line of the river, winding along the edge of the palmerie, past kasbah after kasbah, and in every open space the kasbah cemeteries showed as patches of desert littered with small, up-ended stones, mute testimony to the countless thousands who had lived and died here over the centuries. We came at length to a fork ; a little-used piste turning off to the right and running south over low hills. There was no signpost, but we took it, relying on the map.

Julie was driving again. I could see her face in the light from the dashboard ; an intent, serious, competent face. Her black hair was grey with dust, her eyes narrowed as they peered ahead along the beam of the headlights. The stony, desert country ground past us, always the same—an unchanging yellow in the lights, and then suddenly black as it disappeared behind us. Her hands were brown and slender on the dusty ebony of the wheel and every now and then she beat at her knees to restore her circulation. A bitter wind blew in through the chinks in the windscreen, but our feet were warm in the heat of the engine, which came up from the floorboards with a musty smell of dust mixed with engine oil.

Looking at her, I wondered what she'd do now that her brother was dead. She'd have to do something, for I was pretty sure that George would have left her nothing but a few pictures. George hadn't been the saving type. He'd spent money as he made it—always travelling, always painting.

I was remembering how I had first met them. It must be seven years ago now, when I was in Tangier. Their mother had died and left them some money, and they'd come out to Tangier because in Tangier there are no taxes. I had helped them get their money out. That was how I'd met them. Julie had been little more than a schoolgirl then, wide-eyed, excited by everything, deeply concerned at the poverty she saw side-by-side with the rich elegance of the crooks and tax-evaders who occupied the villas on La Montagne. They had stayed for a few months, and then they had gone to Greece and on to Turkey and Syria. Occasionally Julie had sent me a postcard —from Baghdad, Cairo, Haifa, and one, I remember, from Lake Chad after they had done a trip from Algeria right across the Sahara. It wasn't difficult to understand why Julie had stayed with her brother. He had given her all the excitement and colour she had wanted. And it had suited George, for he was interested in nothing but his painting.

She glanced at me suddenly and our eyes met. " What are you thinking about, Philip?" she asked. " About what an odd trip this is?"

" No," I said. " I was thinking about you."

" Oh," Her mouth spread into a smile and the corners of her eyes crinkled with laughter. But she didn't say anything further, just sat there, her gaze on the faint track of the piste.

" I was wondering what you were going to do now," I said after a while.

She shrugged her shoulders. It was a very Latin shrug. But she didn't answer my question and I was conscious of the stillness between us. It was as though we had suddenly touched each other and then as quickly withdrawn. I felt a softening in the marrow of my bones and I sat back, watching her face, absorbing the straight line of her nose, the smallness of her ears, the way her hair curled at the back of her neck. I'd never thought of her quite like that before. When I had first met her she had seemed very young and then, when they had descended on the Mission three months ago, she had just been George Corrigan's sister. That was all.

And now . . . Now I didn't quite know.

T.S.L.

" What's that? Up there." Jan's voice cut across my thoughts, tense and excited. He was leaning forward over my shoulder and pointing through the windshield. We were climbing now, and far ahead, high up where the dark shadow of a hill cut across the starry velvet of the sky, the yellow pinpoint of a fire showed.

Our radiator was boiling by the time we reached it. It was a petrol fire flickering ghostlike out of a pile of stones beside a battered jeep. Four men were huddled round it. Three of them were town Arabs, but the fourth was a Berber and behind him his two camels stood motionless, hobbled by the foreleg. I signalled Julie to stop and called out to them, enquiring if the piste led to Foum-Skhira.

The Arabs stared at us nervously, whispering together, the whites of their eyes gleaming in the headlights. It was the Berber who answered me. " *Iyyeh, sidi.*" Yes, Foum-Skhira was beyond the mountain. The piste had been washed away by the rains, but it was almost repaired now. The souk at Foum-Skhira had also been washed away. He shook his head gloomily. " Thanks be to Allah I have left that place."

The three Arabs had got to their feet. They were moving nervously towards their jeep, which still carried the American Army star. " I'm going on," Julie said.

" No, wait . . ." But already her foot was pressed down on the accelerator and as we moved off she said, " I didn't like the look of them. I'm sure that jeep wasn't their own."

I had been thinking the same thing, but I didn't say anything and we climbed steadily up the mountainside. Out on the top it was bitterly cold. There was nothing between us and the snow-capped peaks of the Atlas, and the sense of space was immense. We stopped where the road dipped down on the other side. The sky was already paling in the east. We made some tea and watched the sun rise, turning the dark hills first pink, then gold, then a hard, arid brown.

I took over the driving then and we started down the mountain, which was black in shadow and cleft by the start of a deep gorge. Below us lay a brown valley broken by the green of a palmerie, which was shaped like a fist, with the forefinger extended and curving towards the base of the mountain away to our right. From the centre of the fist rose the sun-baked walls of a kasbah. It was Kasbah Foum-Skhira. and close by were the forts of the French Post.

Away to the south the valley opened out, vanishing into the morning haze as though running straight out into the sands of the Sahara: it was like a broad estuary, and on the far side—ten, maybe fifteen miles away—the containing hills were ruler-straight as though cut from the bed of an ancient sea. The sky was palest blue, the earth almost yellow in the clear, dry air. The piste leading to Foum-Skhira was a faint line drawn across the valley floor like the tracing of a Roman road in an aerial photograph.

We swung down in sharp curves until we came to a crumbling cliff and looked down a thousand feet into the black depths of a gorge. The piste seemed to hang on the very edge of the drop and as we rounded the cliff, we came upon a road gang cutting their way through a fall of rock. "Look!" Jan gripped my arm, pointing down towards the entrance to the gorge. A walled kasbah with four mud towers, two of which had crumbled away, was picked out in the slanting sunlight. And beyond it, on the edge of a stream bed, was a little cluster of tents.

Kasbah Foum! It couldn't be anything else, standing like that in the entrance to the gorge. And those would be Ed White's tents. I glanced at Jan. Though his face looked tired under the dust-white stubble, his blue eyes gleamed with excitement. "We're almost there," he breathed.

But it was half an hour before we were driving into Foum-Skhira. The Post consisted of two large forts with a big, open space like a parade ground between them and a single European house. One of the forts was white, with adobe roofs that made it look like a mosque. I learned later that it had been built by the Legion. The other, built by native Goumiers, was of mud with embrasured walls and little square towers like a Kasbah. They were both of them empty and as we drove past they had the silent, deserted look of lost cities. A Tricolor fluttered from a white flagstaff outside the European house.

I suggested to Jan that we make contact with the French officer in charge of the Post first. But he said, " No. Drive straight on to Kasbah Foum. If those were White's tents,

I'd like to find out what he's doing before I talk to the French."

I drove on, past the European house, down towards the palmerie where ruined mud walls marked the site where the souk had been. There were camels hobbled there and mules, and there was a large crowd of people who stood and stared at us, not curiously and not hostilely, but with a strange air of waiting for something. It was the same when we skirted the walls of Ksar Foum-Skhira, the village of the kasbah. The place teemed with people who stood and watched us go by in silence. The women, clustered round the well holes, let go of the ropes so that the long poles for lifting the water stood curved against the sky like the gaffs of dhows. But all the palmerie seemed deserted and the cultivated patches had a neglected look, the little earthen banks to contain the water flattened almost to the ground.

Dust rose in choking clouds through the floorboards as we ran along the edge of the palmerie. Gradually the trees thinned and fell away so that we could see the dried-up stream bed we were following. "There it is!" Jan cried, leaning forward. "Right at the entrance to the gorge. And there's the old city and the watch tower just as Marcel described it to me."

I screwed up my eyes, seeing for the moment only the white glare of the piste and the black bulk of the mountain slope down which we had come. And then I saw it—the little kasbah with its two ruined towers standing out yellow against the black, shadowed immensity of the gorge. I could see the watch tower, too, and all the hill below it was strewn with the debris of an old city. In places the walls still stood, a yard thick and some twelve feet high, and one stone archway remained intact. But all the rest of it had been thrown down as though by some natural upheaval. And yet it was impressive, for this was a land of mud buildings, and I wondered who these people were who had built in stone.

Just short of the kasbah was the huddle of tents we had looked down on from above. We were very close now. A flash of light momentarily dazzled me. It was a mirror reflecting the sun. A man stood, watching us, a razor in his hand and half of his face white with shaving soap. He wore a singlet and green-khaki trousers tucked into half-length boots.

"He looks American," Jan said, and then his gaze switched to the mouth of the gorge.

I pulled up outside the tent and we got stiffly down, our clothes white with the coating of dust we'd picked up crossing the valley. My eyes felt gritty and tired. It was hot already and there were flies and the smell of bacon frying.

The man who had been shaving came towards us. He was tall, broad-shouldered, slim-hipped, with a young, rather square face and a crew cut. He was undoubtedly American —his features, his clothes, everything about him. He was wiping the soap from his face as he came.

"Are you Mr. White?" Jan asked.

"Yeah." He waited, watching Jan uncertainly.

"I believe you were recently in touch with a firm of French lawyers in Rouen."

"That's right. You must be Wade, I guess." There was interest, but no enthusiasm in his voice.

"Wade was in touch with you then?" Jan's tone had sharpened.

The man frowned. "You mean you're not Wade?" He sounded puzzled.

"No, I'm not Wade," Jan said, and then he nodded towards the ruined fort. "Is that Kasbah Foum?"

"Yeah."

There was a short, awkward silence. The two of them stared at each other. Jan's gaze shifted to the tented camp and then followed the broad track that ran up into the entrance of the gorge. The track looked as though it had been made by a bull-dozer, for where it passed below the kasbah it had been levelled out by thrusting aside the stones and rubble of the old city.

"Well, what do you want?" White's tone had hardened. He looked very young with his fair, cropped hair and freckled face—very young and very Nordic.

"Would you mind telling me what you're doing up there?"

"What business is it of yours?"

Jan reached into his breast pocket and brought out the crumpled envelope. " I hold the deeds to this property," he said.

White stared at him. His mouth had opened in an expression of surprise. But he shut it suddenly and his whole face hardened, so that he looked big and tough and a good deal older. " Is that so?" He seemed to tower over Jan as he took a pace forward. " What the hell goes on here? Is everyone screwy? Yesterday it was a Greek telling me the land belonged to him. Now you come here and tell me——"

" Was the Greek's name Kostos?" I asked.

White seemed to notice me for the first time. " Yeah, that was his name. Kostos." The name seemed to bring the anger that was in him to a sudden head. He swung round on Jan. " Now you get the hell out of here. Both of you. D'you hear? I got a concession from the Sultan's Government. That's good enough for me. If you think you own the land, then you go an' tell them so. Okay?"

" I have the documents here," Jan said quietly. " All I want to know is what you're doing up there. You're a prospector, aren't you?"

" Goddammit!" the other exploded. " I'm not interested in documents. The guy who came yesterday had documents. You go an' sort it out with the authorities." His voice was excited, nervous. " Jesus! I got enough trouble, what with the Ay-rabs bellyaching because I use bull-dozers instead of employing them and Captain Legard at the Post getting scared I'll upset the water. Now you and this Greek telling me I've got no right to operate here."

" I didn't say that," Jan put in mildly.

" All right. You didn't say it. But that's the inference, isn't it? Now suppose you get out. I've work to do."

Jan stood there, uncertain what to do next. The man seemed oddly belligerent. " Why don't you talk it over," I suggested to White. " You haven't looked at the documents yet."

" I looked at enough documents yesterday."

" If Kostos showed you any documents they were forgeries," Jan said. His voice had risen slightly and his shoulders were beginning to move excitedly. " Kostos is a crook and if you——"

" You're all crooks as far as I'm concerned," White cut in.

" That's not a very nice thing to say." It was Julie. The American looked at her, screwing up his eyes against the sun. I don't think he'd noticed her before. " I'm sorry," he said. And then he turned to Jan again and added, " I don't know who you all are, and I don't much care. I'm telling you the same as I told the Greek yesterday—go and sort it out with Caid Hassan and the authorities."

" If you'd just look at these deeds," Jan began, but the other cut him short. " What sort of fool do you take me for?" he cried. " Do you thing I'd start work here, spending my own dough, without finding out who owns the place? It belonged to a man called Duprez. It was given him by the Caid here. And Duprez is dead. I found that out from his lawyers. He's dead and he passed the deeds on to a guy called Kavan. Now, according to the Greek, Kavan's dead, too. Anyway, he never got his title to the property confirmed by the Caid, which he had to——"

" But I am Kavan," Jan said.

White opened his mouth to say something and then stopped.

" You'd better know our names," I said. " This is Dr. Jan Kavan, the man to whom Duprez gave the deeds of Kasbah Foum."

" I don't believe it," he said. " Wade wrote me he'd be bringing the deeds out with him. Why should Kavan come here and not Wade? Kavan never took any interest in the place. The lawyers didn't even know where he was. And the Greek said he was dead."

" Well, he's not dead," I said a little irritably. " This is Dr. Kavan, and he has the deeds with him. And this is Miss Corrigan."

He stared at her for a moment and then turned back to me and said, " And what about you?"

" My name's Philip Latham."

" I mean, what's your interest in this?"

" I haven't any," I told him. " I'm an English missionary out here."

" A missionary!" He stared at me, open-mouthed.

" There's a most delicious smell of bacon," Julie said, pointedly sniffing at the air.

He stared at her, still frowning. "Oh, sure—yeah." He looked at the three of us uncertainly. He was bewildered and a little uneasy.

"We've been travelling all night," Julie said.

That was something he could understand. He seemed to relax and a gleam of warmth came into his eyes. "If you haven't had chow . . ." His friendly nature asserted itself. He turned and shouted, "Abdul!" And then he laughed awkwardly and said, "I forgot. I'm cook this morning, I guess." And he glanced a little angrily round the camp.

"Are you on your own?" I asked. There was accommodation for at least four in the tents.

"Yeah. Yeah, I guess so."

"Where's the rest of your party?" I was thinking of the Arabs with their jeep parked beside that fire in the mountains.

"Oh—they left this morning. . . ." He stared at us and then added quickly, "To get stores and things, you know." He turned back to the mirror. "I'll just finish shaving: then I'll see about some food." He gave a little laugh for no apparent reason except that he seemed nervous. There was a streak of blood on his chin where he had cut himself. He slapped irritably at a fly that was trying to settle on it.

"Would you like me to cope with breakfast for you?" Julie asked hesitantly.

He glanced at her and then nodded. "Sure. Go ahead. There's tinned bacon, biscuits, jam and coffee." He watched her disappear into the cook tent, glanced quickly at us and then turned back to the mirror again.

"You're mining up here, aren't you?" Jan asked.

"I told you— I've got a concession from the Sheriffian Government."

"What are you mining?"

"That's my business."

Jan started to ask another question, but then stopped and stood staring up the newly-made track to the entrance to the gorge. An uneasy silence developed between us. The morning was very still. There wasn't a breath of wind and the air was clear and crisp with that freshness that occurs in desert country before the sun bakes the land to arid heat.

" What about a wash?" I suggested.

Jan looked at me and nodded. " Yes. A wash would be good." We got our things and scrambled down the steep bank where a few dwarf palms thrust dusty fronds above the sand. Then we were in the rock bed of the stream and the only vegetation was the feathery sprays of the tamarisk and the needle-pointed tufts of the reeds. A heron rose from the edge of the muddy-flowing stream, its wings beating slowly, cumbersomely. Occasional banks of dark sand were white-crusted and marked by the feet of birds and when I rinsed out my mouth I found the water was slightly salt.

" He was expecting Wade," Jan said suddenly. And then, after a pause, he added, " He doesn't believe I'm Kavan."

" He'll get used to the idea," I said.

He bent down and washed his face. As he stood up he said, " I was right, you know."

" What about?"

" Wade was going into partnership with him."

" You mean he was double-crossing Ali?"

He nodded.

" You may be right," I said as I towelled my face. " The point is, what do we do now?"

" First I'm going up to have a look at the gorge." He was standing with his towel slung round his neck, staring towards the entrance which was a black canyon of shadow.

" Well, you'd better have breakfast first," I said.

" Yes, of course." He nodded, laughing excitedly. Then he turned to me, his expression suddenly serious. " Philip. You've no idea what this means to me; to be actually here, at Kasbah Foum. It was like a dream come true. Back in England, as things became more difficult, I thought of nothing else. It was my dream—a sort of El Dorado." He laughed a little self-consciously and, in a more practical tone, added, " After we've looked at the place, perhaps you'll come with me to see Caid Hassan?"

" Of course," I said. " But I think we'd better see this Capitaine Legard first. You don't want to upset the French."

Julie joined us then. " Breakfast is ready," she said. She washed her hands and face and then came and stood beside us.

" It's a queer, wild place." She said it a little breathlessly, as though she was uneasy about it. " Why do you think the others left him?"

" How do you mean?" I stared at her and saw that her eyes were troubled. " They went to get stores. You heard what White——"

But she shook her head. " I've been inside the big tent. All their things are gone. And there are three empty beds there. You remember those men sitting round that petrol fire on the other side of the mountain?"

" The three Arabs with the jeep?"

" Yes. They came from here. I'm certain of it. That was his jeep. They were frightened. They stole the jeep because they were frightened and wanted to get away." She stared up at the entrance to the gorge. " I don't like it, Philip. He's frightened, too. I can feel it. He's trying to hide something, but he's frightened."

" Who? White? Nonsense," I said. " You're imagining things."

" No." She shook her head. " I'm not imagining things. There's a queer atmosphere about the place. And those people down by the souk." She hesitated and then said, " A little boy came into the tent while I was cooking. Apparently Abdul used to give him scraps to eat in the mornings. He told me he sleeps up in the ruins of that kasbah. His father keeps his flock of goats there. He daren't bring them down into the palmerie in case they get stolen. Since the souk was destroyed they're very short of food here."

" Why?"

" I don't know." Her voice trembled slightly. " There's a feeling of. . ." She didn't seem able to put it into words.

" Oh, come on," I said. " You're tired and you need some food."

She looked up at me uncertainly. Then she smiled and, with a sense of relief, I saw the smile spread from her lips to her eyes. " I expect you're right. Let's go and have breakfast. Maybe I'll feel differently afterwards."

We breakfasted under the extended fly-sheet of the larger tent and from where I sat I looked through into the tent, to the three empty camp beds. I, too, began to feel Julie's sense of uneasiness. It wasn't only the fact that the tent looked deserted. It was White himself. He was oddly talkative. And once started, he talked quickly, eagerly, as though he had to go on talking to keep his mind off other things. He talked about himself, about North Africa—about anything that came into his head. He was from the Middle West and he had worked with Atlas Constructors for eighteen months, building the big American bomber base at Sidi Slimane near Fez. " Hell! That was a tough job. But I needed the dough. That eighteen months made it possible for me to come down here with my own outfit."

" You'd been prospecting here before, I suppose?" Jan said.

" Prospecting?" White frowned. " No, I hadn't been prospecting."

" But you knew the place? You'd been down here——"

" No. I'd never been here before."

Jan stared at him. " But how did you know . . ." He stopped, a puzzled expression on his face.

But White didn't want to talk about Kasbah Foum. He slid quickly away from the subject and began talking about Morocco. He talked about it with an odd disregard for the French as though he had no idea what the country must have been like before they came. And yet, he knew more about the history of the Berbers than I did, and when Julie asked him about the old city that lay in ruins on the slopes above us, he talked with authority. " I'd say it was six or seven hundred years old," he said. " Maybe more." And he went on to describe the ruins in detail, a sudden enthusiasm in his voice as though they touched him personally.

In his view the people who had built it had come in from the desert. " It's a very complicated history down here in the south. And it isn't helped by the fact that it's been passed on by word of mouth from generation to generation. Some of the officers of the A.I. have done some good work on reconstructing it, but I guess nobody will ever really know. Basically, it's quite simple though," he added. " Nomadic tribes move in from the desert, become date farmers and goat-herds in the palmeries, get soft and then themselves fall victim to another wave of tough guys coming in from the desert. It's a cycle that went on repeating itself. But the people who built this city, they were something bigger. As you see, they built in stone."

He had been staring up at the ruins as he talked, but now I saw his gaze shift to the track running into the gorge. It had become very hot and the whole place seemed to brood in the shimmering light.

"And what about the kasbah?" Julie asked.

"The kasbah? Oh, that's later. Much later. It was the first kasbah built here in the valley. Legard says it was originally called Kasbah Foum-Skhira. Then, when the palmerie developed and they built a bigger kasbah and a new village, they called that Kasbah Foum-Skhira, and the deserted fort here became just Kasbah Foum. To differentiate between the two, I guess."

Jan leaned forward and touched my arm. He had the deeds of Kasbah Foum in his hands. "Will you check through this and see if it says how far the property extends?" he asked me.

It took me some time to decipher it, for the ink was very faint in places. As far as I could tell, it took in all the shoulder of the mountains on which the watch tower and the kasbah and the old city stood. It took in both sides of the stream from well below the camp and included the whole of the entrance to the gorge.

"How far back into the gorge does it extend?" Jan asked.

"As far as the first bend."

He nodded. "Good!" And then he looked across at White who had been watching us curiously. "You know Caid Hassan, I suppose?"

"Is that the old Caid at Foum-Skhira?"

"Yes. Have you met him?"

"No."

"But it is Caid Hassan. I mean, it's the same Caid that ruled here before the war?"

"Oh, sure. Legard says he's been Caid here for more than forty years."

"That's all right." Jan folded the deeds up and put them back in their envelope. Then he got to his feet. "Come on, Philip. Now we'll go and look at the place."

"Just a moment," White said.

Jan turned to face him.

"You say you're Kavan?"

"Yes."

"Did Wade get in touch with you?"

"Yes. But I wouldn't let him have the deeds."

"I see." He stared at Jan, frowning again. "I'm surprised he didn't write me again and let me know." He said it more to himself than to Jan and then he gave a quick tug to the waistband of his trousers and turned away as though dismissing the whole matter. "Go on up there if you want to," he said.

But as we went back up the track, I glanced back and saw him standing by his tent, watching us. His face had a sullen, worried look. Julie had noticed it, too. "He's like a child with a toy," she said. And then she added, "But the odd thing is, he's glad we've come. He doesn't want to be here alone."

We had a look at the kasbah first. It was built with its back against a section of the old city wall. The sand had drifted in from the desert, piling up against the walls, and there were goat droppings everywhere, dried and powdery. There was nothing of interest there. We climbed down to the track and walked up it into the entrance to the gorge. "Do you know where the mine entrance was?" I asked Jan.

He nodded, his eyes searching the dark cavern of the gorge, comparing it with the mental picture he had been given. We crossed the sharp-cut line between sun and shade, and immediately we were in a damp, chill world of cliffs and tumbled rock. Ahead of us, in a crook of a bend, stood a plantation of fig trees, their stems twisted and gnarled and white like silver. And on a ledge above, a little almond tree clung in a froth of white blossom.

All above us to the right was a great spill of rock. The track had been slashed through the base of it and the debris shovelled into the bed of the stream, damming it up to form a lake. The water was still and reddish in colour. Skirting the base of the slide, we came upon two bull-dozers, white with dust. They looked insignificant in that huge, natural chasm— forlorn pieces of man-made machinery. They had been cutting into the slide to expose the face of a shallow cliff of grey rock, piling the rubble out into the lake so that there was a big artificial platform.

Jan made straight for the cliff face White had been exposing. "This is the spot," he said. "He's almost reached it. Marcel said the mine shaft was at the base of this cliff." He looked back at the towering cliff that formed the opposite side of the gorge as though to check his bearings. "Yes." He nodded to himself. "Another few days and he would have exposed the entrance." He stood there, staring at the cliff. "Marcel should have been here," he murmured. "He should have been the person to open it up, not an American. He would have opened it up and used it to help the people here." His eyes were clouded. In his mind he was back in that cellar in Essen.

"What's this?" Julie asked, holding out a lump of rock to him. I think she wanted to distract him from his thoughts.

He stared down at it. One half of the rock was a strong reddish colour. "Iron oxide," he said. "What you'd probably call red ochre." He moved back a little way, staring up at the slope of the slide above us. "It looks as though it's fallen from up there." He pointed high up the slope to a crumbling cliff from which much of the slide had come. "I hope there isn't another fall whilst we're——" He stopped, turning to face the entrance to the gorge, his head on one side, listening.

A car was coming up the track from the camp. We couldn't see it because of the slide, but the sound of its engine was thrown back to us by the cliff opposite, beating in upon the stillness of the gorge. It grew rapidly louder. And then a jeep appeared, roaring and bumping round the base of the slide. It stopped beside the second bull-dozer and a European got out. He wore a light grey suit with a brown muffler round his neck and a wide-brimmed town hat.

It was Kostos. His suit was crumpled and dirty, and his narrow, pointed shoes were covered wih a white film of dust. He looked uncomfortable and his city clothes seemed out of place against the towering background of the gorge.

"So! It is you, Lat'am, eh?" He glanced at Julie, and then his small, dark eyes fastened on Jan. "Hah!" He was suddenly smiling. "For a minute I do not recognise you without your beard."

"How did you know we were here?" I asked him.

He tapped the side of his nose, smiling. He was so close to

me that I could see the skin peeling from his cracked lips and the individual hairs of stiff stubble that darkened his chin. " Not a sparrow falls, eh? Even 'ere in the desert."

" Well, what do you want?"

" What do I want? Don't try to be stupid with me, Lat'am. You know what I want." He moved across to Jan, leaning slightly forward and speaking confidentially as though he might be overheard. " Come now, my friend. The papers. They are of no use to you. You cannot make claim to this place just because you have Duprez's papers. Duprez is dead and any successor to the ownership of the property must be confirmed by Caid Hassan."

" I know that," Jan said.

Kostos chuckled. " Maybe you know it now. But you do not know it when you take the papers from that poor devil Kavan, eh?"

" What makes you think I took the papers from him?" I think that at that moment Jan was amused that the Greek still took him for Wade.

Kostos looked at him and there was a little gleam of triumph in his eyes. " You do not kill a man for nothing, my friend." His tone was gentle, like a kitten's purr.

" Kill a man!" Jan stared at him with shocked surprise. Knowing how it had happened and that it was an accident, the idea that he might be charged with murder was still quite beyond his grasp.

" You don't suggest Kavan *fell* overboard from your boat, do you?"

" What do you mean?" Jan's face was suddenly white. " Who told you anyone fell overboard?"

" So! You do not listen to the radio, eh?"

" No, we haven't got one," I said. " But we saw the newspaper report. It was inaccurate."

Kostos spun round on me. " You keep out of this, Lat'am. It is nothing to concern you. I make you an offer in Tangier. You remember? That is finish. You lie to me. But now I have a stronger hand, you see, an' I deal direct." He turned back to Jan. " This is a new development, my friend. The body of Dr. Jan Kavan, Czech refugee scientist, has been washed up on the coast of Portugal. That is what the radio said. It is two nights ago and they give your description—all very accurate, except for the beard which is gone now." He moved a little closer to Jan. "The police would be interested to know what motive you had."

"How do you mean?" Jan's body was rigid, his mouth slightly open.

"If I tell them about the deeds you get from Kavan, then they know it is murder—they know you push him overboard."

"No." The denial burst from Jan's mouth. "I didn't push him. It was an accident. And it wasn't——" He checked himself as though a thought had suddenly occurred to him.

"Now, perhaps you understand, eh?" Kostos was smiling. "We make a deal, you and I. You give me the papers and I keep silent. Maybe I help you get out of Morocco safe. But if you do not give me the papers, then I——" He stopped and turned at the sound of footsteps echoing along the cliffs of the gorge.

It was White. He wore an old fleece-lined flying jacket, open at the front to expose the dirty white of his T-shirt. "What's going on here?" he demanded. And then he recognised Kostos.

"Oh, so you two have got together, have you?"

Kostos smiled and looked across at Jan. "Yes. That is just about what we do, eh?" He jerked the muffler tighter round his neck. "I give you to tonight, my friend. I will be 'ere——" he glanced at his heavy gold wrist-watch——"at five o'clock. If you do not meet me then, ready to come to an agreement, then I will know what to do, eh?" He smiled and nodded and walked back to the jeep. The engine started with a roar that reverberated through the gorge and then he went bumping and slithering over the rocks at the base of the slide and was lost to sight.

"Who was that frightful little man?" Julie asked. "What did he mean about——"

"I'll tell you later," I said quickly. I was looking at White, wondering how much he had heard.

He seemed to hesitate a moment. And then he half shrugged his shoulders and turned and walked over to the nearest bull-dozer, his tall, slim-hipped body moving easily, rhythmically as though he belonged in this wild place.

"White!" I called after him. "Do you know how we contact the Caid?"

But he climbed on to the seat of the bull-dozer without replying, and a moment later the engine started with a shattering roar. The tracks moved and the dull, rock-burnished steel of the blade dropped to the ground, scooped a pile of rock out of the slide and thrust it to the edge of the dumping ground. The gorge echoed to the splash and rumble of a ton of rock spilling down the slope into the water.

I tapped Jan on the shoulder. "We'd better go down and see Capitaine Legard at the Post. He'll take us to the Caid." I had to shout to make myself heard above the reverberating roar of the bull-dozer.

He nodded and we went back down the track to the camp. "Do you think it is true, what Kostos said?" he said.

"He'd hardly have invented it," I said.

"No, I suppose not." He looked worried. "It must be Wade's body that was washed up. But why should they mistake Wade for me?"

"Don't forget they're convinced Wade is alive," I pointed out. "And your papers showed that you aren't unalike. The body wouldn't have been in too good shape." I hesitated and then said, "Was Wade wearing any of your clothing?"

"I don't know." He hesitated. "He could be. You know what it's like in a yacht—oilskins, windbreakers, sweaters, everything gets mixed up. One's too tired . . . Maybe he was wearing something of mine." He said it slowly, considering the matter, and he walked with quick, nervous strides, his eyes fixed on the ground. "If it's true what Kostos said," he murmured half to himself, "then officially I'm dead."

"You'll have to explain that it's Wade's body that's been found in Portugal," I told him. "And you'll have to explain how he died."

"That means publicity." The words seemed to be jerked out of him. "There mustn't be any publicity. It was publicity that started it last time. I told you that. I must keep my name out of the papers. At all costs there mustn't be any publicity."

"That can't be helped," I said. "The man's body has been found and his death will have to be explained."

He didn't seem to hear me. "If I'm dead," he murmured to

himself, " then it's Wade who is alive. It's as simple as that."
He said it almost wonderingly. And then he strode on ahead
until we came to the camp. He seemed to want to be alone.

And when we drove down the piste towards Foum-Skhira
he was strangely silent. It was a queer day now. It seemed to
have changed. The strength and clarity had gone out of the
sun and the sky was no longer blue, but opaque and hazy. A
little wind had sprung up from the mountains and it blew the
dust from our wheels out in streamers in front of us. We
stopped at the house where the Tricolour flew. There was a
sign-board half-hidden by sand. One arrow pointed to the
mountains—Agdz, 44kms.; the other south towards the
desert—Timbuctou, 50js. . . . Fifty days! A dog raced
out to meet us as we stopped. He stood barking at us
furiously, a big, rangy animal, oddly reminiscent of the
medieval hunting dogs depicted on old tapestries.

" Look!" Julie cried. " A baby gazelle." It was in a wire
enclosure; a small deer, beautifully marked with long, straight
horns.

A Berber servant came to the door of the house and stared
at us. I called out to him, asking for Capitaine Legard, and he
pointed to the fort, telling us to go to the Bureau.

The sun had disappeared completely now. Yet there was
no cloud. It seemed to have been overlaid by an atmospheric
miasma. It had become very cold and the wind had risen
further, driving little sifting runnels of sand before it. The
whole great open space between the two forts seemed to be
on the move as the powder-dry top surface of sand drifted
along the ground. We were shown into the Captain's office
by an immensely large, black-bearded orderly wearing a turban
and a blue cloak. He was a Tuareg, one of the Blue Men
of the desert.

By comparison, Legard seemed small and insignificant. He
was short and stocky with sallow, tired features. There was
no heating in the stone-floored office and he sat huddled
behind the desk in a torn and dusty greatcoat with no
insignia of rank on the shoulders. A khaki scarf was muffled
round his neck. He glanced at Julie and then pulled himself
to his feet, staring at us in silence from behind thick-lensed,
horn-rimmed glasses. The glasses caught the light so that

it was impossible to see the expression of his eyes. But I felt he resented our intrusion. Moreover, though he might look insignificant, he conveyed a sense of power, as though whatever he wore or however ill he looked, he was conscious of being the ruler in this place.

Faced with the authority of the man, Jan remained silent, leaving me to explain who we were and why we had come to Foum-Skhira. "We hoped you would be willing to take us to see the Caid Hassan," I added.

"Caid Hassan is an old man now," he said. "Old and sick." He got Julie a chair and went back to his seat behind the desk. "Also, you come at a bad time." He made little explosive noises with his lips and stared at Jan. "So! You are now the owner of Kasbah Foum, eh?"

"It has to be confirmed by the Caid," Jan said.

"C'est ça."

He stared at us from the protection of his glasses and the stillness of the room seemed to crowd in on us. His hostility and the chill drabness of the office with its bare, map-lined walls had a depressing effect on me.

"And if the Caid confirms your title, what do you intend to do about this American?" He said "this American" with undisguised contempt.

"I understand he's been granted a mining concession," Jan said.

Capitaine Legard grunted. The grunt seemed to express what he thought of people in Rabat who granted mining concessions in his territory. There was silence again, and then he said, "You have documents to prove your ownership of the property, monsieur?"

Jan produced once more the crumpled envelope and passed it across the desk. Legard pulled out the deeds and examined them. Then he glanced at the covering letter. He read it slowly, carefully. Then he looked up at Jan. "This letter is from Marcel Duprez?"

"Yes." Jan cleared his throat. "Perhaps you knew him, Monsieur le Capitaine?"

"Non. But everybody has heard of him. Capitaine Marcel Duprez was one of the finest officers of les Affaires Indigènes." There was sudden warmth in his tone. "Tell me, monsieur, how was it he came to leave you this property? Are you a relative?"

Briefly Jan explained how the war had brought them together and the part Duprez had played in helping him to get information out to the British. And as he talked, I saw Legard's face soften and relax. " And you were with him when he died?" he asked. And when Jan had described the scene in that cellar in Essen, Legard nodded his head slowly. " He was a fine man," he said quietly. " I am sorry he died like that. He was what the men who sit at desks in Rabat call an officer of the *bled*—of the country. It seems that he was not an executive type but only a leader of the people. He understood the Berbers as few of us will ever understand them. If he had not been half-dead with dysentery and undergoing a cure in France, the Germans would never have captured him." He shrugged his shoulders and again those little explosive noises blew his lips out. He glanced at his watch and got quickly to his feet. He seemed suddenly alert and full of vigour. " Alors. We will go back to the house. We will have a drink and you will perhaps tell me the full story. Then I wil' phone mon commandant. He will be interested. He served with Duprez. He was with him when they took Foum-Skhira Duprez told you the story of that, eh?"

Jan nodded.

" Eh bien." He took a battered and dusty pill-box officer's hat from a nail on the wall and led us out through the drifting sand to his house. Like all houses in Morocco, it was built for intense heat. The floors were tiled, the walls cold, white expanses of plaster, their severity relieved by a few hand-woven rugs. There was a gramophone and some books and a small collection of brass sugar hammers, beautifully inlaid with copper and silver. When Julie admired them, he said, " Ah, yes. Once Foum-Skhira was famous for its silver craftsmen." He turned to Jan. " There is an old story that your Kasbah Foum was built on the site of a smelting place —for extracting silver from ore. But——" He shrugged his shoulders. " Like all these stories, it has come down by word of mouth only. Maybe it is true. Duprez excavated some old fire-places there and now there is this American . . ."

He shrugged his shoulders again and took us through into

his study. There was a big desk with a field telephone on it, and the walls were lined with books. Magazines, some of them American, littered the floors. On the mantelpiece were some family photographs framed in silver and above it a delightful oil-painting of a Paris boulevard. He saw me looking at it and said, "That one I picked up in a little gallery I know on the Left Bank. It is by a man called Valere. He is not much known yet. But I think he is good. In the other room I have another by him and also one by Briffe. But this is the one I like best. It is a great pleasure to sit here at my desk and look at Paris, eh? I am a Parisian, you see." He laughed and then turned to one of the bookshelves. "Regardez, monsieur." He pointed to a beautifully bound collection of volumes, all on art. "I like to look at the works of the great painters, even if I can never afford to own one. I like pictures." He turned abruptly away, as though he had revealed too much of himself. "Alors, mademoiselle. Qu'est ce que vous voulez boire? Vermout? Cognac? I have a good cognac that I have sent out to me from France."

"I'd like a cognac then," Julie said. He pulled up a chair for her and then shouted for his Berber servant, who came and poured paraffin on the pile of wood in the grate so that it went up with a roar as he lit it. Legard poured us our drinks. "Santé!"

"Santé!"

The fire blazed with heat. The room was suddenly warm and friendly.

"What is the best way for me to contact the Caid?" Jan asked.

"Ah, that is a little difficult, monsieur. I would take you myself, but . . ." He shrugged his shoulders. "It is as I have said—you come at a bad time. I cannot leave the Post until the food trucks arrive. I have two trucks bringing food here to these people, and they have both broken down." He made rude, angry noises to himself. "Our transport is all from the war. It works, but it needs servicing." He began to cough. "Like me," he said as he recovered, and he grinned at us sardonically. "The trouble is that everything—even the wood for the fire—has to come across the Atlas from Marrakech."

"Could you provide a guide then?" Jan said. "I have to see Caid Hassan. It's urgent."

Legard looked at him, frowning. "You have waited ten years, monsieur. What is the hurry?" And when Jan didn't answer, he smiled and said, "Ah, it is the American that is worrying you, eh? Well, he is worrying me, also." He leaned quickly forward. "Things were difficult enough here before. The date crop failed. For two years now we have what is called the Marlatt scale pest here in the palmerie. We have sprayed from the air at the time when the insect comes out to moult, but it is no good." He shrugged his shoulders. "Then this fool arrives, paying three Arabs incredible wages to run his abominable machines. I asked him to clear the rock by hand with local labour. He refused. He did not seem to understand that the people here needed the money."

"His Arabs have left him," Julie said.

"Yes, yes, I know." He had risen and was pacing up and down excitedly. "They departed early this morning." He stopped and stared at us. "But do you know why? Does the American say why they left?"

"He said they left to get stores," I told him.

"Pff! You do not send three indigènes to get stores when one would do."

"Maybe they were told to go," I suggested.

"Who by?"

"Isn't the Caid's son, Ali, here in Foum-Skhira?"

He looked at me hard. "How did you know that, monsieur?"

I told him then about the visit we had had from Kostos.

"Ah, oui. That man Kostos!" He resumed his pacing. "Merde!" The word burst out of him with explosive force. "Everything goes wrong this year." He swung round on his heels so that he faced me. "Did you see the souk when you came in and the road up the mountain? First the dates and then the rain. And now Ali is here." He started to cough again and winced, pressing his hand against his belly. He leaned on the desk for a moment and then walked slowly round to his chair, his body bent, and slumped into it. "Eh bien," he murmured, "my relief will arrive soon."

"You're not well," Julie said.

He looked across at her and smiled wanly, shrugging his shoulders. "Every year I go to Vichy to take the cure. I am late this year, that is all." He shouted for the house-boy who came running with a glass of water, and he drained it at a gulp.

"Is it dysentery?" Julie asked.

He nodded. "Oui, mademoiselle. The Amibe. With us it is an occupational disease. We do not always stay in the Posts. We have to visit all parts of the Territory, and sometimes we must drink bad water. For the indigènes it is different. They are immune. But for us . . ." He shrugged his shoulders again.

"About this man Ali," I said. "Can't you arrest him? I understood . . ."

"Oui, oui, monsieur. I can walk into the kasbah now, this morning and arrest him. But it would disturb the people, and things have been difficult here lately. Maybe when the food trucks arrive . . ."

The field telephone on the desk buzzed. "Pardon, monsieur." Legard lifted the receiver. "Oui, mon commandant— ici Legard . . . Oui . . . Oui . . . Oui, mon commandant. . . ." He looked across at us, the instrument still held against his ear, and his eyes fastened on Jan. "Oui. Exactement . . . Vraiment?" His tone was one of astonishment. For a moment there was silence whilst he listened to the voice at the other end of the line, and then he said, "Je le ferai. . . . Non, non, ils sont justement arrivés. . . . Oui, oui, je comprends parfaitement." He asked about the food trucks then and after a short conversation on the subject, he nodded. "Oui, je le ferai . . . Ca va bien. Adieu, mon commandant." He put the receiver down slowly on to its rest. Then he stared at the three of us, a little startled, a little angry. "Your papers, monsieur," he demanded, looking at Jan and holding out his hand. When they were handed to him, he went through them slowly, glancing up every now and then as though to check that they really did relate to the man sitting opposite him.

"And yours, monsieur," he asked, addressing me.

He checked my passport and then he looked up at the two of us and said, "I regret, but I have orders to retain your papers temporarily. You are to remain in this district until you have permission to leave."

" What exactly is the trouble?" I asked.

" There is no trouble. It is solely a matter of routine." He pushed back his chair and got to his feet. " If you require accommodation . . ."

" We sleep in our vehicle," I said.

" Bon. Now, if you will excuse me, I have to leave for Agdz."

" Don't you want to see my passport?" Julie asked.

" It is not necessary, mademoiselle."

" But if it is a matter of routine." She held out her passport.

" I repeat, mademoiselle. It is not necessary." He shouted for the house-boy. " If there is anything you require for your comfort," he added formally, " Mohammed will see that you have it." He indicated the Berber boy and then ordered him to escort us out.

Disconcerted by the abruptness of his change of attitude towards us, we went without another word.

Little runnels of sand had drifted under the front door despite the sacking that had been placed there. And when Mohammed opened it for us, we were met by a cold blast of wind that flung a cloud of stinging sand in our faces. We thrust our way out, too battered by the impact of the storm to think. The door closed behind us and we hesitated, huddling together for protection. The palmerie had disappeared completely. The Foreign Legion fort was no more than a vague blur in the sand-laden atmosphere. The whole surface of the ground seemed to be on the move, rustling past our feet and climbing into the air with a singing sound on each gust, swirling upwards higher than the flagstaff.

We fought our way to the bus, hauled open the door and staggered inside.

" What happened?" Julie asked us as she got her breath back. " What was that phone call about?"

" I think the police have discovered that Jan didn't come straight out from England," I said.

But she shook her head. " No, it wasn't that. Legard is an officer of the A.I., not a policeman, and Jan was a friend of

Capitaine Duprez. His attitude wouldn't change because he was in trouble with the immigration authorities."

" No," I said. " But it would if his Commandant had thrown doubt on Jan's identity." I glanced at Jan. He was sitting on the berth, his head in his hands, frowning. " Well, what do we do now?" I asked him.

He lifted his head and looked at me almost in surprise. " We find Caid Hassan. That's the first thing. Afterwards . . ." He shrugged his shoulders a little wearily. " Afterwards, I don't know. But first we'll see the Caid. As soon as the storm is over."

I glanced at my watch. It was just after twelve. And at five Kostos would be at the camp again.

II

Though we had parked in the lee of the Foreign Legion fort, the sand still found its way into the interior of the bus. I would have liked some sleep, but sleep was impossible. We just sat and watched the sand whirl past the windscreen, sifting like water over the long snout of the bonnet. A jeep passed us, battling against the swirling clouds of sand like a little mechanical toy. Legard was at the wheel, muffled in his Spahis cloak. He was driving towards the mountains.

" Why did he have to go to Agdz?" asked Jan. " He said he couldn't leave the Post until the food trucks arrived."

" Well, I'm glad I haven't got to drive through this in an open jeep," Julie said.

" He'll be clear of it in the mountains," I pointed out.

" Why don't we go to the mountains then?"

I glanced round at her. She had her eyes closed and she looked tired. " We could go back into the house," I suggested.

" No, we can't sleep there. Besides, we need some food."

" All right. I'll drive up to the foot of the mountains then." I leaned forward and pressed the starter button.

" Why not go to the Kasbah Foum?" Jan suggested.

" If you like."

It wasn't easy driving. Sand was sifting along the ground so thick that it was difficult to see the piste. It was like driving through a dead world. But at length the palm trees thinned, and as we climbed towards Kasbah Foum, the weight of the sand lessened. Soon we could see the mountains, a vague shadow looming up ahead of us like a heavy cloud formation photographed in sepia. There was the watch tower and the ruined city, and there, straight ahead of us, was the kasbah and the dark gash of the gorge.

In that queer half-light the place looked inhospitable, almost hostile. There was a deadness about it. The tumbled graveyard of the ancient city seemed to be spilling down the hill on to the kasbah. The gorge was a yawning cavity in the mountains, remote and sinister. I glanced at Jan. Those last lines of Browning's came into my mind: *And yet dauntless the slug-horn to my lips I set, and blew. Childe Roland to the Dark Tower came.*

I pulled up close to White's tent and switched off the engine. The camp was deserted, but from the entrance to the gorge came the sound of a bull-dozer working, carried to us faintly on the wind. "We'll have some food and then you'd better get some sleep," I told Julie.

As soon as we had finished lunch, Jan left us, walking quickly up the track to the gorge. To Julie and I who watched him go, he looked a small and pathetically lonely figure against the immensity of the mountains. "What will happen to him?" she asked.

"I don't know," I said.

Her hand touched my arm. "How deeply are you involved, Philip?"

"With the police?"

"Yes."

"Oh, I shouldn't get more than ten years," I said, trying to make a joke of it. But her eyes looked worried. "Get some sleep," I said. "There's nothing to be done about it now."

She hesitated, and then she nodded and went through into her compartment of the caravan. I stretched myself out on the berth behind the driving seat and pulled a rug over me. I must have slept, for I woke up with a start to the sound of a car drawing up alongside. It was a jeep and for a

moment I thought it was Legard. But then I saw there was a
Berber at the wheel, and it was Kostos who climbed out of
the passenger seat. He saw me and waved his podgy hand.

"Lat'am. Where is Wade gone to?"

"Wade?" And then I laughed because the name sounded so
odd now. I pointed up to the mouth of the gorge and he
nodded and climbed back into the jeep which shot off up the
track. I glanced at my watch. It was just after five. The wind
had died away and all the sky over the palmerie was shot with
red and gold and a soft blue violet as the sun sank.

I pulled on my shoes and hurried up the track. The gorge
was already beginning to get dark and there was a damp chill
about the place. It echoed to the thunder of machines and as
I rounded the base of the slide, I saw that both bull-dozers
were in operation. White was driving one and Jan the other,
as though they had settled their differences and gone into
partnership.

The jeep was parked close to the point where the rubble was
being tipped into the water. Beside it stood Kostos and the
Berber driver. The Berber, in his white djellaba with the hood
drawn up over his head, seemed so natural, so much a part
of the scene, that he emphasised the incongruity of the
European in his crumpled suit and the great, blundering
machines. Every time Jan's bull-dozer rumbled past him,
Kostos moved forward, shouting and gesticulating in his
endeavour to make himself heard above the roar of the diesel
engine. As I came up, Jan stopped and switched off his engine.
Seeing this, White stopped his engine, too, and in the sudden
silence the Greek's voice, raised to a scream to make himself
heard, was like the cry of some wild bird.

". . . do not stop, we will leave at once, do you hear?"
Kostos was waving his plump hands and his face was red
with the effort of shouting. It was rather comic.

And then I saw that the Berber standing beside him was
Ali d'Es-Skhira.

"We would like to talk to you privately," Kostos said.

"Anything you have to say, you can say to me here," Jan
answered.

Kostos hesitated, glancing quickly round at White and
myself. The movements of his head were jerky. "Well, what

have you decided?" His voice sounded small and peevish against the silence of rock and cliff and water.

Jan didn't say anything. He stared down at Kostos from his seat at the bull-dozer, and his gaze shifted to Ali. The only sound was the soft tinkle of water seeping through rock.

" Come on now," Kostos said. " You make your mind up, eh"?

" I've made up my mind. The answer is No."

Ali took Kostos by the arm and they conferred together in a whisper. And all the time Ali was looking at Jan. Finally he spoke to him in French. " You are not the man I am expecting to meet here."

" No," Jan said. " He's dead."

Ali nodded his head. His face showed no surprise. " But you have the deeds of Kasbah Foum?"

" Yes."

Again Kostos and Ali conferred together. " C'est ça." Ali nodded and folded his hands in the sleeves of his djellaba. " My friend says that the original offer still stands," Kostos announced. " For the papers, five hundred thousand francs."

There was a silence. Nobody moved, nobody said anything. It was like a tableau. Then Ali turned his head slowly and gazed at the cliff face, now rapidly being cleared of debris. His features were impassive. Only his eyes betrayed his interest. They were dark and brown, but they gleamed in the fading light.

He glanced at Jan, staring at him as though to imprint the shape of his face on his mind. Then he turned without a word and climbed into a jeep. Kostos hesitated, looking from one to the other of us uncertainly. He seemed nervous, almost reluctant to leave. He was a European, and I suddenly got the impression he was uneasy. Then he turned, ducking his head in a quick, awkward movement, and scuttled back to the jeep, his thin-soled shoes making a frail, scraping sound on the rocks. The jeep drove off and we watched it go, not moving or speaking until the sound of it died away and was lost in the stillness.

" He knows now," Jan said to me.

I nodded. " Yes."

" The wind has dropped, hasn't it?" His voice trembled

slightly. " I think we should try and see the Caid right away."

" We should have gone before," I said.

He nodded. " Of course. But it seemed a pity that this bull-dozer should not be operating. And we're so close to the entrance now." There was warmth and excitement in his voice again. " White doesn't know the exact location of the entrance. But I do. Marcel gave me bearings. Another two days' work . . ." He stopped there, his excitement damped by my silence. " What's the matter, Philip? You're worried about Ali. Is that it?"

" Yes," I said. " It's a pity we didn't see the Caid this afternoon. So long as Ali thought you were Wade, there was no reason for him to oppose the visit. But now . . . it may be dangerous."

" I'm sorry." He climbed down off the bull-dozer. " I didn't think . . ." His shoulders moved awkwardly and he made a gesture with his hands that embraced the cliff-face, the whole gorge. " I was too excited."

Ed White came over to us then. " It looks like you really have got the deeds of Kasbah Foum," he said.

Jan nodded.

" I see." He stood staring at us for a moment. " That makes a difference, doesn't it?" He seemed about to say something further, but instead he turned and walked slowly back across the rubble and climbed up on to the driving seat of his bull-dozer again. The engine started with a roar and the lumbering machine turned back towards the cliff-face. " Come on," Jan said, gripping my arm. " We must see the Caid right away."

" It'll be night before we get there."

" I know, I know. But that may help." He glanced back as a beam of light cut the gloom of the gorge. Ed White had switched on his headlights. " I was a fool. I forgot all about Kostos coming here at five. Once I got on that bull-dozer . . . It was good to be doing something constructive. I worked with a bull-dozer in Germany for a time—before they discovered I had other uses." He laughed quickly, nervously. " We'll go and have some tea with Julie. You English are always less pessimistic after you've had some tea. Then we'll go to Kasbah Foum-Skhira."

" We'll need a guide," I said.

He didn't say anything and we walked in silence out of the gorge. The sun had set and a velvet twilight was rapidly descending on the valley. But the palmerie was still visible and I could just make out the brown of the kasbah towers rising above the dusty green of the palms. I wished we had visited the place in daylight. " If Legard had taken us there it would have been——"

" Well, he didn't," Jan said sharply.

" No, but——" There was no point in dwelling on it. The palmerie had faded into the dusk already. Everything was very still. It seemed impossible that the pale surface of the land could ever have been whirled up into the air in a cloud of sand; it looked solid and petrified in the half-light. " What are you going to do about White?" I asked him. " Don't forget he holds a concession."

" Oh, we'll probably come to some agreement. I like him. He's easy to get on with. He's a construction engineer and he fits this sort of country. If the Caid confirms my title to the place . . ." He didn't finish. I think that the "If" was too big.

We walked on in silence and as we neared the camp I saw something move along the darkening bed of the stream. It was a black, compact mass of movement. I strained my eyes and it resolved itself into a herd of goats being driven by a small boy. Jan had seen it, too, and he said, " Perhaps the boy would guide us to the kasbah?"

" No," I said. " A boy's no good. He hasn't the necessary authority. They might not admit us. But if we could get his father . . ." I was thinking that a man who had a herd of goats would almost certainly be conservatively minded and a supporter of the Caid's policy rather than of Ali's fanaticism. I turned off the track and scrambled down the bank. Jan followed us.

The boy had stopped now and was watching us nervously. I called to him in his own language to come and speak with us, but he didn't move. And when we came up to him he stood, regarding us with wide, solemn eyes. He was like a startled animal and at any moment I was afraid he would turn and run. But the goats had stopped and were nibbling at the reed tufts. The boy was watching them all the time and I knew that so long as the goats were there, the boy would remain. They were in his charge and the responsibility was a heavy one, for they represented considerable wealth in this starved, arid land.

I explained to him that I wanted to speak with his father, but he stared at me out of his large, awed eyes and said nothing. I repeated my request slowly and clearly. He looked at the goats as though he were afraid I might spirit them away by magic whilst I held his gaze with my strange talk. Then his eyes came back to me as though fascinated. Probably I was the first European who had ever spoken to him.

In the end I put my hand in my pocket and pulled out two hundred franc notes. I held them out to him. He smiled shyly, eagerly, and shook his head. But his eyes remained on the notes. Again I asked him if he would fetch his father for me.

I knew he understood and I waited. His gaze alternated between my face and the notes in my hand. Then suddenly he leaned forward, swift as a bird, grabbed them from my fingers, and with a little shriek of excitement went scampering away after his goats which had gradually merged into the dusk as they drifted from reed tuft to reed tuft.

We watched him rounding them up with shrill cries of *Aiya, Aiya,* driving them towards the ruined kasbah. "Will he bring his father to us?" Jan asked.

"I think so," I said, and we went on to the caravan.

We had just settled down to tea when the boy's figure went flying past, bare feet scuttering over the sand, scarcely seeming to touch the ground; a small, flickering shadow in the gathering dusk.

I turned the bus then and switched on the sidelights, and soon afterwards the boy appeared with his father. He was an oldish man, tall and slightly stooped, with a long, pale face heavily lined with years of sun and sand. We exchanged greetings and I invited him into the caravan. He sent the boy off and, after slipping his feet out of his sandals, he climbed in and seated himself cross-legged on the berth. From an inner pocket he produced the two hundred franc notes I had given his son and held them out to me. "My son is not to be paid for bringing his father to you, sidi," he said.

I insisted that he return the money to the boy and then Julie brought the coffee I had asked her to make and we talked. His name was Moha and he was the chief of a small village at this end of the palmerie. He was a man of some substance, with fifty goats and more than a hundred palm trees, and he had a daughter married to the son of the Khaïlifa, the Sultan's representative at Foum-Skhira. He talked about the failure of the date harvest and how a year ago French experts had examined the trees and then the " machine like a bird had arrived and covered the date palms with smoke."

" And didn't it do any good?" I asked.

" *Insh'Allah*! " He shrugged his shoulders and smiled. But the smile didn't extend to his hard, grey eyes. " The French officer has told us that it is the only hope for the trees and we believe him because he is wise and like a father to us. But this year I have no dates, sidi. No man is sure any more."

It was the perfect situation for a man like Ali to exploit. I asked him if he knew that the Caïd's son had returned to Foum-Skhira. He nodded and I was conscious of a stillness about him, a sudden mental wariness. His eyes were hooded by the pale lids and the curved, predatory beak of his nose made him look like an old hawk.

" Do you know why he has returned?" I asked. But he didn't answer. He had finished his third cup of coffee and, according to Berber etiquette, he would now take his leave. " You are a friend of Caïd Hassan," I said.

He nodded, gathering his djellaba about him.

" We wish to see him tonight. It is important. Will you take us to him?"

" He is a sick man, sidi."

" I know. But we have to see him. Will you take us?"

" Tomorrow perhaps."

" No." I said. " It must be tonight. At least guide us as far as the kasbah."

He stared at me, his eyes narrowed slightly. Then he shook his head. " He is sick," he repeated.

Jan got up then. " Ask him," he said, " whether he was here when Lieutenant Duprez drank tea with Caïd Hassan between the lines."

The Berber's eyes lit up suddenly as I asked him the question. "*Iyyeh, sidi.* I was there."

I told him then that Jan had been Duprez's friend, that he had been with him when he died, and he stared at Jan, smiling and bowing as though greeting him for the first time. "He has a message for Caid Hassan from Capitaine Duprez," I added. "It is important." And then I asked him again if he'd take us to the kasbah.

He got to his feet then. "Very well." He nodded. "I will take you to Caid Hassan."

I opened the door for him and he stepped out into the night. Jan followed him. Julie caught hold of my arm. "Do you have to go with him, Philip?"

"You'll be all right," I said. "Ed White will be down from the gorge soon and——"

"It's not that," she said quickly. She was staring up at me. Then she turned away. "Well, be careful. This place isn't like the mountain villages round Enfida." She picked up the coffee things and went through into the kitchenette.

I stepped down to the ground and closed the door. The little lit world of the caravan seemed suddenly small and remote, an oasis of light in the desert of darkness that surrounded it. The sky was clear and the bright starlight showed us the shape of the mountains crouched above the camp. The sound of White's bull-dozer came down to us from the gorge. There was no wind, but already the air was cold, with that still, frosted cold of a land where the soil had no humus to absorb and retain the heat of the sun.

We followed the piste down until, looking over my shoulder, the bus was no more than a yellow pinpoint of light in the immense black shadow of the mountains. Then we entered the palmerie and the trees hid even that small indication of human existence. We were alone in a cold, alien world.

It was very dark under the palms and we stumbled along countless small earth banks built to retain the water in the cultivated patches where millet would be grown. But finally we came out on to the bank of a deep irrigation ditch. The path was like a switch-back, but the going was easier. Occasionally a star was reflected below us. It was the only indication that there was water in the ditch. We followed the glimmering white of Moha's djellaba through a world of almost complete blackness. All my eyes consciously saw was the still, fantastic shapes of the palm fronds standing darkly against the stars. My feet seemed to develop a sense and a feel for the ground. They found their way by a sort of instinct that was quite divorced from the control of my brain.

We came to a bridge of palm trunks spanning the ditch and there our guide told us to wait whilst he went into his village. We could hear him beating on the wooden door of his house and there was a dog barking. Then there was silence again. " I suppose you've got the deeds with you?" Though I kept my voice to a whisper, the sound of it seemed loud.

" Yes," Jan said. " And Marcel's letter."

I didn't say anything. I was thinking that the only documents establishing his claim to Kasbah Foum were on him at this moment. I didn't like it. If the guide sent a runner on ahead of us . . . If Ali knew . . . I felt a shiver run down my spine. It was cold and very quiet standing there on the edge of that ditch in the palmerie. It was like being in a dead world.

A shadow moved in the darkness. It was our guide, the white of his djellaba almost hidden by the blanket he had wrapped round himself. He led us on along the top of the ditch without a word and soon we caught the faint beat of tam-tams far ahead. The sound was a guide to our progress and as we neared Ksar Foum-Skhira the harsh, lilting chant of the singers joined the rhythmic beating of the drums. *Yaiee-ya Yaiee-ya Yaiee Yai-i . . . Yaiee-ya Yaiee-ya Yai-ee Yai-i-ee*. The chant was repeated over and over again with only slight variations. It was insistent like the drumming of the wind or the singing of a sand storm.

We reached a well with its pole uplifted against the stars and then we were on a beaten track with walls on either side. And when we came out into the open again, the noise of the tam-tams and the singing was suddenly very loud. *Aiee-ya Aiee-ya Aiee-yaiee-ya*. We were close under the walls of Ksar Foum Skhira now and there were people about. I breathed a sigh of relief. *Aiee-ya Aiee-ya Aiee-yaiee-ya*.

We crossed an open space and ahead of us, on a slight rise, the darker bulk of the kasbah showed in the darkness. We passed through the arched gateway of an outer wall, crossed an open courtyard of sand and came to the main entrance, barred by a wooden door. Our guide beat upon the wood and the noise seemed very loud, for the kasbah had the stillness of a place that had been deserted for a long time. A kid bleated softly somewhere in the darkness and from near the outer wall came the rude belching of a camel. A light showed through a crack and then the wooden securing bar was lifted and the door was pulled back with a creak of hinges. A swarthy, bearded man, his head swathed in a turban, stared at us suspiciously. He carried a carbide lamp in his hand—an elementary light made of a metal container with a long spout rising from it, at the end of which was a two-inch jet of flame that wavered in the draught.

Our guide explained that we wished to see the Caid. The thick, guttural sounds of the Arab dialect were tossed back and forth between them. " My companion," I said, indicating Jan, " was a friend of Capitaine Duprez. He has a message for Caid Hassan."

The turbaned porter held the flame high so that he could see us. The light gleamed on his brown, inquisitive eyes. Then he nodded and stood aside for us to enter. The door closed behind us, the wooden securing bar was dropped into place and, with a quick little gesture that was part welcome and part a request to follow him, the keeper of the gate led us into the black cavern of a passageway. From nails on the wall he took two more carbide lights. The place was like an underground tunnel, dank and chill with walls and roof of mud so that it looked as though it had been hewn out of the earth.

We passed a rectangular opening that was a doorway leading to a courtyard. I had a glimpse of stars and the outline of one of the kasbah towers. We turned left here into another passageway. A yellow gleam of light showed at the end of it. It was the entrance to a room and, as we went by, I saw the glow of a brazier and figures huddled round it. The only lights were the carbide flames flickering from their wall hooks. Steps led upwards then—a staircase that followed the square walls of a tower. And suddenly we were out in the open on a roof top. Below us stretched the darkness of the palmerie and away to the right the shadowy bulk of the walled village of Ksar Foum-Skhira, from which gleamed little points of light—the gleam of braziers and flickering flame lights in rooms that had only holes in the walls for windows.

We crossed the roof top and entered the open doorway of another tower. There was a shallow flight of earthen stairs and then we were in a square room with two thick window embrasures, the small, square openings of which were closed by broken wooden shutters. The place was very cold and had a musty smell. It was completely bare. The floor was of hard-packed earth and the walls of dried mud. The ceiling was high, raftered with the soft wood of palm stems. The man who had brought us here lit the two carbide lamps, hung them on hooks provided in the walls and then left us without a word, taking our guide with him.

It was bitterly cold. The temperature was just on freezing and a little wind was driving in through the cracks in the shutters and the carbide flames flickered wildly. " They'll bring cushions and rugs in a minute." I said.

Jan nodded, glancing uneasily about him. " Can I smoke?" " Yes."

He brought out a packet of cigarettes and lit one. The only sound was the whistle of the wind in the chinks of the shutter and the singing from the village and the beat of the drums, which was so clear that they might have been in the courtyard below. *Ai-yai-yee Ai-yai-yee Ya-ee Ya-ee Yai-i.*

" There's a fire in Ksar Foum-Skhira." Jan said.

I went over and peered through one of the broken shutters. In some courtyard of the village flames were flickering in a lurid glow that lit up the corner of a tower and the piled-up walls of some houses. " They have to have a fire to heat the drums and so stretch the hides to the required pitch." I said.

The drums were beating faster now. The tempo of the singing increased, became shriller and then stopped abruptly. The drums went on for a few seconds and then ceased on a beat. In the sudden silence we heard the murmur of voices below us in the kasbah and then the scuffle of sandals on the stairs. Men crowded into the room, their arms piled with cushions and silks and hand-woven rugs. A big square of carpet was spread out on the earthen floor, the cushions were arranged round it and draped with rugs and silks. A brazier was brought, a red glow of warmth, and stood in the corner. A copper kettle was set on it. A great silver tray was placed on a low table that was barely six inches from the ground. Coloured glasses were carefully arranged and a silver tea chest and a white cone of sugar were placed beside it.

One of the men who had carried these things up was Moha and I reminded him that we were relying upon him to guide us back. He nodded and disappeared with the rest of the men. The room was suddenly empty again. We sat down cross-legged on the cushions and waited.

The minutes ticked slowly by. I found myself wishing the singing would start again in the village. Harsh and primitive though it was, at least it was a reminder that there were human beings around. The kasbah seemed quiet as the grave.

But at last there was movement again on the stairs and then an old man entered, walking slowly. He wore a spotlessly white djellaba of soft wool, the hood neatly arranged to frame his features. His beard was white and rather sparse, cut like a goatee, but extending along the line of the jaw almost to the ears. His skin was pale, far paler than mine, and his eyes were a steely blue. He was of pure Berber stock, unmixed with Arab or any of the desert races that so dilute the Berber blood of the south. " *Merhba bikum!*" His gesture of greeting had great dignity. He motioned us to sit and himself sank on to a cushion, folding up neatly and gracefully despite his age. Summoning one of the two men who had entered with him, he bade him make the tea for his guests, at the same time apologising to us in French for not doing it himself. He then make us a little speech of welcome in a frail voice that only occasionally paused to search for the right word. " You should have given warning that you were coming to visit me," he finished reproachfully. " I would have arranged a difa for you."

" It is very kind of you," I replied. " But things are difficult for you now."

" Yes, I know. But for our friends it is still possible to entertain them as I would wish. It is my people who suffer." He paused and then said, " You were with Monsieur le Capitaine this morning?"

I nodded.

"Did he say when the food would arrive for my people?" I explained about the two trucks that had broken down.

"Yes, yes, I know," he said. "But why does he have to go to Agdz? Is he gone to bring the food here?"

I couldn't tell him that Legard had gone to Agdz because of us. "Yes," I said, "he has gone to bring the food trucks."

"Good. But he must come soon. The people lose so much of their supplies in the disaster of the souk." He said this to himself rather than to us, nodding his head slightly. His age showed then, for he looked suddenly peevish and irritable.

"They'll be here to-morrow, I expect," I said.

He shrugged. "*Insh' Allah!*"

"I believe your son is here in Foum-Skhira?" I said.

"My eldest son, you mean? Ali?" He nodded. "Oui. There is dancing in his honour in Ksar Foum-Skhira to-night. You know him perhaps?" His eyes had clouded.

"Yes, I met him in Tangier."

The pale lids closed almost wearily. In those dropped lids I saw suddenly a similarity between the son and his father. He sighed and changed the subject, talking about the rains and how the souk had been destroyed. And then the tea was made and the hot, sweet, mint-smelling glasses were placed in our hands. "Alors," the Caid said, "you say that you are friends of the Capitaine Duprez."

I explained that it was Jan who was Duprez's friend and that he had been with him when he died. The old man nodded and motioned the men, standing like shadows in the doorway, to withdraw. Only the man seated behind the silver-laden tea tray remained. He was small-bodied with a cast in one eye, but he had the old man's features and he was called Hassan, so that I presumed he was one of the Caid's sons.

"Now," the Caid said. "You have came to talk with me about Kasbah Foum, eh?"

I nodded to Jan to go ahead, and he told him how he had met Duprez, how they had worked together against the Germans in Es 1 and how Duprez had died there.

The old Caid shook his head and sighed. "It is a sad end for him," he said.

"He was serving France," Jan pointed out.

"Mais oui. He always served France. He was a Frenchman. But he should have died here. This was his home and my people were his people also. He was a fine man." Remembering what Ali had told me, I was surprised at the warmth in the old man's voice.

The man behind the tea table rose and replenished our glasses. "It is many years ago then that Monsieur le Capitaine died." There was a hard shrewdness in the old man's eyes as he stared at Jan. "Why is it only now that you come to tell me how it happened?"

Jan tried to explain why he had not come before, what his life had been since the war, but it was clear that the Caïd didn't really understand. He was not ignorant of the world beyond Foum-Skhira, but to him it was a French world. The complications of other European powers were largely outside his knowledge. "I think," he said, "that you have come because the tall, fair man from America with the big machines is arrived to work at Kasbah Foum."

"No," Jan said. "I came because I had to. I did not know about the American." He produced the battered envelope and another smaller envelope containing the letter from Duprez. The Caïd waved it aside. "I have been told," he said, "that you are not the man to whom Capitaine Duprez handed the papers. It has been suggested that you killed the man to whom he gave them. First, before I see the letter Capitaine Duprez wrote, you must give proof that you are in reality the man who was with my friend when he died."

"How can I do that?" Jan asked. "What can I tell you that will prove it to you?"

The old man thought for a moment. "Tell me exactly how he looked and what he told you of his talks with me."

For several minutes Jan talked, telling him about Marcel Duprez quoting long speeches that Duprez had made to him, about the Caïd, about Foum-Skhira, about the Berbers and the country of the south. Only occasionally the Caïd interrupted him to clarify a word or to ask a question. Jan was still talking when there was a disturbance at the foot of the stairs below the room where we were seated. Several men were talking, quickly, angrily, in Berber, and then there was the light patter of sandals on the earthen stairway.

The Caid turned his head towards the entrance, his forehead contracted in a frown.

The footsteps ceased. The figure of a man stood in the doorway. His brown djellaba merged into the black rectangle of the entrance so that he was no more than a vague shape in the darkness. His face was hidden in the hood of his djellaba, but his eyes caught the light of the carbide flames and glinted, as did the curved silver knife at his waist; the eyes and the knife were all that was visible of him. "*Skun ya?* Who is that?" the Caid demanded.

"Ali." And the man stepped forward into the light, his head and body only slightly bowed in respect for his father.

"Why do you disturb me? Can you not see that I have guests?" The Caid's voice quavered slightly.

"It is because you have guests that I have come," Ali d'Es-Skhira answered. He had moved to his father's side, towering over the old man who seemed suddenly shrunken and much older.

"Where have you been? What trouble have you been stirring up among the people?" The old man's voice sounded frail and peevish. And when Ali did not answer, he said to him, "Go. I will talk with you later."

But Ali did not move. Tangier and his own rebellious nature seemed to have destroyed all the respect and obedience due from a Berber son to his father. He pointed to us and said, "These men come like thieves in the night, O Sidi, to steal from us the wealth of Kasbah Foum." He was still speaking in the Arab dialect and his voice throbbed with violence. "They are evil men and your people have need of their share of the wealth the foreigner may find in the gorge. Do not be deceived by them. They are thieves."

"We are not thieves," I answered him in his own tongue, and his eyes blazed at me in the flickering light as he realised that I had understood.

"You thought that my friend was the man you had employed to purchase the deeds of Kasbah Foum," I continued, still speaking the Arab dialect. "But this afternoon, when you came to the gorge, you realised that he was not that man, but the true friend of Capitaine Duprez. That is why you have come here now in haste—because you are afraid that your father will discover the truth and will know that this man is the man Duprez chose to prevent you from using Kasbah Foum for your own selfish purposes and not for the benefit of the people of Foum-Skhira. It is you, Si Ali, who are the liar and the thief."

He took a step forward, his sudden in-drawn breath sounding loud in the stillness of the room. " It is the talk of a man who is not sure of himself, sidi," he said to his father and gave a quick laugh.

Caid Hassan's eyes were closed, his body relaxed as though trying to gather energy together inside himself. At length he turned to Jan and opened his eyes. " You have told me much that has convinced me," he said, speaking in French again. " Alors, monsieur, one final thing. Did my friend tell you how it happened that I gave him Kasbah Foum?"

" Oui," Jan said.

" Then tell me the whole story, and I shall be convinced."

" You took tea with him in the middle of the battle," Jan said. " It was then that you first learned of his interest in Kasbah Foum and the ruined city." The old man nodded and Jan continued.

It had been in the spring of 1934, at the very end of the pacification. The tribes of the district of Foum-Skhira were particularly warlike. Their resistance under Caid Hassan had been stubborn and the fighting had dragged on. Marcel Duprez, then a lieutenant, was among the French forces. He had been an officer of the A.I. in Algeria and four years before he had come in alone from the desert to prepare the way for the pacification and persuade the tribes that resistance would be pointless. He knew them all. One afternoon, when both sides had withdrawn after a day of particularly savage fighting, he had calmly walked out into the No Man's Land between the two forces, accompanied by two Legionnaires. They were unarmed and all they carried was the paraphernalia for making tea.

He had set his brazier down midway between the two forces and, after quietly performing the ceremony of the making of the tea, had called upon Hassan and his chiefs to come and drink it with him. And they had come, knowing the officer and admiring his bravery. And over the tea table he had persuaded the Caid and his chiefs that the French must win in the end and that there was no point in continuing the fight. He had then talked about their history and, in particular, the history of the ruined city. As the sun was setting, terms were agreed, but for the sake of his young warriors' pride Caid Hassan had insisted on continuing the battle for one more day, though it was decided that the fighting should not be pressed by either side. Duprez had then gone back to the Legion's lines and all next day the two forces fired on each other with a great deal of noise, but little loss of life. And in the evening Hassan had come to capitulate.

"You were taken to the tent of the general commanding the Legionnaires," Jan added. "But you refused to surrender to him. You said you would only surrender to the officer who had come out and served tea to you. They told you that Marcel Duprez had been wounded in the day's fighting. When you heard this, you insisted on being taken to the hospital tent where he lay, and there, with the general looking on, you surrendered to Lieutenant Duprez." Jan stopped there and stared at the Caid. "That is how Marcel told it to me. It was because of his interest in the place and his plans that you gave him Kasbah Foum. Also, he loved your people."

The Caid glanced up at his son. "Well, Ali, is that correct?" he asked.

Ail said nothing. His face was impassive, but his eyes glinted angrily in the flickering light.

"Say whether it is correct or not," the Caid said, and there was an edge to his voice.

"It proves nothing," Ali answered. "Legard or the Commandant at Agdz could have told the story to him."

"And all the other things he has told me?" The Caid stared up at his son and I was conscious again of the tension between them. Then he held out his hand to Jan. "Give me the letter Capitaine Duprez wrote."

Jan handed him the letter. Lights were brought and placed at the Caid's feet and, whilst he bent forward to read the letter, our glasses were re-filled for the third time. The Caid held the letter in such a way that his son, leaning down over his shoulder, could not read it, and when he had finished it, he folded it up and slipped it inside his djellaba. "This is not a simple matter," he said, speaking slowly in French. "There is an old belief that silver was once mined at Kasbah Foum and that belief has been revived because of this American. I had hoped that it would be Capitaine Duprez who developed that place. He would have used it for the benefit of the people here. He had plans for hospitals and schools. I had hoped that perhaps I was giving him the means to make those plans come to life. But now he is dead and you are here in his place. How do I know I can trust you?"

Jan's eyes were steady as they met the old man's gaze. "I have come to live here," he said quietly. "Morocco is my home now. I have no home anywhere else in the world." He leaned forward slightly, a note of earnestness in his voice. "If there is wealth at Kasbah Foum, it shall be developed for the benefit of the people here. That is what I promised Marcel, and I shall keep my promise."

He had spoken seriously and with force. The old man nodded. But he was still uncertain. "You are not a Frenchman," he said. "And you have only recently arrived in Morocco." He hesitated and then added, "What you say may be the truth at this moment. But a man easily changes his mind when his roots are not deep in the soil of his promise."

"I have come to live here," Jan repeated. "Morocco is my country now."

The Caïd glanced up at his son and then stared at Jan. It was as though he were weighing up the two men in his mind. There was a long silence. Finally he said, "Allah be my guide in this. It shall be as Capitaine Duprez wished it. I will give you——"

"No." Ali's hand descended on his father's shoulder, gripping hold of it, digging his powerful fingers into the old flesh. "These men are strangers. They want the silver. Nothing more. They do not love our people."

"I do not believe it," the old man said, trying vainly to pluck his son's hand from his shoulder.

"Do this thing," Ali said, "and, as Allah is my witness, there will be trouble among the people."

I stared at the scene with a sense of shock, scarcely able to believe that this was a son speaking to his father. In strict Berber etiquette the man should be as a child in the presence of his father, even to the point of making a request through an intermediary. Yet Ali's manner was openly hostile, even contemptuous. The others in the room had noticed it, too. They were whispering and muttering among themselves whilst the two men—father and son—stared at each other. They were like two adversaries who had battled a long time. Finally the Caïd gave a little sigh and his eyes, as they turned away, had the vacancy of the very old; it was as though they looked beyond the flickering walls, back through the dim vistas of the past. Slowly he pulled himself to his feet. Ali made no move to help him. His face was cruel with the look of satisfaction. " My father is tired," he said in French. " I must ask you to leave and permit him to rest."

We waited for the Caïd to speak. He stood there a long time, staring into vacancy. And all he said in the end was, " Yes, I am tired now. We will talk of this some other day."

Jan started to say something, but Ali silenced him with a gesture. He took his father's arm and led him out. The Caïd did not protest. But he paused in the doorway and looked back. His eyes fastened on Jan. And suddenly they weren't vacant any more. They were intensely alive as though he were examining Jan's features for a sign by which he could come to a decision. " *Barak allaho fik*!" he murmured. " Allah bless you! " His voice was gentle, like a monk saying a benediction. And then he was gone.

They brought lights and escorted us down the narrow stairs, across the open space of the roof top and into the bowels of the kasbah. A hand gripped my arm in the half dark. " I don't like it," Jan whispered. " Ali is in control here."

His words echoed my thoughts. We were in the dark tunnel of the entrance passage now. It was intensely cold and I tried to convince myself that that was why I was trembling. We passed the rectangular gap lit by the red glow of the brazier. Figures were huddled around it, as they had been when we arrived. They did not seem to have moved. It was just a brief glimpse and then the carbide flames were flickering on blank walls again, silhouetting the cowled, shadowy figures round us.

With a sense of relief I heard the scrape of the securing bar, the creak of the heavy wooden door. There was a rush of fresh air, a murmur of polite farewells, and then we were out in the cold, bright glitter of the star-studded night.

I turned, surprised that we were, in fact, outside the kasbah. For a moment the carbide flares lit the passageway and the swarthy, aquiline faces of our escorts, framed in the cowls of their djellabas. They were outlined for an instant, motionless like a tableau, and then the door thudded to and we were alone. It was only then, whilst the wooden securing bar was being dropped into place, that I realised we had been shown out without our guide.

Jan had noticed it, too. "Where's Moha?" he asked. His voice was a hoarse whisper. "Do you think . . ." He didn't finish the sentence, but I saw his hand reach into his breast pocket to make sure he still had the deeds there. "Do you remember the way back?" he asked.

"I think I can find it," I said. We had started to walk across the courtyard. We reached the archway and there ahead of us was the dark, towering shape of Ksar Foum-Skhira. There was no singing now. The village seemed as quiet as the grave. We came to the first of the wells and then we were under the shadow of the walls.

We stopped there as though by mutual consent and stood listening. There was no breath of wind and in the stillness my ears picked up small sounds—the grunt of a camel, the cry of a child; sounds that were innocent and yet, because they were not of our own world, disconcerting. "Do we have to go back through the palmerie?" Jan said. "Couldn't we cut across the Post and get on to the piste?"

The thought had been in my own mind, too. We both of us felt the need for open country round us. "All right," I said and we turned back, skirting the walls of Ksar Foum-Skhira, moving slowly, feeling our way in the darkness. Once we stumbled into a caravan of hobbled camels who champed and belched in the darkness, shifting their positions with nervous grunts.

We were on the south side of the village now and the going was slow, for we were in an area of intense cultivation and all the ground was criss-crossed with small earthworks about a foot high to retain the water when the irrigation ditches were allowed to flood. The palms thinned out and we were suddenly in soft sand. Here the desert had moved in on the palmerie, killing the trees and half burying them in steep dunes. We were a long time getting through the dunes, but at last we came out on to hard, flat desert and there, straight ahead of us, were the walls of the ruined souk.

After that we had no difficulty in finding the piste. We struck away from it to the right, making straight for Kasbah Foum, taking our bearing from the shape of the mountains hunched against the stars. The going was rough and uneven and we stumbled repeatedly over stones or fought our way through patches of dry, brittle scrub. It seemed a long time before we saw the faint glimmer of light that marked the position of the camp. We made steadily towards it and gradually the light separated into two lights and we could see the shape of the bus and, beyond it, the tents.

We couldn't have been more than two or three hundred yards away, when there was a sudden cry—a yell that rose to a scream ; high-pitched, sudden and frightening. It was cut off abruptly. I checked at the sound of it and in the same instant the headlights of the bus were switched on. They cut a great swath through the desert night and figures leapt to view, a huddle of Berber men bending over something on the sand of the piste. They straightened up and stood like frozen figures caught in some fearful act that should have remained cloaked by the night.

The horn began to blare then and they broke and ran. I was running, too, now. I shouted something—something in English. I caught a glimpse of White peering out of his tent. There was a stab of flame and the crack of a gun. Then he started to run. We were all running—running towards a still body that lay in a tight bundle on the piste. By the time I reached it, the man's assailants—three or four of them—had vanished into the darkness that lay outside the beam of the headlights.

The body lying on the piste was alive. I saw that at a glance. The man was breathing heavily, his heaving chest thrusting the air out in great gasping sobs. But there was blood on the sand. "I didn't hit him," Ed White panted. "I fired over their heads to scare them."

"Of course," I said and turned the man over.

It was our missing guide—Moha. There was a cut above his right eye that extended across his forehead and into his hair. It looked as though a stone had hit him. But down by his waist his djellaba had been ripped open with a knife and there was more blood. Jan thrust me aside, tearing the djellaba apart to expose the torn flesh of the man's buttocks. He examined the wound quickly and then nodded and said, "He's all right. Just a flesh wound." He sat back on his haunches, staring at the inert body. The man was still panting as though he had just flopped down after winning a race. "Why did they attack him?" he asked, twisting his head round and looking up at me.

"I don't know," I said. "We'd better get him up to the camp."

As we lifted him up, I saw he had something tightly clutched in his right hand. It was a roll of paper. I prised the fingers from their grip on it and then we carried him to the larger of the two tents, where we laid him on one of the camp beds. Julie joined us there, carrying a bowl of water and some bandages. Whilst she set to work to bathe the man's wounds, I took the crumpled paper over to the pressure lamp. It was written in Arabic, the writing thin and shaky, but recognisably the same as the writing on the deeds of Kasbah Foum. It was signed Caid El-Hassan d'Es-Skhira.

I touched Jan on the shoulder as he bent over the knife wound in Moha's body. "Here's the answer to your question," I said. "He was attacked because he was bringing you this."

"What is it?"

"Confirmation of your title to Kasbah Foum."

"But I thought the Caid——" He almost snatched the paper from me and stood staring down at the writing. "Does this mean Kasbah Foum belongs to me?" he asked, and he held the paper out to me so that I could read it.

"Yes," I said, peering over his shoulder. "The letter states quite clearly that the Caid agrees to Duprez's choice of a successor to the title and requests the authorities to make the necessary registration. It further states that so long as you live, neither he nor any member of his family shall have any interest in the property." I hesitated.

"What is it?" he asked quickly.

"He doesn't mention your name anywhere. He simply refers to you as 'the bearer of the deeds.' "

"Probably he couldn't remember my name." He was holding the paper tightly in his hand as though afraid it might vanish. "Does it make any difference, do you think?"

"I don't imagine so. You have the deeds and you have his letter confirming the title. It should be all right."

He shook his head slowly. "I don't understand, Philip. I never thought he'd agree to it so quickly. I thought he'd want to talk to Legard and make some enquiries . . . What do you think made him do it in such a hurry?"

The man on the camp bed groaned and moved. I turned and saw that he had recovered consciousness. "Maybe that's your answer," I said. "The old man knows his son only too well."

There was a movement in the entrance to the tent. It was the goat boy from the old Kasbah, Moha's son. He stood there with wide, shocked eyes, staring at his father. Then he looked at us and there was anger and fear on his small, immature features. It was best that the boy knew the truth of it and I asked his father what happened.

Apparently Moha had received a message from the Caid to attend him in his room. He had found him alone on his couch writing a letter. This he had handed to Moha with instructions that it should be delivered to us with all possible speed. He had left with it at once, but, as he came through the palmerie, he realised that he was being followed. He was past his village then and all he could do was run on in the hope of reaching our camp before his pursuers caught up with him. He had almost made it.

We patched him up as best we could and then drove him down the piste to the nearest point to his village and escorted him to his house. Afterwards we drove back to the camp and had a meal. That night I insisted on Jan moving into Ed White's tent. The American was the only one of us who had a gun. I had Julie lock herself in her own compartment and

I was just settling down in the passenger seat where I should be within easy reach of the controls, when the door was flung open. It was Jan. He was half-undressed. "What is it?" I said, for he was excited about something.

"This." He threw something into my lap.

It was a small blue book—a British passport. And when I opened it I saw that it was Wade's. "Where did you get this?" I asked him.

"It was in my suitcase."

"But——" I stared at it. "How could it be in your suitcase?"

"I think Kostos must have put it there this morning. You remember there was nobody at the camp that first time he came here. We were up in the gorge."

"But why should he return it to you like that?"

"I don't know. That's what I wanted to ask you."

It occurred to me then that Kostos, suspecting Jan of murder, was getting rid of the one piece of evidence that involved him.

I didn't tell Jan this, but long after he'd gone back to the tent I was still thinking about it.

The passenger seat made an uncomfortable bed and I slept little. Nothing happened during the night and when dawn broke and showed me the empty expanse of desert leading down to the palmerie, I transferred myself to the bunk and slept through till almost midday.

By the time I had washed and shaved and had some coffee, Jan and Ed White were coming down out of the gorge for their mid-day meal. They were talking together and laughing as though they had known each other all their lives. Julie came out of the cook tent and stood beside me, looking up the track, watching them approach. "I'm glad," she said. I glanced at her and she added, "If Ed hadn't been as nice as he is . . . It could have been horrible here if they'd hated each other. They're so completely unalike.'

"I don't know," I said. "They have things in common. They're both strangers in a new country. And there's the mine. They're both absorbed in Kasbah Foum."

"Philip!" Jan's voice reached me on the light breeze. He seemed excited. "We've found it," he shouted to me. "We've found the entrance to the mine. There's just one corner of it exposed now, but by tomorrow we'll have cleared it entirely."

" Fine," I said and sat down on the step of the bus and lit a cigarette, looking down across the sand and the dusty green of the palmerie to the Post gleaming white in a sudden shaft of sunlight. I was thinking that Legard would be back and wishing I had Jan's power of concentration, his ability to shut his mind to everything but the immediate problem.

" Jan's right," Ed said. His eyes, too, were aglint with excitement. " I guess we'll have the entrance fully exposed by tomorrow. After that, all we got to do is to clear the rock fall inside the shaft."

Their enthusiasm should have been infectious. But I felt strangely flat. Whether it was the place or just the fact that I saw the situation too clearly, I don't know, but my gaze kept turning away from the gorge down the piste towards the Post.

It was an odd sort of day, almost English. Julie had laid the table out in the open under the fly of the big tent. The air was cool, despite the periodic bursts of sunshine, and there was a lot of cloud about, especially towards the west, where it was banked up in great cotton-wool piles of cumulus. " I've been ransacking your stores," Julie said to Ed. " I opened up some of your tinned turkey. I hope you don't mind."

" Why should I?" Ed laughed. " That's what it's there for —to be eaten. Besides I owe you people a debt of gratitude anyway. If Jan hadn't turned up when he did, it would have been a week or more before I found the entrance."

Julie was standing over the table. " You boys are so interested in what you're doing, I'll bet you haven't any idea why I'm serving a turkey dinner." There was laughter in her eyes.

Jan stared at her with a puzzled frown. It was Ed who suddenly laughed out loud. " I got it," he cried. " I got it." And he thumped the table with his fist. " By God, it's Christmas Day." And he jumped to his feet and dived into his tent, coming out with a bottle of cognac. " Merry Christmas!" He was laughing as he held the bottle up.

" Do you mean it's the twenty-fifth to-day?" Jan's voice

sounded surprised, as though time had crept up on him unawares.

Julie put her hand on his shoulder. " And tomorrow will be the twenty-sixth. Your wife will be in Ouarzazate tomorrow. Remember?"

He nodded. " Tomorrow." He repeated the word as though it were something unattainable and I saw him glance towards the Post.

Julie turned to Ed. " Afterwards, I'll drive you down to the Post. There's probably some mail for you."

" Oh, don't bother." He turned to Jan. " We got more important things to talk about."

" But you must have your mail on Christmas Day," Julie said. " There'll probably be some presents——"

Something in the expression of his face stopped her. He was standing with the bottle in his hand looking round at the tent. " I've been too much of a rolling stone, I guess. And I've no family anyway." He came over to the table. " Come on, let's have a drink." And he began to pour us each a cognac.

We drank a toast and then we started to feed. Every now and then Jan glanced uneasily down the piste towards the palmerie. It was as though he were waiting for something to happen, for tomorrow—the future—to catch up with him.

About halfway through the meal he suddenly stopped eating, his eyes staring down towards Foum-Skhira. I turned in my seat and saw a little puff of sand scurrying along the edge of the palmerie. It was a French truck driving fast along the piste towards us. " Do you think Legard is back?" he asked me.

The truck drew up by the tent in a cloud of sand. The bearded orderly from the Post was at the wheel. " Bureau," he shouted, pointing urgently towards Foum-Skhira.

I got up and went over to him. " Who wants us to go to the Bureau?" I asked the Berber.

But he insisted on sticking to his limited French. " Bureau," he repeated. " Vite, vite, monsieur." It was clear that for official business he regarded French as the only language to talk to Europeans.

I asked him again who wanted us, whether Legard was back, but he remained obstinately silent, merely repeating, " Bureau, monsieur."

" Ca va," I said and went back to the others. " I think we'd better go and see what's happened," I told Jan.

He nodded and we continued our meal in silence, whilst the orderly sat stolidly waiting for us in his truck. When we had finished I got to my feet. " I'll drive you down, shall I?" Julie said. Ed sat watching us. His freckled face was puckered in a frown. Jan drew me to one side. " I'm just going to have a word with Ed," he said. " Then I'll join you. We've come to an understanding—a sort of gentleman's agreement. I want him to realise that whatever Legard's instructions about me, he's free to go ahead on his own." He turned back to the table then, and Julie and I went out to the bus.

As we climbed in, she said, " I've got something for you, Philip. I wanted to give it to you before the meal, but I couldn't because of Ed." She went through into her section of the caravan and came out carrying one of George's canvases. She turned it round so that I could see it. It was a painting of the ravine at Enfida, showing the Mission house as a small white building above the green of the olive trees. " It's just to remind you of us—to hang in your room when you build your new Mission."

I looked at her, feeling a sudden lump in my throat. I took a step forward and then stopped. " But you've so few of his paintings. I couldn't possibly——"

" Please. I want you to have it. He would have wanted it, too. I told you, he was doing a painting for you when—when it happened."

She held the canvas out to me and I took it, still staring at her. Her eyes were wide and close to tears. A pulse beat in her throat. " I don't know what to say," I murmured. " I haven't words to thank you."

" Just remember where I have asked you to hang it."

I looked down at the painting, not knowing how to tell her what I felt. And then Jan came in. Julie went past me to the driving seat and started the engine. We drove past the tent where Ed White sat alone and down the piste towards Foum-Skhira, the orderly trailing us in his truck.

The day had clouded over completely now and the wind was getting up so that all the sky beyond the palmerie was brown with sand. It was like it had been the day before. But the wind was from the other direction now and as we ran along the edge of the palmerie, we were sheltered from the drifting sand and all we experienced of the rising wind was the thrashing of the palm fronds as the soft, springy trunks bent under the thrust of it, though away to the left, between us and the mountains, the sand was on the move everywhere. We didn't catch the full force of it again until we drove past the remains of the souk and out into the open space between Ksar Foum-Skhira and the forts. And here, besides the sand, the windscreen became spotted with rain.

There was a Citröen parked outside the Bureau and we drew up beside it. "That's not Legard's car," Jan said. "He had a jeep."

"Maybe somebody gave him a lift back," I said. But I noticed as we walked past it that it wasn't an Army car. Under its white coating of dust it was black. I had a sudden sense of being trapped and glanced quickly at Jan. He was frowning and his eyes were looking around him uneasily.

The orderly hurried past us, his cloak flapping in the wind. We followed him into the passageway of the Bureau. He went straight to Legard's office, knocked and went in. I hesitated, trying to catch what was being said, but they spoke softly. And then the orderly emerged again and beckoned to us.

Julie went in first and then Jan. They both stopped and there was a look of shocked surprise on Jan's face. Then I, too, was inside the office and the sense of being trapped was overpowering.

It wasn't Legard sitting at the desk in there. It was Bilvidic. He rose as he saw Julie. "Mademoiselle Corrigan?" he asked.

Julie nodded. "We were expecting to see Capitaine Legard."

"Ah yes. But he stayed to organise his food trucks. My name is Bilvidic, of the Sûreté in Casablanca." He paused and regarded Jan, who had turned automatically towards the door as though seeking escape. But the door had closed and, standing against it, was a man who was obviously a policeman in plain clothes. He was tall, thick-set, with sallow features and a flattened nose. Bilvidic motioned Julie to a seat. " Tell me, Mademoiselle Corrigan, how long have you known this gentleman?" He indicated Jan.

" Not very long," Julie answered. " Why?"

" And all the time you have known him as Dr. Kavan?"

" Yes."

" And you agreed to drive him down here to Foum-Skhira?"

" Yes."

" Why?"

" Miss Corrigan has nothing to do with this business," I said quickly. " If you want to ask questions, please put them to me."

" Very well, monsieur. Since you wish it." Bilvidic's grey eyes stared at me frostily over their little pouches. " Why did you lie to me? Why do you say this man has flown from England? You knew that we would check."

I looked across at Jan. But he didn't say anything. He was standing with his hands clasped behind his back, his head slightly bowed ; quite still like a man considering a problem.

Bilvidic, waiting, produced his pack of American cigarettes and lit himself one. " Eh bien," he said, and sat down on the corner of the desk and inhaled the smoke from his cigarette. " Since you do not wish to talk, I will tell you what we have been doing. First we check with Paris and London. There is no Dr. Kavan leaving London Airport on the night of the 18th. There is no Dr. Kavan leaving Orly Airport in Paris for Casablanca on the morning of the 19th." He glanced at Jan. " But you were on that flight from Tangier to Casablanca and you are shown on the list of passengers as having booked through from Paris." He made little clicking noises with his tongue and his eyes switched to me. " Why did you do it, Monsieur Latham? It was stupid of you. Now you must come to Casablanca for questioning." He turned to Jan. " Alors, monsieur. Your name is Roland Tregareth Wade, yes? And you are the owner of the yacht that is wrecked near Tangier on the night of the eighteenth."

I waited for Jan to deny it, but he didn't speak. " What's the charge?" I asked and my voice sounded nervous for I thought it would be murder.

But Bilvidic said, " There is no charge. He is being held for questioning. That is all. And we have to be in Casablanca by the morning."

" By tomorrow morning?" It was over three hundred miles across the mountains. " It means driving all night. If there's no charge, surely it isn't as urgent——"

" My headquarters insist that we are there by the morning."

" But why?"

" It is nothing to do with us, monsieur. I do not wish to drive through the night any more than you do. Nor do I enjoy being here in the desert for Christmas Day," he added sharply. " It is because of the British authorities. This man——" he nodded towards Jan "——has been masquerading as Dr. Kavan. They insist that the matter of his identity is resolved immediately. If you do not like it, then you have only your Government to blame."

" But I tell you he *is* Dr. Kavan."

" Non, non." He shook his head. " It is no good, monsieur. Undoubtedly he is Wade." He tapped a sheaf of notes that lay in front of him on the desk. " You see, the body of Dr. Jan Kavan was washed up on the coast of Portugal near Cape St. Vincent four days ago."

There was a sudden silence in the room. Jan had moved forward slightly as though to ask a question. But now his eyes were fixed on the floor again. I was conscious of the tenseness of his body.

Bilvidic rose and moved behind the desk. " Tell me, monsieur, how much did Kavan tell you about himself when he applied for the post of doctor at your Mission?"

" Not very much," I said. " Just that he was a qualified doctor and that——"

" He did not tell you he was a famous scientist? Ah, well then, you would not appreciate the interest this matter has aroused. It is in all the British papers. But now that his body has been discovered his disappearance is no longer a mystery."

" If you're certain the body was from the *Gay Juliet*, then i is Wade's body." I looked across at Jan. Why the devil didn't he say something? "What makes them think it's Kavan's?" I asked Bilvidic.

"It is definite, monsieur. We have a full report at head-quarters. The state of the body, of course, was not good. But the general description is exact, and he is wearing a windbreaker purchased in Dur-ham, which is where Kavan worked. It even had the name Kavan on it and in the pocket is a watch inscribed in Czech which was given to Kavan by his wife." He shook his head. "There is absolutely no doubt, monsieur. But the British insist that we check the identity of your friend here, and also there is the matter of illegal entry into Morocco."

"Listen, monsieur," I said. "I assure you that this man is Kavan. There were two men on the boat—Kavan and Wade. It was Kavan I pulled out of the sea at Jews' Bay."

He shrugged his shoulders. "Tell me one thing," he said. "Did you ever meet this Dr. Kavan—when you engaged him to be your doctor, for instance?"

"No. It was all arranged by letter."

"Exactly. In fact, you have never seen the real Dr. Kavan. You have no idea what he looks like."

"I assure you——"

But he cut me short, leaning quickly forward. "Have you had occasion to call on this gentleman's services as a doctor?"

"No, not personally, but when——"

"So you do not know if he is a doctor or not. Have you ever heard him speak Czech?" I looked across at Kavan. "Well, have you, monsieur? Has he ever spoken one word of Czech since you have known him?"

"It's no use, Philip," Jan said quietly, speaking in English.

"Oh, don't be a fool. All you've got to do is talk to him in your own language."

"I know."

"Don't you realise what this may lead to?"

He didn't answer me, but turned away towards the window and stood there, staring out at the drab expanse of rainswept sand. He seemed suddenly to have withdrawn from the room.

I was angry and a little scared. "Are you crazy?" And when he still said nothing, I turned back to Bilvidic. "I give you my word that this man is Kavan," I told him in French.

He frowned, annoyed at my insistence. "You admit, monsieur, that he is the man you rescued from the sea at Tangier?"

I nodded.

"And he is also the man who shared your room at the Hotel Malabata, the man you put on the plane at Tangier Airport?"

"Yes."

"And yet you still insist that he is Kavan?"

"Yes."

"Very well." He shrugged his shoulders. "Then we will settle it finally." He nodded to the plain clothes man standing against the door, and he opened it and disappeared. There was a momentary silence as we waited, and then footsteps sounded on the bare concrete of the passage. There was the man's heavy tread, and also the shorter, lighter tap of a woman's heels.

We were all of us facing the door as it was thrust open and she entered. It was Karen Kavan and she stopped in the doorway, her face frozen with the shock of seeing us there. Her gaze went straight to Jan. But he made no move. He just stood there, looking at her, his face expressionless. She turned to me then. There was a desperate, bewildered look in her eyes—it was as though she was pleading for me to tell her what to do.

And then Bilvidic's voice cut the stillness of the room. "One question, Madame." He pointed to Jan. "Is this man your husband?"

I saw her hesitate. I thought she was going to tell him the truth. But then Jan turned away again towards the window and her face froze so that there was no sign of recognition in it. "No." She was looking straight at the detective, her face white and strained, just as it had been in the café by the waterfront in Tangier, and she was twisting at the gold band of her wedding ring. Her features might have been chiselled out of stone, they were so controlled.

"Have you ever seen him before?"

"Yes." Her voice was scarcely above a whisper.

"What is his name, please?"

Again the momentary hesitation. "So far as I know it is Monsieur Wade."

"Thank you." Bilvidic nodded and the plain clothes man opened the door for her. She paused a moment. Then she went quickly out, and Jan made no move to stop her going. He had turned at the sound of her footsteps, that was all, and he stood there, staring at the open doorway through which she had passed, his face empty of all expression. I couldn't stand it. "For God's sake!" I cried. "Tell them who you are. Have them bring your wife back again. Don't you see what you're doing to her?"

I had spoken in English, but he replied in French. "It is useless." His voice was harsher now, suddenly determined.

I stared at him. If he had just said one word to her. I turned to Bilvidic. "Monsieur. I want you to bring the girl back. These two——"

"Philip!" Jan's voice was suddenly angry. "This is nothing to do with you. Keep out of it. You hear?" He turned to Bilvidic and said in French: "You say I'm not under arrest?"

"No."

"I have important work to do here. We're opening up a silver mine. Since I'm not under arrest, is there any reason why I should have to come to Casablanca with you?"

Bilvidic shrugged his shoulders and smiled coldly. "If you refuse to accompany me voluntarily, then I have orders to arrest you on a charge of entering Maroc under another man's name and with another man's papers."

"I see." Jan hesitated and then turned towards the door. "Very well. The sooner we get started the better," he said and his voice sounded tense. I listened to his footsteps going slowly down the passage. He didn't pause as he went out to the waiting car.

"Monsieur?" Bilvidic was looking at me. His assistant came in and he ordered him to follow Jan. I glanced at Julie. She was looking pale and a little scared. "What do you want me to do, Philip?" Her voice trembled slightly. "There must be something I can do?"

"Do you think you could drive the bus alone as far as Ouarzazate?"

"Of course."

"Go to the Gîte d'étapes there and phone the British Consul at Rabat. Tell him the whole thing. Make him understand that this man is Dr. Kavan."

"But how do you know——" She stopped abruptly. But she had said enough. I suddenly realised that she, too, wasn't certain about Jan's identity. "I'm worried about you," she said. "Not him."

"Just do as I ask."

She nodded. "Yes, of course. And then I'll come on to Casa."

"It's too long a drive."

"I'll leave the bus at Ouarzazate and come on by C.T.M." And then she smiled. "Don't worry. I'll be there to bail you out."

Bilvidic must have understood the gist of what we had been saying. "If you are going to Ouarzazate, mademoiselle," he said, "then perhaps you will be so kind as to take Madame Kavan with you. She also has to go to Ouarzazate . . ."

I slipped out of the office and walked down the passage. I had seen Karen standing by the open door of one of the other offices. She heard me coming towards her and turned. Then she went back into the office. When I reached the door she was standing by the window, staring out at the desert. She couldn't see the car from there. She was staring out at nothing, deliberately trying to avoid me. She was quite still and her face was set hard like a mask.

I went over to her. "Why on earth did you say he was Wade?" I said. "Can't you see it doesn't matter any more? You're safe. You're both of you safe. There was no point in it." She stared at me as though I were a stranger to her. "For goodness' sake tell them the truth. I don't know what Jan's idea is, but it'll only land him in real trouble. Come back now and tell Bilvidic who Jan is."

But she made no move. "If that is what he wants, he would have spoken to me." She said it flatly and without hope.

"He doesn't understand," I said. "He doesn't know what he's doing. A body has been found in Portugal and sooner or later the police will——"

"It is my husband's body." Her voice was toneless as though she was repeating something in her sleep.

"Oh, for God's sake!" I said, and I caught hold of her and turned her towards me. "Go out to the car and talk to him. Tell Bilvidic the truth."

She stared up at me, her eyes wide with sudden hostility. I thought for a moment she was going to struggle, but then her body went slack under my hands and her eyes were blank. It was as though she had withdrawn completely inside herself. "Don't you understand?" I cried, shaking her. "If you let the police go on thinking he's Wade, he'll face a serious charge. Wade had a motive for killing your husband. For God's sake tell them who he is."

But she said nothing and her face remained quite blank. I let her go then with a feeling of hopelessness. Years of living in a Police State had taught her this one refuge—silence. But surely there was some way I could persuade her. "You're not in Czechoslovakia now," I said. "Please try and understand that I want to help you."

She remained quite still, her lips tight shut. It was as though I hadn't spoken. She was as obstinately silent as Jan had been earlier. I felt a sense of futility and exasperation. "Can't you understand how the police——" I stopped there, for footsteps sounded in the passage.

"You are ready, monsieur?" It was Bilvidic. He had paused by the open door, waiting for me. I glanced at Karen. There were tears welling from the corners of her eyes. I was shocked. I'd never seen her cry before. "Tell him now," I said.

But she turned her head away. It was a movement of denial, a final refusal. "Come, monsieur," Bilvidic said.

I turned then and went to the door. There was nothing more I could do. "Madame," Bilvidic said, speaking to Karen. "I have arranged with Mademoiselle Corrigan for you to travel with her. There is not room for more than four in the Citroën. She will take you to Ouarzazate."

"Thank you, monsieur." Her voice was no more than a whisper.

Bilvidic hesitated. Then he touched my arm and led me out to the car. "La pauvre petite," he said and his voice was softened by sudden pity for her. " She had hoped so much that her husband wasn't dead."

I didn't say anything. There was no longer any point. The two of them together had effectively convinced Bilvidic. I was glad Karen was going with Julie. It might help, and anyway it meant that she and Jan wouldn't be sitting side-by-side for hours on end in the enclosed space of the car stubbornly refusing to acknowledge each other. When we reached the Citroën Jan was already seated in the back with the second police officer. It was raining and the wind was thrashing through the palmerie. There wasn't a soul in sight. The forts, the souk, the track leading down to Ksar Foum-Skhira —it was all empty and lifeless.

" It is strange weather for this country," Bilvidic said. " I have never known such a winter." He said it for the sake of making conversation. He motioned me into the passenger seat and went round to the other side of the car. He glanced towards the mountains, his eyes shuttered against the rain. Then he shrugged his shoulders and climbed in behind the wheel.

Jan was sitting, staring straight in front of him. He didn't look at me. He didn't seem to be looking at anything. His eyes were quite blank and he seemed to have withdrawn inside himself as his wife had done and again I was conscious of this as something learned in a country that was outside of my experience, in a Police State. It was as though the line of mental contact between us had been suddenly cut.

The engine roared and we swung round, slithering on the wet sand, spraying it up behind us. I glanced back and saw Julie and Karen walking out towards the bus. I looked at Jan again. But he hadn't moved. He was staring straight ahead ; not at the piste, nor at the mountains—rather at the future that was in his mind. A jagged line of lightning stabbed the darkness of the sky above the gorge and the noise of thunder went rumbling through the hills. Then the rain came down and the mountains were blotted out.

III

A gust of rain swept over us as we went out past the Foreign Legion fort. It drummed on the bonnet and stabbed into the sand. A grey murk enveloped us. Looking back I saw the old bus turn and begin to lumber along in our wake. The rain came in gusts. Nobody in the car talked. The only sound was the click-click of the windscreen wipers. The wheels spun in a soft patch, flinging sand up in sheets like a brown spray. I wondered how the bus would behave on the sticky surface of the piste. It was a heavy vehicle for a girl to drive and the going would be bad through the mountains unless the rain eased up. "You should have let me go with Mademoiselle Corrigan," I told Bilvidic angrily. I was thinking of the section of road overhanging the gorge where the road gang had been working.

He shrugged his shoulders. "I am sorry. But it is not possible. They will be all right."

A heavier gust hit the car. The wheels slithered and spun. The rain was turning the powdered sand of the piste to a thick, red paste. The mountains were blotted out entirely. I glanced back. I could see nothing but wet sand and rain through the rear window. The bus, like the mountains, had disappeared from sight and I cursed the Frenchman under my breath. It was no weather in which to make two girls drive a heavy vehicle over mountains on a narrow, treacherous track. Once more I tried to persuade him to let me change places with Karen and keep Julie company in the bus, but he shook his head. "Non, monsieur. We must be in Casablanca by this morning."

"You'll never make it in this weather. You might just as well . . ." The full weight of the storm hit us then and the rest of the sentence was drowned in the roar of the rain. It sheeted down, bouncing on the bonnet, drumming on the roof, cutting visibility to practically nil. The wheels churned in the mud of the piste. The car slithered and swayed. And then the rain slackened again and there were the mountains right ahead of us.

We reached the harder surface at the foot of the mountains and began to climb. Away to the left I saw the watch tower above Kasbah Foum, and the debris of the ruined city gleamed blackly through the rain. Sections of the track were running with water and in places there was a soft surface of mud. The car had front wheel drive and the engine laboured as the wheels spun in the soft patches. We reached the spot where the road had been repaired and I looked down into the black gulf of the gorge. The whole place seemed to be streaming with water and, on the remote fringe of visibility, I saw the towers of Kasbah Foum looking withdrawn and hostile as they stood guard over the entrance to the gorge.

" If we could have had two more days." There was a note of bitterness in Jan's voice as he said this and he was leaning forward in his seat, peering down the mist-wrapped length of the gorge.

Then we had turned the corner under the cliff overhang and the gorge was behind us. Far below us down the mountain slope, I glimpsed the bus nosing its way across the flat valley floor. Then it was lost in a curtain of rain. " They'll never make it," I said as the Citroën's wheels spun again on a soft patch and Bilvidic fought the wheel to regain control of the car.

" Then they will stop and wait," he replied impatiently. " The girl is not a fool. She will not try it if it is not possible."

But I wasn't sure. Julie knew it was important for her to contact the British Consul. She'd go on as long as she thought there was a chance of getting through. And Karen was with her. Karen would want to go on, too. " I think we should stop," I said.

" No."

" They could go over the edge in these soft patches."

" Stop worrying, monsieur. They will be all right. They will be going up-hill. Downhill, it would be different."

" You forget that the bus has rear wheel drive. You can easily skid the back wheels . . . "

" They will be all right. I tell you," he repeated angrily. And then he was fighting the wheel again and suddenly the whole road ahead was blotted out by another storm. It swept down on us like a cloudburst, drumming on the car, beating at it as though trying to flatten it into the mud of the piste. A little spill of stones slithered in a trickle of water down the bank to our right. It had become very dark and all we could see was the rain and a few yards of mountain stretching ahead of us. The rain was solid like a million steel rods thrust at an angle into the ground. The car juddered, the engine roared. Mud spurted up past my window as the wheels clawed at the surface.

I glanced back. I didn't know what I imagined I would be able to see. I was scared for Julie. I wanted to reassure myself that the bus was all right. But I could see nothing—only the rods of rain gleaming dull like steel against the utter blackness of the storm. I turned and gripped Bilvidic's arm. " You must wait," I shouted at him. " You must wait for them."

He glanced at me quickly, his eyes sharp and alert, measuring my mood. But he drove on. It was then that I became conscious of Jan's increasing restlessness in the back. He kept twisting round and peering out through the rear window. Once, when I turned round, I met his eyes. " Do something!" he said. He looked worried. He was thinking of Karen back there with Julie in the bus.

We turned a bend that overlooked the gorge and began to climb a straight stretch of track beside a shallow rock cliff down which rainwater streamed, glistening blackly. " Do something to stop him, can't you?" he said urgently. We were coming up to the point where the piste hair-pinned round the very head of the gorge. I caught hold of Bilvidic's arm, " You must stop," I shouted at him. " If you don't stop . . . ." There was a blinding flash of lightning and the crash of thunder right overhead.

" Attention, Georges!" Bilvidic threw my hand off as he called the warning to his assistant. I heard Jan struggling in the back and then I reached for the ignition key. Bilvidic caught hold of my hand. The car swayed wildly. We were coming up to the bend now and as I flung him off and grabbed again for the key, the wheels hit a stone and suddenly the rock wall of the cliff closed in against my window. There was a crash and I was flung forward, striking my head against

the windscreen. The car stopped dead. "Imbecile!" Bilvidic
screamed at me. "Imbecile!"

I struggled back into my seat, momentarily dazed. "Look
what you have done!" Bilvidic's face was white with anger.
All the right-hand wing and the front of the bonnet were
crumpled.

"If you'd stopped when I asked you——" I said.

He gave an order to his assistant. It wasn't really necessary
for he already had Jan pinned down by his arm. The starter
whined. But nothing happened. Bilvidic kept his finger on the
button. The motor went on and on, but the engine didn't
fire. It was completely dead. The rain was torrential, water
pouring everywhere, glistening on the rocks, running in little
streams. Now that the engine was silent, we could hear it:
the hiss of the rain, the drumming of it on the tin body of the
car, the little rushing noises of water carrying small stones
down the mountain.

And then suddenly all movement ceased inside the car. The
rain had lifted slightly and we could see the bend ahead. A
brown flood of water was pouring across it, frothing white as
it plunged on down the gorge. All the water from the slopes
that formed the very beginning of the gorge was collected
in the bottom of the V to form a torrent that was slowly eating
into the piste. Already there was a jagged gap and, whilst we
sat and watched, it widened as the rocks that formed its
foundation were shifted and rolled down into the gorge. There
had been a culvert there once, but that was gone, or else the
weight of water was too great. And every minute the volume
of it and the noise of it seemed to grow.

Jan began struggling again in the back. "Let me go!" he
shouted. "Philip. We must get back to the bus."

Bilvidic gave an order to his assistant. One of the rear
doors of the car was thrust open and I saw Jan standing there
in the rain, staring back down the piste. "In all the years I
have lived in Morocco," Bilvidic said, "I have never known
a storm like this." He got out of the car then. He had given
up all hope of reaching Casablanca. The piste was hopelessly
cut. It would take several days to repair it. I scrambled across
the driving seat and got out. "I think we should get back and
stop Mademoiselle Corrigan from coming up," Bilvidic said.

I nodded. "Come on!" Jan called to me. He had already started off down the piste. Bilvidic and his assistant were searching in the car for their raincoats. I started to run after Jan, splashing through the water that ran almost ankle-deep down the rutted surface of the track. I was soaked through and steaming by the time I caught up with him. Side by side we went back down the piste, loping down with long strides, our shoes slithering and squelching through the mud and water. Neither of us spoke. We were both intent on getting back down the mountain as fast as possible. The rain died away, but we scarcely noticed it. We were hurrying down through a dead world of mist and streaming rock, and the sound of water was all about us.

The mist gradually lightened and a gleam of warmth softened the blackness of the mountain sides. A wind sprang up, the mist swirled streamers over our heads, and then abruptly it cleared and we were in bright sunshine. All the wet, glistening landscape of rock smiled at us. But above and behind us the sky was black with storm.

And then we saw the bus. It was caught on a bend far below us. The sound of its engine, revving violently, came up to us faintly on the wind, an angry sound like a buzz-saw. But we lost it almost immediately in the roar of a small avalanche of stone on the other side of the gorge.

"The sooner we're out of these mountains the better," Jan panted.

We had reached the section that had only just been repaired. All along under the cliff face little cascades of rock had built themselves up into small piles and the outer edge of the new-made piste was already sliding away into the gorge. Kasbah Foum was picked out in sunshine as we had first seen it and from far below came the steady, insistent roar of water.

We found the bus at the next bend. It had slewed half across the track, its wheels deep in mud. Karen was kicking rocks under the spinning tyres as Julie revved the engine. The engine died away as they saw us coming down the track towards them. Karen stood quite still, almost breathless, as though she couldn't believe it was true.

Jan had stopped. I glanced back over my shoulder. Bilvidic and his assistant weren't in sight yet. They knew we

couldn't escape. " Listen, Philip." Jan gripped by arm. " I'm
going back to Kasbah Foum. The whole valley is cut off now.
It may be several days . . ." He was staring down towards
Karen. " In two days we might have that shaft opened up."
" That won't do you much good," I said. " Not now."
" Who knows?" He looked up at me and he was smiling.
He seemed suddenly to have found himself. It was as though
at this moment, with his wife standing there waiting for him
to come to her, anything was possible. " I'll take Karen
with me," he said. " At least we'll have a little time together . . ." He glanced back up the track. The rain was
closing in again and visibility was lessening. Then he started
down towards the bus. " Karen!" he called. " Karen!"
She came running to meet him then. They were both
running and he was calling her name and she was answering
him, her eyes shining, her face suddenly quite beautiful. They
met in the rain and the mud there and he caught her in his
arms, hugging her to him.
And then they parted, almost guiltily, as though they hadn't
a right to be so happy. They stood there, looking at each
other a little shyly, their hands locked, talking quietly.
I turned away, looking down towards Kasbah Foum. I
could just see the top of the watch tower. The tumbled rocks
of the mountainside would be hard going. Then the rain
swept over the tower, blotting it out. " You two had better
get going," I said. " It's a goodish way to the camp."
" Oh, we'll make it before dark," Jan answered. He said
it as though he were going on a picnic, his voice was so full
of happiness.
" What do you want me to tell Bilvidic?"
" Tell him Monsieur Wade has gone down to Kasbah
Foum." He laughed, but I knew he meant it. He was looking
up at the curtain of rain that was sweeping over us and there
was an obstinate set to his mouth. Then he called to Karen
who had run back to the bus and was speaking urgently to
Julie. Jan ran down to her and took her hand, and together
they crossed the Piste and dropped on to the steep slope of
the mountainside. " Don't forget please," Karen called back
to Julie.
In a moment the two of them had disappeared into the

driving mist of rain. "What happened up there?" Julie called out to me from the cab of the bus. "Couldn't you get through?"

I climbed in beside her and was in the middle of explaining to her about the crash and the piste being washed away when a voice hailed us out of the rain. It was Bilvidic. He was panting and his thinning hair was plastered down by the rain. "Where's Wade?' he demanded, his eyes searching the roadway and the limited area of mountainside visible in the downpour. He wrenched open the door of the bus. "Where is he?" he demanded angrily.

"He's gone to Kasbah Foum," I told him.

"I don't believe you. Why should he do that? He cannot go down the mountain in this weather. Georges!" His assistant came running and he ordered him to search the vicinity. "The fool!" he exclaimed angrily. "He cannot go far in this rain. He cannot sleep on the mountain." He looked at Julie. "And where is Madame Kavan? Why is she not with you?"

I started to explain, but Julie stopped me. "She's not very well," she told him. "She's resting."

"Where?" Bilvidic demanded suspiciously and he began to climb into the bus.

"Non, non, monsieur," she said quickly. "I cannot allow you to disturb her. She is lying down on my bed in the rear compartment. She is quite exhausted, poor thing." And then she added, "It was a great shock to her to discover that that man is not her husband. She had hoped . . . You understand, monsieur?"

Bilvidic nodded, clicking his tongue sympathetically. "Of course, mademoiselle. I should have realised." He jumped back on to the piste and began to walk up it, shouting, "Wade! Wade!"

I turned to Julie then. "Why did you say that, about Karen?"

"She asked me to. Bilvidic would be suspicious if he knew she'd gone off to Kasbah Foum with a man who is supposed to be a stranger to her."

"It's madness," I said.

Julie shrugged her shoulders. " It was what she wanted, anyway."

That meant it was what Jan wanted. " So he's determined to go through with it," I said and leaned back in the seat staring at the water streaming down the piste and wondering what would be the end of it all. The storm was passing now and in a moment there was a gleam of sunshine. Bilvidic abandoned the search then. " He cannot get out of the valley unless he walks. And if he does that one of the Military Posts will soon be notified." He stood for a moment staring down towards Kasbah Foum. Then he turned abruptly " Now we will go back to the Post. I must phone the Chef de Territoire."

With him guiding me, I started to back the bus down the hill. There was no room to turn and I had to go on backing until we reached the level sand at the foot of the mountains. And there we bogged down. The piste was a sea of mud, and even the sand beside it was impassable, for it was layered with two inches of glutinous paste that filled the treads of the tyres.

Finally Bilvidic left with his assistant for the Post. It was beginning to get dark and Julie and I watched the two Frenchmen go, sitting in the bus in our stockinged feet, thankful we hadn't got to trudge three miles through that mud.

We spent the night where we were, and in the morning the sun shone out of a clear sky. The air was clean and fresh after the rain. We did the chores and then sat around waiting for the piste to dry, not talking much, just enjoying the sense of being alone. It was the first time Julie and I had been alone together and I think we both felt that these were precious, stolen hours. " You might have been in Casablanca now," Julie said once. " I loathe Casablanca."

Everybody loathes Casablanca. The thought of the place emphasised the clean beauty of this desert country. The fact that we were cut off here gave it an unreal quality. I glanced at her, seeing the smooth, clear-cut line of her features, the black hair swept back and softly curving to her shoulders. She looked as fresh and sparkling as the day. " When we've got ourselves out of the mess we're in, I'd like to come down here again and travel through this country."

She looked at me. "Like this?" And I knew she meant the two of us and the old bus. She smiled. "Yes, let's do that." And she looked away again towards the mountains.

The desert sand dried quickly and by midday we were able to travel on it. As I drove across the open space between the forts, I saw that the French truck was still parked outside the Bureau. Its bonnet was up and both the orderly and Bilvidic's assistant were working on the engine. There was a big crowd gathered by the ruins of the souk. They stared at us in silence as we drove by, a sullen, menacing group. And as we skirted Ksar Foum-Skhira along the edge of the palmerie there seemed a brooding stillness. There was nobody drawing water at the wells and, apart from a few children, nobody moved outside the walls.

"The village looks deserted," Julie said. "It's too quiet." Her voice sounded taut and strained and I remembered her reaction on our first arrival.

"They're short of food," I said. "That's all. As soon as the piste is open again and the food trucks——"

"It isn't that. Something's happened. They wouldn't all be gathered round the souk like that if it hadn't."

I thought her sudden change of mood due to the fact that in a few minutes now we should have rejoined Jan and Karen and that the reality of the situation would have closed round us again. "I'd rather be here than in Casablanca anyway," I said, trying to make a joke of it.

But all she said was, "I wish Legard were here."

The camp looked empty when we reached it. The sides of the tents had been rolled up; clothes and bedding were laid out to air in the sun. The stream was much wider now, a surging flood of rust-red water. As we got down, Karen appeared at the entrance to the cook tent and waved to us. I barely recognised her. She was wearing a pair of Ed White's khaki trousers and a bush shirt several sizes too large for her. She was barefoot, trousers rolled up almost to her knees and the waist held in by a broad leather belt. "You look like a castaway," Julie said.

She laughed. "I'm cooking. Isn't it wonderful!" She tossed back her hair, her eyes sparkling. I tried to see in her the girl who had sat waiting in José's café in Tangier. But it was impossible. She was somehow different, more alive, almost beautiful. " Where's your husband?" I asked.

" He is up in the gorge." The laughter died out of her eyes. " And please, you must not call him my husband. He has told Ed that his name is Wade. We are sleeping in different tents and we came here together only because we got separated from the rest of you coming down the mountain." She hesitated. " I have to be very careful not to give Jan away. I keep my eyes on the ground and never look at him when he is here. It is not easy after so long."

" Good God!" I said. I was appalled at the self-control required. It shocked me that he'd asked it of her. " And what about Ed?" I asked. " Is he convinced?"

" I don't know whether he is convinced or not. He doesn't say much. He thinks only of the work up there in the gorge. I don't think he cares."

" Jan's being a fool," I said. " You know about this body they've found. You realise the risk he's running?"

She nodded. " Yes. I realise."

" Have you talked to him about it?"

" Yes, we have talked."

" And you didn't try to dissuade him?"

" No." She hesitated, and then said, " Please. You must try to understand. They think Jan Kavan is dead. It is the answer to everything." She stared up into my face, her eyes pleading. " You saved his life. You got him out of Tangier. You must help him now."

" How?" I asked. " What does he want me to do?"

From the entrance to the gorge came the muffled thud of an explosion. Karen turned her head sharply, an anxious expression on her face.

" What are they doing?" Julie asked.

" Blasting. He and the American. They have cleared the entrance to the mine and they are blasting to break up the rock falls inside the shaft so that they can clear it away by hand. He warned me what they were doing, but I don't like it. When we came down last night we went too far to the right and had to come down the shoulder of the gorge. All the rock there is crumbling away and the stones kept moving under our feet."

" Have you been up into the gorge?" I asked her.

" Yes." She gave a shudder. " I don't like the place. It is cold and a little frightening. I prefer to cook." She said it with a little laugh. And then she looked at me, her face serious again. " That American—why is he so afraid?"

" Afraid of what?" I asked.

" I don't know. But last night, when we got here, he was waiting for us by his tent with a gun in his hand. He was terribly pleased to see us. I think he's frightened to be here by himself."

" I'm not surprised," Julie said. " I would be myself."

They were both of them looking up towards the gorge. Then Karen began to collect the blankets and fold them. Julie went to help her and I walked up the track into the gorge. Water was pouring in a cascade over the lip of the lake. It was a violent brick red. The whole gorge was full of the sound of water seeping down from above and it was cold and dank despite the noonday heat of the sun. The bull-dozers stood idle. There was no sign of Jan or Ed White. But the rubble had been cleared from the base of the cliff to expose a round opening from which a cloud of rock dust drifted. It was like the entrance to a cave. " Jan!" I shouted. " Jan!" There was no answer, but back from the wall of the gorge opposite came the echo—*Jan! Jan!*

I walked towards the entrance to the mine. A little pile of clothing lay beside a plain deal box which was marked in red —EXPLOSIVES: Danger—Handle with Care. The top of it had been ripped off to expose cartridges of dynamite with slow-match fuses. The dust was thick by the shaft entrance, hanging like an iridescent cloud where the sunlight struck through from above. There was the sound of a stone shifting and Ed White appeared, staggering under the weight of a rock he was carrying. " Oh, it's you, Latham." He dropped the rock on to a pile they had made just outside the entrance. " I thought I heard somebody call." He glanced up at the cliff top on the far side of the gorge, and then he gave a quick, nervous hitch to his trousers and came over. He was stripped to the waist and the dust had caked on the sweat of his body in a white film. He had his gun fastened to his belt. " Well, we've made some progress since yesterday. We've cleared the entrance and we're working on the rock falls now. But we need some local labour. Wade thought you might help there. You know the language."

"He's told you then?" I asked tentatively.

"About his name? Yeah, he told me."

"It must have come as a bit of a shock to you."

He looked at me for a moment and then said, "Between you and me I don't care what he calls himself. All I'm interested in is getting through those falls before my dough runs out. This is a new country and what a man was before he came out here doesn't interest me. All I know is I like the guy and we get on together. Have done from the first. Which was more than I expected from the tone of his letters," he added. And then he hitched up his belt and turned away towards the entrance to the shaft.

At that moment Jan emerged, blinking in the sunlight. "Philip!" He came quickly forward. He, too, was stripped to the waist and the dust was white on his thick, hairy body. "I'm so glad you've come. We need your help." He stopped and his voice was suddenly nervous. "Bilvidic isn't down at the camp, is he?"

"No."

"That's all right." It was almost a sigh of relief. "Look! We need men up here. There's tons of rock to be hauled. We need twenty men at least." The eagerness was back in his voice again. "I thought if you could go down and have a word with Moha, maybe we could hire men from his village." He seemed to have no thought in his mind except the opening up of the shaft. "Come here. I want to show you something." He switched on the big torch he had slung on his belt and dived back into the shaft.

"What is it?" I asked Ed, for Jan's voice had been excited.

"He's found traces of silver," he said and he pushed me towards the shaft entrance. "You go ahead. I'll follow." I climbed the piled-up debris and ducked into the entrance to the shaft. It was dark inside and the air was thick with dust. The yellow light of Jan's torch flashed ahead. We went in about forty feet and then we were crawling over piles of broken rock. "You see," Jan said. "The roof collapsed. We're having to blast and clear by hand. Now. Look here."

He had stopped and was directing the beam of his torch into a cavity half blocked by the fallen roof. "We've just cleared this." He gripped my arm and thrust me forward.

The cavity seemed to be a long, narrow fissure in the rock. I couldn't see it very well. Only a small part of it was so far exposed. But it ran well back, for the beam of the torch failed to reach the end of it. "What is it?" I asked.

"Part of the mine," Jan said. "It's where a seam of ore has been removed."

"How do you know?"

He shifted the beam of the torch to the sides of the fissures. "See the marks of their tools. And look at this." He pulled a piece of crumbled rock from his pocket. "That's polybasite— a complex ore, but one where the extraction of the silver is a simple, quite primitive process. Probably that's what Marcel found."

I turned to Ed. "Do you agree with him?"

"I wouldn't know," he said. "But if he says so, then I guess he's right. He's like a walking encyclopaedia. All I know is that this mine must date way back. It wasn't being worked five hundred years ago when the landslide sealed this shaft." He started to back out again. "Come on. The sooner we have those natives on the job, the better. I want to get through this fall."

We scrambled back over the debris and then we were out in the open again, blinking our eyes in the bright sunlight. Once more I saw Ed's gaze go straight to the cliff top on the far side of the gorge. "Look at him—the bastard!" he cried, and his voice was pitched a shade higher than normal.

"What is it?" I asked, shading my eyes.

"Can't you see him? Look!" He took my arm and pointed. "I noticed him there for the first time yesterday. He was sitting there all day and again today—just sitting there, watching us."

I saw him then, a small, turbaned figure, sitting cross-legged and motionless in a natural niche right at the top of the cliff. "Who is he?" I asked.

"How the hell should I know? They change the guard about midday and a new guy takes over. They never move.

They just sit there, watching us." He turned away to get his clothes. " It gives me the creeps."

I looked at Jan. " Ali?"

" I imagine so." He hesitated and then drew me aside. " Did Karen tell you?"

" About the name? Yes, she told me. Look, Jan," I said. " This is crazy. You'll never get away with it."

He gave me a quick, sidelong glance. " All right, it's crazy," he said. " But I don't have to convince anybody. They're convinced already."

" And what about the British authorities?" I asked.

But he smiled and shook his head. " Their only worry would be if they discovered I was alive. So long as I'm dead they don't have to try and explain the disappearance of another scientist." He looked up at me anxiously. " It's up to you now, Philip." And then he added with sudden violence, " Don't you see? This is the perfect solution."

I shook my head. He seemed utterly blind to the real problem. " You seem to forget that a body has been washed up."

" Well, it was an accident, wasn't it?" And then he added quickly, " Whether I'm Wade or Kavan, I've still got to explain that."

" I suppose so," I said. " But you've entered Morocco illegally."

He nodded, but he didn't seem worried about it. " I think I can make them understand. If Kostos keeps his mouth shut, I know I can. And if we could prove this mine . . ." He glanced towards Ed White who was pulling on his clothes. He was frowning again. " Did Karen tell you what happened when we arrived at the camp last night? Ed met us with that German Luger of his in his hand. He seemed scared stiff. He was all packed up, too, ready to clear out."

" Why? Because Ali has men watching him?"

Jan nodded. " That and something that happened yesterday afternoon. He had a visit from the Caïd's younger son—the man who made tea for us when we visited the kasbah that night. He rode out on a white mule to give Ed a message from his father."

" Well, what was the message?" I asked.

" The man only spoke a few words of French. But he kept pointing to the Post——"

Ed White's shadow fell between us. " I got the idea anyway," he said. " I was to get out, and quick."

" Why?" I asked.

" How the hell do I know why? Could be that the food trucks haven't arrived and the people are getting sore. Could be that your friend Ali is just trying to scare me. I don't know. But I can tell you this; I was plenty scared last night." His gaze swung again to the watcher on the cliff. " Those three Ay-rabs I had working for me were paid good dough. They wouldn't have quit for nothing." He shook his head angrily, buttoning up his bush shirt. " I suppose Miss Corrigan is down at the camp now?"

" Yes."

" At least those two girls ought to go down to the Post. I don't mind staying on here so long as you guys are with me. But they should be down at the Post. They'd be safe there."

His attitude made me feel uneasy. " What are you expecting to happen?" I demanded.

He pushed his fingers up through his hair. " If I knew that, I wouldn't be so Goddamned jittery."

Jan had scrambled down the rock tip to the water to wash the dust off his body. He was out of sight and for a moment Ed and I were alone. There was something I had to find out and now was the time to do it. If Jan had really convinced Ed, then there was just a chance he could get away with it. I hesitated, wondering how to put it. " Sooner or later," I said, " the police will want a statement from you."

" From me? What about?"

" About him," I said, nodding towards Jan.

" Well, they won't get much out of me." He seemed to consider the matter. " The only intelligent comment I could make is that he doesn't seem British the way you do. And he talks differently." He said it slowly, as though it were something that had been on his mind for a long time.

" He's Cornish," I said, remembering the details of Wade's passport.

" Cornish? Oh, you mean dialect. And then he's knocked

around a bit. I guess that would make him different." He nodded to himself, frowning slightly. And then he shrugged his shoulders. " Well, Mrs. Kavan should know. I feel sorry for that girl. When she came down here she must have been thinking there was a chance that her husband was alive. Instead, it's a stranger, impersonating him. That's not very nice, is it?" He had been staring down at his boots, but now he looked up at me. " Wasn't Kavan going to act as doctor at your Mission?"

" Yes," I said.

He nodded, staring at me, and then turned away. " What I've seen of the people here, they could have used a doctor." Jan climbed up from the water and he called to him: " Come on. Let's get some food."

Jan picked up his clothes and joined us. " Pity about that shaft," he said, glancing back over his shoulder. " Fortunately Ed had that dynamite and he knows how to use it. But even so, it may take several days to break through the falls."

I knew he was thinking about Bilvidic and I asked him how long he thought he'd be allowed to stay up here. " I don't know," he said. " I hope he'll leave us here until the piste is open. He knows I'm here. That orderly from the Post rode out to the camp on a mule this morning to check that. And he knows I can't get out—not unless I walk, and the Military would soon be informed if I tried to do that." His eyes lifted to the slope of the mountain above us. It was very steep and about five hundred feet up there was a sudden cliff face, not high, but sheer and crumbling. It shone red in the sunlight. " I didn't like it when I first saw it," he muttered. " But now that we're blasting . . ." He shook his head and turned and started to walk down the track towards the camp.

" It's the Ay-rabs that worry me," Ed said. " Legard's away and with the piste cut, God knows when the food trucks will get through. And now there's this discolouration of the water."

We had reached the entrance of the gorge and in the sunlight the water pouring down the stream-bed was almost the colour of blood against the yellow of the sand. " How far does the discolouration extend?" I asked.

"Right down into the palmerie," Jan said over his shoulder. "There was quite a rush of water coming out of the gorge last night."

None of us spoke after that and we walked down to the camp in silence. We were thinking about the water and the watcher on the cliff top. For the moment I had forgotten about Jan's personal problems. But it was impossible to forget about them once we had reached the camp, for Karen was there to remind me. She ignored Jan completely. He might not have been there, and not by a single glance, even when Ed's back was turned, did she betray the fact that she was conscious of him. Her self-control was so rigid that I began to understand how it must have been for her in Czechoslovakia.

Lunch was laid out in the open under the fly of the big tent as it had been on Christmas Day. But the atmosphere was very different. There was a sense of strain. As though conscious that she was partly responsible, Karen announced at the end of the meal that she had arranged for Julie to take her down to the Post. "It will be better if I go." She said it to Ed, but it was directed at Jan. He stared at her for a moment and then turned abruptly away.

"What about you?" I asked Julie.

"I'll drop Karen and then bring the bus back here."

"No, don't do that," I said. "Stay down at the Post. It'd be safer."

"My view is we should all go down to the Post," Ed announced. "When Legard gets back——"

"No," Jan said, almost violently. "I'm damned if I'll leave here now. A day's work might see that shaft opened up. And if it is a workable mine . . ." He hunched his shoulders, staring up towards the gorge. He was thinking that it would give him a stake in the country. That was the thought that was driving him.

"Well, of course, I see your point," Ed said. "I'm pretty interested myself to know whether there's still silver to be got out of it. But that isn't the reason I'm here, as you know. The way I see it——"

"Then what is the reason?" Jan demanded.

"Exactly what I told you." He sounded surprised. "I never knew there was a chance of finding silver——" He checked himself. He was staring at Jan with a puzzled frown. "Didn't you bother to read my letters?"

Jan's eyes widened slightly with the shock of realising that he had nearly given himself away. It was Karen who covered up for him. "But I thought you were a prospector, Ed? When we stopped at Agdz on the way down I heard Capitaine Legard talking about you to Monsieur Bilvidic. He said you had been granted a mining concession."

"That's right." Ed was grinning to himself like a boy. "It seemed the smart thing to say. I didn't want people asking a lot of questions."

"But if you're not a prospector," Julie said, "what are you?"

"An archaeologist."

"But why ever didn't you tell us?"

He shrugged his shoulders, still grinning. "Nobody bothered to ask me." And then he turned to Jan. "Anyway, you knew. I explained it all in that second letter. Or didn't you get it?"

"But I thought you were a construction engineer," Karen cut in. "You were telling me last night——"

"Sure. That's right. I am a construction engineer. But I got a bee in my bonnet about this place Kasbah Foum. Look," he said, facing the two girls. "Maybe I'd better explain. Archaeology is a sort of a hobby I picked up in college. Old cities and things; they fascinated me. Well, a friend of my father's was a collector of books and he used to let me browse around in his library when I was a kid. There was an old manuscript there that particularly intrigued me; it was the diary of an Englishman who had turned Muslim and lived in North Africa as an Arab trader in the early fifteen hundreds. It was an incredible story—of wars and love-making and long camel treks through the desert. In it, he described a great stone city built at the entrance to a gorge down here south of the Atlas. He had traded from that city for several years and he knew it well. And this is what interested me. He described a shaft or tunnel running into the cliff face at the entrance to the gorge. There were rooms cut back into the rock from the sides of this tunnel and these had been used partly as the city treasury and partly

as an arsenal. He went to Mecca and on to Arabia, and some
years later he came back to the same city. It had been sacked
and was partly in ruins. And a great landslide had poured
down the mountains, completely covering the entrance to the
tunnel." He glanced round at us. "Well, two years back I
got this job at Sidi Slimane air base and I came down here—
just out of curiosity. And there were the ruins of the city
and there was the slide he'd described." He had turned his
head so that he could see the entrance to the gorge. "I just
had to find out whether that shaft did exist and, if so, what
was in it."

"But it's fascinating," Julie said. "You might find all sorts
of treasures there."

"Maybe," Ed said. "On the other hand, the people who
sacked the city may have looted the treasury. But whatever
I find, when it's opened up, I shall be the first man to set foot
in there for almost five centuries. That's pretty exciting. At
least to me." He turned and glanced at Jan. "That's why my
angle on this is different from yours. A few days one way or
the other won't make any difference to me. But if I open it
up and there's trouble—well, I don't want a lot of ignorant
natives getting in there and maybe busting up stuff that's
priceless. There could be things in there dating back to . . ."
He laughed. "Oh, I don't know—to the first nomadic
infiltration from the desert."

"Not if it were originally the shaft of a silver mine," Jan
said.

"No. That's right, I guess."

A silence settled on the table. I was thinking how strange
it was that these two—the Czech refugee and the American
construction engineer—should be working together to open up
this shaft for two such different reasons.

Jan got suddenly to his feet. "You do what you like," he
said to Ed. "But I'm going straight on clearing the debris
out." He turned to me. "Will you go down and see Moha
about labour for me, Philip?"

"Now wait a minute." Ed, too, had risen. "Get this
straight, Wade. Our interests don't conflict. But mine come
first. Okay?" He was much taller than Jan and he had moved
towards him so that he towered over him. "If I decide that we

wait until Legard returns and things have settled down——"

"All right," Jan said. He was looking up at Ed and then his eyes shifted towards the gorge. "I understand your point. But suppose we have another rainstorm like we did last night? It could bring the whole mountainside down and cover the entrance again."

"Yeah. It could."

"The mine won't run away any more than your antiques will, if they're there. But if the mountain comes down . . ." He stared up at Ed and then said, "I think we should push straight on with opening up the shaft."

Ed stood there, considering it. His gaze, too, had shifted to the gorge. In the end he nodded. "Okay," he agreed. "Maybe you're right."

"I'll go and see Moha," I said. "How many men do you want?"

"As many as he can let us have," Ed answered. "Twenty at least."

"And how much are you prepared to pay them?"

"Whatever he asks, within reason. I leave that to you."

I had Julie drive me down in the bus to the point on the piste nearest the village, and then I entered the palmerie and crossed the irrigation ditch by the bridge of palm logs. Even here the water was strangely red, instead of its normal muddy colour. I knocked at the wooden door of the chief's house and was admitted by one of his sons and taken to an upper room. Moha lay on a bed of cushions and rugs. There was little light in the room and it was very cold. The lines on his face were more deeply etched, the gash on his forehead a brown scab of dried blood. His wound, he said, did not worry him except that he could not sit and if he walked it started to bleed again. He lay there, watching me, and I had the feeling that I wasn't welcome.

Briefly I explained the purpose of my visit. He didn't answer for a moment, but just lay there, staring at me. At length he said, "The people are angry, sidi. They will not come to work for the man of machines who has destroyed the water." He raised himself up on one elbow. "My father and his father and his father's father have lived here in this place. In all the time we have been here, the water has never been like it is now. The people are afraid to drink it. They are afraid that their trees will be finally destroyed."

I tried to explain to him that it was only mineral discolouration, that it would soon pass, but he shook his head and murmured " *Insh'Allah*." His people might need money, but nothing I could say would make him send them up to work at the mine. I offered them as much as five hundred francs a day—an unheard of figure—but he only shook his head. " The people are angry. They will not come."

In the end I left him and walked back to the bus. I didn't tell Julie what he had said. It had scared me badly, for in the south here water was the same as life, and, if they thought the water had been poisoned, anything could happen.

As we drove up to the camp we passed several villagers, sitting on the banks of the stream bed. They stared at us as we went by, their tough, lined faces expressionless, their eyes glinting in the sunlight. " Where did they come from?" I asked her. " They weren't there when we drove down."

" They came out of the palmerie. There are some more over there." She nodded to the open country between ourselves and the mountains. There were about twenty or thirty there, sitting motionless as stones in the hot sun.

" Which direction did they come from?" I asked.

" I didn't see. They were just suddenly there."

Karen was alone at the camp when we drew up. " Where are the others?" I asked her. " Up at the gorge?"

She nodded and I walked up the track. The sun's light was already slanting and the gorge was black in shadow. I had to go into the shaft to find them. There, in the light of the torches and amongst the debris of the rock fall, I told Ed what Moha had said. " Until this matter of the water is cleared up," I said, " you won't get any of them to come and work for you. I think we should get down to the Post." And I explained about the group of villagers who were waiting within sight of the camp. " I don't like it," I said. " It may be just curiosity, but I had a feeling they were expecting something."

We stood there in the torchlit darkness arguing for some time. Jan was angry. Time was running out for him and he desperately wanted to get through that rock fall, to know what was on the other side. But time meant nothing to Ed and he was all for packing up the camp and getting down to the Post. " If we can't get labour, then we can't and that's that. The only thing for us to do is go down to the Post and wait for Legard to return. He'll have a talk with the Caid and then maybe we'll get somewhere."

We went out into the daylight and they washed and put on their clothes. Jan was in a sullen mood. When he was dressed, he walked over to the entrance to the shaft and stood there looking at it. I didn't hear what he said, but I guessed he was cursing that fall of rock. Twenty men could probably have cleared it in a couple of days. As it was, he'd have to leave it. He turned suddenly and stared at me. " If only we could have got down here two or three days earlier." He said it as though it were my fault that we hadn't.

" Come on," Ed said. " There's no good beefing about it."

" What about the bull-dozers?" I asked him.

" We'll pile all the gear and that box of explosives on them and take them with us. I'm not leaving them to be fooled around with by curious villagers. Come on. Give me a hand and let's get started. It'll be dark before we get down to the Post, anyway."

We had just started to collect the tools when we heard the sound of footsteps in the entrance to the gorge. We stopped, all three of us, for they were a man's step, but light, as though he had sandals on his feet.

But it wasn't a Berber. It was Kostos. He saw us and jerked himself into a shambling run. His clothes were white with dust and his shoes were cracked and broken, the thin soles breaking away from the uppers. He was shabby and tired and frightened. " Jeez!" Ed exclaimed. " He looks like a piece of white trash."

" Lat'm! Lat'm!" Kostos came to a halt and his eyes watched our faces nervously. " I must stay 'ere. I must stay with you." He was out of breath and his eyes seemed to have sunk back into the dark sockets as though he hadn't slept for a long time. He was unshaven and the blue stubble of his chin emphasised the pallor of his face. A drop of sweat ran down the bridge of his sharp nose and hung on the tip.

"What's the trouble?" I said. "Why do you suddenly prefer our company to Ali's?"

His body shivered. It may have been the coldness of the gorge, for his clothes were all damp with sweat. But he had a scared look. "Caid Hassan is dead," he blurted out. "Ali is in control of Foum-Skhira."

"Hassan dead!" I exclaimed. "But we saw him only . . . How did it happen?"

"I don't know. I am not there, you see." He said it quickly as though it were something carefully rehearsed that he had to be sure of saying. "I am in the village, in a pig-sty of a house. It happens suddenly. That's all I know."

"When?"

"Last night."

I glanced at Jan. His face was hard. He was thinking of the old man who had found it necessary to send him the confirmation of his title to this place secretly because he was afraid of his son. He looked as though he could kill Kostos. "We don't want you here," he said angrily. "Why don't you go to the Post if you're scared?"

"Because at the Post are two men from the Sûreté. I don't like to be so close to the Sûreté." Kostos looked at me almost pleadingly. "You understand, eh, Lat'am?" And then his tone changed to truculence as he said, "Well, I am 'ere now. So what you do? It is a public place, this gorge. You cannot throw me out of it." He looked at Ed and his small, black eyes fastened on the holster at his belt. "I see you 'ave guns. That is good. You will give me a gun, eh? I am very good shot with a pistol."

Ed laughed. It was a hard, tense laugh. "What do you think we are—an arsenal?" He turned and looked at me. "Is this guy nuts or something?" He was trying to shrug the whole thing off, but the tremor of his voice betrayed him.

Kostos noticed it, too. He crossed over to Ed and caught hold of his arm. "Please now. You give me a gun. You give me a gun and I stay here and——"

"Are you crazy?" Ed threw his hand off angrily. "We haven't got any guns. This——" He tapped the Luger at his waist. "This is the only gun in the place."

"The only gun!" Kostos stared at him, and then his eyes darted quickly round at Jan and myself. "But you have women to protect. You must have guns. You couldn't be such fools . . ." His voice died away as he saw from our eyes that it was the truth. "Oh, Santo Dios!" he cried, reverting to Tangier Spanish, and he wiped his brow on a filthy handkerchief, his eyes darting round the sides of the gorge as though looking for a way out.

Jan moved slowly forward then. "What's happened to make you so scared?"

"Nothing. Nothing." Kostos backed away from him. "You keep away from me. You keep away."

"What about that passport?"

"I never had your passport."

"Don't lie. Why did you slip it into my suitcase when you came up here that first morning?"

"All right. I tell you. Because I want no part of any killing. The passport is too dangerous."

"And now you come running up here." Jan was still walking towards him. "Let's have the truth now. You're scared of something. You've seen something or done something that has frightened you out of your wits. What is it?" He lunged forward and caught Kostos by the arm. "Why have you abandoned Ali? What's he done that's frightened you?" His grip tightened on the Greek's arm and he began to twist it back. "Come on now. Let's have the truth."

"Look out!" I said. "He may have a knife." I had seen the Greek's other hand slide under his jacket.

Jan flung the man away from him and turned angrily back towards us. He pushed his hand up through his hair. "I can't believe it," he said. "The old man dead. He was ill, I know, but . . ." He turned again and stared at Kostos, who was standing there, breathing heavily, his eyes watching us uncertainly. "He knows something. I'd like to beat the truth out of the swine."

"I think you'd better go down to the Post," I said to Kostos.

"No. I am staying here."

"Then suppose you tell us——"

"Philip!" It was Julie's voice and it rang shrilly through the gorge. "Philip!" There was a note of panic in it and I started to run, the others close behind me.

Julie stopped as she came round the base of the slide and saw us. Karen was with her and they stood there, panting. "What is it?" I cried. "What's happened?"

"I think it's Ali," she panted. "There's a whole crowd of them coming up out of the palmerie. Some of them are on mules. They're heading straight for the camp."

"Julie saw them first," Karen said. "I was in the tent. She called to me and then we began to run, up here."

"Okay," Ed said. "Let's go and see what it's all about."

We didn't have to go far. From the entrance of the gorge we could see them swarming over the camp and round the bus. "Goddammit!" Ed cried. "They're looting the place." He had unbuttoned the holster of his pistol and was pulling it out.

"Better put that away," I said, "till we find out what they want."

"Do you think I'm going to stand by and see my whole outfit vanish under my nose?"

I tightened my grip on his arm. "How many rounds have you got on you?"

He stared at me. "Only what's in the magazine," he said sullenly and began cursing under his breath.

Just twelve rounds and there were a hundred men milling around the camp. "Then I think you'd better regard that gun as being for purposes of bluff only."

He nodded sullenly, staring at the scene with hard, angry eyes. A murmur of sound came up from the camp. They were like wasps round a jam pot. They were looting the food and all the time a man on a white mule was shouting at them. It was Ali and he was trying to get them to follow him up towards the gorge. The crowd increased steadily. It was being joined by little groups of men coming in from the desert and up out of the palmerie. A wisp of smoke rose in a blue spiral from the cook tent. It drifted lazily up into the still air and then died away as the tent disintegrated. The other tents were on fire now and then the bus was set alight. We could hear the crackle and the roar of the flames above the steady murmur of the mob.

"The bastards!" Ed cried. "The bastards!" His eyes glistened with tears of rage and frustration. I kept a tight hold of his arm. The situation was explosive enough.

A hand touched my sleeve. It was Julie. She was staring at the bus which was now well alight and I knew she was thinking of her brother. It was her last link with him, apart from a few paintings scattered up and down the world. "Why are they doing it?" she whispered. "Why are they doing it?"

"The Caid is dead," I said. "And they think the water is poisoned." I turned and glanced back at the gorge. The sides were too steep to climb. We should have to retreat back into it until we could climb out. "Come on," I said to the others. "We'd better get started. I don't think they will attack us."

Jan nodded. "Yes. We'd better go." The mob was breaking away from the tents now and starting up towards us, packing close round their leader on his white mule. They weren't shouting. They were, in fact, quite silent, so that we could hear the sound of the flames. Their silence was full of menace. "Come on," Jan said, and we went back hurriedly into the gorge.

But when he came to the bull-dozers, Ed stopped. He had his gun out now. "I'm staying here," he said. He looked very young and a little frightened. But his tone was obstinate.

"You'll only get hurt," I said. "Come on now. There are the girls to think of."

"Okay," he said. "You go back with the girls. But I'm staying here."

"Don't be a fool," Jan said.

Ed stared at him sullenly. "These machines represent all the cash I got in the world. If you think I'm going to run off and let these bastards . . . Latham. Will you stay here with me? I don't speak their language. But if you were here, maybe we could——"

"No," Julie said. "Please, Philip. Don't stay."

But Ed caught hold of my arm. "You're not afraid to face them, are you? I've got a gun. I can hold them off. If you'll only talk to them, explain to them."

" All right," I said, and I turned to Jan and told him to get the girls back up the gorge.

" Do you rate a couple of bull-dozers higher than your own life, or Philip's?" Julie demanded. " Please, Philip. Let's get out of here."

" It's all right," I said. " You go on. I'll just have a word with Ali and see what I can do. They won't harm us."

She turned and faced Ed. " Damn you!" she cried. " Damn you and your bloody bull-dozers." She was crying with anger.

" I'm sorry, Miss Corrigan," Ed said, his voice quiet and restrained. " I appreciate how you feel. But those bloody bull-dozers cost me eighteen months' work. No man likes to pass up eighteen months of his life without a fight." He looked at me. " You do what you think best, Latham."

" I'll stay, for the moment," I said, and told Jan to take Karen and Julie back up the gorge. Julie hesitated, her jaw set, though her face was white and frightened. " Please," I said. " I'll be with you in a few minutes."

I turned to face the mob that was now coming into the gorge round the base of the slide. As I did so, I caught sight of Kostos. He was beside the bull-dozer nearest the mine entrance and he was bending down, stuffing something into the pockets of his jacket. " Kostos!" I shouted. " Get back with the others." And as he didn't move, I shouted, " What are you doing? Get back with the others."

He straightened up then and his pale, haggard face was twisted in an evil, frightened grin. He held out his hand so that I could see what he had been picking up. He held a stick of dynamite. " One gun is not enough," he said. " I like to be certain." And he bit the slow-match of the cartridge off short.

" Kostos!" Ali's voice rang through the gorge. He had halted his white mule just in sight of us, sitting it very still. He was wearing a turban now like his followers and it gave him height, so that he looked a commanding figure with his aquiline face and his blazing eyes. His exile hadn't made him a stranger to the land that had produced him. He belonged, and sitting there, with the sides of the gorge reared up on either side of him, he looked like some virile leader out of the Old

Testament. The tribesmen were bunched together behind him. "So. This is where you are hiding. Come here! At once! You hear me?" He had spoken in French, but Kostos didn't move. And when he saw that the Greek wasn't going to come, he turned and gave an order in Berber to the men who were mounted on mules close behind him. They thumped the flanks of their mounts with their bare heels and came riding forward at a trot, their voluminous clothes billowing out behind them.

I shouted at Kostos to come down and join us, for there was panic in his face. He was city bred with no sense of this country or these people, and I was afraid he'd light the fuse of that stick of dynamite and fling it without thought for the consequences. If he did, the Berbers would attack. There would be no holding them. But instead, he broke and ran, flinging himself at the steep slopes where the fig trees grew.

"Don't shoot," I warned Ed. "For God's sake don't shoot." He had the gun in his hand and it was aimed at the men who were riding their mules towards us. But he didn't shoot and they swept past us, headed towards Kostos.

The mob was now packed tight in the entrance of the gorge and Ali was coming forward again, his mule stepping daintily on the stones of the track. The men of Foum-Skhira closed up behind him, shoulder to shoulder like a herd of goats. They were mostly young men and they were silent as though awed by the place and by what they were doing. I called on them to halt and began to speak to them in their own tongue, telling them that what they were doing was a wicked thing, that the wrath of Allah would fall upon themselves and their families if they did harm to anyone. I started to explain that there was nothing wrong with the water, telling them that if they wished I would drink it myself. And all the time I didn't dare look round to see how far up the gorge Julie and the others had got, though I was conscious of the movement of rocks and the scrape of feet as Kostos was hounded up the slopes.

Ali's voice suddenly cut across mine. "Monsieur. These people are angry. They have no food and the water is bad. This place belongs to Foum-Skhira and they believe there is

great wealth here that will save them from starvation. Leave
this place and you will not be hurt. But if you stay, I cannot
be sure what my people will do."

That mention of " my people " reminded me of the Caid's
death and I called out to them again in Berber: " Men of
Foum-Skhira! Two nights ago I saw Caid Hassan. Because
of this man "—I pointed to Ali—" he was not permitted to say
what he wished. He had to send a secret messenger. That
messenger was set upon by the men of Ali. They tried to
kill him. Now Caid Hassan is dead and I must tell you . . . ."

" Silence! " Ali screamed at me in French. " Silence! " And
then he was shouting at his followers, screaming at them in a
frenzy, inciting them to attack. And they answered him with
a low murmur like an animal that is being roused to fury.

" We'd better get out of here," I cried. But Ed didn't need
to be told what that low mob growl meant. " I guess it's no
good," he said, and his voice was resigned.

And as we backed, so the mob advanced, and the sound
that emanated from their throats filled the gorge like the growl
of a monster. Then, suddenly, they rushed forward. We
turned and ran for it.

The others were already well up the side of the gorge on a
shelf of rock that slanted up from the bend. And, as I ran, I
glimped Kostos, cut off from the rest of the party by his
pursuers and being forced out along the cliff top above the
entrance to the mine.

Ed, just ahead of me, turned and looked over his shoulder.
And then he stopped. " It's all right," he said as I halted beside
him. " They're not following us." I turned and stared back.
The gorge was full of weird howls of triumph and blood lust.
But it wasn't directed against us. All their warlike instincts
were concentrated on the two bull-dozers. " Goddam the
bastards! " Ed breathed. The men of Foum-Skhira were
clustered round the machines like ants. They shouted and
yelled and as though by magic the bull-dozers moved. They
trundled them down across the tight-packed rocks of the
dumping ground and toppled them into the water. There was
a splash and then the waters closed over them and the place
was suddenly as God had made it again.

And then they moved towards the entrance to the mine shaft. Ali was already there. He had got off his mule and was standing in front of the entrance. My eye travelled upwards and I saw Kostos balanced precariously on the rocks of the slide almost directly above him. He must have dislodged a stone, for Ali was looking up now. Whether the two men could see each other I don't know. I think it likely, for Kostos wasn't looking at the Berbers creeping over the rocks towards him. He held a stick of dynamite and he was looking down at Ali and the scene below him.

A pinpoint flicker of flame showed for an instant in his hand.

My eyes went involuntarily upwards. Not four hundred feet above, the crumbling cliff, that Jan had pointed out to me, towered above him. The flicker of flame was replaced by a wisp of smoke. I wanted to shout, to tell him not to do it. The men were packed tight below him. It was murder. Stupid, unnecessary, pointless murder. His arm swung back and the wisp of smoke curved through the air. From where we were Kostos was no bigger than a puppet and the wisp of smoke curving downwards into the close-packed mob looked as harmless as a feather floating through the air.

It fell into the centre of the crowd which mushroomed out away from it with an instinctive sense of fear. We could see it sizzling away on the ground now, and I felt a sudden relief. Kostos had left too long a fuse. It would injure nobody. But then Ed gripped my arm. "The dynamite!" he whispered hoarsely. "Do you see it? That box."

It was a small, square patch of yellow close beside the sputtering wisp of smoke. I saw it for a second, and then there was a flash. It was followed instantly by a great, roaring burst of flame. The whole area of beaten rock on which the mob stood seemed lifted skywards. Rocks were flung up and men flattened to the ground. I saw Ali thrown backwards into the mouth of the shaft. And whilst the rocks were still rising in the air, the sound of that explosion hit us and the blast of it rocked us on our feet. It was an ear-shattering, indescribable crash in that confined space. And the noise went on, hammering at the cliff faces, rolling upwards over the mountain slopes, and drumming back at us in a stupendous cacophony of sound, whilst the rocks stopped heaving upwards and began to fall back to the ground.

The sound of the explosion began to diminish as the echoes reverberated back from farther and farther away. And just as a deep, mutilated silence seemed to settle on the gorge, there was a rumble like thunder out of the sky. I looked up. And then Ed's hand clutched my arm and I knew that he'd seen it, too. The sky was blue. There wasn't a cloud to mar the pastel shades of sunset. But against that blue the cliff face where Kostos stood was slowly, lazily toppling outwards. It was catching the reddening rays of the sun so that the rock glowed. It was like something in Technicolor, remote and rather beautiful.

But the sound was not beautiful. It grew in volume, a great, grumbling, earth-shaking roar. The whole clip was toppling down, hitting the slopes below and rebounding. It was as slow and inevitable as a waterfall, and the dust rose like spray.

I glanced round me in sudden fear, expecting all the cliffs around us to be toppling. But it was only that one cliff and below it Kostos stood, his body twisted round so that I knew he was looking upwards, seeing the ghastly thing he had let loose, but standing transfixed, knowing it was death that was pouring down upon him in the form of millions of tons of rock and unable to do anything to save himself. And below, by the entrance to the mine, the men of Foum-Skhira lay dazed, barely aware of what was descending on them from above.

All this I saw in a flash and then my gaze returned to the mountainside. The cliff was hidden now by a cloud of dust that shone red in the sunlight, and below it, the great tide rolled like a tidal wave, and as it rolled it seemed to gather the mountainside with it, so that the whole slope on which Kostos stood was thrust over the lip of the cliff, taking him with it, still oddly standing erect staring up at the main body of the landslide.

And in that split second in which my eyes recorded his fall, the whole gorge was suddenly filled by chaos. The sound pounded at the ground under our feet. Pieces of cliff from the farther side were shaken loose. Small avalanches were started.

And all the time the noise gathered volume, the dust rose white like steam till it caught fire in the sunlight, and all the mountain poured into the gorge, thundering and crashing and filling it with rock.

Long after the movement had slowed and the weight had gone out of the sound, Ed and I stood there, incapable of action, stunned by the terrible vastness of it. It had a sort of horrible fascination. It took an effort of will power to make me turn my head and look behind me, up the gorge, to see that the others were safe. Thank God, they were. They were in a little huddle as though clinging to each other, and they were as motionless as we were.

I looked back again at the scene of desolation and felt slightly sick. The dust was settling now and the sunset colours on the mountain top were flaming into vivid beauty. And into the dark cavern of the gorge a stillness was creeping, not a graveyard stillness, but the deep, satisfied stillness of Nature. And then, clear across that stillness, came a cry. It was a high, piercing cry, and I heard the name of Allah. Down by the gorge mouth, clear of the outer spill of the slide, was a little knot of men. They were waving their arms and calling down curses on our heads. One of them, a big, bearded man, was shaking his fist at us and clawing his way towards us across the debris of the slide.

I turned and started up the slope of rock towards the others. "Come on," I shouted at Ed. "Hurry, man. We've got to be out of this gorge by nightfall."

He caught the urgency of my voice and came hurrying after me. "There's only a handful of them left," he said breathlessly as he caught up with me. "And anyway it was that damned Greek that caused the explosion. It was nothing to do with us."

"They don't know that," I said. "He was a European. That's all they know. If they catch us in these mountains at dawn . . ." I didn't bother to finish the sentence. I needed my breath, for we were climbing at a desperate rate to join up with the rest of the party.

IV

The trek out of that gorge was a nightmare. It wasn't that we were followed. The men who had screamed their need of vengeance at us were fully occupied searching the debris for their dead. But the sun was setting fast and if darkness overtook us before we had climbed out of the gorge, we should be trapped there, and when dawn came we should be hunted down amongst the rocks of the mountainsides and killed.

The ledge up which we were moving gradually narrowed until it finished abruptly at a sheer rock climb of twenty feet or more. It sloped slightly and there were hand- and foot-holds, but except for Ed we were all wearing shoes, and we had nothing with which to rope ourselves together. Below us was an almost vertical drop of some four hundred feet to the bottom of the gorge. We paused there a moment, looking back. The slide filled the whole mouth of the gorge and water was already building up against this natural dam to form a wider and deeper lake, red like a gaping wound. The flowing robes of Berber men moved ghostlike amongst the debris of the fall, searching for their dead.

There was no going back and we turned to face the cliff of rock that towered above us. "We'll never get up there," Karen said.

"Sure you will," Ed said cheerfully. "There's nothing to it." He had her take her shoes off. "I'll be right behind you," he said as he started her off. His tough, rubber-soled boots gripped the rock as he climbed, encouraging her all the time, sometimes bracing her foot with his hand. Jan stood with his head back, watching her until she reached the top. "Come on," Ed called down to us. "It'll be dark soon." He climbed back down the face of the rock and met Julie halfway, helping her up as he'd helped Karen.

The climb wasn't really difficult, but it took time. The sun had already set before we had all gathered at the top. The gorge was cold and dark now, and, above us, the slopes of the mountain seemed to stretch into infinity. We started up,

climbing as quickly as we could. But we made slow progress.
Karen slipped a great deal in her leather soles and Jan was
out of training for this sort of thing. "Latham!" Ed called
back to me. "I'll go ahead to find the track. It'll be too
dark to see soon. I'll call directions down to you. Okay?"

It was the only thing to do. "Yes, you go ahead," I told
him.

He was fit and seemed to have the feel of the mountains.
He climbed fast and in a few minutes he was lost to sight over
the brow of a hump. Darkness fell swiftly. It was odd the
way it came. Our eyes adjusted themselves to the diminishing
light and even when the stars were out I could still see my
way ahead. Then I looked down to negotiate a tumbled patch
of rock and when I looked up again I could see nothing—only
the vague shape of the mountain humped against the studded
velvet of the sky.

I shouted and Ed's voice hallooed back to us, very faint and
far away. Sound was deceptive, curving round the larger
rock buttresses, so that we worked too much to the left and
found ourselves up against a cliff. It took us a long time to
negotiate it and then, when we could climb again, we found
ourselves in an area of massive great rocks as big as houses
with deep gashes between that appeared as dangerous as
crevasses in a glacier. We called and called, but could hear no
response.

I worked away to the right then, calling all the time. But
a wind had sprung up from off the top of the mountain and we
heard nothing. I kept on working to the right, hoping to get
downwind from Ed and hear his calls, but I must have gone
too far, for we reached an area where the rocks were piled in
absolute confusion. I tried to cross this, still attempting to get
down-wind, but it was a very bad patch. Loose rubble slid
away from under our feet and even some of the bigger rocks
showed a tendency to move. And then, as I was climbing
round an extra large piece of rock, my foot braced against it,
the thing moved. I shouted a warning to the others and
clutched hold of the ground above me. The rock crunched as
it moved. I could see it as a vague shape moving gently over
on to its side. It hung there a moment and then moved again,
dropping away out of my field of vision. We stood there,

braced against the slope, listening to the sound of it crashing and banging down the mountain, gathering stones in its path so that there was a rustling, slithering sound of rubble behind it. There was a heavy splash and then silence.

I knew then where I was. I had come much too far and we were right out on the face of the new slide with the broken, crumbling cliff above us. It was already past nine. We had been clambering and stumbling across the face of the mountain for almost three hours. I tried to estimate how far across the face of the slide we had come. " Do we go forward or back?" I asked Jan, trying to remember which side of that cliff face was the better going.

"' If we go forward," Jan said, " We'll be on the route Karen and I came down last night. With luck I might be able to find my way back to the piste."

" And if we go back?"

" I don't know." His voice sounded nervous. We were both thinking about the chances of getting across the slide without disturbing it and starting the whole new slope on the move.

I asked the two girls which they would prefer to do. They both agreed. " Let's go on." And so we inched our way forward across the face of the slide, scarcely daring to breathe, let alone put our weight on to any of the rocks. Stones clattered down, little drifts of scree and dirt were started. Occasionally a larger rock shifted and then went bouncing and thudding down the slope. And each time the sound ended in a splash of water.

It took us nearly two hours to cross the face of that slide and all the time the retina of my memory carried the picture of how the slide had been after Kostos hurled that stick of dynamite. The picture was appallingly vivid and every time I heard a stone shift or a trickle of rubble start, my heart was in my mouth and the sweat stood cold on my forehead. And each time I cursed myself for having led them too far to the right, for not having realised that we hadn't climbed above this obstruction.

But a little after ten-thirty we came out on to undisturbed mountainside and lay there, panting and exhausted, with a bitter cold wind drying the sweat of physical and nervous exhaustion on our tired bodies.

After that Jan took the lead. We moved very slowly. He was just about all in and so was Karen. She was slipping a lot and she had cut her head open on a rock. Her hand, when I helped her over a bad patch, was sticky with blood.

About an hour later we heard Ed calling from higher up the mountain. The sound of it came to us quite clearly on the wind. But I knew it was a waste of breath to answer him and we climbed doggedly on until we found the piste. I left the others there and trudged on up to the bend where the piste had been repaired. From that point I was able to make contact with Ed. A few minutes later he joined me. " Where the hell have you been?" he demanded. " I've been waiting up there for hours, bawling my head off. What happened to you?"

I explained as we went down to join the others. "Well, thank God you're here now," he said. " I'd just about given you up. Once I heard some rocks crashing down . . ." He didn't say anything for a moment, and then he murmured, " It's a terrible business, that landslide. There must have been thirty or forty of them buried under it. But it wasn't our fault," he added quickly.

"They're not to know that," I reminded him.

" No, I guess not."

When we rejoined the others, we found them discussing whether we should make for the Post or go on up over the pass towards Agdz. It was over forty kilometres to Agdz and the Berber tribesmen from Foum-Skhira could easily overtake us on the piste. At the same time there would probably be a road gang working on the break in the piste higher up the mountainside. There might be transport there. But even so, it was a stiff climb and I wasn't sure we could make it. " What do you think, Ed?" I asked.

There was a long pause and then he said, " I didn't tell you this before, but the reason why you lost me was that I had to stop calling down to you. I'd almost reached the piste when I heard mules coming up from the direction of Foum-Skhira. They were Berbers and they passed quite close to me, about ten of them, going up towards the pass and riding hard."

That decided us. We headed downhill, back towards Foum-Skhira and the Post.

T.S.L.   H

It was then just on midnight. It didn't take us long to reach the foot of the mountain, but from then on the going was heavy in the deep sand of the piste and our progress became slower and slower, our stops more frequent. According to the map it was five kilometres from the foot of the mountains to the Post, but it seemed infinitely farther and it took us nearly three hours. And for the last hour of that journey we could hear the sound of wailing from Foum-Skhira. It was a high-pitched, quavering sound, strangely animal in the darkness of the night, and it grew steadily louder as we approached the Post.

At last the dark shape of the first fort loomed up, the domed roofs curved like some Eastern temple against the stars. We left the piste, making a wide detour round it, so that we approached the Post from the south. We went slowly, not talking, moving cautiously. They might have a lookout posted to watch for us. I didn't think it likely, but it was just possible. A dog barked—a sudden, harsh sound in the stillness. And beyond the sound of the dog was the remote, persistent sound of the women of Foum-Skhira keening for their dead.

I think we were all a little scared. We were bunched close together and I could just see that Ed had his gun in his hand. We were braced mentally against the sudden, blood-curdling yell, the rush of an attack out of the night. It is easy to be frightened at night in a strange country among a strange people. Darkness should be the same everywhere. But it isn't. This was desert country. These were desert people. We could feel the difference in the sand under our feet, see it in the brightness of the stars, the shadowed shape of the bare mountains. The chill of it was in our bones. It was as alien as the moon, as cold and naked. And the agony of that death-wailing froze our blood. The dog barked incessantly.

" Goddammit! " Ed muttered. " Why can't that bloody dog keep quiet? "

A hand gripped my arm. It was Julie. " I wish we'd crossed the mountains and made for Agdz," she whispered.

We were in the open space between the two forts now. The shape of one of the towers was outlined against Orion. " Where do we go now? " Ed asked. " The Bureau? "

"That's no good," I said. "There won't be anybody there."

"No, but there's the telephone. We need to get on to the Commandant at Agdz, and quick."

"Well, we can try," I said. "But they probably lock the Bureau at night."

"What about Bilvidic?" Jan asked. "He'll be at the house, I imagine."

We turned the corner of the fort and struck the beaten path that led to the Bureau. The French truck was still parked outside. The door of the Bureau was locked. "Let's try the sleeping quarters," Ed said. "Maybe your friend Bilvidic is there." The guest rooms were built on to the Bureau in the form of an L. The door was locked and Ed beat on the wooden panels with the butt of his gun. The noise seemed shatteringly loud in the night stillness. The dog's barking became frantic. The sound of the wailing continued unchanged —insistent and agonised. The building outside which we were clustered remained silent as the grave.

"We'd better try the house," Jan said.

Ed beat once more upon the door, but nobody answered, and we trudged, coldly, wearily, through the sand to the house. The dog barked his fury at us from the wired-in enclosure. Once more Ed shattered the night with the hollow thudding of his gun-butt against wood. A window was thrown open and a voice demanded, "Qui va là?" It was Bilvidic. I never thought I should be glad to hear his voice. "I'll come down immediately," he said as soon as he discovered who we were.

It was bitterly cold standing there waiting outside that door. The sweat lay against my body like a coating of steel. The dog had stopped barking now and there was utter silence except for the sound of wailing which came to us loud and clear on a chill breath of wind. A light showed between the chinks of the heat-contracted woodwork of the door. The bolts were drawn back and there was Bilvidic. He peered at us in the beam of the torch he carried. "Come in," he said. His face was puffed with sleep and his voice sounded irritable.

It was as cold inside as it was out, except that there was no wind. "You must phone Agdz immediately," Ed said in his halting French. "They must send troops. Something terrible has happened." He glanced quickly round the room. It looked bare and chill in the hard beam of the torch. "Where's the telephone?"

"The telephone is broken," Bilvidic said. "It is cut when the piste is destroyed."

So that was that. "We should have gone over the mountains," Jan said.

"If we'd done that we might all be dead by now," I answered sharply.

Karen had slumped into an easy-chair. "It's so cold," she said. She was shivering and I glanced at Julie. Her face was pale and she looked desperately tired. We were all of us tired.

Bilvidic's assistant joined us then. He was angry at having been got out of bed. "What's happened?" he demanded. "Why have you returned here at this time of the——"

But Bilvidic cut him short. "Georges. Go to the Capitaine's room and bring the cognac and some glasses." He turned to us. "First you have something to warm you and we get a fire lit. Afterwards we talk, eh?" He went to a door leading out to the back and shouted, "Mohammed! Mohammed! Venez ici. Vite, vite!" My estimation of him soared then, for he must have been consumed with curiosity and a man is seldom at his best when rudely woken in the small hours.

Mohammed came and was ordered to produce a fire immediately. We moved into Legard's study. Paraffin blazed in the wood-piled grate and Bilvidic handed each of us a quarter tumbler of neat cognac. "Eh, bien. Now we will talk. What happened last night at Kasbah Foum? There were rumours that the Caid was dead and that several indigènes had lost their lives. What happened, monsieur?" He was looking at me.

I told him the whole thing then, sitting there by the fire, sipping my drink, my body gradually relaxing with the warmth.

When I had finished he sat quite silent for a long time. He was frowning and his fingers were beating a tattoo on the desk where he was seated. At length he said to me, "Do you know this country? Do you understand the people here?"

"No," I said. "This is the first time I have been south of the Atlas."

He clicked his tongue. "That is a pity, for I also do not know it. This is a military area and there is seldom any reason for us to come down here." He scratched his thinning hair. "It is a pity because it would be helpful if we had some idea what they would do. It is an extraordinary situation, quite extraordinary." He was using the word in its literal sense. "First there is the failure of the dates, then the piste is cut so that the food trucks, which are delayed anyway, cannot get through. Then they are frightened by the change in the colour of the water that feeds their palmerie and the wells. Their Caïd is dead. And now this. It is too much—too much for any primitive and warlike people." He looked across at me. "I agree with you, monsieur. There is likely to be trouble." He paused and scratched his head again. "The question is—what do we do? Soon they will know that you are here."

"If we could get to Agdz," Ed said.

But Bilvidic shook his head. "Unfortunately, the only vehicle here has something the matter with it. And you cannot go on foot. It is a long way. Also it is too dangerous." He pulled a pack of American cigarettes out of the pocket of his jacket which he was wearing over his vest. He made a spill from a strip of paper and lit it from the fire. Then he started pacing up and down, taking quick, nervous puffs at the cigarette.

I leaned back and closed my eyes. The drink and the warmth of the fire were enveloping me with sleep. I seemed to slide away into darkness, engulfed by a beautiful lethargy.

I awoke to the sound of voices raised in argument. I opened my eyes and blinked in the brilliance of the light. It was morning and the room was full of sunshine. Jan lay asleep in the chair opposite me. The grate was piled white with wood ash. A single log was still burning, its flames obliterated by the brightness of the sunshine. "I have sent a runner to Agdz by mule," Bilvidic was saying. "What else can I do?"

"But it'll take him all day to get there," Ed cried.

"Perhaps." Bilvidic shrugged his shoulders. "But there is a chance that he will find transport up there where they are repairing the piste. Also I have told him to get the road gang to try and repair the telephone."

"Yeah, but that'll take hours. Meantime anything can happen."

"What's the trouble?"

Ed swung round. "Take a look out of the window."

I crossed the room and peered out. The open space between the forts was full of people. They stood or sat in little isolated groups, silently watching the house as though waiting for something to happen. And from the direction of Foum-Skhira came the sound of tam-tams beating. It was a sound without rhythm, an insistent, urgent tattoo like drums beating to quarters. I glanced at my watch. It was just after nine. "You should have woken me earlier," I said.

"There was nothing you could do," Bilvidic declared quietly. "There is nothing any of us can do now except wait here and hope they do not attack."

"Attack?" I stared at him, my brain still dulled with sleep. "Do you mean you think they may attack the Post?"

He nodded his head slowly. "Yes. I have just had a visit from Hassan—that is the Caïd's second son, the man who is now, in fact, the Caïd. He came at some risk to himself to warn us that he had not the influence to hold his people back and that we were in imminent danger."

"They know we're here at the Post then?"

He nodded. "I cannot understand how they know, but they do." He swung round at the sound of the front door opening. It was Georges. He carried a rifle slung over his shoulder. "You found the armoury then?" Bilvidic said.

But Georges shook his head. He had searched the Bureau building, but he had failed to find it. The rifle he had found in the orderly's room, but there had been no ammunition with it. Bilvidic went through into the main room where Julie and Karen were peacefully asleep in easy-chairs with blankets wrapped round them. He pulled open the door leading to the back premises and shouted, "Mohammed! Mohammed!" But there was no answer. We searched the whole place, but there was no sign of him.

"Looks like he's cleared out while the going was good," Ed said. "Isn't there somebody else around here to tell us where they keep their weapons?"

"Only the orderly," Bilvidic said. "And that is the man I sent to Agdz."

"But there is a Military Post," I said. "There must be some troops here."

Bilvidic shook his head. "Not at the Post. Farther south there is the Camel Patrol. But here Legard has only two orderlies and the other is away."

"And you didn't ask the man you sent to Agdz where the armoury was?"

"Why should I? I had no reason then to believe that we should be attacked."

"But we told you there'd be trouble. We told you that a party had been sent out into the mountains——"

"Yes, yes, but that does not mean they will attack a French Post. It is many years now since a Post was attacked."

"Monsieur. Here. Quick!" It was Georges and his voice was urgent. He was standing by the front door, his head on one side. "Listen! Do you hear?" He turned the key in the lock and pulled open the door. We heard it then. It was a sound like the sea breaking along the sands, the murmur of many voices and the tramp of many feet. The tattoo of the tam-tams had ceased and in its place was the single, menacing beat of a drum giving the time to an army on the march. And then we saw them, coming up out of the palmerie just to the left of the souk. They were a great mob of people and they flowed over the sand towards the house like a tide. There must have been a thousand or more, including the children running on the outskirts. I felt my heart hammering and my mouth was dry. If they attack in a body . . . I glanced at Julie, still sleeping peacefully in her chair.

"What are we going to do?" It was Jan. He had come through from the study and was standing, looking first at his wife and then through the open door at the advancing mob. "We must do something." He rubbed his eyes, half-dazed with sleep, blinking owlishly. "Shall I wake them?" He was looking at the girls again.

"Let them sleep on," I said. "There's no point in their knowing about this till they have to." I turned to Bilvidic. "Exactly what arms have we got?" I asked.

He put his hand into his pocket and brought out a French service pistol which he tossed across to me. " That is Legard's. We have plenty of rounds for that. Also Georges and I have each an automatic with a full magazine and one spare."

" And I have my Luger," Ed said.

Four pistols! I stared out of the door at the approaching mob. It wasn't much if they really meant business. " We ought to move to the fort," Ed said.

But Bilvidic shook his head. " It is too big. We could never hold it."

" But we could hold one of the towers."

" Yes, but we must be near the telephone. That is essential."

" The Bureau then," I suggested.

But again he shook his head. " They could come at us across the roof from the fort. Here we have an all round field of fire. It is not good, but it is the best we can do. Close the door now, Georges."

The door slammed to. The key grated in the lock. We could no longer hear the angry sound of the mob. Only the beat of the drum penetrated the room. " I think," Bilvidic said to me, " that you should get all your people upstairs." He was staring at the advancing mob, searching it with his eyes narrowed over their little pouches. " I do not think they have a leader. Without a leader they will not attack unless they are given cause. They have only been told that you are here. They do not know. And if they do not see you, then they will begin to doubt and lose their nerve. Get your people upstairs." His voice was more urgent now. " Vite! Hurry! And when you are up there, do not show yourselves at the windows."

" But that leaves only the two of you down here," Ed said. " If they once get inside this place . . ." He hesitated. " What makes you so sure they won't attack?"

Bilvidic turned and looked at him. " I know about mobs, monsieur," he said in a quiet voice. " In Casablanca I have had to do with many riots. Now hurry, please."

I knew he was right. It was no time to argue, anyway. I woke Julie and Karen and bundled them up the stairs, explaining the position to them as we went. Jan followed close at my heels and Ed was behind him.

There were Venetian blinds in one of the upper rooms and

through the slats we watched the mob slow down and come to a halt in front of the house. Bilvidic was right. It had no leader. It was moved only by the sense of being a mob. Those behind pushed forward and spilled out to the sides, spreading round the house. The people who had been watching and waiting in the space between the forts moved into the herd as though drawn by instinct. The inarticulate murmur of the mass gradually died into silence. It was like a brute beast standing with his head down, wondering whether to charge.

I could pick out individual faces now. They were curiously blank. Many of those in front were young men. They were awed by the stillness of the house, by the Tricolor floating from its flagstaff and by the looming mass of the forts behind, mute evidence of France's mastery of this land. A little knot gathered in the centre and a young man was pushed forward. He was too young to have any hair on his face and he was scared. But he had women behind him who goaded him on and he suddenly clutched the silver hilt of the knife at his waist and ran forward.

But all he did was to peer in at the windows and then he ran back to the crowd, which opened out and sucked him into its bosom. He was shaking his head and then the mob had closed up again and I could no longer see him. But it wasn't a silent crowd now. The people were talking and becoming individuals again in the process. It was no longer a headless, dangerous mass, but a thousand individuals all full of their own opinions. Looking down on it was like looking at some disease through a microscope. It writhed and seethed, splitting up into little eager groups.

The danger, for the moment, was over.

I breathed a sigh of relief, for there were women in the crowd, many of whom would have lost menfolk in the disaster at Kasbah Foum. If this bonfire was to catch fire, it was they who would set the match to it. And the mob was armed. Apart from the knife which every Berber carries at his waist, I counted at least two dozen, perhaps more, with long-barrelled, old-fashioned guns.

" What will they do now?" Julie asked. And it was only then, as I glanced at her and saw her face close to mine, that

I realised that I had my arm round her shoulder. " Nothing,"
I said. " They will talk and talk. And then they will get
hungry and go home."

A buzzer sounded downstairs. It was an odd, mechanical
little sound in the stillness that had descended on the house.
It stopped and then started again. I heard the scrape of a
chair on the tiles and a man's tread as he crossed the main
room towards the study. " By God, it's the telephone," Ed
cried. " We're through to Agdz." And he went clattering
down the stairs. I shouted at him to stop, but all he said was,
" I want a word with the Commandant myself."

" Ed! Come back!" I flung myself down the stairs after
him.

The stairs descended into a recess between the main room
and the study. As I reached the bottom Ed was already in the
study. Bilvidic was seated at the desk with the field telephone
pulled in front of him and the receiver to his ear, and behind
him, framed in the window, was the lined, gaunt face of an
old Berber. He was staring into the room and he saw Ed
moving towards the desk, his mouth opened slightly to reveal
a solitary tooth, like a fang hanging in the muzzle of an old
dog; and then the face was gone and I heard Bilvidic saying,
" Oui, oui, tout de suite."

" Let me talk to him," Ed said. I think he thought they'd
take more notice of an American.

But Bilvidic waved him away. " Get back upstairs."

There was the sudden crack of a gun and a splintering
crash. A bullet thudded into the woodwork above my head.
Glass from the shattered window-pane rained on to the desk.
Bilvidic shouted to us to get down. But Ed was standing dazed
in front of the desk with blood welling from a cut on the side
of his head and trickling down his face. He turned slowly
to the shattered window. A big, wild-eyed man was standing
staring at us, the long-barrelled gun with which he had fired
the shot still smoking in his hand.

Ed's reaction was instantaneous. His hand grabbed at his
Luger. " Don't fire!" Bilvidic screamed at him. " For God's
sake don't fire!"

For an awful moment there was a stillness in the room.
Then Ed lowered the gun. He put his hand up to the side of

his head and stared at the blood on his fingers. "He tried to kill me," he said in a dazed voice.

I didn't say anything. Bilvidic wiped the sweat from his forehead. "If you had fired," he said slowly in a small, quiet voice, "the lust for blood would have entered into that mob out there. You would have been committing suicide—for yourself and for all of us." He turned to me. "You take the gun, monsieur; and get him upstairs out of sight of these people."

Ed turned to me then and gave a little shaken laugh. "I'm sorry," he said. "I guess I shouldn't have come down." He glanced towards the window, listening to the roar of the crowd who had become excited at the sound of the shot. Blood dripped from his chin to the floor. Then he turned to Bilvidic who was busy explaining to the man at the other end of the line what had happened. "Monsieur. You must get them to send troops. That's what I came down to tell you. We need troops here, and we need them quick."

Bilvidic looked at me and nodded towards the door. "Get him upstairs," he said. "And get one of the ladies to see to that cut." And then he was back on the telephone. "Ullo. Ullo. Monsieur le Commandant? Est-ce que vous avez . . ." Ed stood there listening to Bilvidic's request for a military detachment to be despatched immediately.

"Come on," I said.

He nodded and moved towards the door, his handkerchief held to the side of his head. "Well, at least they know what's going on. They'll send troops now."

I got him back up the stairs and handed him over to Julie. Fortunately it was only a superficial cut from a piece of flying glass and it had missed his eye.

"So they know we're in the house now," Jan said when I had explained what had happened.

I nodded. "I'm afraid so."

He turned on Ed. "You damned fool!" And then he was looking at Karen. He was scared and angry, for he was standing by the window and the roar of the crowd came up to him.

"It wasn't his fault," Julie said. "He did it for the best." She was bandaging Ed's head with a strip torn from a sheet.

I went over to the window and looked out at the crowd. They were like cattle, bawling and milling around, waiting to stampede. And then suddenly, above the solid, heavy roar came a liquid sound, a ululation made with the tongue like a yodel. It was just a little sound at first, but it swelled rapidly, a female sound that swamped the male.

My blood ran cold, for I knew that sound. I had heard it in the High Atlas. But then it had been a greeting, a ceremonial welcome. Now I was hearing it for the first time as I had been told it was really used ; a repetitive sound like the singing of crickets to drive the men to a frenzy of excitement, to goad them into battle.

I went to the window and saw that the women were gathering together, closing up behind the men, their mouths open, their tongues moving ; and the shrill, insistent cry gathered greater and greater volume.

I turned then and ran down the stairs.

"Where are you going?" Julie cried out.

I didn't answer her. I think I was too scared of what I knew had to be done to say anything. But she seemed to sense what was in my mind, for she came after me. "No, Philip. No." She caught hold of my arm. "Please."

Bilvidic met me at the foot of the stairs. His face looked very pale and he had his gun in his hand. "You can give the American back his gun," he said.

"You know that sound then?"

"I know what it means—yes. But it is the first time I have heard it." He smiled a little wryly. "Get your men down here. The ladies should remain upstairs. We may beat back the first rush. After that . . ." He shrugged his shoulders. Ed came down the stairs then, his face very pale under the blood-stained bandage. Bilvidic made no attempt to blame him for what was going to happen.

I stared out of the window at the gathering men standing silent, staring at the door. That throbbing, tongued cry of the women seemed to fill the air. "You understand mobs," I said, turning to Bilvidic. "There must be something that would stop them?"

"Yes," he said, his pale eyes staring into mine. "If I went

out there and faced them and told them why their men had been killed in the gorge—that would stop them."

"Then why don't you do it?" Julie said quickly, breathlessly.

"Because, mademoiselle, I do not speak Berber, only Arab, and the mass of them would not understand that." His eyes came back to me and I knew he was thinking that I must speak Berber since I'd been a missionary at Enfida.

"That's what I thought you'd say." I turned and walked towards the door.

But Julie caught hold of my arm. "Not alone. Not like that."

"I must." I was trembling and my stomach felt cold and empty.

"I won't let you." She was dragging at my arm.

"Let me go." I cried.

"I won't." Her face was white and her dark eyes looked at me with a steady gaze. "I love you, Philip."

I stared at her and a sudden glow of warmth filled me. It was as though her declaration had set light to something inside me. I felt suddenly calm and at peace. Gently I released her fingers from my arm. "You'd better have this," I said, and handed her Legard's pistol. And then I walked to the door and opened it and went out into the hard sunlight and the noise to face the stare of a thousand hostile, half-animal eyes.

They were bunched out fifty feet back from the house, a compact, solid mass of men that thinned out towards the edges, spreading in a crescent round the house as though formed by instinct into some old order of battle. I was not conscious of their individual faces. They were just a blur in the hot sunlight, a solid mass of flowing robes that ranged from white to brown and matched the arid sand. I was only conscious that they were of this naked land, a living and integral part of it, and that I was an alien

I tried to marshall my thoughts, but my mind was a blank as I walked out towards them. I couldn't even pray. And they watched me walk out to them like a herd of animals, pressed shoulder to shoulder; and there wasn't a single individual among them—they were a mass and they felt as a mass, not thinking, only feeling. That mass feeling seemed to hang in the air. I sensed it physically, the way you can smell something mad. And behind it all, behind the evil expression of their mass feeling, was that damned female noise, that many-tongued liquid, frenzy-making sound, beating at my brain, thrumming through it until I could feel it against the raw ends of my nerves, stretching them beyond the limits of strain.

And I was afraid; desperately, horribly afraid. My mouth felt dry and there was a weakness in the marrow of my bones. I prayed God to stop me being afraid. But the prayer was not a real prayer and I stopped and looked at the sea of faces, that blur of figures, and I was afraid then that they would know I was afraid.

For a moment I could say nothing. I could think of nothing. I stood there twenty paces from them and stared at them. And they stared back at me, silent and motionless, but strong in the strength of their mass feeling. And behind them was that sound that seemed an expression of the very wildness and primitiveness of the land.

And suddenly it maddened me. I was angry, with myself and with them, and my anger killed my fear. I found my voice then and heard myself shout at them for silence in their own language. I shouted several times for the women to be quiet and gradually the sound lessened and died away. Abruptly the silence was complete, the whole crowd of them so still that I could hear the small sound of the breeze blowing through the dark green sprays of the tamarisks that acted as a windbreak for the house.

I had them then. I could have talked to them. But my eye was caught by an individual face. It was the bearded, wild-eyed face of the man who had fired into the study. He was standing right in front of me and as our eyes met, I was conscious of the hatred and violence that seethed inside him, and it appalled me. He had his gun clutched in his left hand and with his right he pointed a finger at me. He cursed me in the name of Allah. "You have killed my son and my brother and my brother's son," he accused me.

"I have not killed anyone," I said. "The men who came

to Kasbah Foum died because of Ali d'Es-Skhira." My voice
was steady and it gave me confidence. I began to tell them
exactly what had happened there in the gorge. But in spite of
myself I found I was speaking to this one man and not to the
whole crowd of them, and I saw his face become set and
wooden as he made himself deaf to what I was saying.

Slowly he shifted the gun to his right hand and slowly he
raised it to his shoulder, moving it slightly so that the long,
heavy barrel pointed straight at me. I tried to ignore him. I
tried to look at the sea of faces, to talk to them as one
composite individual. But my eyes were fascinated by the
round hole of that barrel. It didn't waver and it pointed
straight into my eyes and I heard my voice falter and slow.
His eyes were looking straight at me along the barrel.
They glinted with sudden triumph, and in that instant I knew
he was going to fire.

I ducked, flinging myself sideways. There was a report and
the bullet hit my shoulder, spinning me round. Somehow I
kept my feet. Pain shot through my arm and my whole body
seemed to grow numb with the shock. I could feel the
blood flowing. I could feel, too, the blood lust of that
crowd growing.

What came to me then, I don't know. I would like to think
that it was courage. But it may only have been the instinct
of survival, the knowledge that if I failed to face them now,
they would charge and trample me underfoot. I felt suddenly
quite cool and a little light-headed, and I was walking towards
them.

I walked straight towards the man who had fired at me,
never shifting my gaze from his face. His eyes stared back
at me for a moment and then I saw guilt and fear in them and
he looked down, shuffling his feet and beginning to back away
from me. The crowd opened up, so that a narrow gully
formed in the mass of it. I walked straight into it. They could
have killed me then with their bare hands, but nobody moved,
and I felt the power of dominating them, of holding their
attention with what I was doing.

The man backed until he could retreat no farther. He was
held there by the weight of people behind him. I walked
straight up to him and took the gun from him. I didn't say

anything to him. I just turned my back and walked out till I was clear of them. The concrete signpost stood at the entrance to the house. I swung the gun by the barrel and brought the breech down across the post, using all the strength of my sound arm, and the stock splintered and broke off. I tossed the useless thing on the sand and walked down the path and in through the open door of the house.

In the sudden shade of the room I could see nothing. I felt my brain reeling. I heard a murmur like surf as the crowd gave voice to its reaction and the door closed, shutting it out. A hand touched mine. I heard a sob. And then my legs gave under me and I passed out.

When I came to I was lying on the couch. There were voices talking. "But there must be troops down here." It was Ed speaking. "How else would you hold the country? If you're properly organised you should be able to have troops at the top of the pass by——"

"I tell you, there are no Goumiers nearer than Boumalne." Bilvidic's voice sounded cold and angry. "That is more than a hundred and fifty kilometres away, and they are not motorised."

"What about the Legion?"

"The Legion is in Indo-China. All our troops are in Indo-China."

"Oh, to hell with that for a story. You'll see. The Commandant knows there's trouble. He'll have troops here fast enough. It's just a question of whether they get here in time."

I closed my eyes, wondering what there was about the Americans and the French. They always seemed to get on each other's nerves. I felt a little weak and my left arm was cold. It had been bared by cutting away the sleeve of my jacket and shirt at the shoulder. I moved it gently, flexing my fingers. The muscles seemed all right. I was conscious of somebody close beside me. Fingers gripped hold of the arm and there was a stinging pain in the wound halfway between elbow and shoulder. I cried out, more with surprise than with pain, and Julie's voice, close to my ear, said, "I'm sorry. I thought you were still unconscious. There's no damage. It's just a flesh wound and I'm swabbing it out with iodine.

The bullet nicked your arm." Her voice was cool and soothing.

"I lost my nerve," I said.

"Don't be silly." She gripped the arm as she began to bandage it.

But I was remembering how I had ducked and the man had fired. "If I'd walked up to him, he'd never have fired. I let him dominate me." My voice sounded shaky.

The others crowded round me, salving my wounded pride with kind words. "It requires courage, mon ami, to face a mob like that," Bilvidic said. There was a warmth in his voice that soothed me, but I had a feeling that if he'd been the one who had spoken Berber, he would have outfaced them.

As soon as Julie had finished bandaging my arm, I swung my feet off the couch and sat up. "What's happening outside?" I asked.

"C'est ça," Bildivic said. "You have given them something to talk about. For the moment they are no longer a mob."

I got up and went over to the window. It was true. They were no longer bunched together in a solid mass. They had split up into groups. Some were sitting down well away from the house as though content to be merely spectators. Others were drifting back to Ksar Foum-Skhira. "It is very hot to-day." Bilvidic had come to my side. "I do not think they will do anything during the heat of the day." There was a note of reservation in his voice.

"And afterwards?" I asked.

"Afterwards . . ." He spread his hands with a Gallic shrug. "Afterwards, we shall see."

"Where's the man who fired at me? Is he still out there?"

There was a momentary hesitation, and then he said, "He has gone back to the village."

"Because he was ashamed or afraid, or what?"

It was Jan who answered. "He couldn't stand their taunts."

"Their taunts?"

He nodded. "They jeered at him because you had taken his gun from him."

"If you hadn't taken his gun away, he would have reloaded it and killed you," Bilvidic said. "They laughed at him and threw stones at him because he had been afraid of you." He turned abruptly away as though he were afraid to talk about the incident. " I think we should have some food."

We split into two watches, one half keeping guard, the other half feeding. The time passed slowly. It was a weird business. We dared not go out of the house and, it seemed, the mob dared not attack it. We played through all Legard's records on the gramophone, opening the windows so that the people outside could hear our music and would know that we weren't afraid. By midday the crowd had thinned to no more than a few hundred who sat or lay stretched out quite peacefully on the sand. The rest had gone back to Foum-Skhira. We had lunch and played cards. It was cool in the house, but we could feel the heat outside—the heat and the stillness. " Why the hell don't they send those troops?" Ed cried, suddenly throwing down his cards. " This waiting is getting on my nerves."

Nobody answered him. The waiting was getting on everybody's nerves. " They must have a garrison at Agdz. Why don't they send them?" ·

" Oh, shut up," I said angrily. My arm was stiff and painful. That and the waiting was making me irritable.

A sound drifted through the open windows, the beat of drums coming faintly across the sands to us from Foum-Skhira. The tam-tams had started again. And almost immediately that harsh, wailing chant of the women took up the rhythm. *Ayee-ya-i-ee Ayee-ya-i-ee*. Ed, who had been pacing up and down, stopped to listen. " Can't you do something? Get on the phone again to Agdz. Tell them to hurry. Tell that darn fool commandant——"

" What is the good?" Bilvidic asked. His voice was calm. " He knows what the situation is."

" Jesus!" Ed's fists were clenched with anger. " Are you going to sit there and do nothing while they whip themselves up into a frenzy again? Will you telephone Agdz or will I?"

Bilvidic shrugged his shoulders. " Do as you please," he said. " But I assure you that everything that can be done——"

" Okay. Then I guess it's up to me." And Ed turned and stumped off into the study.

Bilvidic looked almost apologetically at the rest of us. " He is very young," he murmured. " It is over forty kilometres from Agdz to this place and the piste is cut up near the pass."

" They could send planes," Jan suggested.

Bilvidic turned down the corners of his mouth. " This territory is controlled by the A.I. It is a military responsibility. They will handle it themselves."

" Well, they'd better hurry," Jan muttered. He looked across at Karen. Bilvidic was watching him. " It's a pity you had to bring Madame Kavan into this," Jan said.

We listened to Ed trying to get through to Agdz. He tried for almost a quarter of an hour. Then he came back into the room. " The line's out of action again."

Bilvidic nodded. " Yes, I know. I tried to telephone them after Latham was wounded. I could not get any reply."

" Why the hell didn't you tell me?"

" There is no point in telling you," Bilvidic answered quietly.

Georges called down the stairs then. He was acting as lookout on the roof. " There are some riders coming in now," he said.

" Troops?" Jan asked hopefully.

" No. Berbers on mules."

We went to the windows. They were riding in across the open space between the forts, their robes billowing out behind them. They paused to speak to some of the people squatting on the sand. Then they rode on towards Foum-Skhira. " I guess those are the guys that passed me up on the mountain road last night," Ed said.

" It is possible." Bilvidic was staring through the window towards the palmerie. Then he turned abruptly. " Georges. Go back to the roof. Watch the palmerie."

" Oui, oui. Ça va." His assistant hurried back up the stairs.

" Let us continue our game of cards," Bilvidic said and took up his hand again.

But we couldn't concentrate any more. The drums were beating faster now and the sound, though faint, seemed to throb through the room. It was nearly four. " I'm going to make some coffee," Julie said. Her voice sounded small and taut. She and Karen went out together into the kitchen.

We had ceased all pretence at playing. We were just sitting, listening to the drums. "It won't be long now," Jan murmured. He rubbed his hand across his face. "It's funny," he said to me, speaking softly. "For more than five years I have been wishing for Karen to be with me. And now . . ." He half closed his eyes. "Now I wish she weren't." He looked across at Bilvidic who had joined Ed at the window. "I'm sorry for him, too." The detective came towards us across the room. "Are you married?" Jan asked him.

Bilvidic nodded. "Yes, and I have two children also—a boy aged eleven and a girl nine."

"I'm sorry," Jan said.

Bilvidic's face softened into a friendly smile. "It does not matter. It is my work. There is always some danger. The boy—François," he added, "is in France now. He has gone to Dijon to stay with his grandmother for the New Year."

The drums were growing louder and a moment later Georges called down that the mob was coming out of the palmerie. Bilvidic muttered a curse as we went towards the windows. "It is those men who came in from the mountains. They have whipped up the people into a fury again." The mob looked different this time as it swept past the ruins of the souk. It was led by a man on mule-back, and it seemed to have more purpose. "There is going to be trouble this time." Bilvidic turned to the stairs. "Georges! Can you see anything moving on the piste from Agdz?"

"No, nothing. Un moment. Yes, I think so. Just one man; riding a mule, I think."

Presumably it was a straggler from the party who had already arrived. "Ecoutez!" Bilvidic said. "There is to be no shooting. You understand? No shooting. We retreat up the stairs and then up to the roof. Only then do we fight. As long as there is no shooting we have a chance."

Julie came in with the coffee. She poured us each a cup and took the rest upstairs. We drank it scalding hot, conscious of the growing murmur of the advancing mob. It wasn't such a large mob, but it seemed more compact. It was bunched up behind the man on the mule and there were very few women in it. Knives flashed in the sunshine as they neared the house.

Several men carried swords and one a lance. There were guns, too.

There was no hesitation this time. They came straight on towards the house. The leader trotted his mule up to the door and shouted, " Give us the men who killed Ali. Give us the slayers of the men in the gorge." He was a tall, bearded man with dark, aquiline features. He was the man who had shaken his fist at us from the entrance to the gorge after the slide.

" Get up the stairs," Bilvidic said to me. And when I hesitated, he added, " There is nothing you can do to stop them this time. Get upstairs. Georges and I will hold them. Take everybody up to the roof. Hurry, monsieur. I don't think they will hurt the women."

The man was looking in at us now. I saw recognition in his eyes and the blaze of a fierce hatred. He shouted something and then his face vanished abruptly. The next instant a lump of concrete was flung with a crash through the window. He was screaming at the crowd and they answered with a deep, baying roar, split by wild cries as they swarmed forward.

" Up the stairs, all of you," Bilvidic shouted.

We backed away from the room. I motioned Jan and Ed to go on ahead. The two Frenchmen were also backing across the room, their guns in their hands. The tide of the Berber mob rolled against the house, breaking against it, lapping round it. Windows crashed in, the frames splintered under heavy blows. Men climbed through over the sills. The door fell open with a crash. The room was suddenly full of them.

Bilvidic and Georges were in the archway between the main room and the study. The Berbers, finding themselves in unfamiliar surroundings, hesitated—uncertain and suspicious like animals. They stood, silent and baffled, facing the two Frenchmen. Their momentary stillness was full of fear.

Then the study windows were broken in and Bilvidic was forced to move back to the stairs. The tribesmen thrust forward, milling into the alcove between the two rooms. A gun was fired and a bullet slapped the wall above our heads. Bilvidic was backing steadily. It was only a matter of time. I turned, gripping my gun, and ordered everybody up to the roof top. "Keep down though," I shouted. "Keep down below the parapet."

A ladder led from the top storey on to the flat roof. Julie was waiting for me there and our hands gripped. Karen went up and then Jan and then Ed. We were alone on the landing with the guttural jabber of the Berbers lapping the house. She was looking up at me and my grip on her hand tightened. And then suddenly she was in my arms and our lips touched, a kiss that was without passion, that was a physical expression of what we were suddenly feeling for each other, of the love we had found. Then the door behind us was flung open and crashed to again as Bilvidic and Georges thrust their shoulders against it and turned the key. "Montez! Montez!" Bilvidic shouted. "Up on to the roof. Quick!"

I pushed Julie up and followed quickly after her. And as my head emerged into the slanting sunlight, I heard Jan shouting something excitedly. Georges followed me and then Bilvidic. The noise of the mob milling round the house was terrifying. A gun fired and a bullet whined over our heads. I pulled Julie down. Bilvidic and Georges were hauling up the ladder whilst blows rained on the door they had locked against pursuit. It splintered and burst open and at the same moment they dropped the trap-door leading on to the roof.

And then I heard what Jan was shouting. "Look! Philip. Look!"

I lifted my head above the parapet. A lone horseman was galloping across the open space between the two forts. It was a French officer. He rode bent low over the horse's neck, his round, pale blue hat screening his face, his cloak streaming out behind him. The horse, a big black, was lathered white with sweat and dust.

Julie and I stood up then. It was so magnificent. He was riding straight for the house, urging his horse on as though he intended to ride the mob down.

The roar of voices that circled the house gradually died as the horse, almost foundering, was pulled on to its haunches on the very edge of the thickest of the mob where they milled around the front door. "Abdul! Hassan!" The rider had singled out two men from the mob and ordered them to take charge and clear the crowd from the doorway. "You. Mohammed. Drop that gun!"

It was Legard. His body sagged with exhaustion, his eyes blazed with tiredness. His horse could barely stand. Yet he and the horse moved into the mob as though they were reviewing troops on parade. Here and there he singled out a man and gave an order.

In a moment the mob was moving back away from the house. They were going sheepishly, their eyes turned away from the Capitaine. They were no longer a mass. They were just a crowd of rather subdued individuals moving quickly away from the scene, anxious to avoid recognition. They were like children and he scolded them like children. "Moha! Why are you not looking to your goats? Abdul! You should be teaching the children today. Youssef! Mohammed!'

He picked them out, one by one, riding his horse in amongst them. He seemed to know them all by name and what they should be doing. And at no time was his voice raised in anger. It was only pained.

"Mohammed Ali. You here, too? Why do you make me ride so hard today? Yakoub. I have been to get food for you and now you have brought me back."

He knew them all and they ducked past him, their heads bowed in respect and contrition. " *Llah ihennik, O Sidi*—Allah keep you in peace, O master." And they scuttled away across the sands in ones and twos, like whipped dogs with their tails between their legs.

The noise of the mob died into the whisper of individuals and then into silence. Even the voices immediately below us, searching for a way up to the roof top, became subdued and receded into silence. One by one the men who had invaded the house came out, and Legard sat his horse, watching them—and to them he said nothing. They murmured their greetings, grovelling before the sternness of his face, and then they slunk away.

The last to come out was the man who had been their leader. He stood for a moment facing Legard. Neither spoke and the man's head dropped and he ran quickly to his mule and left.

We rigged the ladder then and went down. Legard was standing in the door of the house surveying the wreckage as we came down the stairs. He looked at us in silence. He was drooping with tiredness and I saw that it wasn't only the dust of travel that made his face grey. He looked desperately ill. His eyes glittered as they fastened on us. "Imbeciles!" he cried, his voice savage with anger. "You are here two days and you cause trouble." He began to cough. "My relief has arrived and now I have to come here and deal with this. All because of you, because you are so stupid that you . . ." His words were lost in a fit of coughing. He staggered forward to the settee and collapsed into it, clutching at his stomach, his eyes half closed. "See to my horse," he croaked. "Somebody see to that poor devil of a horse." He began to cough again.

Bilvidic sent Georges out to look after the animal. "What can I do for him?" Julie whispered.

"Get him some water," I said. I went over to him. "Monsieur le Capitaine," I said. "I'd like to thank you—for us all."

His eyes stared at me coldly.

"I'd like to thank you, too," Ed said. "But why the hell did you have to come alone?" he added. "What happened to the troops?"

"What troops?" Legard asked harshly.

Ed turned to Bilvidic. "Didn't the Commandant promise to send troops?"

"Why should he?" Legard pushed himself up on to his elbow. "What did you want troops for? These men aren't vicious. They're like little children. Anyway, there aren't any troops. We have no troops down here."

Ed hesitated and then he grinned and shrugged his shoulders. "Okay. Whatever you say. But thanks all the same."

Legard didn't say anything, but I saw the severe lines of his mouth relax into the ghost of a smile which spread up into his eyes so that they were slightly crinkled at the corners and he looked younger and less ill. Julie brought him the water and he gulped it down. "Alors." He pushed himself up into a sitting position. "Now explain to me everything that has happened. I have already sent for Caïd Hassan and for the

Khailifa. What happened? Monsieur Latham, suppose you tell me."

"Caid Hassan is dead," I said.

"Yes, of course. I had forgotten." He closed his eyes, screwing them up as though they were still half-blinded by sun and sand. "It is a pity. He was a fine old man." He pressed his fingers against the balls of his eyes and then got to his feet with an abrupt, determined movement. "Bilvidic. A word with you, please." The two Frenchmen went through into the study.

A sudden stillness descended upon the room. It was an uneasy stillness and I glanced across at Jan. He was standing with his back to the fire, his hands behind him, the palms open to the blaze. The muscles of his face were rigid and his head was thrust a little forward. He was frowning and there was a look of concentration on his face as though he were listening to their conversation. But the curtain had been drawn across the study entrance and all we could hear was the drone of their voices. There was a question I wanted to ask him, but I couldn't because Ed was there.

Mohammed came in, his sandals slapping the tiles as he crossed the room. He went into the study and announced that the Khailifa and the old Caid's son had arrived. "Tell them to wait for me at the Bureau," Legard said and Mohammed went out again. The stillness of the room became unbearable. Ed walked over to the window and stared out towards the mountains. "Well, that's that, I guess." He was speaking to himself.

Jan's head jerked up. "How do you mean?"

"Well, it's obvious, isn't it? That shaft will never be opened up now." He was still gazing towards the mountains, seeing in his mind again the landslide thundering into the mouth of the gorge. "All that work for nothing."

"You mean you're giving up?" There was a note of surprise in Jan's voice.

Ed turned towards him with a quick, irritable movement of his body. "What else can I do? I can't clear that slide away. There's too much of it."

"We know the position of the shaft. We could tunnel down to it."

"How? I've no equipment and I'm just about broke."

"We could use local labour. As for money, there's the insurance on your bull-dozers."

"They weren't insured. I didn't think there was any reason to insure them."

He had turned back to the window. Silence descended again on the room. Jan was standing very still. His hands behind his back were clenched now and I saw that his gaze had shifted back to the entrance to the study. And then the curtains were pulled aside and Legard and Bilvidic came out. "I will arrange for the mules to be ready at nine o'clock," Legard said. "Ca va?"

Bilvidic nodded. Legard picked his blue stiff hat up off the table where he had flung it and slung his cape round his shoulders. As he went towards the door he paused and looked at Jan. "At least, monsieur, you seem to have succeeded in carrying out Duprez's wishes." He stared at him for a moment and I realised with a shock that Jan was incapable of meeting the man's gaze. Then Legard twitched his cloak closer round his body and went out. The door banged to behind him.

The sun had set now and night was closing in. The room was growing dark and I could no longer see Jan's face clearly. My shoulder hurt and I was feeling drained of energy, wishing we were away from the place. Bilvidic shouted for Mohammed and ordered him to light the lamps. But even in the soft lamp-glow the room had a cold, alien look. The sense of tension was still there.

And then the telephone buzzer sounded. Bilvidic went through into the study to answer it. He was gone a long while and when he came back he paused in the archway between the two rooms. He was looking at Jan. "Monsieur Wade. You will please come through into the study. There are some questions I have to ask you. You, too, Latham," he added, turning to me.

The moment I had been dreading had arrived. I pulled myself to my feet. Jan was already following Bilvidic into the study. Karen was staring after him, her body rigid, her face pale and taut with strain. Her small hands were clenched as though she were trying to will with all the strength of her body that everything would be all right.

I went through into the study, conscious that my footsteps sounded very loud on the bare tiles. Bilvidic was already seated at the desk. " Asseyez-vous, monsieur." He waved me to a chair. " That telephone call was from Casablanca. I have orders to phone through a preliminary report on this matter to my headquarters tonight." He pulled out his pack of American cigarettes and lit one. " Monsieur Wade." He was looking across at Jan. " From the time you entered French Morocco until I confronted you with Madame Kavan you had assumed the name and identity of Dr. Kavan. Why? Explain please." He was the policeman again: cold, precise, logical.

I looked at Jan. His hands gripped the arms of his chair and his body was braced. He hesitated momentarily. It seemed an age. Then he shifted his position. " Because I had to," he said.

" Why? " Bilvidic's voice was still and hard.

" What else was I to do? Kostos had taken my passport. But I still had Kavan's papers and I had to get to Kasbah Foum." His voice sounded nervous.

" Why did you not report the loss of your passport to the authorities? The International Police were the proper people to deal with the matter."

" But that would have taken time. Listen, monsieur." Jan leaned forward and the nervousness was suddenly gone from his voice. " I was with Kavan over two weeks in the confined space of a small boat. He told me the whole story—how Duprez had given him the deeds and had made him promise to get his title to Kasbah Foum confirmed before Caid Hassan died. If he didn't, the property, with all its potential wealth, would have passed to Ali. You know the sort of man Ali was. He would have used that wealth against France. He would have purchased arms. Kavan was dead. I accepted his responsibility as though it were my own. It was the least I could do." He stopped then. He was breathing heavily.

" Nevertheless," Bilvidic said, " you should have reported the loss of your passport to the police."

" Damn it, man. Don't you understand? " Jan's anger was

genuine. "Kostos was waiting for me there on the beach at Tangier. The matter was urgent. Latham understood. That was why he agreed to get me out on Kavan's papers."

"Very well, monsieur. It is understood. But why do you have to go on calling yourself Kavan?"

"What else could I do? I was here in Morocco on Kavan's papers. Besides, Caid Hassan wouldn't have confirmed the title to anyone but Kavan."

"Ah. That is the real point, eh?" There was a cold glint in Bilvidic's eyes. "You had to be Kavan in order to obtain the title to Kasbah Foum."

"Are you suggesting I arranged for Kostos to steal my passport?" Jan demanded. "Do you think I enjoyed getting out of Tangier the way I did and coming down here under an assumed name? It was dangerous. But I had to do it." He got up suddenly and walked over to the desk, leaning on it and staring down at Bilvidic. "What you're implying is a motive of personal gain. What you should be considering is the alternative. Your troops are all fighting in Indo-China. Caid Hassan is dead, and if Ali were now alive and the owner of Kasbah Foum . . ." He thrust his head forward slightly, staring at Bilvidic. "Be thankful, monsieur, that it has turned out the way it has. If there is silver there, then it will be developed for the benefit of the people. It was what Kavan wanted. It is what I promised Caid Hassan."

I glanced at Bilvidic. The whole thing was so logical that I almost believed it myself. The detective was staring at Jan. He didn't say anything and a silence settled on the room. Jan had turned away from the desk. I wondered how long he could stand the silence. There were beads of sweat on his forehead. And then I saw Bilvidic relax in his chair. He drew gently on his cigarette. "Perhaps you will go and join the others now," he said to Jan. "I would like a word with Latham alone."

Jan hesitated and glanced at me. He looked tired. Then he turned without a word and went out through the curtains. I moved uneasily in my chair, turning to face Bilvidic. He was watching me, his cigarette held vertical between two fingers and a thumb. "How is the shoulder?" he asked me. "Painful?"

" A little," I said, waiting.

His face softened to a smile and he offered me a cigarette. " There are one or two questions I would like to ask you. First, who suggested that method of getting him out of the International Zone—you or he?"

" I did."

He nodded. " That is what I thought. I have seen your security report. Perhaps you have had previous experience of that method, eh?"

" Perhaps," I said.

He shrugged his shoulders. " Well, that is for Tangier to worry about. Now, this matter of Kavan being lost overboard from the yacht. Did our friend tell you how it happened?"

" Yes."

" In detail?"

" Yes." I explained when he had told me and he nodded. " Good. He would have been tired then. Will you repeat it to me in the exact words he used, as far as you can remember them." I did so and he sat for a long time, tapping his pencil against his teeth. " Have you sailed yachts at all?" he asked suddenly.

" Yes," I said. " Quite a lot when I was a boy."

" And do you believe this story? Could a man fall overboard like that—or would it be necessary to push him? Remember, the storm was finished."

" You don't need a storm for a thing like that to happen," I said. " It can happen quite easily." I was determined to convince him on this point. " The guardrails are often no more than thirty inches high—less than a metre," I explained. " Even in a quiet sea a man can go overboard, if he's careless —especially if there isn't much wind and the boat is rolling." He made no comment and I added quickly, " In this case, though the storm was over, there was still a big sea running. If you make a quick move out of the cockpit in such conditions and the stern of the boat falls away in a trough . . ." He still said nothing. " They were both very tired," I said. " That was confirmed by the log."

" Ah. So you have seen the log, eh? Where is it? Has he got it?"

" No."

" Where is it then?"

I explained how I had burned it and he said, " Why? Why do you do that?"

" He asked me to."

" Why?"

I didn't know what to say. For a moment there was a tense silence. And then he gave me the answer himself. " Was it because he was afraid Kostos might get hold of it?"

" Yes," I said. " Yes, I think that was it."

He leaned slowly forward across the desk. " Why should that matter, monsieur?"

It was a trap. I realised that too late. There was no earthly reason why Kostos shouldn't have seen the log. If it were Kavan who had gone overboard, then the writing in the log would have remained unaltered. I couldn't think of anything to say. Bilvidic waited a moment and then he got up and crossed the room and pulled back the curtain. " Wade. A moment please." Jan's eyes were fixed on my face as he came in, walking jerkily, his hands thrust into his pockets. " There is something I don't understand," Bilvidic said. " Why did you ask Latham to destroy the log?"

Jan's hesitation was only momentary, then he turned slowly to face the detective. " It was the handwriting, monsieur," he said in a tone of surprise. " I could not take Kavan's identity and still carry about with me all those pages of my own handwriting."

It was so simple, so logical. I felt a sense of relief. Bilvidic wasn't to know that the decision to get out on Kavan's papers had been taken after the log had been destroyed. The detective turned back to the desk. " Now then," he said, " let us get this down in the form of a statement." He looked across at me. " I think perhaps, Latham, you would be more comfortable in the other room. Keep warm by the fire." His expression was almost friendly.

Julie and Karen were standing by the hearth. There was no one else in the room. The lamps and the fire gave a glow of warmth to the bare walls. Karen turned and moved slowly, almost reluctantly to meet me. " Is it all right?" she asked in a whisper.

" Yes," I said. " I think so."

Her lips trembled slightly and then she turned away her head. I think she was close to tears. Julie's fingers closed on my hand. " You're cold," she said. " Come and get warm."

Ed came back soon after and we sat and waited in silence. It seemed a long time before Jan came out. He was talking to Bilvidic. " And you'll make it clear that I had no alternative, won't you?"

" I don't think you need worry," Bilvidic answered.

" Thanks. And I'm glad you reminded me about the yacht." He came towards us then, and he was smiling.

" Monsieur White." Bilvidic's cold, official voice cut across the mood of relief that had filled the room. " If you will come in here, I would like a short statement."

Ed went into the study and as the curtains fell to behind him, Jan came towards Karen. " Well, Madame." For the first time since I had known him I saw him completely relaxed. His blue eyes were twinkling. He looked young, almost a boy again.

" It's all right then?" Karen whispered.

" Yes," he said. " Everything is going to be all right now— for always, darling." Their hands touched and gripped. " You understand, Karen," he said. " We shall have to start courting again. After a decent interval, of course." And then he turned to me. " Philip. You will be best man at our wedding, eh?" He was suddenly laughing. " Tell me. What is the opposite to your saying—It never rains but it pours?" But he didn't wait for an answer. " Listen. *Gay Juliet* was insured for £15,000. As Wade I collect that money Isn't that damn funny?" His laugh was a little nervous, as though it were all too good to be true. " You come and help us open up that shaft, and after that we'll do something about your Mission."

The door opened behind us and Jan and Karen moved quickly apart. It was Legard. He put his cloak and his hat on the table and came over to the fire. He stood warming himself for a moment and then he turned to Jan. " I have been talking to Caïd Hassan's son," he said. " He was present at your meeting with his father." He paused and then added significantly. " He speaks French."

The sudden look of shock on Jan's face showed me that he had understood the implication.

Legard stared at the fire for a long time and then he gave a little shrug. "Eh bien," he said. "Perhaps, if you stay here long enough, you will cure me of the amibe, eh?" He looked at Jan, his tough, leathery face unsmiling—but the corners of his eyes were crinkled up. Then he walked to the door and shouted for Mohammed to bring him some water.

THE END